Praise for

DESCENDANT OF THE CRANE

"A gripping tale full of intrigue, unpredictable twists, and betrayal—
this is the Chinese fantasy readers have been waiting for."

—HAFSAH FAIZAL, *New York Times*–bestselling author
of the Sands of Arawiya duology

"This is my favorite kind of story: lyrical, romantic, politically
complex, but most of all, driven by an iron-willed heroine who
will do what must be done—no matter the cost."

—KRISTEN CICCARELLI, internationally bestselling author
of *The Last Namsara*

"A beautiful debut with thrilling politics and strokes of magic."

—LORI M. LEE, author of the Gates of Thread and Stone series

"You'll be drawn in by this marvelously vivid world . . .
and keep turning the pages for the plot twists!"

—TRACI CHEE, *New York Times*–bestselling author
of *The Reader*

"*Descendant of the Crane* soars from page one."

—RACHEL HARTMAN, *New York Times*–bestselling author
of the Seraphina series

"Hesina is a heroine for the ages—brilliant, determined,
and fierce. It is impossible not to root for her."

—LAURA SEBASTIAN, *New York Times*–bestselling author
of *Ash Princess*

DESCENDANT
OF THE
CRANE

ALSO BY JOAN HE

The Ones We're Meant to Find
Strike the Zither

DESCENDANT OF THE CRANE

JOAN HE

Roaring Brook Press
New York

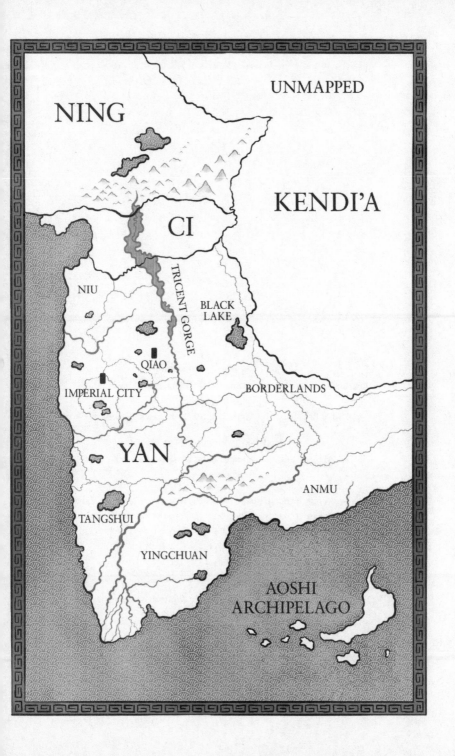

Published by Roaring Brook Press
Roaring Brook Press is a division of Holtzbrinck Publishing Holdings
Limited Partnership
120 Broadway, New York, NY 10271 • fiercereads.com

Our books may be purchased in bulk for promotional, educational, or
business use. Please contact your local bookseller or the Macmillan Corporate
and Premium Sales Department at (800) 221-7945 ext. 5442 or by email at
MacmillanSpecialMarkets@macmillan.com.

Library of Congress Control Number: 2022908763

Originally published in hardcover by Albert Whitman & Company, 2019
First paperback edition, 2022
Book design by Aurora Parlagreco
Printed in the United States of America

ISBN 978-1-250-81590-3
1 3 5 7 9 10 8 6 4 2

To my dad

I

TREASON

A well-conceived costume is a new identity, the father used to say as he put on his commoner's cloak. *From now until I return, I am no longer the king.*

Teach me how to make a costume, begged the daughter.

He did that, and more. By candlelight, he divulged every way he knew of escaping the palace, for King Wen of Yan loved the truth, and little was found within the lacquer walls.

ONE

*What is truth? Scholars seek it. Poets write it. Good kings
pay gold to hear it. But in trying times, truth is the first thing
we betray.*

ONE of the ELEVEN on truth

Truth? Why, it's a lie in disguise.

TWO of the ELEVEN on truth

No night was perfect for treason, but this one came close. The
three-day mourning ritual had ended; most had gone home to
break the fast. Those who lingered in the city streets kept their eyes
trained on the Eastern Gate, where the queen would be making her
annual return.

Then came the mist. It rolled down the neighboring Shanlong
Mountains and embalmed the limestone boulevards. When it descended into the bowels of the palace, so did the girl and her brother.

They emerged from the secret passageways the girl knew well—
too well, perhaps, given her identity—and darted between courtyard compounds and walled wards, venturing toward the market

sectors. When they arrived at the red-light district's peeling archway, an ember sparked in the girl's stomach. Some came to the seediest business quarter of the imperial city to buy warmth. But she?

She had come to buy justice.

Her brother held her back before she could cross. "Milady—"

If he called her "milady" out here, he might as well call her Princess Hesina. "Yes, Caiyan?"

"We can still go back."

Hesina's fingers closed around the glass vial dangling from her silk broad-belt. They *could*. She could let her resolve fade like the wisp of poison bottled in the vial. That would be easy. Figuring out how to live with herself afterward . . . not so much.

Grip hardening, she turned to her brother. He looked remarkably calm for someone risking death by a thousand cuts—crisply dressed despite the rough-hewn *hanfu*, every dark hair of his topknot in place.

"Having doubts?" She hoped he'd say *yes*. At fifteen, Caiyan had passed the civil service examinations. At seventeen, he'd become a viscount of the imperial court. At nineteen, his reputation was unparalleled, his mind more so. He wasn't renowned for making bad decisions—unless they were in her name.

"How would you find the way?" asked Caiyan, countering her question with one of his own.

"Excuse me?"

Caiyan raised a brow. "You're hoping that I'll say 'yes' so you can proceed alone. But that wasn't our agreement. I am to lead the whole way, or I don't take you to this person at all."

Our agreement. Only Caiyan could make treason sound so bland.

"I won't be able to protect you." Hesina scuffed one foot over the other under the hem of her *ruqun*. "If we're caught . . . if someone sees us . . ."

A man bellowed an opera under the tiled eave of a dilapidated inn, and something porcelain shattered, but Caiyan's voice still cleaved the night. "You don't have to protect me, milady." Red lantern light edged his profile as he looked into the distance. "He was my father too."

A lump formed in Hesina's throat. She *did* have to protect him, in the same way her father—*their* father—had. *You can't possibly touch all the lives in this world*, he'd told her that winter day ten years ago when he'd brought the twins—slum urchins, one thin girl and one feverish boy—into theirs. *But if you can lift someone with your two hands, that is enough.*

Hesina wasn't lifting Caiyan up; she was leading him astray. But when he reached for her hand, she held on, to her dismay. The confidence in his grip grounded her, and they crossed into the district together.

They entered a world of slanted teahouses and inns, brothels and pawnshops clustered like reeds on a panpipe. Men and women spilled out of the paper-screened doors, half-clothed and swinging certain appendages. Hesina averted her gaze and pressed closer to Caiyan.

"It'll get better up ahead." Caiyan had once called streets worse than these home, and he guided them around peddlers with impressive ease. He didn't pay any mind to the occasional beggar, not even the one who tailed them down the block.

"Beware the night," cried the man, shaking coins in a cracked pot. Hesina slowed, but Caiyan tugged her along. "Beware the rains, the crown, and the Sight!"

"Ignore him." Caiyan's gaze glowed with focus. "He speaks of the bygone dynasty."

But on a night like this one, the past felt uncomfortably close. Hesina shivered, thinking of an era three centuries ago, when peasants had drowned in summer floods and perished in winter famines. The relic emperors had pursued concubines, conquests, and concoctions for immortality, while their imperial soothsayers Saw into the future to crop resistance before it could sprout. As for the sick and the starving, too weak to resist, the sooths placated them with visions of the brilliant tomorrows to come.

And they did come—at the hands of eleven scrappy outlaws who climbed the Ning Mountains, crossed the Kendi'an dunes, breached the imperial walls, and beheaded the last relic emperor on his very throne. They emancipated serfs and set them to work on dikes and embankments. Storms calmed. Floods drained. They opened the doors of education to women and commoners, and their disciples circulated the former outlaws' philosophies in a book called the *Tenets*. The people of Yan called them the Eleven. Legends. Saviors. Heroes.

"Beware the devil of lies."

Of course, heroes cannot be forged without villains: the emperor's henchmen, the sooths. The Eleven rooted them out by their unique blood, which evaporated quicker than any human's and ignited blue. They burned tens of thousands at the stake to protect the new era from their machinations.

Whatever the reason, murder was murder. The dead were dead. Hating the sooths, as the people continued to do, made little sense to Hesina. But occasionally, like now, with the beggar barking ominous warnings, her pity for the sooths spawned into fear, eating away at her conception of a sooth until it collapsed and a new one rose in its place: a faceless head attached to a charred body, an eyeless, toothless monster straight from the Ten Courts of Hell.

By the time Hesina eradicated the image, the beggar was gone and another had taken his place, resuming the chants—in an all-too-familiar female voice.

"Beware the one you leave behind."

Oh no.

Hesina whirled as a hooded figure strode toward them.

"My, my. What do we have here?" The newcomer circled Hesina. "I like the linen *ruqun*. Very commoner-esque. As for you . . ." She flung aside Caiyan's cloak and frowned at the plain *hanfu* beneath. "*This* is how you try to pass as a sprightly nineteen-year-old in search of a romp? What are you, a broke scholar?"

Caiyan readjusted his cloak. "We're going to a music house."

The newcomer placed a hand against her hip. "I thought you said 'brothel.'"

"I said no such thing."

"I could have sworn—"

"I thought," Hesina gritted out, overcoming her shock and glaring at Caiyan, "you were to say *nothing* about this to *anyone*."

Caiyan, in turn, glared at the newcomer. "You said you wouldn't come if I told you."

"You should have known better!" cried Hesina, and Caiyan pinched the bridge of his nose.

"I know, milady. Forgive me."

"Now there, Na-Na." The newcomer lowered her hood and fluffed out her braids. Pinned back like a pair of butterfly wings and woven through with bright ribbons, the braids were a signature part of Yan Lilian's style. So was the mischief in her eyes, a shade of chestnut slightly lighter than her twin Caiyan's. "The stone-head tried. It's not his fault that I blackmailed him. Besides, did you really think I'd let you commit treason without me?"

Hesina wasn't sure whether to be angry or miserable. "This isn't a game."

"You *promised*." Caiyan sounded mostly miserable.

Lilian ignored him and faced Hesina. "Of course it's not a game. It's a dangerous, important mission befitting a threesome. Look at it this way: you need one person to hear this forbidden wisdom, one to watch the door for intruders, and one to beat up the intruders."

"Send her away," Hesina ordered Caiyan.

Lilian danced out of Caiyan's reach. "I *could* still tell all your high-minded court friends that the illustrious Yan Caiyan reads erotic novellas in his spare time. Who's the latest favorite? Wang Hutian?"

Caiyan made a strangled sound. Lilian laughed. Hesina watched their shadows lengthen under the moonlight.

They were losing time.

"Let's walk," said Lilian, as if reading Hesina's mind. She linked their arms. "You can try to get rid of me on the way."

Hesina knew better than to try. They proceeded in silence, the low-lying shops on either side giving way to taller, pillared structures. The song of zithers and *pipa* lutes replaced drunken improvisations.

"You shouldn't have come," Hesina finally said.

"What's life without a bit of danger?"

"Be serious."

"I am, Na-Na." Like a real sister, Lilian still used Hesina's diminutive name long after she'd outgrown it. "Father might be gone, but he won't be forgotten. Not with us here."

"That's . . ." Comforting. Frightening, that Hesina had more loved ones to lose. "Thank you," she finished hoarsely.

"Well, we might not be here for much longer, since meeting with this person *may* end in death by a thousand cuts."

"Lilian!"

"Sorry. Sorry. Pretend I didn't say that."

Ahead of them, Caiyan stopped in front of a three-tiered building. From the outside, it resembled one of the celestial pagodas rumored to exist back when gods walked the earth. But inside, it was every bit a music house. Beaded curtains fell from the balustrades. Private rooms blushed behind latticework screens. The namesake music—plucked and bowed—gusted through the air, fanning Hesina's anxiety.

"Don't look anyone in the eye," Caiyan instructed as they crossed the raised threshold and came into the antechamber. "And don't take off the hood of your cloak," he ordered, right before lowering his.

"Welcome to the Yellow Lotus," said a madam, weaving toward them through flocks of painted girls and boys. Her smiling, moonlike face dimmed when she neared Caiyan. "First time at this establishment, I presume?"

Lilian coughed.

"Let's see . . ." The madam scanned the courtesans. "The White Peony might be to your liking—"

"We're here to meet the Silver Iris," cut in Caiyan.

The madam frowned. "The Silver Iris is our most highly sought-after entertainer."

"So I've heard."

"She has mastered the golden triad of calligraphy, music, and dance."

9

"Again, so I've heard."

"She is choosy with patrons and has limited hours." The madam leaned in and, with a long, emerald-varnished fingernail, extracted a loose thread from Caiyan's cloak. "Her gifts are wasted on the likes of you."

Hesina gulped.

Without batting an eye, Caiyan withdrew a brocade purse. "Is this enough?"

The madam snatched it, loosened the drawstring, and peered in. Hesina couldn't tell what the woman was thinking, and as the madam bounced the purse up and down in her ringed hand, she sweated through her underclothes.

At last, the madam scrunched the purse shut. "Come with me."

As she led them up a set of purple *zitan*-wood stairs and rapped on one of the many doors lining the second-floor corridor, Hesina pinched her own wrist. For five nights, she'd tormented herself with questions. Was it right to do this? Was it wrong? If it was, then was she angry enough, sad enough, selfish enough to see it through regardless? She didn't know. She'd gotten this far, and she still didn't know. But now only one question remained: Was she brave enough to hear the truth?

Hesina knew her answer.

The madam rapped again, harder, and a husky voice unfurled from within. "Yes?"

"You have guests."

"How many?"

"Two," said Lilian. She leaned against the wall beside the door. "I'll be right out here."

"Have they paid?"

The madam moistened her lips. "They have."

"Leave them, then."

Nothing happened immediately after the madam departed. The doors didn't open. Demons didn't descend from the beamed ceiling to exact their punishment, but as they waited, Hesina's mind produced demons of its own. Maybe they'd been followed. Maybe someone had recognized her. Maybe—

The doors parted, and her demons fled before treason's face.

It was an exquisite face. Ageless. Pearlescent. Silver-lidded eyes skimmed past Hesina and landed on Caiyan. Rose-tinted lips crimped in displeasure, and Hesina had all of a heartbeat to wonder *how*, exactly, Caiyan was acquainted with a courtesan before she was ushered past the doors. The courtesan bolted them, the ivory dowel falling into place like the final note of a song.

Hesina, unfortunately, was much too prone to nervous laughter. In an attempt to ignore the tickling tension in her chest, she fixated on the chamber. A gallery of *pipa* hung on the walls, their scrolled necks knuckled with ivory frets, strings drawn tight over their pear-shaped bellies. Four-word couplets papered the remaining space. To her embarrassment, Hesina only recognized one from her studies.

Downward unbridled water flows;
Upward unrealized dreams float.

"I assume you'll want to skip the tea."

Hesina nearly jumped at the Silver Iris's voice, which was as metallic as her name.

"That's correct," said Caiyan, standing against the door.

"Then let's have a little demonstration, shall we?"

That won't be necessary, Hesina imagined saying with grace and magnanimity, but it was a lie, and the Silver Iris knew it. A hairpin was already in the courtesan's hand. She pushed her finger into its needle-sharp tip, then held the pin over an unlit candle. A bead of blood fell and burst on the wick.

A wisp.

A spark.

A flicker.

The wick ignited into blue flame.

Hesina's vision swam. The flame blurred, but stayed blue.

Blue. Blue. Blue.

"A nice parlor trick, don't you think?" asked the Silver Iris. Her tone was conversational, but her gaze picked Hesina apart, straight to the core of who she was: a descendant of murderers.

Hesina's stomach clenched. She wasn't supposed to think the Eleven cruel. They'd built a kinder era, a fairer era—one where individuals were judged by their honest work, not the number of sooths and nobles they knew. Everyone was promised rights by the law— everyone but the soothsayers, who had manipulated the public for so many centuries. Death by a thousand cuts was considered kind for them . . . and for the people who employed the sooths for their gifts.

People like Hesina.

The Silver Iris sat and gestured for her to do the same. Weak at the knees, Hesina sank onto the silk-cushioned stool. She realized, somewhat belatedly, that she had yet to reveal her face. The disguise seemed silly now. A child's game. She looked to Caiyan in question while the Silver Iris swaddled her finger with a handkerchief.

The courtesan spoke before Caiyan could. "So tell me, Princess Hesina." She balled up the bloodied handkerchief and tossed it into the brazier at their feet, where it promptly burst into flame. "What is it that you wish to see?"

TWO

Too much of a thing—be it success or power—rots the heart.
ONE *of the* ELEVEN *on soothsayers*

They had no hearts to begin with.
TWO *of the* ELEVEN *on soothsayers*

With shaking hands, Hesina pushed back her hood.

She had come to see the future. The unknown. Yet for a second, all she could see was her father, lying in the iris beds, wearing his courier costume. She wasn't sure how long she'd waited. Waited for him to rise and yawn, to tell her how lovely it was to stroll through the grounds in disguise. Waited for herself to wake when he never did.

That day, Hesina had watched as the Imperial Doctress took up a scalpel, splitting the dead king's stomach like a fish. There was nothing to find, not at first. The Imperial Doctress concluded that the king's death was of natural causes before puttering off to the adjacent chamber.

If only she had stayed a second longer to witness the golden gas rising from the slit. If she had *believed* when Hesina tried to show her the wisp in the vial, then Hesina wouldn't be here. Her hands wouldn't be clenched in her skirts just as they'd been clenched around the Doctress's robes.

Her voice wouldn't be so strained when she asked the Silver Iris, "Who killed my father?"

The Silver Iris blinked once. "Killed?"

"Yes, killed!" Hesina choked up. "The king didn't die a natural death. The decrees lie."

But she would show the kingdom the truth. With the Silver Iris's Sight, she would find the assassin, press them into the *tianlao* dungeons, and maybe then, when she had a life for a life, this nightmare would—

"I See golden gas rising from a pile of shards," the Silver Iris started. Hesina leaned in. "But I can't See who killed the king."

Hesina's heart dove like a kite without wind.

"What I can See is the person who will help you find the truth."

"A representative?" Hesina couldn't mask her disappointment.

"Yes." The Silver Iris smoothed an embroidered sash over her knee. "You could call him that."

Hesina wound the cord connecting the vial to her broad-belt around her thumb. If she chose to follow a path of formal justice for her father's killer, the Investigation Bureau would look into Hesina's claim that he'd been murdered. Once they'd officially forwarded the case to the court, the Minister of Rites would assign a representative to both the plaintiff—in this case, her—and the defendant.

"Well?" prompted the Silver Iris. "Would you like to hear?"

Princesses were not so different from beggars. Hesina had learned to take what she could get. "Yes."

The Silver Iris's doe-like eyes roved over her. Hesina squirmed, well aware there was nothing impressive about her appearance. She lacked the hunger for knowledge that flamed in Caiyan's eyes, the mirth of Lilian's lips. A visiting painter had once said that Hesina had her mother's face, but they both knew she'd never wear it as well as the queen. Hesina thought she heard similar sympathy in the Silver Iris's voice when she finally said, "A convict."

"A . . . convict." The cord had cut the circulation to Hesina's thumb. She unwound it, pins and needles replacing the numbness. Her father's justice . . . handed to a convict.

She almost laughed.

"I'm sorry." Hesina's composure would have made her tutors proud. "There must be a mistake."

The Silver Iris drew back. "No mistake. A convict will represent you in court."

"That's impossible." *Only* up-and-coming scholars, selected from a pool of hopeful civil service examinees, acted as representatives in trials. The court was a stage on which to prove their intellect; the reward for winning the case was a free pass through the preliminary rounds of the examinations. The Eleven had made it so to give every literati a chance to rise, regardless of family background. But what did a criminal have to gain from such a system?

Hesina's disbelief condensed. "Please look again."

"You think I'm lying."

"What? No." Hesina didn't believe the Silver Iris would lie, not really, for the same reason people trusted sooths in the past. Though books and libraries on the specifics of their powers had been destroyed in the purge, select legends had lived on to become common knowledge. One was that sooths couldn't lie about their visions without shortening their life spans. How else, argued scholars, could the relic emperors have controlled them?

"Why not?" The Silver Iris rose and turned her back to them. A cascade of colors tumbled out from the hidden layers of her lilac skirt. "Do you think I'm scared of shaving a few years off my life?"

She loosened her sash, and the *ruqun* puddled onto the lacquered floor.

First came the hand-shaped bruises, flowering over her bare back. Then came the burn marks. Hundreds of thin, puckered lines, as if someone had bled her with a knife and watched her smoke for the fun of it.

"Some would rather see us alive than cut to a thousand pieces or charred at the stake," she said as Hesina's throat closed. "You assume I tell the truth because I fear death, but the dead are lucky. They cannot squirm or shudder." She made for her wardrobe. "Nor can they be forced to say the things you want to hear."

The brazier at Hesina's feet was still spitting flame, but her toes had gone cold. She shouldn't have come here. The Silver Iris had bled for her and Seen for her, but Hesina had given her no choice, just like the patrons before her. She staggered out of her seat.

"I . . . I'm sorry. I never . . . I never meant . . . We'll leave—"

"A convict." The Silver Iris slid on a different *ruqun*—this one sheer and crimson—and tied it shut with a braided cord. "The one with the rod. That is all I can see. My blood is diluted. Few of us are as powerful as our ancestors. But you already knew that, didn't you?"

Meaningfully, she met Hesina's gaze in the bronze mirror atop her vanity.

Hesina's mouth opened and closed. No words came out.

A rap sounded at the door, then Lilian's voice. "Someone's coming up the steps."

"You should go now." The Silver Iris opened a drawer, withdrawing a tiny pot. She unscrewed the top and dabbed a fresh coat of silver over her lids. "I have patrons to tend to."

"Y-yes," stammered Hesina. "We'll go. I . . . I'm sorry."

She backed up. Caiyan joined her side. He held the door open for her, but suddenly Hesina couldn't move. A question rooted her, climbing up her esophagus like a weed and choking her mind:

"Why tell me anything?"

"What makes you so certain I haven't been lying to you all this time?" asked the Silver Iris, gaze chilly.

Because Caiyan said you wouldn't. Because rumor said lying would cost you.

"Because you showed me more than I deserve," said Hesina truthfully. "And . . ." She bit her lip and looked away. *Naive*, the Imperial Doctress had called her. *Reckless.* "And because I want to trust you."

Because I feel sorry for you.

The Silver Iris sighed. "Come here."

Hesina went over cautiously, and the Silver Iris held out her index finger.

The prick from the hairpin was gone. As small as the wound was, there was no way it could have healed so quickly, and Hesina goggled at the smooth, unmarred skin, flinching when the Silver Iris's breath brushed her ear.

"Your histories only tell you how our powers hurt us," whispered the courtesan. "But there are benefits to speaking true visions too."

She drew back, leaving the shell of Hesina's ear hot and cold all at once. "Why are you telling me this?"

When the Silver Iris studied her this time, the ice in her gaze had thawed to pity, as if she were the human and Hesina were the sooth. "For the same reason you believe me: I am sorry for you."

* * *

They left the red-light district at two gong strikes past midnight. Left and right through the eastern market, merchants packed up their stalls, loading *jiutan* of sweet-wine congee and fried bean curd back onto wagons. Hesina drifted through the traffic, a ghost, as Caiyan pacified angry mule drivers and palanquin bearers.

"Hey, watch it!"

"Are you trying to lose a leg?"

"I'm terribly sorry," said Caiyan. "Excuse us. Pardon us."

"Tell your missy to grow a pair of eyes!"

"Wait up, Na-Na," called Lilian.

Hesina didn't stop. She needed to think, and she couldn't think standing still.

A convict with a rod was to be her representative.

The Silver Iris had told the truth.

But now what?

Her feet brought her to the abandoned tavern from which they'd come. Her hands filled a pitcher at the counter pump. She dribbled water down the throat of the concrete guardian lion at the entrance, and the statue rotated aside at the base.

One by one, they descended the tight drop. The dark waxed over them as Lilian rotated the statue back in place, and Hesina suddenly knew her next steps.

"I need to become queen." She made her declaration to the humble dirt walls of the underground passageway. Her voice echoed, hollow as the feeling in her chest.

"Of course you'll become queen," said Lilian, referring to the rites of succession that passed the throne from deceased ruler to eldest child.

"When your mother returns from the Ouyang Mountains, you can ask for her blessing," said Caiyan, referring to the tradition of parental validation that all heirs, imperial or not, observed before staking their claims.

The twins went back and forth as they walked down the tunnel. Rites. Traditions. Rites. Traditions. Neither seemed to realize that Hesina had said she *needed* the throne, not that she *wanted* it.

She envied Lilian, who was allowed to spend her days overseeing the imperial textiles. She envied Caiyan, who positively breathed politics. She even envied her blood brother Sanjing, who led the Yan militias. The throne never stood in the way of *their* hopes and dreams.

But for the first time in her life, Hesina had a use for power.

"I want an official investigation." Her father would have wanted the truth delivered by the codes of the *Tenets*. That meant going through the Investigation Bureau, not a sooth. "I want a trial." The ground rose beneath their feet as they approached the end of the passageway. "I want the people to see the truth unfold in court."

"So you really think there's a convict with a rod?" asked Lilian as they emerged from a miniature mountain range situated in the center of the four-palace complex.

There was only one way to find out.

"Go on without me." Hesina turned north, toward the dungeons.

Caiyan caught her elbow. "It's best to visit at a less suspicious hour."

Lilian took her other elbow. "For once, I agree with the stone-head. Commit one act of treason at a time."

Better yet, commit no treason at all.

Hesina shook them both off. "I didn't say I was going to make him my representative *right now*."

If only it were that simple. To prevent the rich and powerful from hiring the best scholars and winning every case as they had during the relic dynasty, the *Tenets* ordered that plaintiff and defendant each be assigned a representative at random. As a result, Hesina couldn't choose her own representative. It was treason. Convincing the only person in charge of the selection—Xia Zhong, Minister of Rites, Interpreter of the *Tenets*—happened to be treason too.

But that, Hesina decided, was another problem for another night.

"What are you going to do in the dungeons, then?" Lilian was asking when Hesina emerged from her thoughts. "Examine his *rod*?"

Caiyan cleared his throat.

Hesina patted Lilian on the arm. "I'd save you the honors."

"I'm holding you to that."

"It's late, milady," said Caiyan, changing the subject. "The prisoners won't be going anywhere. Wait for tomorrow, when your mind is clearer."

Don't wait, growled the fear in Hesina's belly. She'd been too late to save her father, too late to stop news of his "natural death" from circulating the kingdom.

But Caiyan had a point. The night was balmy with the last of the summer heat, and Hesina's senses had begun to fog. Their trip into the red-light district felt like it'd taken place an eon ago, and she couldn't hold back her yawn when they reached the Western Palace, home to the imperial artisans.

Under a medallion-round moon, Lilian bade them good night. The woodwork of her latticed doors was stained fuchsia and gold, bright like the textiles strewn, hung, and piled within. It was like looking into another world, a too-short glimpse of a life Hesina could not have. The doors slid shut, and Hesina and Caiyan continued on, traveling under the covered galleries that converged like arteries at the Eastern Palace, the largest of the four and the heart of court. The sunk-in ceilings dropped lower as they passed the ceremonial halls of the outer palace, the corridors narrowing as they approached the inner.

Caiyan stopped Hesina short of the imperial chambers. "Lilian and I will stand by you no matter what you choose to do."

The words were bittersweet, reminding Hesina of something her father might say.

"Thank you," she whispered. "For everything."

Caiyan hadn't doubted the gas in her vial. She'd run to his rooms in hysterics and he'd sat her down and outlined her options. Steady, reliable Caiyan, a friend, a brother, who received her gratitude with a short bow. "Get some sleep, milady."

"You too." But then Caiyan headed in the direction of the libraries, which made Hesina doubt he would.

Alone, she made for her chambers. The path to the imperial quarters was intentionally convoluted, designed to confuse intruders. Tonight, Hesina felt no better than one as the knit of lacquer corridors enmeshed her within the screened facades. Some of the images stitched upon the translucent silk were of water buffalo tilling rice paddies, but most were of the Eleven's revolution. Gold thread fleshed out the flames engulfing the soothsayers and shimmered in the pool of blood spreading from the relic emperor's severed head.

Hesina's breath went ragged. *Don't fear the pictures, Little Bird,* her father would have said. *They're simply art.* But now she was as bad as the emperors of the past. She had used a sooth. Worse, her true heart sympathized, and she was too cowardly to speak it.

Hesina tried to look ahead. A mistake. The list of tasks awaiting her was daunting. Find the convict with the rod. Persuade Xia Zhong to choose him as her representative. Secure her mother's blessing *and* commence her reign by telling the people their king had been murdered.

She would be an unforgettable queen—*if* she didn't die by a thousand cuts first.

As Hesina neared her chamber, her blood slowed to a crawl. Light was seeping out from under the doors. She'd blown out all her candles—she was sure of it—which could mean only one thing:

Someone was inside.

Pulse fluttering, she laid a hand atop the carved wood. Her options were few. Walk away, and her visitor would think she'd been gone all night. Enter, and she'd have no choice but to explain her whereabouts.

On second thought, perhaps she *hadn't* blown out her candles. Hesina very much hoped that was the case as she pushed in.

"Sanjing?" Her mouth fell open while the doors swung shut. "What are you doing here?"

Candlelight rippled off the scales of her blood brother's laminar armor as he rose from her daybed. He was still in full military dress, hair pinned in a sloppy topknot, curved *liuyedao* sheathed at his leather broad-belt.

He stalked past her embroidered screens and around her sitting table. "You first, dear sister. What have you been doing *elsewhere*?"

He closed in. Too late, Hesina realized the state of her

22

appearance—brown cloak, wild eyes, the fumes of sin city clinging to her hair.

She backed away, but her brother was quicker. He grabbed a handful of her cloak, frowning when his fingers met linen instead of silk. He brought the fabric to his nose, and her heart hammered. She tried to slow it. Sanjing was kin. He wouldn't betray her to death by a thousand cuts.

"You went to the city. And you reek of incense."

Hesina's fear frayed into annoyance. *She* was the older sibling, and she drew herself up to her full and very average height. "Glad to know you care about my whereabouts. What next? Will you supervise who I speak to?"

"Why would I? You already have a devoted chaperone." Sanjing released the cloak, and Hesina retreated to her desk. "Or should I say, manservant."

She straightened her paperwork. Decrees, proposals, memorials— all matters that fell to her while she acted as unofficial queen before the coronation, and in the absence of her mother's blessing. But no matter how Hesina concentrated, she couldn't stop trembling. *Elevens*. Why did Sanjing have to be here, now of all times? "His *name* is Caiyan."

"Really? I still prefer the sound of manservant. Has a nice ring to it."

Her hands stilled on a copy of the *Tenets*. It was solid, thick with hundreds of essays on the Eleven's beliefs. It withstood the pressure of her fingers as she dug them into the spine.

She could be cruel. Dredge up the past they'd both agreed to bury, say the words guaranteed to drive him away. But in the end, she simply set down the tome with a heavy *thump*. "Why are you here, Jing?"

"Again: Why *weren't* you?"

"I went to find justice."

"For?"

Her limbs were cold, her head heavy. She was too tired for this. Maybe that's why she told the truth. "Father."

She drew the vial from the folds of her cloak. The golden gas shimmered in the candlelight.

"What is that?" asked Sanjing, squinting.

"Poison."

He hissed in a breath. "Why am I learning this now?"

"You *really* thought he died from natural causes?"

"I didn't think the Imperial Doctress had a reason to lie." Sanjing scrubbed a hand over his face. "Six's bones. What are we going to do?"

Hesina's hopes lifted at the *we*, but it wasn't enough. The better question was what *could* they do. It was their word and a vial against a kingdom already convinced its king had passed peacefully. Again, she needed the throne. She needed power. Once she had both: "Open an investigation."

"With the Bureau?"

"Where else but the Bureau?"

Sanjing narrowed his eyes. "What about the war?"

"What *about* the war?" Then Hesina caught herself. "Don't call it that."

"What would you rather call it? A pissing match?" She cast him a warning glance, and he responded, "We're alone, Sina." Sanjing planted his hands on the desk, boxing in the space between them. "What we call it doesn't change the nature of the 'bandit raids' along the Yan-Kendi'a border. They're planned attacks from Kendi'a, and the commoners will realize that sooner or later."

"They mustn't." The *Tenets* forbade war, and understandably so. The relic emperors had conscripted hundreds of thousands of serfs to wage extravagant campaigns against the other kingdoms of Ning, Ci, and Kendi'a, and the commoners of this era hadn't forgotten the bloodshed. They praised Sanjing whenever he won skirmishes—*skirmishes* being key. Every century or so, some Yan king or queen would disregard the Eleven's pacifist teachings and decree war, sending hamlets and provinces across the realm into revolt.

"Yan has water," said Sanjing. "Kendi'a does not. Their lands grow drier and drier with the years. Invasion is inevitable, and we need to be ready to meet it with an army. The *Tenets* forbid wars fought for gain; we fight for self-defense. But starting a war *and* officially declaring that the king was murdered? Don't you see the issue?"

No, Hesina did not. "The people will want to know who killed their king," she said, more certain of this than anything else.

Her brother's eyes flashed. "They'll want a *scapegoat*, Sina."

"They're better than that."

"What makes you so certain?"

"Father loved them." In the same way he loved her—regardless of her flaws, teaching by example.

"Father wasn't always right."

Hesina stared at her brother as she would a stranger. When had they grown so far apart that they'd stopped seeing eye to eye on this too?

"We should start by examining the poison on our own," Sanjing continued. "Find the truth for ourselves—"

"What's wrong with you?" Hesina hadn't shouted, but Sanjing stiffened as if she had. "Why do you have so little faith in our court?"

His expression hardened. "Because of this."

He tugged papers out from under his breastplate and tossed them onto her desk. They spread like the wings of a crane, scattering on impact. Some landed on the floor.

Under the heat of Sanjing's gaze, Hesina bent and gathered the papers that had fallen. She stacked them with the rest, shuffling everything into place, and grudgingly gave her attention to the contents.

"I didn't want to show you this," said Sanjing as she tried to make sense of what she was reading. "I figured it'd make you worry. But it's time you opened your eyes."

The papers were pages torn from a copy of the *Tenets*. But the characters scrawled between the vertical columns of text weren't commentary or critique. They were reports—fine-grained accounts detailing the security and transportation systems of several borderland towns, information that would have been very helpful to a Kendi'an raiding party.

Only a Yan official could have written these letters.

"My scouts confiscated several suspicious bundles before they could cross into Kendi'a. These letters were hidden among the tariff reports, in a chest stamped by the Office of the Imperial Courier. Someone in this palace has been helping the Kendi'ans terrorize our villages. Someone *wants* a war. Hand them a murder case, and they'll hand you a Kendi'an."

Sanjing sounded far away. His words circled Hesina's head like wasps. Or gnats. It was the latter, she decided, setting the letters down on the desk. Gnats were harmless. "There are hundreds of officials in this court, most of them unimportant," she said. "One person cannot obstruct the course of justice."

"And what if they *are* important? What if they have friends?"

All conjecture. Hesina waved it aside. "You have no way of know-ing. Besides, if we withheld cases from the Investigation Bureau for every small quibble, would we still have a court?"

"This is different. A king has never been killed before."

"He was our father before he was the king. We owe this to him. Enough." Hesina raised a hand before her brother could go on. "Ride to the borderlands. Take five thousand militiamen and women with you, and see if you can quell the raids for the time being."

"Really, Sina?"

"Yes. That's an order from your future queen."

Sanjing shook his head. "You'll regret this."

So much for "we." What had Hesina expected? Sanjing was no Caiyan. If something didn't go his way, he abandoned course. Weeks, months, *years* of his cold-shouldering reared in her mind, and with a bitter laugh, Hesina said, "One of us has to love Father and what he stood for. He believed in the people, he believed in the courts, he believed in truth, and he believed in the new era. I will too."

A long silence passed between them.

"Fine." The shadows fell from Sanjing's face as he straightened. "I'll go."

The cowlick sweeping above his right brow was more prominent in the light. He was General Yan Sanjing, prodigy of the sword arts, master of strategy, commander of the Yan militias, but he was only sixteen, one year Hesina's junior, and for a moment, her heart wavered. Perhaps she'd been too harsh—

"I hope ruling is everything you ever wanted." He wielded his words like his sword: with precision, stabbing into her insecurities. "I hope this investigation is too."

"Don't worry." She went to the door and held it open for her brother. She could walk any path, with company or without, as long as the justice her father deserved and defended waited at the end. "It will be."

THREE

Justice cannot be bought.

ONE *of the* ELEVEN *on trials*

It's a luxury, plain and simple.

TWO *of the* ELEVEN *on trials*

The letters were stained along the edges. Hesina hadn't noticed by candlelight. It was only when she'd stacked them all to the thickness of a pamphlet, and when the night drained out of the sky, that she saw the moss-green tint around the width.

The pages had been torn from a special edition of the *Tenets*. It was the only identifier she had, and the only one she wanted. Sanjing had planted a seed of suspicion, but she didn't have to let it grow.

She pushed the letters away. Put them in a drawer. Opened the drawer and read them again, fingers drumming against the edge of her desk.

She summoned one of her pages. "Find whatever handwriting samples you can from members of the court," she ordered. *Damn Sanjing, and damn his paranoia. Damn the letter writer too.* "Bring them to me along with a report on the officials with connections to Kendi'a. Any connections," Hesina said firmly before the page could ask. How was she to know what might tantalize a person into betraying his own kingdom?

"Understood, *dianxia*. Will that be all?"

Hesina palmed her eyes. "That will be all."

Once the page left, she put on her oldest dress, a plum-colored *ruqun* with an unraveling hem that wouldn't mind being dragged through a few dungeon puddles.

* * *

Simplification had been the defining word of the Eleven's reign. One and Two, the first co-rulers of the new era, had hacked away any relic excess they could. They pared down the complex written language invented by nobles to bar commoners from learning. They forbade tailors from spinning *hanfu* and *ruqun* from precious metals that could be used to fill coffers. They dissolved the imperial alchemy, dedicated to developing an elixir of immortality for the emperor. Monthlong festivals turned into weeklong festivals. Elite military sects were absorbed into the militia.

But the underground dungeon system remained an elaborate labyrinth of crypts, cells, and torture chambers. The relic emperors had filled them with rebel leaders and commoners. The Eleven had filled them with sooths.

Now most of the cells were empty. The handful of sooths who had escaped execution either lived like the Silver Iris or had scattered to the far reaches of the other three kingdoms. Only common criminals remained, such as the robber across from Hesina.

They sat in an old interrogation chamber, perfectly sound-proofed for private conversations but aesthetically compromised by the bloodstains on the wall. The convict slumped in his chair, mute as a toad. His head was cast down, a shock of brown hair curtained over his eyes, making it hard to tell what he was feeling or thinking—or if he was even breathing. At least, in this way, Hesina couldn't see his bruises and lament over the terrible first impression she'd made.

Nothing had gone as planned. Convicts weren't allowed personal possessions, and the gnarled, crooked rod discovered in the robber's cell apparently qualified as such. Hesina had stopped the guards from crushing it under their boots, but she'd been too late to spare the robber from their fists. Now she placed the rod on the table between them. She hoped—yet doubted—the peace offering would be enough.

The convict took the rod without a word.

Hesina cleared her throat. "Forgive me." She hedged on the side of sounding overly formal. She didn't want her emotions to betray her as they had in front of the Silver Iris. "I know this is all very"—*strange*—"sudden."

Silence.

"You must have many questions."

Evidently not.

With a breath, Hesina began to explain the circumstances of her father's death. The words came slowly, then fast, tearing out of her as if they, too, were trying to outrun that day in the gardens.

She finished by describing the golden poison. Her chest heaved for air.

"As you can tell, the king didn't die a natural death, contrary to what the decrees . . ." Did convicts look at decrees? "What the rest of the kingdom knows. Once I open an investigation, the Bureau will see the truth in the evidence. When they forward the case to the court, I'll need a representative, and"—*how long could she beat around the bush?*—"well, when that time comes, would you be willing? To be that representative?"

Silence upon silence upon silence.

Hesina's hands went clammy. She took inventory of other things, like the color of the convict's hair. It was brown like clay, at least three shades lighter than the lamp-black fuzz Yan babies were born with.

Maybe he wasn't Yan. Maybe he couldn't understand a thing she'd said. It wouldn't be the first wrench in her plans, but it'd be the most unfortunate. How was she to make him appear like an examinee hopeful if he wasn't literate?

"Excuse me." Hesina whispered, as if he were dozing and she didn't want to wake him. "You do understand the language, don't y—"

Her breath hitched as his gaze snapped up.

Beneath all the swelling and discoloration, the robber was surprisingly young. His eyes, like his hair, were oddly pigmented, gray as stone, impenetrable as they captured hers.

Without warning, he took her right hand. She almost yelped as he pressed a finger to her palm and drew out the shaky characters of the common tongue.

I AM A LOWLY MERCHANT ROBBER. I CAN'T HELP YOU.

This was a start. "I'll support you in any way that I can."

WHY ME?
WHY SEARCH?
WHY THE ROD?

His grasp tightened as her hand closed. Cocking his head to the side, he examined her. He tapped on her knuckles, and after fighting to pace her racing heart, Hesina reluctantly uncurled her fingers.

YOU CAN'T SAY.

The writing stopped, then continued.

HOW WILL YOU TRUST ME WHEN YOU DON'T TRUST YOURSELF?

Gone were the uneven strokes and crude lines of someone unfamiliar with the language.

He was one to speak of trustworthiness. "Honesty on matters of the trial is all I ask for," Hesina said with confidence she didn't feel. Could he see the secrets she held under her tongue? Or had the lies stained her teeth?

AND IF I REFUSE TO BE YOUR REPRESENTATIVE?

"Then you refuse." Her stomach dropped when she imagined the scenario—having courted treason all night only to walk away empty-handed. "You have that right."

A PERSON OF PRINCIPLE.

WHO LIES FOR THE TRUTH.

Hesina held his impassive gaze. *Well?* she thought as the seconds passed and it became clear that he'd seen her for who she truly was. Her father had taught her honesty, but deception had been her first language. *Well? Can you work with a hypocrite?*

He drew the characters slower this time, as if he was making up his mind. He lifted his finger, and Hesina hardly dared to breathe. She looked down, even though the words were invisible, and searched for an answer in the tingles of his touch.

DO YOU KNOW HOW TO DUEL?

* * *

"A duel?" asked Caiyan after Hesina recounted her conversation with the convict.

It was the next day. After morning court, they'd met in the king's study, sitting around a *zitan* game table on squat, jade stools carved to resemble napa cabbage heads.

"Yes, a duel." Hesina considered the pieces on the ivory *xiangqi* board. "He said he'd only represent me if I won."

"He's mocking you," concluded Lilian. "Or flirting with you. Or both."

"His motives are unclear," rephrased Caiyan. "But if he didn't want to represent you, he wouldn't have set terms at all. What do you think, milady?"

Think before you act, Hesina's tutors always said. They made it sound so easy. In reality, Hesina acted more often than she thought, and her cheeks warmed as she recalled the course of their conversation. "He seems honest enough." And shady enough. "I think I can trust him to keep his word." Though she didn't even know if he could speak.

But the Silver Iris hadn't lied about the rod, the one and only in the entire dungeons. And the convict was clearly more than the merchant robber the prison documents claimed he was. Hesina remembered the strokes of his finger. The flush on her face extended to her neck. She quickly pushed her chariot three squares over, lining it up with another and entrapping Caiyan's emperor.

"I'm still peeved that you met him without me." Lilian's voice rose from the daybed, where she lay on her back, an ankle propped on one knee and a cat's cradle made of hair ribbon webbed between her fingers. Cyan and ochre blotched her apron. It'd been a dyeing day at the workshops.

"With any luck, you'll see him in court," said Hesina.

"Rod and all?"

"Please," said Caiyan as he blocked the course of Hesina's chariot with a black-powder keg, simultaneously endangering her steed. "It's barely midday."

Lilian snorted. "Says the reader of erotica."

Caiyan sighed, but Hesina thought she caught a glimmer of a smile in his dark eyes. With a tug of jealousy, she looked back to the game board. Bickering was never so simple between herself and Sanjing.

"I'd recommend brushing up on your swordsmanship if you're going to duel, milady."

"*You'd* recommend?" Lilian hooted with laughter. "At least Na-Na can use a sword."

"That's debatable," reminded Hesina. She was a flapping *yuan-yang* duck next to Sanjing's hawkish skill with the sword. But Lilian had a point. Hesina had never witnessed Caiyan holding a weapon, and she'd seen him injured only once. It wasn't a memory she wanted to revisit.

With her double chariot formation foiled, Hesina resorted to the black-powder keg reserved for protecting her own emperor.

Caiyan advanced a foot soldier. "There's a hole in your plans, milady."

Hesina half-heartedly defended her emperor with a chancellor. "Do tell."

Caiyan's foot soldier crossed the river running down the middle of the board and was promoted. "Let's say a trial is declared after the Investigation Bureau reviews the evidence and narrows down the suspects. You win the duel, and the convict agrees to be your representative. How will you convince Xia Zhong to pick him for you?"

"That's easy." Lilian fluttered a hand. "Spout something convincing from the *Tenets*. Passage 1.1.1: 'A minister must serve!' Passage 1.1.2: 'A queen must have a convict with a rod as her representative!'"

Caiyan shook his head at Lilian's impersonation while Hesina suppressed a giggle. Xia Zhong did, in fact, interpret the Eleven's teachings of asceticism to the literal extreme. Word in the palace was that his roof was leaking; there were more mice droppings in his rice bags than rice; he slept on a praying mat, kept only one brazier running in the winter, and had been wearing the same underwear for ten years. For the minister's sake, Hesina hoped the last one wasn't true.

"I'll think of a way," she said to Caiyan. Hopefully soon.

"You won't be able to bribe him."

Even a monk had to want *something*.

"Sure," said Lilian when Hesina voiced as much. "He'd probably ascend if you brought him the original *Tenets*."

He wouldn't be the only one. Scholars all over Yan would worship Hesina if she recovered the version penned by the Eleven themselves. It had disappeared shortly after the fall of the relic reign, and Hesina was as likely to find it as she was to find the mythical Baolin Isles.

Caiyan won the game, and Hesina rubbed her temples. "Only the *Tenets*?"

"I mean, it's Xia Zhong." Lilian flung away the cat's cradle and stretched out on the daybed. "Elevens. I could never live like that."

Yet she had. The twins didn't share much about their past, but Hesina saw its fingerprints whenever Lilian took up the warmest spot in any room, and whenever Caiyan filled his empty rice bowl with tea and drank down the last grains. They lived life as if they might lose its comforts someday, as if they remembered what it was like to be without shelter, food, and father.

But Hesina wasn't like the twins. Losing her father wasn't like returning to a world she'd once known. She'd been unprepared.

She was alone.

Slowly, she pushed away from the square *zitan* table. She climbed a short set of stairs to the floor-to-ceiling windows lining the study's upper half.

The sweet smell of overripe peaches rose from the imperial gardens below. Each palace followed the same layout: courtyards placed within courtyards, halls nested within halls. Her father's study was the exception to the standard sprawl. Half of it rested atop an outcrop of granite, giving Hesina her favorite views of the four gardens—koi, silk, rock, fruit—and their respective ponds, connected by covered galleries zigzagging between mountain formations and thickets of jujube trees.

Hesina's chest locked. Had her father looked out these windows eight days ago as she was looking now? Had the smell of summer peaches lured him to the gardens through the secret passageway behind the shelves? He had left his favorite tortoiseshell chair askew, his wolf-hair brushes dipped in ink. Abandoned on his desk, scattered and waiting, were a three-legged bronze goblet, a snuff bottle, a copy of the *Tenets*, left open to One of the Eleven's biography. Hesina had agonized over whether to leave them be or accept that her father was never coming back.

In the end, she'd taken everything on the desk, along with the courier costume he'd been wearing at the time of his death, and boxed them away. Boxed away her grief too. Placed it out of dust's reach, where it would remain like new.

"Na-Na . . ." An arm wrapped around her shoulders, and Hesina let Lilian pull her in. "You can always slow down. Rely on us. We're here for you."

It wasn't the same. Her father had filled her nights with shadow puppets, dress-up, and maps of secret passageways. Year after year, he boosted her onto his shoulders—her very own throne—and together they'd watch the queen's carriage fade into the mist, whisking her back to the sanatorium in the Ouyang Mountains, where the air and altitude could preserve her failing health. Afterward, the king would take Hesina into the persimmon groves. They'd eat fruit picked straight off the branches until they bloated, and Hesina would cry, missing a mother who would never miss her.

Her tears had blinded her to the unconditional love right in front of her. Now, justice was her only way to say *thank you*. To say *goodbye*. To say *I love you too*.

Caiyan joined them on the second level. He placed a hand on each of their shoulders, and the three stayed that way until a distant drumbeat passed through the air. Horns blared into the chorus, and a gong struck a single, deafening note.

The twins stepped back at the same time Hesina pulled away.

She walked out of the study, telling herself not to run, not to rush. Only fools were eager to receive disappointment. But the sound of the gong resurrected the little girl she had been, and she became a fool again as she climbed the steps of the eastern watchtower, first at a steady pace, then a jog, then a run.

She burst through the doors, cut through the startled guards, and leaned over the granite parapet. The watchtower stood a whole *li* from the city walls, but Hesina was tall enough now to see the line of carriages on her own. It slithered through the Eastern Gate like a serpent scaled in mourning white, horned with banners flying the imperial insignia, wending between crowds of commoners.

Hesina's heart filled and emptied all at once. Her mother had finally come home.

FOUR

There should be six, one for each ministry, granted office on the basis of merit.

ONE *of the* ELEVEN *on ministers*

They're the last line of defense against corruption.

TWO *of the* ELEVEN *on ministers*

Standing on the terraces, with commoners and nobles blanketing the Peony Pavilion below, Hesina couldn't remember the warmth of her father's study. Blades hung in the air as her mother made the slow ascent up the terraces, the people rippling as they bowed. Summer had ended with the return of the queen, and autumn, the season of death, began.

The imperial children awaited her in the same order they always did, with Sanjing to Hesina's right and Rou, the Noble Consort's son, to her left. For reasons Hesina could not understand, Xia Zhong had deemed Rou closer to a trueborn offspring than Caiyan and Lilian. The twins stood behind with Consort Fei herself, who rarely left her lodgings in the Southern Palace. When she did, she wore a screened headpiece that covered her entire face. The headpiece was the source of many rumors. Hesina would know; she'd fed some herself.

To be fair, she'd been young. Four when she'd first seen Rou—a two-year-old toddler then—from afar. Six when she learned the truth—that in the Southern Palace, behind the wisteria vines, there lived a consort, and Rou, the boy in blue, called Hesina's father his own.

Her first taste of betrayal went down about as well as a bowl of tortoise blood tonic. Her father had lied. The boy *wasn't* a visiting prince from the kingdom of Ci. The queen *didn't* have all of the king's love. Hesina hadn't spoken to her father for weeks. Then, when it hurt more to stay angry, she forgave him, but a knot remained in her heart, and blaming someone else was the only way to untie it.

So she blamed Consort Fei and Rou. It wasn't right. But it was easier.

Well, easier when Rou wasn't trying so hard to catch her eye. Hesina's dread mounted as she sensed him working up the courage for words. Finally, as the queen reached the final terrace landing, he offered Hesina a smile and said, "Good luck, Sister."

It was the exact sort of gesture that made her feel terrible in comparison, and she acknowledged Rou with a stiff nod. Later, she would wonder what the good luck was for. Meeting with the queen? Asking for her blessing? Or good luck in general, because her half brother was kind like that?

Not that it mattered. Luck was never on Hesina's side when it came to her mother.

The queen reached the final landing, immaculately wrapped in a voluminous *ruqun* of the deepest blue. She had a face like ceramic—arresting to behold yet quick to fracture, her mouth carved downward as she dismissed everyone but her two trueborn children.

Hesina and Sanjing followed their mother to the red lacquered threshold rising before the palace's front hall. There, she refused Hesina's offered arm and took Sanjing's instead. It could have been worse. At least Hesina hadn't been shamed in front of all the commoners.

The humiliation continued. When they reached the queen's chambers, their mother rejected Hesina's cup of tea and chose Sanjing's instead. Her entourage of maids pretended not to notice and continued fanning the queen. Hesina pretended not to care.

"My blessing, is it?" Her mother's hair, quilled with gold pins, was jet-black like Hesina's. Time didn't touch her, or these chambers, which had been painstaking preserved for the few days a year she visited.

Being here made Hesina feel six again. The orchids hanging from the beamed ceiling looked like sneering faces, and her knees ached with the memory of kneeling against the russet *huanghuali* floors. "Yes," Hesina answered, keeping her voice flat, cool, and stripped of hope.

"Do you have a trusted scribe?"

But a little always crept back in. "I do. I can summon—"

"Good. You may forge the blessing, because you will never receive one from me."

The maids stopped fanning, then sped back up.

Hesina braided back her nerves. She needed the validation of this blessing. "I am ready to fulfill my duties, Mother."

Her mother considered the teacup in her hand with disinterest. "You speak of the coronation as if it's inevitable." With a *clink* of porcelain, she set the cup back down. "I may yet choose to stay."

The chamber froze.

Mother. Staying. Ruling as regent.

Hesina hadn't considered the possibility, but maybe it wasn't a bad thing. If she told her mother the truth about the king's death, the queen would surely want to find the assassin too. What did crowns and thrones matter then?

The Imperial Doctress, who serviced the queen just as often as the maids, placed a steaming porcelain bowl on the side table. The tang of ginseng tunneled up Hesina's nose. "Be reasonable, Your Highness. You can't stay away from the mountain air for long."

"You should focus on getting better, Mother," Sanjing added, standing at the queen's side. He belonged there, unlike Hesina, and she stiffened as his gaze drifted to her. "Sina will be a good ruler."

The queen barked a laugh. "You speak on your sister's behalf, but do you know half her thoughts?"

As if she knew herself.

The queen canted her head in her daughter's direction, and Hesina's spine went rigid. "You. Why do you want to rule so badly?"

A week ago, Hesina wouldn't have been able to answer. This fate had chosen her. It was only now, seventeen years later, that she chose it back. For truth, for justice, and for her father.

But she wasn't in a habit of opening up to her mother. "Why *shouldn't* I want to rule?" After all, she'd been groomed for this her entire life. Sacrificed normal interests for lessons in calligraphy, cosmology, and diplomacy.

"If you're doing this for your father, there's no use."

Hesina blinked. "What do you mean?"

The queen lifted a hand, and a maid immediately began to massage it. "Nothing you do will bring him back."

What did her mother think she was, a child? Someone who still believed in the myths tutors told their pupils, that enough studying could make them an immortal sage or give them the power to raise the dead?

Before Hesina could reply, the Imperial Doctress tutted and nodded at the steaming bowl of tonic. "It's growing cold," she said, as calmly as she had when insisting that the king had died a natural death.

But this time, Hesina wouldn't back down. She seized the bowl of tonic and dropped to a kneel, bowing her head. "Please, Mother. Accept this."

Accept me.

The Imperial Doctress was wrong. The concoction hadn't grown cold. Heat seared through the pads of Hesina's fingers and gnawed at the bone. She held on, presenting the bowl as her piety. All the queen had to do was take it.

As Hesina's arms grew leaden, a knock came from the chamber doors. A maid hurried to open them, and the visitor entered, his *hanfu* hem skirting into Hesina's limited range of vision as he approached.

"This had better be important, Minister Xia," snapped her mother.

Xia Zhong?

Hesina didn't believe it. Not even when she heard the Minister of Rites say, "I wouldn't intrude if it weren't," or when he knelt beside her, the scent of wet, cold tea leaves emitting from his person.

"I came as soon as I learned of your return," said Xia Zhong. "It's on the matter of succession."

Hesina tensed. *He knows.* About her treason, her visit to the dungeons. He'd seen her duplicitous heart, so unlike her father's. He'd come to declare her unfit.

"She isn't ready." Her mother's rejection pinched, but it would be nothing compared to death by a thousand cuts. Hesina's head spun. She struggled to follow along when the minister recited:

"Passage 2.1.3: 'No ruler, young or old, can know everything there is to know. The realm is large, the commoners many. Without the guidance of their advisors and ministers, even the most experienced of kings and queens turn incompetent.'"

No one spoke when he finished.

Then the queen did. "Get out of my chambers," she ordered, just as Hesina understood the meaning of the passage. Xia Zhong hadn't come to denounce her. Quite the opposite, he was *encouraging* the queen to give her blessing.

Wait.

The minister bowed low. He got to his feet, one knee at a time, and paid the queen the utmost respect by facing her as he retreated. As the doors closed, Hesina wished she had the power to call him back. But it was pointless—her mother had made up her mind.

Hesina's temples tensed as she ground her teeth. She began to lower the bowl.

The weight of it suddenly lightened in her hands.

The porcelain parted from her fingertips.

"If this is what you want, then take the crown. Take my blessing."

Head still bowed, Hesina dared to hope.

"You can bring this kingdom to its knees, for all I care."

The bowl, concoction and all, crashed to the floor as her mother let go.

The queen laughed, and coughed, and coughed as she laughed. Half the maids tended to her while the other half huddled around Hesina to clean up the shards.

Hesina remained kneeling. There was a time when she would have cried as she blamed herself, the illness, anyone and anything but her mother for her porcelain heart.

That time had passed. As the dark green liquid spread over the varnished floor, Hesina laid one hand over another, pressing them palm down to the floor and her forehead to their backs in a final *koutou* to the queen. Because of her, Hesina could risk everything and more for her father. Because of her, she had no regrets.

* * *

"Xia Zhong! Wait!"

It wasn't queenly to shout, but Hesina didn't care. The minister turned as she hurried down the covered gallery.

"Thank you," she said when she reached him. For someone who supposedly subsisted on tofu and leeks, he walked at an impressive speed. The Northern Palace—home to the relic emperors' harems in the past, now the offices of ministers—lay just past the rock gardens.

Xia Zhong bowed, the wooden beads at his neck clicking as they swung forward. "A minister does what duty demands."

"Please, at ease." Hesina helped him upright.

The minister hadn't aged well. His nose was sharp and defined, his frame tall and thin, but his skin was creased and sagging, his bald scalp dark with liver spots. His eyes bugged, draped with bags so heavy that they pulled red into the rim, giving them a fishlike quality.

His court robes, too, had seen better days. The black cloth had faded to charcoal, the malachite cuffs bordering on mold green. The smell of damp tea leaves enveloped Hesina again. She tried not to gag.

Xia Zhong took a step back as if sensing her discomfort. "Can I help you, *dianxia*?"

DESCENDANT OF THE CRANE

Her automatic answer was *no*. She'd come to thank him, not to flaunt her incompetence.

But he'd already seen her at her lowest. He'd spoken for her. His words had carried a torch down to the deepest, darkest dungeon of her self-doubt. He wasn't a friend, but perhaps, if Hesina played her cards right, he could be an ally.

"I'd like some advice." She invited Xia Zhong to walk, and they started down the gallery and through the rock gardens. The twisted pumice boulders on either side of them were supposed to evoke auspicious characters such as *longevity*, but all Hesina could see were the nooks and crannies where she and her father had played hide-and-seek. "If, let's say, my father didn't die a natural death . . ."

She braced herself for derision, for scorn.

None came.

"If he were murdered," she ventured, "would the people have the right to know?"

"Passage 3.4.1: 'A suspected case of misdemeanor, private or public, personal or institutional, must be forwarded to the Investigation Bureau of the province in question.' The Bureau deliberates, not you or I. If the Bureau can find enough evidence and suspects, then the case goes to trial, and the people must be notified by the law of the *Tenets*."

If only she'd had Xia Zhong to convince her brother. "What if the political climate is . . . unstable?"

"Passage 3.4.2: 'Justice is a muscle. Without faith, it weakens. Without use, it decays. Without challenges, it does not strengthen.' Small cases have their challenges, *dianxia*. So do large ones."

Hesina always considered the *Tenets*, with their sooth-hating passages, as propaganda. Even her father had cautioned her against reading the book too literally. But the passages were like weapons in Xia Zhong's hands. It stunned her. It awed her.

"If there's nothing else," said the minister as they neared the end of the gallery, "I must be going now."

"There is something else."

They came to the Northern Palace moon gate. Through the circular opening of cutout limestone, Hesina glimpsed the minister's residence. Just like rumors claimed, the roof was missing half its tiles.

Xia Zhong didn't invite her in. Hesina didn't blame him.

They stood under the gallery eave, the minister waiting for her to speak. She collected her courage, building it like a house of twigs. "I have a favor to ask you."

"Is it in accordance with the *Tenets*?"

She could not lie. "I don't know."

"Then I can't help."

"Wait," Hesina said as Xia Zhong started to go. She thought she caught a flash of annoyance in his red-rimmed eyes, but it was gone when she looked again.

"I know a boy. A boy of immense talent and skill." The lies came easily this time. Too easily. Hesina almost grimaced when she imagined what her father would think. "He made some mistakes. His life was hard, and he was desperate. But his dream always was to pass the civil service examinations. Become a servant of the state."

She layered emotion to her voice, infused the story with truth. She'd known a boy like this, after all. It was Caiyan.

But Caiyan had never robbed a merchant of five hundred pieces of *banliang*. "Now he's wasting away in the dungeons. I could pardon him, but he is without a home and family. I'd be releasing him to rot on the streets. The only thing that can save him now is a ticket past the preliminary exams."

Xia Zhong shook his head before she had even finished. "No."

"Please. If my father's case makes it to trial, pick him for me as my representative."

"I said no." The minister slipped past her.

Hesina balled her fists. She'd lost count of all the sunny days she'd stayed in to read another treatise or commentary on the *Tenets*, reciting the passages to her tutors. It couldn't have been for nothing. If Xia Zhong could use the words of the dead, then so could she.

"Passage 5.7.1: 'The death sentence for petty crimes such as theft and vandalism will be lifted because the potential for such persons to contribute remains.' Passage 4.6.3: 'The examination system will not discriminate on the basis of gender, class, or background.' Passage 5.2.2: 'Everyone, under the new era, will have an equal chance at a self-sustainable living.'"

Xia Zhong stopped in his tracks.

"Passage 2.4.1," she added for good measure. "'A minister serves.'"

A gale swept down the gallery, bringing the first of the fallen gingko leaves to Hesina's feet.

"Name. Quickly," snapped the minister when she didn't speak. "Before I change my mind."

Name.

Name.

She had no name. She'd made up this elaborate story about a boy whose name she didn't even know. *Demons take her.* "Cell 315."

She wanted to disappear into the ground as he left without a word.

* * *

Three letters appeared on Hesina's desk the next day.

One was from the Investigation Bureau; they had received her case on the king's murder and would notify her if it proceeded to trial.

Another was from the Imperial Cosmologist, who'd selected an auspicious day for her coronation, two nights away.

The last was from Xia Zhong.

Hesina unfolded this one slowly, apprehension drying her mouth to lotus paste.

Passage 2.4.1: 'A minister serves.'
If a trial is declared, consider Convict 315 your coronation gift.

FIVE

War is thievery on a grand scale.

ONE *of the* ELEVEN *on war*

*The emperors think it's a game. They sit on their thrones and
watch people die on their behalves.*

TWO *of the* ELEVEN *on war*

Downward slash.

Do you know how to duel?

Palm the hilt.

Come to me when you're ready.

Transition into leftward swing, leading with the torso.

Win.

Forearm to eye level.

And I will represent you in your trial.

Cut right.

"You're doing it wrong."

Hesina lowered her sword.

Sanjing came up from behind. He adjusted her grip. Then he
led her arm in a series of strokes. "Your opponent isn't a log to

be hacked at, but a painting to be finished. The tip of the sword should always fall sure. Keep your wrist loose for a wider range of motion." He stepped back. "Try again."

"Stop favoring your dominant side," he barked after her third repetition. "It makes you predictable."

Hesina cut right and returned to her center. "You always win," she grumbled. A breeze combed through the courtyard, teasing apart the willow fringe on the white limestone walls. "That makes you predictable too."

Sanjing crossed his arms. "I can't help being brilliant."

Hesina snorted, then smiled. The tension between them had eased—for now. "Why are you here?"

"Thought I'd stop by before heading west. Carrying out your orders to delay a war, if I remember correctly."

Her smile slid. "Now?"

She noticed her brother's attire. Leather pads covered his legs. A thatch cloak for wicking away the rain fell over his shoulders. He was dressed to ride.

She waited for Sanjing to speak, but he simply paced to the courtyard's center, where an ivory table, speckled with black and white stones, displayed an unfinished game of Go.

After studying positions, Sanjing lifted a white stone. "A messenger hawk from the Yan-Kendi'an border post just arrived." Placed it. "We've lost a village. It's gone."

"To another raid?" Then Hesina realized how ridiculous that sounded. People lost cattle and oxen and grain stores to a raid. Sometimes money. Sometimes lives.

Not villages.

"Explain, Jing." Fear and frustration bolted through her gut— frustration because she should have had the answers, and fear because it felt like she never would. No matter how much Hesina learned, her kingdom was too large. She would always be blind to its corners. "What do you mean by 'gone'?"

"What do you think I mean?" Sanjing's eyes burned black. "Nothing is there. No livestock. No people. Everything is gone without a trace."

He raised a black stone, gripping it as though he aimed to hurl it. Hesina drew back, and the fire in her brother's gaze abated.

He placed the stone on the board beside a white one. "Some say it's the work of sooths."

"Jing . . ."

"What? Don't believe me?"

Hesina lowered her gaze to the game board in case Sanjing saw her skepticism. Yes, the sooths were hated for their Sight. In the relic era, it'd enabled them to rat out countless individuals who harbored the mere thought of rebelling.

But what kept the hatred flowing, from mouth to mouth, generation to generation, was the rumor that the sooths could perform magic. The specifics of what and how were lost to time. The handful of sooths caught in the centuries since the purge certainly didn't have magic. If they did, wouldn't they have saved themselves from death by a thousand cuts?

Now her brother expected her to believe that sooths were responsible for the disappearance of an entire village. That magic was real. Not only that, he expected her believe that sooths were aiding Kendi'a. If he said this kind of thing on the streets, then Yan would descend into chaos. The people might just believe in the assassination of the king without Hesina's help.

Something clicked into place, and comprehension unlocked like a door. "I see how it is." She lifted her eyes from the game board and let them rest on her brother's. "Your scare tactics won't work on me. No matter what you say, I'm not sacrificing justice for Father."

"The sooths—"

"—*aren't* making the villages disappear. When was the last time you encountered a sooth?" Days ago, for Hesina, but that didn't diminish her point. "When was the last time *anyone* encountered one with power stronger than the Sight? There are no magic-wielding sooths, Jing. Not after the purge. There are sandstorms, and there is your undying paranoia."

"You think I fear for *myself*? You—" Her brother bit back his words. His knuckles whitened around the pommel of his *liuyedao*. "You're unbelievable."

"And you're delusional." One of them had to be.

"Yes." Her brother let out a humorless laugh. "It seems that I am. So what's the secret to making you listen? Should I spout passages from the *Tenets*?"

Tenets? Hesina blinked. Where had that come from?

"Anyway, congratulations," Sanjing said without much cheer. He turned to the moon gate to go, then stopped. "I'm sure you won't miss me at your coronation, but on the off chance you do, Mei will attend in my place."

"She's not going with you?"

"She has better things to do, like watching over a certain inexperienced queen from the shadows."

"I don't need her," said Hesina, partly out of spite, and partly because she knew what Commander Mei meant to her brother, who had plenty of admirers but not many friends. It was the one thing they had in common. "I have guards. I have . . ."

"Who?" her brother scoffed. "Your manservant?"

"It's been ten years, Jing." Ten years since their father had adopted the twins, ten years of enduring Sanjing's jealousy. He accused her of replacing him with Caiyan. She accused him of being petty. But the closer she grew to Caiyan, the further she grew from Sanjing, and Hesina had to wonder—was everyone's heart like her mother's? Was love a resource to be split, sometimes unequally?

She sat on the table's matching ivory stool and rested her sword over her lap. They'd moved from the war to Caiyan, from one argument to another. But at least she was used to this fight.

"Caiyan's been nothing but civil toward you." Especially after what Sanjing had done to him that winter day on the lake. "You don't have to like him, Jing. But you can accept him."

"I can't accept a person I don't trust."

"Give me one good reason why you don't trust him."

"He's a bad influence." His jaw tensed as Hesina snorted. *Bad influence* and *Caiyan*. She'd never thought she would hear those words together. "It's because of him that you . . ."

"I what?"

"Forget it."

"*What* were you going to say?"

Sanjing looked away. "You went to the red-light district."

The sword slipped off Hesina's lap. Without realizing it, she'd risen from the stool. "You're spying on me."

It wasn't a question.

First the comment about the *Tenets*. Now this.

For a second, she thought her brother would deny it.

He didn't. "Only because you refuse to tell me anything."

"Well, no wonder. Why would I confide in a little boy who can't mind his own business?"

The words worked. Her brother whipped around and strode

away, so fast that Hesina couldn't even catch the expression on his face.

Good. She collapsed back onto the stool and let out a damp exhale. All the emotions she'd been holding back trickled out: Vexation—how dare he spy on her? Relief—he didn't know the worst of what she'd done. And finally, defeat—he'd never know that she kept him in the dark for his own good. Instead he'd head straight for the stables and ride out hard. He'd think she didn't care, without giving her the chance to prove him wrong.

Hesina rose. She lifted her sword and went through the sequence again, practicing until blisters bubbled on her palms, the skin wounds distracting from the pain inside.

She could wait. Wait for a trial to be declared. Wait for her skill to sharpen. But all she wanted was to fight. With swords, not feelings, and with someone she could win against, someone other than her brother.

※ ※ ※

In the prison exercise yard, sunlight highlighted the half-healed cuts and bruises on the convict's face. He shifted his hold on the wooden sword's hilt, the sleeves of his dungeon fatigues in tatters.

Hesina adjusted her own grip, ignoring the sweat on the wood. She wasn't nervous. Couldn't be nervous. She would have this convict as her representative, or she would have no one at all.

She drew her sword and judged the distance between them.

Steady.

Breathe in.

Hold it.

Now.

She dashed.

Crack. Wood struck wood. Gravel flew out from under their feet as they spun. She pressed into the gridlock of their swords to test his strength. His sleeves gathered at the elbows as he returned the effort.

Measuring them to be equally matched, Hesina whirled backward, recovered her stance, then lunged again. They crossed once more. Sequence after sequence unfolded, and she fell into the rhythm, timing his blows and matching them. The darkening sky drowned out their shadows. The first few droplets pattered onto the gravel, right before sheets of rain split the clouds.

With renewed vigor, Hesina pressed the convict onto the defensive. She knocked his sword upward, creating an opening. He slipped as he stumbled back. The opening widened.

She danced behind him and slashed in from the right. He struggled to maintain his grip. Victory was all around her. Hesina pressed on, backing him into the wall. But as she thrust her blade forward, she saw all the things the rain had brought into sharp relief: his knobby wrists, his bony chest, his eyes, sunken and bruised with sleeplessness.

Equality is not the natural way of the world, whispered her father's voice. *It must be nurtured.*

Her sword struck stone.

The convict's wooden blade streaked her way. Instinct kicked in; Hesina shoved her sword up just in time, but the impact slammed into her shoulder. She braced her palm to the flat of her blade and he leapt away, then came at her as an entirely different swordsman.

His first slash drove her against the wall. His second had her trembling. His third wrenched the hilt from her hands and sent the sword flying across the exercise yard, where it snapped upon striking the cinder-block wall.

He lifted his sword and touched its wooden point to her throat.

Hesina wheezed. How? How had she not read his true ability? Why had he hidden it? Who was he, this self-proclaimed merchant robber who could fight with such power and grace? But the answers were inconsequential. She had lost. The rain rinsed out the world, drenching her.

She had come this far for nothing.

She moved out of the fighting stance, then held still, waiting for him to do the same.

He didn't, not at first. His wooden blade remained pointed at her throat, prolonging the burn of her humiliation. Then he laid down the sword and sighed. "Okay."

Hesina stared.

"You won," he went on. "Well, technically you lost—"

"You're fluent?"

"Huh?"

"You can speak Yan?" *Elevens, he could speak at all?*

"Oh." He scratched his head. "I learned it a year ago. There's not much else to do in prison."

The tips of Hesina's ears warmed. "Then what was all . . . *this*"—she waved her hand—"about?"

"To make you go away." He shrugged. "As I was saying, you lost, but you threw."

"What . . . Why . . . *Wait* . . . I didn't *throw*."

"I've looked better, I'll admit. Attacking my opening probably didn't seem fair."

He closed in, and she stumbled back. The rain had filmed his clothes over his skin, highlighting the raised old scars on his arms and the fine, pointed angles of his face, fox-like in their definition.

His eyes were young, yet dark with a lifetime's worth of wins and losses.

Hesina took another step back. "That doesn't answer my question. Why give me a chance to duel at all?"

He stopped several reed lengths away. "Why not send a champion in your place? Why not threaten me when you thought you had lost?"

"That wasn't what we agreed on."

"Yes. But I didn't expect you to be so—"

He opened his palm. Intersecting the fate lines was something silver and shaped like a dragonfly. The prison master key, freed from the cord of Hesina's sash.

"—honorable." Key in hand, he strode across the exercise yard. "Ideals aren't worth it. Yours cost you the duel."

He was a convict. She was to be his queen. She could have ordered him back or, better yet, had him whipped for his insolence. But instead Hesina sloshed after the convict, mud splattering her *ruqun* skirts as they made for the steps leading back to the underground dungeon. "Why, then, are you agreeing to represent me?"

"Would you believe me if I said that I feel bad for your loss?"

"No."

"I have a hunch that you're going to pardon me. I'm in it for the freedom. Do you believe me now?"

The hunch was correct, but: "No."

"Then how about this? I'm curious." The dungeon's darkness solidified like lard, melted intermittently by torches down the cinder-block tunnel. "A dead king," said the convict. "A deceived populace. A truth seeker. Sounds like a story that could end very well or very poorly, and I want to spectate. Believe me now?"

"You don't have to be *that* honest," muttered Hesina.

"Sorry. That sounded better in my head."

"So is that the truth? You're here to spectate?"

"And help, I suppose."

"You suppose!" She stepped on his heel, and he stumbled.

"To help!" He caught himself, then glanced at her over his shoulder. "To help."

In the dim light, his eyes were like pools of rainwater, reflecting more than they revealed. But they also were clouded with woe, an expression contradictory to the amusement curling at his lips. Someone with eyes like that could have smiled as they bled. Hesina was suddenly overcome with remorse. She wanted to apologize for tripping him, but he turned those eyes and that smile away, facing back around. "Though truth be told, I'm more used to harming than helping."

What he was used to didn't matter. She could tear out his past as a criminal. She would embroider in a new identity, a motivation.

"Let me tell you what you're in this for," she said as they came to his block of cells. "You're a scholar. Your lifelong dream has been to serve the kingdom. But you've had a dreadfully disadvantaged upbringing compared to your peers—"

"It wasn't so bad."

"—and *winning* this case is your one chance of making it to the civil service examinations."

The convict rubbed a hand over the back of his neck. "I see."

"Who are you?" Hesina demanded, quizzing like a tutor.

"A scholar."

"What do you aspire to be?"

"A civil servant."

She nodded in approval, but the convict appeared troubled.

"Er, what am I studying? As a scholar?"

"You're studying . . ." She thought back to all her imperial lessons and picked the topic she'd hated least. "Agriculture."

"Agriculture."

"Yes." She would have her books delivered to him. She would train him herself on the specifics of sheep pedigrees and soybean rotations.

"Can I suggest something else?" he asked as they stopped in front of his cell.

He was rejecting her idea. She found that almost more offensive than when he'd stolen her key.

On the thought of the key . . .

"You said the king was poisoned," said the convict as Hesina reached for his hand. She missed him by a second; their knuckles brushed as he raised the key to the cell padlock. Something in Hesina came briefly undone, just like the lock.

He entered the cell and relocked it from the inside.

"How about I study something related to poison," he said, returning the key through the bars. "Like medicine."

She tried to avoid skin contact as she accepted her key. "Fine. Medicine. You'll receive a pardon once a trial is declared." She didn't *quite* trust him enough to release him now.

He nodded as if he completely understood.

"Until then . . ." Hesina didn't know what to say. Her father's justice was in the convict's hands. It made her vulnerable. Desperate. She forced herself back from the bars. "Who are you?"

"A scholar—"

"No. Your name."

"I have many."

"Which do you prefer?"

The convict ran his teeth over his bottom lip, deciding. "Akira," he finally said.

"Akira." Hesina memorized it, then turned away, disarmed but not defeated. "We'll meet again in court."

SIX

A ruler who abandons their people is no ruler at all.

ONE of the ELEVEN on monarchs

Dress simply. Eat simpler. We were all commoners once.

TWO of the ELEVEN on monarchs

Many gifts came overnight, well wishes for her coronation. Many more would arrive before the day's end. But the thing Hesina wanted most was in her hand.

MEMORANDUM OF THE INVESTIGATION BUREAU
ON THE FIRST DAY OF THE 10TH MONTH, YEAR 305 OF THE
NEW ERA,
AFTER 2 DAYS OF REVIEW,
UNDER THE SUPERVISION OF THE DIRECTOR,
THE BUREAU HAS DEEMED THE FOLLOWING CASE OF
{ THE KING'S MURDER }
SUFFICIENT IN EVIDENCE AND IN SUSPECTS.
MAY JUSTICE BE DELIVERED IN COURT.

"Shall it be posted?" asked her page.

"Not yet." She reread the memorandum, marveling at the words. They were real. They were so real they bled, the fresh ink imprinting on her hands. Hesina finally put the document aside, placing it among the new maps, books, brushes, and scales covering her desk, offerings from ministers and officials of her court.

Tonight. It hit her again, a punch to the gut, that her coronation was *tonight*. Two days ago, she'd been begging for her mother's blessing. Unlike her mother's blessing, the memorandum had arrived quicker than she'd expected. Timely, too, since tonight she was to issue her first decree, a document to set the tone of her reign. What could be more fitting than announcing the trial? Tonight suddenly felt too far away.

Hesina wrote her first decree. Then she wrote her first pardon and handed it to her page along with a small pouch of money, enough for a few nights' lodging in the city.

"Make sure he eats." Ideally, Akira would put on a few *jin* between now and the trial. "As for clothes . . ." Unfortunately, there was no time for tailor-made. "Buy him the best set of scholar robes you can find." Hair! She'd almost forgotten hair. "And have him see a barber. I want him well-groomed."

"Understood, *dianxia*. But there is one thing . . . Is he strong?"

"What?"

"Is he fast?" asked her page. "I'm afraid I won't be able to catch him if he runs."

"Oh." Hesina leaned back in her seat. "Don't worry."

Her page frowned, worried. "A newly freed convict can be unpredictable. Perhaps a guard should accompany us."

Hesina had considered it. She had the most to lose, after all, if Akira slipped away. But she wanted a representative she could trust, not a mule on a tether. If he broke his promise, she would consider it an arrow dodged. "No, it's fine. You won't be able to catch him if he runs, so don't try."

Lilian entered as the page left to his new assignments. "Poor thing. I've never seen someone look so confused. What did you do to him?"

Hesina fiddled with one of her new bronze scales. "Nothing scandalous."

"Good. I wouldn't have wanted to miss out." Then Lilian lifted the *ruqun* hanging over her arm. "I come bearing gifts from the workshop. Do you like it?"

"It looks like a funeral gown." Which, Hesina assumed, meant it was her coronation gown. The entire ensemble—from the billowy sleeves to the brocade *bixi* panel that would hang down the center of the skirts—was white. Bleached of color and of life, cut from coarse linen instead of silk. That was the point, of course. The coronation was more of a commemoration than a celebration, a time to remember that the peace of the present had been built on the blood of the past.

Lilian cocked her head to the side. "It *is* lacking a bit of color. Shall I spruce it up?"

"Please don't." Hesina would cause enough of a stir by revealing the king's true cause of death. She would wear the white, and it would suit her, because while the others mourned the heroes of the past, she would mourn the end of her life as a princess.

It's for Father, she reminded herself after Lilian left and her maids streamed in. When they dusted her face with rice powder, she pretended she and her father were powdering their opera masks. When they helped her into the *ruqun*, she pretended she and her father were trying on costumes. But when they started pulling at her hair, forcing it into some gravity-defying coiffure, Hesina wished her father were really here to spirit her off into a secret passageway.

He would never rescue her again. Instead it was Ming'er, her lady-in-waiting, who swept in and shooed the maids away.

"How you've grown," Ming'er cooed as she took her place by the vanity and set out a selection of pins. "Just yesterday, you were barely the length of my forearm, and you hated being bathed."

Babies were odd creatures, Hesina concluded. "I hope I haven't been too troublesome."

"Oh, my flower. Time is the only troublesome one."

For Ming'er, Hesina tried to smile. Then she glanced down at the array of hairpins before her. Garnet, opal, sapphire. Jewels befitting a queen. But one was missing.

"Ming'er, where's . . ."

Her voice trailed off as Ming'er slowly set the final pin in the center. A crane in flight rose at the end of the white jade length, its wings spread and feathers individually carved, the longer ones tipped in obsidian.

Her father had gifted her this pin as he'd gifted his love: from the moment of her birth, when her hands had been too small to grasp its form. Her eyes moistened. She closed them, hiding the tears as Ming'er combed her hair—one stroke, two strokes, three strokes before the doors flung apart with a *bang.*

Hesina's eyes flew open. Her maids fell to their knees and pressed themselves down in *koutou,* lending her a direct view of her mother.

The queen stood in a shaft of noonday light. Her face was pinched, her hair untamed. The cross-wrapped front of her thin underrobes gaped open, showing the cord of scar tissue at her throat.

Hesina's own throat bobbed as she swallowed. She didn't know what could have possibly left a scar so thick and so complete, a collar in its own right, but the sight of it exposed set her on edge.

Her mother drifted through the sitting room, under the painted beam, past two silk screens embroidered with cranes, and into Hesina's inner chamber.

"Leave us," she said when she reached her daughter's vanity.

Ming'er set down a pin. Hesina's heart sank with it. The dowager queen had given a direct order; Ming'er couldn't disobey. Still, Hesina hated to see the woman she cared for bow in submission. Ming'er drew the silk screens shut as she retreated, enclosing mother and daughter.

The dowager queen lifted a lock of Hesina's hair and began curling it around a dowel, and Hesina tensed at the uncharacteristic gentleness. She should have said something daughterly, but there was no point in pretense with her mother, so she stayed silent and fixed her gaze on the slant of bronze mirror reflecting both their faces.

The resemblance never failed to startle Hesina. With irises more black than brown, skin more olive than peach, and ebony hair that never faded in the sun, each strand straight as bamboo, she and her mother were like the same person at two different points in life.

Today, though, her mother's cheeks were flushed. Her breathing was heavy and laden with a scent that cut through the sweet varnish, something clear yet bitter, like ashes, like ice, like . . .

Sorghum wine.

"So," said the dowager queen before Hesina could ask why she was drinking when the Imperial Doctress had explicitly forbidden it. "I hear you've set the Investigation Bureau on the case of your father's death."

Was this a trick? A test? Hesina wound her fingers in her skirts. "I have."

"Foolish girl." Her mother selected a long and slender opal pin instead of the white jade crane. "He's finally gone. Why change that?"

The words came as a slap. Hesina's heart stung, then tingled with confusion and horror. "Finally gone?"

The dowager queen hummed a melody.

"Father always said you were riveting. Whip-smart. Brave." Hesina should have stopped. Apologized. Taken back her words. But she only made them quieter. "What happened to you?"

Her mother's hand slipped. The hairpin slipped with it, a flash in the mirror as the tip jerked up and caught on skin. Pain exploded over Hesina's scalp. She bit down on a cry, then gasped, "I thought you loved him. I thought you'd understand my actions for once."

Unless she was imagining it, her mother's breathing seemed shaky too. She lifted the pin again, gave Hesina's hair a hard twist, and successfully inserted it. "What happened? It was his time. It was all our times. And yet, we lived. The world loved us once. It no longer does. One day you will know what it means to be forsaken."

Hesina already knew.

But this time, she kept silent.

* * *

On the palanquin ride down the terraces, Ming'er redid Hesina's hair. Hesina should have told her not to bother. No one would care about a lopsided chignon if the dowager queen didn't show for her own daughter's coronation. But in the end, Hesina let Ming'er do her work because it comforted the woman, even if it didn't comfort her.

In the end, Hesina was also right. The people were too busy whispering to notice her hair. Hesina caught snatches of their words as she ascended the Peony Pavilion at the base of the terraces. *What has the daughter done to offend her?*

They would soon find out.

Every coronation since One and Two of the Eleven's had been held outside and shared with the people. In the same vein of tradition, a selected commoner climbed the limestone steps after Hesina. Hesina lowered her head, and the commoner rested the Rising Phoenix over her crown. It was a boulder of a headpiece with spread wings carved out of red coral. Each time Hesina bowed to the setting sun and the rising stars, she worried it'd topple and crush her toes. Miraculously, it stayed.

She straightened to deafening applause. Members of the six imperial ministries prostrated themselves in *koutou* below the pavilion. "*Wansui, wansui, wan wan sui!*" The rest of the crowd followed in suit. "*Wansui, wansui, wan wan sui!*"

May the queen live ten thousand years, ten thousand years, ten thousand ten thousand years.

The Imperial Breeder released a flock of red-crowned cranes; they took to the sky, blotting it white and crimson. Ning and Ci emissaries swarmed forward, offering chests of diamonds mined from the bottom of Ning ice lakes and pearls fished from the Ci clay swamps. The Kendi'ans were missing, but that became the least of Hesina's concerns as dozens of hands fell to her skirts and crying babies were shoved into her face. The people's fervor squeezed like an ill-fitting girdle. Her tutors had all failed. None of them had prepared her for this; she was going to suffocate and die.

"Make way!" Silver flashed through the throng of bodies. "I come to the rescue," Lilian whispered when she reached Hesina's side. She was stunning in a sleek, metallic *ruqun* printed with black medallions. Commoners immediately streamed to her; they worshipped the twins as physical representations of the king's benevolence.

"About time," Hesina wheezed.

"Let's discuss payment."

"Payment? Shouldn't you be saving me out of the goodness of your heart?"

"Yes, but I'm also hungry."

"Have some rodent." Coronation fare was humble, to replicate the days when the Eleven, as fugitives, had subsisted on much less.

"Bah, no thank you." Lilian shuddered. "I'll save the mice for cats."

"I think it's squirrel." Or perhaps raccoon. Hesina thought she'd seen something bushy-tailed in the Imperial Buttery.

"Tell you what. I'll give you a discount. I only *require* three baskets of candied hawthorn berries for my services today."

"Five if you stay."

Lilian grinned, to Hesina's relief. "Deal."

By the time they saw to everyone, the moon had risen. Palace servants carried braziers out onto the pavilion, and under the stars, nobles and commoners alike roasted wild fennel bulbs and squirrel. The imperial troupe put on a reenactment of the last relic emperor's beheading. The imperial engineers revealed their latest fireworks: sun-bright peonies and azaleas bloomed and wilted in the night sky.

Everything was exquisite—or so Hesina assumed. It was hard to enjoy the entertainment when she was its centerpiece. The night was cool, but watching eyes warmed her skin. She willed time to move faster. It didn't, but the moment nevertheless arrived.

A page carried two ewers of yellow wine to Hesina. Mothers hushed their children as she lifted one. Her hand shook under its weight as she poured. Wine splashed onto the ground, a libation to the buried and the dead.

"A toast to the past, and to the sacrifices made for the new era."

Heads bowed for the nine of the Eleven who'd perished before the dynasty's fall, and for the hundreds of thousands of commoners who'd died for the revolution's cause.

Unwittingly, the face of the Silver Iris flashed in Hesina's mind. Tens of thousands of sooths had died for this era, too, but she could never voice her remorse over that.

"And a toast to the future," she said over the lump of guilt in her throat, lifting the second ewer. "My first advisor will be Viscount Yan Caiyan."

Caiyan made his way forward. He nodded at Hesina when he reached her, and it was all the encouragement she needed.

"My first gift will be the commodity we lack most."

Imperial guards carried forth sacks of salt. As an old saying went, water and salt made lifeblood. Yan had been blessed with lakes, rivers, springs, but it relied on Kendi'a for the white crystal essential to food preservation and medicine. Kendi'a's recent incursions had disrupted trade, driving the price of salt in Yan to historic highs, and families wept in gratitude as the guards divvied out allotments.

Impatience soured the moment for Hesina. She could barely contain herself as she waited for the excitement to settle. "My first decree . . ."

She drew a deep breath.

". . . Concerns the king's death. He passed far before his time.

The Investigation Bureau deems there to be sufficient evidence for a trial. The truth must be found, and justice delivered."

The night went thick and airless. No one breathed; no one moved. Hesina searched the sea of faces for a flicker of support. She drowned in the silence.

"A trial?" someone finally asked.

"The Investigation Bureau?"

"What is there to investigate?"

A voice cracked through the others like a cane. "Nonsense!"

It came from a wispy old woman who still wore the white mourning headband. "What are you trying to suggest?" she snapped at Hesina as if she were a misbehaving child. "That the king was murdered?"

Murdered. The word raked through Hesina, overturning her banked fury. "Yes. Yes, there is reason to believe so."

"Lies!" shouted a man. "That's impossible!"

"Who would want to kill our king?"

"The decrees said he died peacefully!"

Faces boiled red. Voices swelled. Hesina's went unheard. Her anger sizzled, smoking into panic.

Who was she fooling? She couldn't do this. She wasn't her father, who inspired empathy. She wasn't her mother, who radiated authority. She wasn't Sanjing, glowing from another victory, or Caiyan, riveting with his rationale, or Lilian, charming her way into hearts. She was just Hesina, the princess who couldn't sit still during her imperial lessons, who found agriculture more interesting than statecraft and legends more engrossing than history. Inadequate as always.

"Dianxia."

Slowly, as if manipulated by some mechanism outside of her

body, her head swiveled from the raging crowd to the new voice at her side.

The imperial guard bowed. "A scout from General Sanjing's seventh borderlands legion has just arrived," she reported. "He demands to see you."

"Now?"

"Yes."

Blearily, Hesina looked back at the people. *Her* people. Except in this moment, their ranks teemed like the enemy, and she was the vanguard they were trying to break down. "Can't he wait?"

"He's already here and"—the guard lowered her voice—"he doesn't have much time. His final wish is to speak to his queen."

As if on cue, hooves clipped against limestone. The sound punctured the din, because the din was quieting. Gasps replaced the shouts. People fell back as the rider emerged. Caiyan tried to shield Hesina from the sight, but it was too late. She had already seen.

There was no way anyone could look the way the rider did and still be . . . alive.

The man had no face. Where there should have been features, there was only black char. He'd been burned so badly that the rope strapping him to his mount had rubbed away the fabric, the *skin*, over his thighs. The flesh beneath was scarlet, and as the horse approached, the ropes exposed more.

Then two white maggots popped out under the man's brow bone. Hesina gasped. The maggots blinked. Not maggots at all.

The man had opened his eyes.

Acid laid waste to Hesina's throat. She wanted to escape. To hide. Instead, she stepped forward. "What happened?"

"They're back." His voice whistled like wind through a bamboo thicket. "They're back, and they're with the Kendi'ans."

"Who?" She took another feeble step forward, nearing the horse. "Who are 'they'?"

They are inhuman. They are—

"The soothsayers."

—monsters.

Hesina couldn't hear the reaction of the crowd. All she could hear, it seemed, was her brother's voice.

They'd lost a village, Sanjing had claimed. It was gone, Sanjing had claimed.

The work of sooths, Sanjing had claimed.

Fear streaked into her revulsion, one marbling around the other, a tumor that blocked her senses, allowing her to catch only a handful of what the man said next.

He'd been captured . . . Kendi'ans . . . drenched him in . . . blood of sooths . . . let . . . burn . . . strapped into saddle . . . given one mission . . .

"—you'll pay." The whistling had turned to gurgling, the man's every breath and word greased with blood. "They wanted me to tell you that you'll pay for your ancestors' crimes."

Then he choked to a stop.

Hesina lurched forward, hand outstretched, while Caiyan shouted for water. As someone rushed in with a goblet, the man slumped forward.

He didn't move again.

Hesina's hand remained outstretched, reaching. For what, she didn't know. She lowered her arm as the shouts started up again, her fingers closing and her nails biting into her palms.

"It was the sooths!"

"It was the Kendi'ans!"

"Our queen is right! Our king was murdered!"

"A trial! A trial! A trial!"

People knelt at her feet, praising her name. Ministers came up, offering her their guidance through the trial. Hesina's jaw locked against a scream. She was queen of a populace united, and she'd never felt so powerless.

II

TRIAL

The king blinked at the mess sprawled upon his daughter's bed. A pouch of millet, a wooden sword, the white jade hairpin he'd given her years ago . . .

What are you doing, Little Bird?

I'm running away.

Without me?

She started to pack. *You wouldn't come even if I asked.* He watched her struggle to fit the sword into the satchel. *You'd say your place is at the palace. But I have nothing here.*

You have Lilian and Caiyan.

Sanjing's mean when I play with them. I'd rather have no friends at all.

The king took the sword out of her grasp. *Here, let me.* He strapped it across her back. *How about this—let's play stone, silk, and sickle. If I win, you stay.*

She frowned as she considered. *You have to too. You have to promise that you'll stay forever if I win.*

He agreed to her conditions. So they played. It was a game of reflexes, which he'd had many, many years to perfect. When he saw her small hand start to form stone, he made sickle, because he wanted her to win. He wanted—as ill-advised as it was—to make a promise he couldn't keep.

SEVEN

When the inner palace is in turmoil, so is the court.

ONE *of the* ELEVEN *on polygamy*

They spend more time in their beds than on their thrones.
What man with twenty concubines wouldn't do the same?

TWO *of the* ELEVEN *on polygamy*

Hesina couldn't remember the last time she'd slept.

At first, it was because she saw the burned rider wherever she looked. His face was the clump of tea leaves at the bottom of her cup. His voice was the whine and creak of her mother's carriage when it rolled out of the Eastern Gate, returning the dowager queen to the Ouyang Mountains the dawn after her daughter's coronation.

Then, it was because she *couldn't* sleep. A queen simply didn't have enough hours in the day. If she wasn't writing letters to Kendi'a, demanding an explanation and requesting negotiations, she was reading about the sooths, trying to understand just how much of a threat they'd be in a purely hypothetical war.

It was thankless research. Books contradicted each other or

stated things she already knew: sooths were evil, not all sooths had magic, and sooths couldn't lie about their visions without truncating their life spans. One tome, which Hesina discounted because it had more pictures than words, claimed that sooths *added* a year to their natural life spans for every true vision shared. Some had lived centuries by virtue of honesty.

Maybe this was why so many books on the sooths had been burned, thought Hesina dryly. Imagine the outrage if schoolchildren found a shortcut to immortality! But if being well read was, in fact, the only way to godhood, then Hesina must have been halfway there. To top off all her paperwork, her page had delivered a report on the court officials with connections to Kendi'a and hundreds of their archived memorials as handwriting samples. The stacks were huge, towering in spires on her desk. As Hesina went through them, more and more people gathered on the terraces outside the palace. Everyone was waiting for the trial to open. There was a murderer roaming the kingdom, and they wanted the person found.

Hesina did too. But she'd also found murder in her own people's eyes, and she couldn't help but unfold, refold, and unfold the Investigation Bureau's memorandum, creasing it like her brow. Justice was a muscle, Xia Zhong had said, but was it strong enough to withstand the people's rage? Was the *Bureau* strong enough?

Some nights, she took her questions to the throne hall. She would stride down the enamel walk of python inlay, ascend the altar-like dais of black lacquer, and sit, a reredos fitted with twelve *zitan* and soapstone panels rising at her back, an empty assembly ground framed with faux gateways and cinnabar pillars spreading before her. Impossibly small beneath an impossibly high caisson ceiling commissioned by the relic emperors, Hesina would ask for advice and expect no reply. Vassals needed sleep, and none of their voices came close to her father's.

But her need for real answers grew as the trial drew closer, and the night before its start, Hesina changed her course, going to the Investigation Bureau instead. She was determined to see it for herself.

Two lines of imperial guards—more heavily armored, it appeared, than their dungeon counterparts—bowed as Hesina made for the stone doors at the end of the hall. Padlocked and chained, each door bore a mirrored carving of the mythical *taotie* face. Bronze charms and paper talismans hung from the beast's protruding horns, meant to ward off the sooths.

Had they ever worked? Hesina reached for a talisman, and the guards tensed. They relaxed as she withdrew her hand, then tensed again as she placed it over the *taotie*'s stone snout.

The stone was cold. She wished for the power to see through it, into the room that processed every case in the imperial city.

"It doesn't do well to forget, my queen."

She turned to see Xia Zhong come down the hall. Light from the candelabra yellowed his skin.

"Do you remember?" He joined her side, rubbing his fingers over his beads. "Nobles used to enter and leave the Bureau as they pleased. They'd hire sooths to see the evidence and suspects in advance, and orators to manipulate both to their desired outcome in court."

"I remember." It was the reason why the Bureau had the level of security it did now, and why no one but the Bureau members were privy to the evidence or the suspects prior to a trial. Plaintiffs, defendants, and their representatives would learn all the information there was to learn in the court.

"Then why are you here?" asked Xia Zhong. "Do you doubt the system?"

"No!" Hesina blurted out. "No," she repeated, quieter. "I just . . . I just wanted to see how it worked. To understand." She glanced at the minister, hoping that he might provide guidance or comfort, be the ally he had been in her mother's chambers. "There is so much I don't understand."

"There is only one thing you need to understand." Xia Zhong reached into the cross folds of his *hanfu* and withdrew a handful of dry tea leaves. He popped them into his mouth and began to chew. "Nothing is ideal. There is better; there is worse. There is less; there is more. Was it better before, when the people believed that the king had died a natural death? Is it worse now, when you have the very trial and representative you asked for? You be the judge, my queen."

"What do you think?" Hesina didn't know what was better and what was worse. The clarity of her goals dimmed as they came within reach.

"A minister dares not decide for his ruler."

"But a minister is supposed to guide and remonstrate."

Xia Zhong turned away from the door. "If you ask me, the only thing you have less of now than you did before is faith."

* * *

"Enough is enough," declared Lilian, slamming a tray of salted duck eggs and braised water chestnuts onto Hesina's desk the next morning. "You need food, sleep, and a change of clothes. Talk some sense into our queen," she ordered Caiyan.

"The life of a queen is busy by nature—"

Lilian pinched his ear. "Sense, I said!"

"—which means you can't manage everything by yourself."

Wincing, Caiyan tugged his ear free, before eyeing the hand-writing samples stacked before Hesina's nose. "The trial must go on, milady. The decree has been shared, the proverbial die cast. The people are waiting. Your representative is too."

"He didn't run?" Hesina was disappointed. *She* would have run, if given the chance. Away from this palace, where faith was something she could possess one day and lose the next.

"No, milady." Caiyan offered his hand. She took it after a second, and he helped her out of her seat. "He's dressed and ready."

"Like you should be." Lilian thrust out a silk-wrapped bundle. Hesina undid the ties.

A dove-gray *ruqun* spilled out. Crimson embroidery trellised up the length of each billowing sleeve and plumed into phoenix tails at the shoulder. The silk was luxuriously heavy, but also cold in Hesina's hand. Its folds slithered through her fingers like eels.

She clenched it.

Caiyan and Lilian were right. She couldn't stall forever. She would have faith, even if she had to borrow it from the two of them.

＊ ＊ ＊

Like the throne room, the court was a vestige from the relic era, its strange design imported from some far, western land across the Jieting Sea. The imperial architects called it a double dome, but Hesina and her father had known better. Between cases, they'd sometimes catch each other's eye and smile, because really, the court was an egg. It had a pointy top and rounded bottom. When ministers pounded their staffs and debated the fate of the realm, it was all happening inside an egg.

But today, if the court were truly an egg, it'd be cracking. Nobles crammed the balustrades ringing the upper half. Commoners in the bottom half merged into a patchwork of grays, browns, and beiges.

A suspended aisle arced between the two halves, starting at the double doors, folding into a short set of stairs, and ending at a dais flanked by witness boxes. Hesina and Lilian walked the aisle together, climbing to the imperial balcony overhanging the dais.

The imperial balcony was largely empty. As a court official, Caiyan's place was in the upper ranks. Sanjing sat in saddles more often than chairs. The dowager queen, for all intents and purposes, lived in the Ouyang Mountains. Hesina's father had been this balcony's one constant, and her throat closed as she remembered all the cases she'd watched from his lap.

Now the court stood for her, sat for her. The director of the Investigation Bureau stepped onto the dais, wearing the standard malachite and black court *hanfu* and winged *wusha* cap. He bowed before the balcony. "May we begin?"

"We may," said Hesina. She scanned the ranks, finding Caiyan. He touched two fingers to his chin; she lifted hers higher. Next she found Xia Zhong, who gave her a nod before returning his attention to the director. The stocky official had unfurled a scroll.

"Welcome to the 305th court," he boomed. "The case in question today is that of the king's murder. The plaintiff is our queen, Yan Hesina. For the first round, we will present the representatives, preliminary evidence, and suspect on the stand. Allow me to introduce the scholars representing both parties. The defendant's representative: Hong Boda of the Yingchuan Province!"

The great doors opened.

The scholar assigned to defend the suspect, a young man of average build, had tried—and failed—to grow a beard. His brows, in comparison, put his facial hair to shame; they were fat like silkworms, inching up as he covered his mouth with a sleeve and yawned.

"Next, we have . . ." The director frowned at his scroll. "A-ke-la of the Niu Province."

And they were already off to a bad start.

"Oh my," whispered Lilian as Hesina cringed. "Is that how you say his name?"

"No." There weren't any Yan characters that could represent the exact phonemes in Akira's name. "It's Akira."

"*Much* better."

Hesina leaned forward in her seat as Akira entered the court. Three weeks had passed since their duel, and she scrutinized him as he ascended the dais. On the whole, he looked . . . almost decent. Like the defendant's representative, he wore the black-and-white scholar's *hanfu*, which was baggy enough to hide most of his sharp angles. Though his hair was an awkward length, too long to leave loose and too short for a topknot, it'd been tied back in a short, brown tail. And the cuts and bruises on his face had mostly faded. Hesina sighed in relief.

Lilian wasn't quite as impressed. "I was expecting more."

"More what?"

"I don't know. Girth. Muscles?"

"Muscles would be *very* helpful in court."

Lilian sniffed. "You never know what might come in handy."

What would be handy right about now was an edible sort of insecticide to kill all the dragonflies in Hesina's stomach. Today was just a formality, she reminded herself. The presentation of the representatives, evidence, and suspect was like the distribution of an exam, and not the exam itself. Keel over now, and she'd miss the real trial.

The director presented the preliminary evidence. The king had been poisoned; Hesina had delivered half of the sample herself. On the day of his death, no one had left the palace. No one had entered. There were other ways of coming and going, as Hesina knew best, but the passageways were a secret between father and daughter. They didn't show up on any map that could be purchased, which reduced the likelihood of a foreign assassin. No, the suspect was someone in this kingdom.

Someone in this *palace*.

The dragonflies in Hesina's stomach multiplied as the director rolled up his scroll. "Finally, allow me to present the first suspect."

He said a title. He said a name. The title and name rang in Hesina's ears like a misplayed note.

It couldn't be.

It made no sense.

How could a concubine who never left the Southern Palace be suspected of killing Hesina's father?

The great doors swung open, and everyone craned their necks, compulsively drawn to the most enigmatic member of the imperial family. Hesina couldn't move. She couldn't even react, astonished as she was when it wasn't Consort Fei who came down the aisle, but her son, Rou.

Whispers percolated through the ranks as Rou ascended the dais. The director frowned. "Do you go by the title Noble Consort or the name Fei?"

"No."

Her half brother's squeak brought Hesina back to herself. A chill prickled over her skin as the director followed his question with, "And are you the one charged with regicide?"

No. Her confusion turned to nausea. Consort Fei. Regicide. The words sounded wrong together, like a wedding ballad at a funeral.

"No," repeated Rou.

"Then why are you here?" demanded the director.

Rou quaked in his shell-blue *hanfu*, and Hesina grimaced when he struggled to project his reedy voice. "There's been a mistake. My mother couldn't possibly have killed my father."

Jeers surged from both the upper and lower galleries. The director swept out his sleeve, and the rumble quieted. "Mistake or not will be up to the court to decide."

"N-no."

"No?"

"I—I can vouch for my mother."

"Yes," dismissed the director. "Any filial son would."

"Please." Rou spun in a shaky circle, looking to the ranks as if they were the walls of a well he had to scale. "She never left the Southern Palace that day. She—"

"An accusation is not a sentence, Prince Yan of Fei."

Hesina's gaze snapped to Xia Zhong. He sat among the other ministers, a dull rock against a bed of gems. But his voice wasn't unkind when he continued, "Your mother has a representative to defend her. Let justice run its course."

Rou didn't appear appeased.

"Enough," said the director. "Representatives, you now have twenty-four hours before the trial begins. You may meet with your parties to prepare your prosecution and defense. Session adjourned."

But no one stood, because Hesina hadn't stood. Standing was a form of leading. How could she lead if she didn't understand what was going on anymore?

"Up you go," grunted Lilian under her breath, helping Hesina to her feet by the elbow. The rest of the court rose, the shuffle sounding like a collective sigh, and something in Hesina's throat unclogged.

She sucked down what felt like her first real breath, then gripped Lilian by the arm.

"Meet me in Father's study. Tell my page to lead Akira to the same place. Go, now."

Lilian pursed her lips. "Can you walk?"

"I'll manage." One way or another, she would make it out of this nightmare of a court.

She took the steps slowly after Lilian left and was one of the last to exit the court through the Hall of Everlasting Harmony. As fate would have it, she didn't get very far before the person she dreaded most called for her.

"Sister!"

At first, Hesina pretended not to hear. But then Rou called again, and her conscience wouldn't allow her to ignore him a second time. She stopped between the last pair of pillars, built of sturdy *huanghuali* and covered in a mother-of-pearl overlay of cranes, phoenixes, and herons in flight. She let Rou catch up.

And she regretted it when he did, because he immediately dropped to the ground and prostrated himself in *koutou*.

"My mother's innocent," he blubbered. "I swear on the Eleven."

He couldn't have picked a worse time. There were still courtiers behind them, watching curiously. Quickly, Hesina hauled Rou to his feet.

"Stop this," she hissed so the others wouldn't hear. "The situation is bad enough as is. You're never going to clear your mother's name if people catch you groveling."

"I-I'm sorry." Rou's pupils were huge with fear, but also with hope. Hesina saw her face reflected in them. "But . . . does that mean you believe me?"

She took him in, this half brother of hers with ears that protruded and a sparse fall of black bangs over a pearlescent forehead. She probably saw him four or five times a year—fewer, if she could help it—and each time he was the same. Genuine. Earnest. Kind.

He made it that much harder to resent him.

"I'll believe whatever the court finds," she said, loudly this time, announcing it to everyone within earshot. Then she turned on her heel, cursing and walking faster when the footsteps continued to trail her.

"Are you trying to outrun me too?"

"Oh." Hesina exhaled as Caiyan came down the hall, regal in his black-and-gold viscount *hanfu*. "It's you."

He fell into step beside her. "Are you okay, milady?"

She nodded stiffly.

"I understand you have some history with the consort," Caiyan said as they wove through the maze of facades. "But don't let it get to you."

Easier said than done. Maybe if Hesina *hadn't* overturned the archives for information on the consort or crouched in the Southern Palace shrubbery for a glimpse of the woman who'd divided her father's heart, these childhood memories wouldn't bead like sweat on her mind.

Inside the king's study, Akira sat on the far window ledge overlooking the gardens. Lilian lounged on her favorite daybed, a green hair ribbon knit between her hands. "Consort Fei, huh? Well, what do we all think?"

Caiyan took up pacing. "The suspect had to have come from inside the palace."

"But seriously, Consort Fei? That's like saying *you'd* murder the king. How would she, even?"

"Poison, clearly."

"You're missing my point, stone-head."

"I see your point." Caiyan reached one end of the room and turned back around. "And I have my doubts. But we should treat her as we would any suspect."

Treat her as we would any suspect.

Hesina stood by the wall of books in the lower study, where the shelves would split down the middle if she removed a certain pattern of tomes. *A secret passageway to the orchard*, her father had said with a wink. It explained the never-ending supply of fresh persimmons on his desk. So many seemingly mysterious things about her father could be explained in simple ways. But why had he broken his vows to the dowager queen for Consort Fei? Hesina would never know.

She knew other things, though, thanks to all the research she'd done on the consort. At Caiyan's words, and the realization that she could never treat Consort Fei as a normal suspect, something floated belly up to the surface of Hesina's thoughts.

"What is it, Na-Na?" cried Lilian as Hesina gripped the edge of a shelf for balance.

"Consort Fei. Her grandfather was an advisor to the previous Kendi'an Crown Prince."

"What are you saying?"

She was saying that Sanjing was right. He'd been right all along, and now, with a mouth too dry for words, she was glad he wasn't here to see this.

"Milady is trying to say the consort is a scapegoat." As usual, Caiyan helped Hesina when she could not help herself. He turned from Lilian and to Hesina. "You don't believe she killed the king."

She'd seen her father carry Rou on his shoulders, just like he carried her. She'd noticed the occasional wisteria sprig from the Southern

Palace caught in the collar of his *hanfu*. Whether she wanted to or not, she'd witnessed his love for Consort Fei. It was a truth no court or representative could ever find.

"Lilian is right," Hesina finally said. "Consort Fei had no reason to kill my father."

Caiyan paced another lap. "Assume many reasons until proven otherwise."

"I'm with Na-Na on this one," said Lilian. "But the commoners hate war. They won't mobilize for it just because the king's killer has some distant connection to Kendi'a. Whoever framed Consort Fei must realize that."

Or, thought Hesina darkly, whoever framed the consort had realized that the people despised sooths far more than war and was capitalizing on what had happened at her coronation.

"Anyway, clearing Consort Fei will be easy." Lilian tossed aside her cat's cradle and sat up. "We'll secure an alibi."

"No." Akira scooted off the window ledge and padded to the lower half of the study. Hesina took a step back as he passed. One stolen item was enough for her.

Lilian arched a brow. "No?"

"This Consort Fei seems secluded. If her only companions are her son, her personal maids, and her guards, then who," Akira said calmly, walking to her father's desk, "would think her witnesses' accounts unbiased?"

"Akira's right," said Hesina as he circled the desk, running a finger along its carved edge. The gesture seemed casual enough, but she never knew what was mindless and what was intentional with Akira. "You saw how the director rejected Rou as a witness."

Lilian groaned. "So what do we do?"

Hesina waited for Akira's answer. Just by being here, the ex-convict had proven himself trustworthy. But trustworthiness wasn't enough. Even with Caiyan and Lilian at her side, Hesina felt like she was staring into the dark maw of a snake she had summoned, the truth obscured by venom and fangs.

Akira's finger came to a rest on the corner of the desk. "We wait."

Lilian crossed her arms. "That's it?"

"Wait." He lifted his finger. "See if the evidence is fabricated, or if the other representative doesn't try very hard. One of those things is bound to happen if the consort really is a scapegoat."

"And if both happen?" asked Caiyan.

For the first time since that day in the dungeons, Akira looked to Hesina, his expression probing like a thread at a needle. "I'll defend the suspect, if you want me to."

Slowly, Hesina released the shelf she'd been gripping. Her shoulders squared. "I want you to."

Caiyan paced by, brow furrowed. "The plaintiff's representative defending the suspect is unprecedented."

Hesina's stomach sank.

Lilian rolled her eyes. "But it's not against the law, is it?"

"It's never been done before," argued Caiyan.

"In other words, no," said Lilian. "For the love of the Eleven, stop picking at fish bones."

Caiyan stopped midstep and turned on Akira. "You're betting on the evidence having holes."

"Fish bones!" cried Lilian, but the corner of Akira's mouth had already knifed up, and Hesina saw something of a robber's deviousness in his eyes as he answered Caiyan.

"I've bet on worse before."

EIGHT

Plaintiff and defendant shall each have a representative, drawn from a pool of rising scholars.

ONE *of the* ELEVEN *on trials*

The Minister of Rites will make sure that the representatives are selected at random.

TWO *of the* ELEVEN *on trials*

Akira was betting on the evidence having holes. Hesina was betting on the Silver Iris's Sight being true. A whole lot of gambling was going on, and she wasn't sure she liked that.

But what could she do? Nothing, other than show up for court the next day to find a pale-faced, bruise-eyed Rou still standing in his mother's place. Evidently, she wasn't the only one who hadn't slept.

The director presented the court with a complete list of evidence and witnesses the Investigation Bureau had compiled against Consort Fei. Hesina's jaw stiffened, and when the director invited the consort's representative to present his defense, she caught herself grinding her teeth.

The scholar dawdled, fluffing out his sleeves and clearing his throat, only to then say, "The defense has nothing to present. The evidence is sound."

"Bleeding emperors," muttered Lilian, taking Hesina's hand.

Hesina closed her eyes, dizzy. Sanjing had known this was coming, and she hadn't listened. She could almost hear his voice, berating her for being so *naive* when she, as the eldest, was supposed to be the wisest.

"Then Consort Fei accepts the charges of regicide?" asked the director.

Two voices sounded at once.

"No!" cried Rou, with anguish so sharp it pierced Hesina's heart.

"Yes," said the representative.

"You understand that this means you forfeit the case?" asked the director.

"I do." The representative projected like an opera singer. "The murder of the king concerns the entire kingdom. I dare not put my own interests first."

The court clapped, as if he'd done the honorable thing, sacrificed his ticket past the preliminary round of the civil service exams for the truth.

"I'm going to vomit," said Lilian.

Hesina wasn't far behind. She swallowed the taste of breakfast—pickled daikon—then opened her eyes to watch Akira ascend the dais.

"Closing remarks?" asked the director, turning as Akira walked behind him.

"Yes." Akira spun with him like a tail to a cat, eliciting gasps when he clapped the director's back. The man froze, slack-jawed, allowing Akira to point at the list of witnesses he clutched. "Can I see this maid you have listed?"

The director's jaw snapped shut. "Insolence!" he cried, jerking away from Akira and straightening his robes.

"I'll take that as a 'yes.'"

The director grumbled, then waved a hand at the doors. The guards opened them for a servant, clad in a cream *ruqun*, the hydrangea-blue sleeve cuffs denoting her as a lady-in-waiting. She floated down the walk, head high as she entered the witness box.

"Repeat your account to the plaintiff's representative," ordered the director.

"I was cleaning my lady's vanity four days ago when I came across her powder," began the maid. "The top of the box hadn't been properly replaced. I was about to close it when I realized the color of the powder was off."

"How did you know the color of the powder was off?" asked Akira, leaning an elbow against the witness box.

The lady-in-waiting regarded him as she might a roach in her rice congee. "Because she uses it every single day."

Akira gestured at Rou. "And would her son be able to confirm the color of this powder?"

"Men wouldn't know such things," sniffed the lady-in-waiting. "At first, I thought my lady had simply switched powders, even though it didn't make much sense. This new powder didn't match her skin tone. Then I heard the Investigation Bureau was looking for anything suspicious. I remembered the color change and brought the box of powder to them."

"Very thoughtful of you," said Akira.

"Desist from the commentary," snapped the director. "Questions only."

"Understood. Wait. Er . . . forgive me?" Akira faced the lady-in-waiting. "By all means, will you please go on?"

Lilian held back a snort.

"The Bureau had the Imperial Doctress examine the powder," said the lady-in-waiting primly. "She said it was poison."

The court fractured with voices, and Hesina's throat filled with shards. She didn't always agree with the Imperial Doctress, but she trusted the woman's loyalty. If the Doctress deemed the powder poisonous, then it very well was. Golden mist or not, *planted* or not, poison was poison. They'd found a hole, all right, and they'd fallen straight into it.

"May I inspect this powder box myself?" asked Akira.

Before the lady-in-waiting could speak, the director inclined his head to the imperial balcony. "My queen," he said. "I believe your representative doesn't understand the rules."

Then he turned to Akira. "Boy, your job is to represent the queen and the queen alone. You've convicted the murderer and won the case. When the preliminary rounds open with the new year, you'll be exempt—"

"Director Lang." Hesina's voice drew the heat of every gaze. She tried not to shrivel like a sprout under the sun. "My representative has the right to examine any evidence that is listed."

The court muttered.

It's never been done before, Caiyan had said.

But neither had an investigation into the king's murder.

Neither had the use of a convict as a representative.

Hesina stood. Everyone in the court rushed to stand with her. She pretended they were her warriors, even if they were just following etiquette.

"The box," she ordered the director.

The director flung out a hand. "The box!"

A page carried a gilded tray to Akira, who lifted a small, ceramic box from it.

"Does the consort have any other boxes like this?" he asked the lady-in-waiting as he flipped open the top.

"No. This is her only box of powder."

Akira sniffed the powder, then swiped a finger through it. "Who said this was poison?"

"I did," muttered the Imperial Doctress from the opposing witness box.

"Can you describe the properties?"

"The powder comes from the desiccated root of *jinsuo*." The Doctress sounded as though she'd much rather be in the infirmary, tinkering over her tinctures. "The plant flourishes only in dry, hot conditions. In the context of our kingdom, that means it's found along certain sections of the Yan-Kendi'a borderlands. If taken with a water-based substance, immediate, painless death is guaranteed."

"And in its dry form?"

"Not poisonous but sure to burn skin through prolonged contact. So I'd suggest wiping that finger."

Do what the Doctress says, Hesina mentally ordered, irritated when Akira did not.

"So it's corrosive," he said.

"Extremely. It can even discolor glass."

Lilian growled something about the Eleven and their mothers. Hesina didn't have enough air in her lungs to do the same.

But Akira seemed unaffected. "I have a task for you," he said, pivoting to Rou.

Rou looked slightly green. "Me?"

"Yes, you." The court tensed at the sudden ferocity in Akira's voice. "Fetch me the consort's most recent trash."

Silence.

The court broke into laughter.

"Enough of this!" bellowed the director, but Rou had already scampered to the doors. The guards, snickering themselves, didn't give him a hard time, and in a flash of blue, he was out of the court.

"What's Akira's endgame?" Lilian whispered to Hesina.

To help me find the truth. But right now? "I have no idea."

The Southern Palace was a twenty-minute walk to and from the court. To burst through the doors less than ten minutes later, Rou had to have sprinted. Red in the face, he huffed up the dais with a woven hemp bag and emptied it at Akira's command.

The director wrinkled his nose as trash spilled onto the marble. "Do you take this court for a pigpen?"

Akira ignored him and knelt by the crumpled knickknacks. He picked up something white. "Was this yesterday's trash?"

"And the day before," said Rou without missing a beat.

Hesina straightened. Where had her half brother's newfound confidence come from?

"Do you agree with your prince?" Akira asked the lady-in-waiting.

She considered the heap. "Yes, I think so."

He stood. "Then why," he said, holding out a white square of silk, "would this facial handkerchief be here?"

He raised the square for all to see, and Hesina squinted along with the rest of the court.

Peach-pink powder smudged the white cloth.

"Is this the color of the powder before the change?" he asked the lady-in-waiting.

"I don't remember."

"But didn't you suggest only men lacked an eye for these things?"

"It could be the switched powder. It could just appear darker on the cloth."

"No." Akira's gaze glinted like whetted steel. "No poisoner would be so foolish as to apply corrosive powder to her own face."

"Maybe she used another box."

"But you claimed she only has one box. Do you doubt your answer?"

Courtiers and ministers whispered among themselves. Hesina caught Caiyan's eye among the viscounts and he, for all the gripes he'd had before, had a set to his brow she knew well. He thought they could win. He was never wrong.

Hope hatched in Hesina's chest. Fragile, delicate hope, almost crushed when she returned her attention to the dais below and saw the director marching over to Akira.

But Akira turned the powder box upside down, and the director stumbled back from a cloud of peach ash. "Enough! That is *enough*!"

Akira peered into the ceramic box, then held it out for the court's viewing. "Look carefully at the inner porcelain. What do you see?"

"Nothing but white!" jeered one courtier.

"Are you certain?"

"Do you take me for a fool?"

Akira's lips quirked. "Of course not. In fact, I think you're very smart for reading my mind. I find it *interesting* that a poison with the ability to discolor glass should leave its porcelain container perfectly white."

The court fell silent.

Hesina's head spun. Had the Imperial Doctress lied? Was the poison not poison at all?

"The poison is real enough," said Akira, handing the empty container to a page. "But I daresay this powder box is a duplicate. The consort probably continues to use her old powder without a clue. I also daresay that the poison has been in its container for no more than a week. If you gave me the time to make a sample, I'd show you what a month of corrosion looks like. Regardless . . ."

Akira's gaze hit like a pebble in water, casting ripples through Hesina's heart, each echoing the same question.

Shall I tell the truth?

She nodded.

Akira turned back to the court. ". . . I think we can agree that this powder was planted."

* * *

Shame was a wildfire. It raged in Hesina's chest as she left the court. Flames of it blistered her throat, consuming her as she made for her rooms. But like a wildfire, it was unsustainable. When there was nothing left of her to eat, it crackled and popped and *grew*.

Shame became blame.

Hesina couldn't escape it. She was to blame for this farce of a trial.

But she wasn't the only one.

She took up her sword and left her rooms as quickly as she had come. Step by step, she gained momentum, blame snowballing around shame, and rage melting both. Nothing and no one could stop her this time. Not the charms, not the talismans, not even the chains on the Bureau doors.

The guards tried to hold her back, but she unsheathed her sword and spun, daring them to unsheathe theirs. When they didn't, she lunged at the door and struck. Another strike, and the chains fell.

She wriggled out of the guards' grasp and shouldered through the halves of stone.

She was met with the sight of the entire Bureau cowering like rabbits, taking up refuge behind the long investigation tables.

They feared her.

The realization stunned Hesina for all of a heartbeat before she hardened. Good. They *should* fear her, because she didn't know what she might do. Her gaze darted from the Bureau members to the tables to the contents of the tables. Her eyes widened.

Slowly, she walked to one of the tables.

It was stacked high with books on genealogy.

This was truth.

She walked to another table, papered with family trees of courtiers from inter-kingdom bloodlines.

This was justice.

She walked to a third table, where a single sheet of paper listed names, from palace servants to ministers, of people with Kendi'an relations.

This was her father's truth and justice.

She rested her fingertips atop that final sheet. It hilled as she drew her fingers in, becoming a small mountain under her hand.

She crushed the mountain.

"Elevens!" A bellow came from the open doors at her back. "What—"

The director stopped in his tracks as she turned.

Heat pooled in Hesina's fists. She advanced on the director, and he fell back.

"*Dianxia*. Please. Allow me to explain—"

He was a buzzing fly, speaking some language Hesina couldn't understand. Her eyes narrowed. She wanted to silence him. She might have, if she'd stared at his face a second longer, those lips of his smacking with excuses. But instead, her gaze caught on a copy of the *Tenets* on the table behind him.

Its edges were stained green.

Green like the letters Sanjing had confiscated.

She fell upon the book like a wolf on a carcass, seizing it and tearing it open.

There. Right in the middle. A folio of torn-out pages, the stationery repurposed for something other than the Eleven's philosophies— something such as letters.

"Whose is this?" Hesina spun on the Bureau. No one replied. "*Whose?*"

"Minister Xia's," a young Bureau member answered shakily, earning a glare from the director. "He lent it to us to ensure that our investigation complied with the *Tenets*."

Xia Zhong.

There was a limit to how much something could break. Hesina's trust had already been broken today. It could not break more. With calm and almost frightening clarity, she suddenly knew why Xia Zhong's copy of the *Tenets* was here, and it had nothing to do with the Eleven's philosophies.

She grabbed the book and left, chest burning as she practically ran all the way back to her rooms. She flung into her study and lunged at her desk, papers going every which way, memorials avalanching.

In the mess of hundreds of documents, she found one authored by Xia Zhong. She wasn't a scholar of the letter arts. Her own calligraphy was lamentable. But she knew enough about it to match the weight and style of Xia Zhong's handwriting to the letter writer's.

She then took the letters and fitted them into the *Tenets*. The torn-out ridges lined up perfectly. The green tint of the letters and of the book became one.

Xia Zhong was the letter writer. Xia Zhong was feeding Kendi'a information, helping them raid Yan's borderland villages. Hesina's shock wore off like medicine; confusion and hurt panged behind her eyes. Why? *Why?*

Even a monk has to want something.

Hesina whirled on her pile of reports on officials with connections to Kendi'a. She hadn't examined it closely before because everyone, it seemed, had some sort of tie to the land of sand and fire, be it an acre of land or a twice-removed cousin. Now she scanned the tiny characters for Xia Zhong's name. He wasn't in the first report, or the second. She flipped to the third and found a list of ministers involved in the Kendi'an salt industry.

Xia Zhong wasn't listed.

He *was* listed, however, in having a role in the Yan salt trade. Hesina inhaled sharply when she saw the numbers. In the last year, he'd purchased two domestic salt mines and invested in four. A significant number. A *dangerous* number, considering that before relations had soured, Yan imported most of its salt from Kendi'a.

Xia Zhong and salt. Xia Zhong and investments. Xia Zhong, with his ratty robes and holey roof, and *profits*.

He was doing this for . . . money?

Hesina collapsed onto the floor, surrounded by scattered papers, something cold and damp in her hand. She uncurled a fist and blinked at the Investigation Bureau's list of names, now compacted to the size of a small stone. She'd been gripping it so tightly that it'd become a part of her. It'd *always* been a part of her, this trial. She'd brought it into existence.

She wouldn't let anyone kidnap it.

She wasn't sure how much time passed before she picked herself up. All she knew was that the sun was going down, and the room was as dark as her mind when she slipped a single letter out of the stack, placed it into her sleeve, and made for the courtyards.

NINE

Wealth should not determine fate.
    ONE of the ELEVEN on social hierarchy

Every kingdom has nobles, but not every kingdom has ones that reign as kings.
    TWO of the ELEVEN on social hierarchy

The gingko trees had shed all at once, leafing the ponds in gold. But the evening was abnormally warm for fall as Hesina traveled through the columned galleries, reminding her of the weather *that* night two weeks ago, when she'd gone into the red-light district. Except this time, she had nothing to hide. She was a queen on her way to a minister, and whether or not he wanted to, he would have to answer to her.

She reached the Northern Palace, where the relic emperors had housed their favorite concubines. Even Xia Zhong's courtyard complex, the shabbiest of all the ministers', exhibited traces of odious elegance. Dragons reared at the upturned roof points, their claws forming hooks from which paper lanterns dripped like mandarins on a branch.

Hesina hung up her lantern with the others and knocked on the latticework doors. They swung apart almost instantaneously, and she stumbled back as a maid hurried out.

The sight rattled her. Had Xia Zhong been plying the maid just as he, or one of his cronies in the Bureau, had plied Consort Fei's lady-in-waiting?

Hesina still had trouble visualizing his involvement. But she'd seen the green-stained *Tenets*. Matched the handwriting. Found a motive. And now, when his voice came from the inner chamber— "Who's there?"—she tasted something as foul as the tea leaves he always chewed.

"Your queen."

The minister hurried out from behind the partition, one arm slid through a patched *yi*. "My chambers are unsightly," he said, shrugging his other arm into the shirt jacket. "You shouldn't be subjected to such filth."

No filth, Hesina decided as she crossed the threshold and shut the doors behind her, could be worse than Xia Zhong himself. "Your chambers will do just fine."

Xia Zhong bowed. She didn't bother relieving him, and he remained hunched as he led her around the partition, inviting her to his inner chambers. Cheap sheep-fat candles smoked on bronze candelabra, releasing a gamy stink as they burned. The low *kang* table—piled with copies of the *Tenets*—looked cheap, too, nicked and scratched and denuded of most of its lacquer. Only the double-edged sword hanging on the wall appeared to be worth something. It was plain and unadorned, but the steel shone of quality.

It wouldn't surprise her, thought Hesina dryly, if Xia Zhong was secretly a swordsman too.

She sat on a threadbare cushion before the low *kang*.

"I'll go make tea," said the minister, backing away.

"Stop right there."

Xia Zhong stilled in his tracks.

"Come," said Hesina, and the minister came. "Sit."

The minister knelt on the cushion opposite the *kang*, the *Tenets* atop it nearly eclipsing him. "To what do I owe this pleasure?"

Hesina answered by reaching into her sleeve and tossing a letter onto the table.

"What is this?" asked Xia Zhong. He sounded like a weary man who'd read too many documents and couldn't possibly look at another.

"I think you know very well."

"I don't understand."

"Then let me explain it to you. You know that Yan's salt mines will never outcompete the Kendi'an ones as long as trade exists between our kingdoms. And yet lately, you've invested in quite a number of mines in the Yan provinces of Yingchuan and Tangshui. It's as if you foresaw inter-kingdom trade stopping because of a war . . . a war you're trying to orchestrate by writing to the Kendi'an court."

The words came out polished, like bones picked clean by carrion birds. Hesina's voice didn't shake, didn't tremble. Anger had cauterized her nerves. Numbly, she went on to say, "You're feeding information to their raiding parties. That is treason."

Xia Zhong didn't react. He merely tucked his hands into his wide sleeves. "Passage 2.3.2: 'Suspicion poisons the heart. A ruler should see her advisors as friends and mentors rather than competitors.'"

To think she'd ever tried to mimic him. "Open it, if you don't believe me."

Xia Zhong drew the letter toward him. "I see you've taken a liking to your *selected* representative."

Hesina pinned the letter down.

Their gazes locked over the table and the paper bridged between their hands. Cunning shined in the minister's fishlike eyes; in the past, Hesina had mistaken it for fanaticism.

"Let's say we're even," said Xia Zhong. With grace, he withdrew his hand from the letter. "You forget these letters, and I'll let you keep the convict."

"I earned my representative."

"Earned?" Xia Zhong laughed like a chirping frog. "My dear," he said, leaning in, his shadow falling over the table. "I *gave* him to you so you would feel comfortable about forwarding your case to the Bureau."

"You—"

"I spoke for you in front of the dowager queen because I knew you would investigate your father's death if given the power."

He pulled back, drawing the breath in Hesina's lungs with him. In speechless horror, she stared at the face of her true opponent.

"Don't look at me like that," said Xia Zhong. The monk was gone. His diction had changed. Even his voice had slickened. "Without a war scare from Kendi'a, the people never would have accepted your investigation as anything more than the whim of a grief-stricken daughter. Consider our purposes aligned. If you are wise, wiser than your father, you will work with me."

"Work with you," Hesina repeated, the words foreign.

"Yes. Give me my war, and I'll give you your trial."

The cushion beneath Hesina couldn't have been more than a finger-width thick, but she suddenly felt as if she was sinking, suctioned into a swamp of desire for control—and shame for even considering the price of it toward him. "The *Tenets* forbid war," she said weakly.

"The *Tenets*?" Xia Zhong's voice dripped with scorn, as if there wasn't a pile of every edition stacked before his nose. The Ministry of Rites existed because of the books. Hesina didn't agree with everything in the *Tenets*, especially when it came to the sooths, but she didn't agree with Xia Zhong either when he said, "The *Tenets* are but paper."

It was the end of an era. Hesina would never be able to laugh at one of Lilian's impersonations of the minister again.

"What use do you have for that kind of money?" she demanded. It made no sense, and she was tired of things not making sense. Ministers earned decent salaries. Xia Zhong had the means to fix his roof or buy a new set of robes without resorting to such measures.

"This is not an interrogation, *dianxia*," the minister said amicably. "I'm offering you a partnership, a deal. A war for a trial. Take it or leave it."

No. She should have said no. But the word wouldn't come. The silence stretched, and a bead of sweat carved a path between Hesina's shoulder blades.

Draw the line. But where was the line? She'd committed treason for this trial. She was blackmailing Xia Zhong for this trial. She kept drawing the line only to cross it. The idea of sacrifice didn't scare her. She was willing to bend.

But then she'd become the sort of person her father didn't respect.

The sweat on her back went cold. She rose and looked down on the minister's bald head, waiting for him to meet her eye. "I won't have the people believing a lie that will cost unnecessary lives. And neither will you. Remember this before you frame another person."

She made sure to leave the letter on the desk. The act spoke for itself. She had more. She could spare this one.

Without a word, Xia Zhong fed it to the candle flame.

✳ ✳ ✳

"I could shove this up his ass," growled Lilian, screwing the end of her poled net into the pebbled banks of the silk ponds. Surrounded by willows that wept into the silk-swathed waters, they were in the quietest section of the imperial gardens. "Or boil him in a vat of dye. The girls and I were thinking of roses and grays for the winter season. How do you think the monk would look in mauve?"

Caiyan sighed, and Lilian snapped, "What? What do *you* have up your ass?"

Without answering, Caiyan turned to Hesina. "Do you have the letters somewhere safe?"

"Yes." She'd placed them under the floorboards of her study, the only place her meticulous maids didn't clean.

"Good. Don't use them."

"She *should* use them," snarled Lilian as she flung her net out into the pond. Yan silkworms cast their cocoons on lily pads instead of mulberry trees, making the collection process as easy as skimming raw silk from the water. But today Lilian looked like she was trying to harpoon a tiger shark.

"Xia Zhong is more than we ever took him for," said Caiyan.

"He is the lesser being of all lesser beings," Lilian shot back. She jerked the net out, clumps of silk caught like white hair, droplets flying into Hesina's face. "He's the descendant of a slug."

Caiyan raised a fist to his mouth and started pacing on the banks. "You don't know how he might retaliate if you push him too far."

"Which is *why*," gritted out Lilian, detangling the silk and tossing it into her collection basket, "we should retaliate *first*."

"Milady, you must proceed with caution."

"To hell with caution! Na-Na—"

"Stop!" The twins froze as Hesina clutched at her pounding head. "Just . . . stop."

Seconds passed, during which an unspoken conversation took place between Caiyan and Lilian. A decision was reached, and Caiyan bowed. "I'll see you at dinner, milady."

As her twin left, Lilian crouched, plucked a stray silkworm from the ground, and helped it back into the water. "Sorry, Na-Na."

"It's fine." Hesina just wanted an answer to her problems, and neither Caiyan's nor Lilian's suggestions felt like one. She crouched by Lilian. "I doubt Xia Zhong will listen to me. He'll just work closer with the Investigation Bureau. It'll get harder to acquit the suspects from here on out."

"Don't be so certain," said Lilian. "Akira seems *very* capable."

What about me? What am I supposed to do?

But Hesina was being silly. She wasn't a princess anymore. Power wasn't wielding the knife on her own but having someone else wield it on her behalf.

With a groan, Lilian stood. "Any word from the Kendi'an court?"

Power, apparently, was also ignoring letters from queens. "No," Hesina muttered, rising with her sister.

"You should bring a party of your strongest warriors to them and make them reply at sword point."

"I wonder why I haven't thought of this before."

"Because you have that stone-head as your advisor, not me. If *I* were your courtier, we'd make all the kingdoms cower in fear."

"You hate court."

Lilian raised a finger. "But I like muscular warriors and threatening people."

Hesina snorted. Lilian giggled. Snorts turned into giggles, and giggles into snorts. Hesina's cheeks ached, as if the muscles required for mirth had atrophied. Right when she thought she might have pulled something, the pebbles behind them clattered and she was forced to school her features into a semblance of regality before facing the visitor.

"Why, if it isn't Prince Rou!" cried Lilian, batting her lashes and causing Rou to flush and stammer and bow to someone equal in rank. Hesina grimaced.

"S-Sister, may I have a moment with you?"

"I'll see you at dinner," said Lilian, departing before Hesina could offer her a lifetime supply of candied hawthorn berries for her company.

Your loss. But mostly, it felt like Hesina's loss as she and Rou stood in awkward silence.

At last, Hesina suggested a stroll to the koi ponds. Rou eagerly agreed. They sat on the shelves of rock, waterfalls cascading around them, and Rou reached into the cross-collar fold of his blue *hanfu*. Hesina stared as he withdrew a handful of lotus seed. First Xia Zhong. Now Rou. Was she the only one who didn't carry food in her clothes?

The koi fled as Rou scattered seed over the pond. Then, slowly, they returned. As they chased the seeds, Rou cleared his throat. "Thank you."

In two words, Rou expressed emotions Hesina couldn't convey in a thousand.

"Don't thank me." It was easier to speak to her half brother as if he were an emissary from another kingdom. *Be gracious.* "He was my father." *Be honest.* "It's my duty to keep innocents from being framed in his name." *Be firm.*

Rou scattered another handful of seed. "It's my duty too."

"I didn't say it wasn't."

Her tone was sharper than she intended, and Rou's gaze dropped to his knees. "I know what the palace thinks of me and my mother. But that doesn't change the fact he was also my father. Which means you're my sister, and I should have helped you."

Hesina exhaled, trying not to laugh.

"D-did I say something wrong?"

You usually do. Rou's kindness always reminded her of her father's betrayal.

Instead of responding, Hesina opened a hand. Rou poured lotus seeds into her palm, covering the fate lines, before closing his fist and scattering the rest over the pond. A second later, Hesina joined him, and together they waited for the koi to come. She was almost sorry when the seed ran out and there was no excuse not to stand.

Silence cemented the space between them all over again as they faced each other. The willows had begun to brown, and a catkin had fallen onto Rou's head. Hesina instinctively reached to flick it out. Then she remembered Sanjing's cowlick. Her hand fell.

"Do you like persimmons?" Rou blurted out.

"I—I do."

"Maybe . . . you'd like to visit our courtyards sometime? They're ripe, and, um, I don't really like persimmons, but my mother does, and she says they're best right now, and, well, she'd like to meet you. She's wanted to for a long time."

How long was long? Hesina dearly hoped it wasn't when she'd still been spying on the consort from her shrubs; then she'd never have the face to visit. "I appreciate the invitation and will keep it in mind. Please send your mother my regards. And . . ." Hesina glanced to the mossy stone at her feet, composed herself, and looked Rou in the eye. "My apologies."

Rou smiled shyly in reply.

As she watched him go, his pale-blue *hanfu* turning ivory in the sunset, determination gripped Hesina. It didn't matter if she couldn't quite bring herself to call Rou a brother yet. She would protect him. She would protect Consort Fei. She would protect all of the innocents in this trial by finding her father's murderer on her own.

TEN

Knowledge is truth.

   ONE *of the* ELEVEN *on edification of commoners*

Give the nobleman a book, and he'll turn it into a weapon
that only he can use.

   TWO *of the* ELEVEN *on edification of commoners*

A snuff bottle.

A book.

A bronze goblet.

A folded courier's costume.

Hesina's stomach lurched as she stared at her father's items. If she was searching for poison, the goblet was the most obvious place to start—assuming she knew *how* to start. A thousand directions existed in an uncertain sea, and the full implication of embarking on a private investigation slammed into her.

Her, against a seasoned court. Her, against the tides of war. Her, against the king's assassin.

Akira had been right to call it a story worth spectating.

With a shake of the head, she shut the chest. Then she gripped the lid, a thought blooming like ink.

Akira.

He'd deconstructed Consort Fei's case so deftly that she'd almost forgotten who he was. A convict. *The* convict with the rod, destined to help her find the truth.

Hesina rose, giddy, and walked to the servants' quarters of the outer palace, where representatives stayed for the duration of a trial.

Akira sat on the floor of his simple room, chair untouched. A pile of medical tomes sat on the floor, too, neglected; he was too concentrated on his rod, peeling it with a paring knife, making more wood shavings, it appeared to Hesina, than anything else. She cleared her throat, and he slowed his carving.

"I—I have something to show you." It hadn't been her intention to stammer, but things never seemed to go as intended around Akira. How was Hesina to speak to her representative? As an equal? A lesser? A servant? A friend?

Might as well get used to ordering him around; that's what queens did, right?

"Come," she said, sighing. "You're moving rooms. Bring your belongings."

The "move" consisted of Akira carrying his rod and Hesina leading the way, a grand distance of two rooms down. She unlocked the door and held it open for him. He stayed under the frame.

A high-ranking maid had recently vacated the chamber. Rumor was that she'd been caught with her fiancé—palace servants weren't allowed to start families of their own. Hesina was usually two months behind on imperial gossip, but this maid was special.

Rather, this *room* was special. Even at a glance, the ornate details set it apart. Budding branches latticed the sitting table's skirt; swirling clouds patterned the divan. Chiseled monkeys scurried across the bed's lacquered headboard, peaches clutched within their hands.

"This is a bit . . . much," Akira said, sniffing the air as he entered.

Hesina thought so too. But she wasn't here for the decor. She made a beeline for the far wall. "You haven't seen the most important part."

She lifted a hanging brocade tapestry and thumped a fist against the *zitan* panel beneath it. The panel fell back, giving way to one of the few secret corridors that started in the outer palace and snaked into the inner palace.

This one, it so happened, went directly to Hesina's chambers.

They stared down the gilded corridor in silence. It was a vestige from the relic era and—Hesina's cheeks suddenly burned—had probably been well-used by the empresses who took servants as lovers in defiance of their husbands' growing harems.

Whatever Akira was to her, he was *not* a lover. *Stranger* was more fitting, considering she hardly knew him. But she did know one thing.

"I'm going to find Father's murderer." She turned to face him. "And I'm going to need your help."

He scratched his head. "I thought I was already helping you."

Yes and no. Hesina had envisioned an honest investigation. A fair trial. Instead, they were battling against lies. Their victories redeemed the innocent, but they brought her no closer to the truth.

Akira sat on the floor by the bed. He took up his rod and started to carve. "It's happening."

"What?"

"The loss of your idealism."

She sucked in a sharp breath. "Is a spectacle all you really want?"

The carving stopped.

She waited for him to meet her gaze, and when he did, she stared into his gray irises until she thought she might lose herself in them.

She broke eye contact first. What should she have expected? Everyone was the same; everyone was waiting for her to fail. But failure wasn't an option, not when her trial was so close to becoming a persecution.

"This"—she jerked her chin at the corridor—"is so we can meet more easily. The other end connects to my private study. I'll bring you the evidence I have. You, on the other hand, are free to come to me anytime. That is . . ." She wouldn't look at him. Wouldn't torture herself by watching him debate his answer. "That is, if you accept."

There. She'd done it. She'd asked for his help without downright begging.

The silence that followed made her wonder if she *should* have fallen to her knees and pleaded.

"Okay." His voice was quiet. Almost gentle. "I'll help you. Just one request."

"Yes?"

"I'd like to keep my head if the truth ends up destroying you."

And with that, he returned to sounding like his usual self, one who'd seen everything terrible in the world and decided nothing was that terrible after all. But whatever Akira had done before—be it merchant robbing or worse—Hesina could look past it. All she'd needed was this one *yes*.

"Thank you." She didn't know what else to say. "Make yourself comfortable. Let me—I mean the servants—let the servants know if you need anything."

No reply.

Wonderful. He probably thought she was utterly unhinged. Bracing herself, Hesina finally faced him.

His head was bowed. The string at the nape of his neck had come undone, and messy locks of ash-brown hair fell over his forehead.

"Akira?"

His breathing had slowed.

Instead of scaring him off, Hesina had bored him to exhaustion.

She gathered the down-and-silk blanket from the bed and knelt before him. He held his rod even in sleep. The detail brought a small smile to her lips, and she settled the blanket over his shoulders.

Something caught her eye as she did. The crossed collar of his *hanfu* had shifted to reveal a dark claw hooking over his shoulder.

No, not a claw. A tattoo of a leaf, the tip of it brushing his collarbone. The rest disappeared over the slope of his trapezius.

Hesina squelched her curiosity—disrobing her representative was the last thing she wanted to do—and carefully tucked the blanket under his chin.

* * *

"Hello."

Hesina spun so fast that she nearly knocked over a candle and set her desk aflame. But it was only Akira standing in her wall. He pulled the panels of the corridor exit shut, and she slumped in her seat with a sigh. "Please knock in the future."

"I did."

Well, she hadn't heard it. Perhaps the sound had gotten lost in her gnashing migraine. The life of a queen was tedious and horrible for her posture; she'd been hunched over paperwork since seeing Akira yesterday and hadn't gotten a chance to deliver the chest of evidence to him yet.

He cocked his head to the side. "You're one of those, aren't you?"

"Those . . . ?"

"A queen who'd be assassinated in broad daylight."

He came closer before she could be properly affronted, invading the wide breadth of personal space Hesina preferred to maintain at all times with strangers. She rushed to organize her desk, but he passed it for her bookshelf.

"You're welcome to any," she said as he surveyed the rows.

Of the many he could have chosen, he slid out her copy of *Assassins through the Ages*.

"Yes, I probably shouldn't have that."

Expression unreadable as always, Akira flipped through the book. "Interesting."

"What is?"

Without answering—a quirk Hesina found infuriating—he set it back on the shelf and took a seat on the floor. "So, how do you want to do this?"

After some wrestling with her desk drawer, Hesina successfully lifted the chest of her father's items. She laid out the contents. The snuff bottle. The tripod bronze goblet. The *Tenets*, open the way her father had left it. She spread the clothes he had worn: the navy courier's *hanfu*, the brocade broad-belt strung with his paring knife, and a knotted cord with a medallion in the center.

She removed the pouch containing the vial last, and hesitated as she slid out the tiny glass bottle. Half of the gas had already been wasted on the Investigation Bureau. The golden wisp was smaller than ever. Swallowing hard, she handed it to Akira.

He turned it to the light. "Mind if I study this further?"

She wanted to protect the vial, keep it out of sight. But she had to trust Akira, so she said, "Do as you please" instead. Then she reached for the bronze goblet. "Here. This might be linked—"

"Hold. Where do these items come from?"

Slowly, Hesina withdrew her hand. "His study. It was the last place he was seen."

"Did anyone else enter the room that day?"

"No. At least, that's what the maids say."

"The guards?"

"They wouldn't know." She wound a tassel on her sash around and around her index finger. "Father always hated having them stationed in the inner palace. But I went to the kitchens after . . ."

I found his body.

Hesina counted to ten. By seven, her throat stopped closing. By nine, her eyes cleared up. But there were not enough numbers in the universe to seal the hole in her heart when she said, "Breakfast is"—*was*—"his favorite meal of the day. But all the cooks and maids claimed he didn't want breakfast that morning."

Akira took the goblet and ran a finger along the rim. "There's a residue."

"Sometimes Father keeps"—*kept*—"a stash of persimmons in the study. He likes to juice them himself."

Then Hesina froze. When had he been poisoned, if no one had delivered food and drink that day?

"Some poisons take several days to act," Akira said. "Or the cup was already coated."

That made sense. Bit by bit, she unwound the cord around her finger.

Akira pulled the *Tenets* close. Together, they studied the pages. It'd been left open to a biography on One of the Eleven. The man had spent his early life as a humble street actor before committing some unspecified offense against the emperor and being slated for execution. The rest of the details—about his escape with ten other convicts and his subsequent rise to leadership—were just as vague.

Hesina wasn't surprised. Legend was the sort of wool that people willingly pulled over their eyes, especially when it came to heroes. One was the best example: an overwhelming chunk of the passage praised his kindness and fairness. This kind, fair man had gone on to kill tens of thousands of sooths, but no one mentioned that.

If Akira had an opinion on One, or any of the Eleven, he didn't show it. He simply rose, taking the book with him, and held the pages over the candle flame on the desk.

"What are we searching for?" Hesina ventured. She felt as though she was in her swordsmanship lessons again, always one step behind Sanjing.

"An assassin's mark." Akira touched the book to his nose. For an alarming second, Hesina thought he might lick it, but he only inhaled from the pages.

"But why would an assassin want to leave a mark?" She feared she was asking the obvious. "Wouldn't that give them away?"

"People think poison is the subtlest method of killing." Akira set the book down and started going through the other items. "In reality, you can arrange a carriage accident just as easily. A poisoner who doesn't dispose of the body wants to send a message."

He handed her the corded medallion before she could ask anything else and turned his attention to the courier *hanfu*.

On her own, Hesina studied the character etched into the jade round. *Longevity.* A generic bauble. There was nothing notable about the cord looping either.

The scream of tearing silk shredded her thoughts. She winced as Akira finished splitting apart the *hanfu*'s seam, but helped him smooth the single layers flat. Nothing unusual appeared inside.

She sat back on her heels and saw her "evidence" for what it really was: a random collection of knickknacks. What could she learn from an ornament or a paring knife that her father wore every day on his belt? Reeling with disappointment, she reached for the last item remaining: the snuff bottle.

A tiny mountain was painted on one side of the alabaster bottle, a crane on the other. With a thumbnail, Hesina popped the jade bead stopper.

"Careful." Akira took the bottle from her and sniffed first. He passed it back. "Just incense."

Hesina raised the soybean-sized opening to her nose. A scent she could have recognized anywhere hit the back of her throat.

Slowly, she lowered the bottle. Her voice rasped when she spoke. "It's Mother's."

Sticks upon sticks of this exact juniper incense had burned while she knelt in her mother's chambers as a child. What did it mean for this snuff bottle to have shown up on her father's desk? Hesina's anxiety grew when Akira didn't say anything for a long, long time.

"Did anyone have reason to kill your father?" he finally asked.

Before, she wouldn't have been able to answer. Her heart had been too raw to entertain the notion. But now the wound had scabbed; she spoke around its rough edges. "Xia Zhong."

She went to her desk and returned with a blank scroll and a brush wet with ink. "He wants Yan to go to war against Kendi'a. Father never would have allowed it."

Her hand shook as she wrote the minister's name, botching three strokes out of ten—not that he deserved any better.

Akira took the brush when she was done. "What about the people close to the king? Like your sister. Lilian, wasn't it?"

Her gaze jerked to him.

He patted his neck. "We had an agreement."

"I'm not so eager to behead everyone," Hesina muttered. Still, she chewed uneasily on her cheek as Akira wrote *Caiyan* and *Lilian* after *Xia Zhong*, his brushstrokes quick and sharp.

"And the dowager queen?"

"Mother couldn't have." Hesina's denial was vehement. It didn't matter if the snuff bottle was the dowager queen's, or if illness of the mind made her say terrible things. Her father had loved her mother. He would have wanted Hesina to defend her. "She's at the mountains for months at a time. In fact, she's there right now."

Akira got to his feet. "Then she won't mind if we search her rooms."

"We—" *Shouldn't.*

But he was already at the door, waiting.

Just a search, Hesina told herself as she reluctantly joined him.

They made sure to travel through the secret corridor and exit through Akira's room. Even then, several servants gawked as the queen emerged, unattended, from her representative's quarters. Heat rising to her cheeks, Hesina averted her eyes and focused on the route to her mother's wing. The sooner they got this over with, the better.

Yet at the dowager queen's opal-inlaid doors, she faltered. While Akira cut across the sitting room, Hesina gingerly stepped around the gourd-shaped stools and matching tables. The curtains were drawn. What little sunlight eked past was rusty red, making the chamber seem like the heart of a slumbering beast that might rouse if startled.

Tap. Tap. Tap.

Hesina jumped as Akira tested the floor with his rod. When he approached the dowager queen's sleeping chambers, he ducked under the brocade curtains.

After a conflicted moment, Hesina did too.

"We shouldn't be here," she whispered as he swept his rod under the vanity, then started opening drawers. The air seemed to palpitate in tandem with her heart. She swore she smelled juniper incense, though none of the censers burned.

"Check the bed" was Akira's answer.

"Me?"

Akira didn't reply, too absorbed in turning over some vials and pocketing others.

Hesina checked under the pillow log. Flipped over the embroidered quilt. She found nothing amiss.

Her relief was short-lived; Akira was already moving into the washroom. Hesina followed, overcome with vertigo when she saw the rosewood tub, raised on rooster feet, sitting in its corner.

"You won't find anything," she tried to tell Akira again. Her voice sounded as hollow as the tub did in response to Akira's rod.

"You might." He went on to examine the poultice cubbies built into the wall. "You're her daughter. Try to think of where she might place something important . . ."

His voice faded as Hesina stared at the tub, a memory appearing as clear as yesterday. It'd been after kneeling for several hours in her mother's sitting room. Petals had skimmed the surface of the water like little skiffs. Clouds of steam rose and parted, unveiling her mother, shoulders bare, eyes closed. Hesina had only peeked into the washroom to ask if she could leave. She wasn't supposed to see the scar around her mother's neck split open, blood weeping against her pruned skin.

She'd tried to back away.

Tripped.

Her mother's eyes had snapped open.

Pain crackled up Hesina's spine, jerking her into the present, where she'd backed out of the washroom and straight into her mother's altar. Rubbing at what was sure to become a hideous bruise, she lifted her eyes to the pillar of stone, carved with the immortal gods the relic emperors had aspired to become.

Her mother's illness of the mind had stumped the Imperial Doctress so thoroughly that she'd prescribed spiritual medicine. It hadn't worked. But the altar had stayed, likely to the dismay of the maids. Altars were a hassle to maintain. They had to be cleaned a certain way. Positioned a certain way.

Which made them the perfect hiding place.

The pain in Hesina's spine fled, replaced by a cold trickle of revelation. With a trembling hand, she reached out and—heavens forgive her—turned the altar pillar.

Its back contained a hollow, and the hollow cradled a bronze chest strung with a silver half-moon padlock. Hesina stared, triumphant to have found something, and terrified for the same reason.

Before she could recover her bearings, Akira came over and lifted the chest.

"A wedding lock," he explained, fiddling with the three dials. "One of a pair, exchanged during a marriage ceremony. The combination is traditionally set to the other partner's birth year."

His gaze flicked to her, expectant.

"265." Two hundred and sixty-five years since the end of the Relic Dynasty.

Akira spun each dial. The lock didn't budge. He looked to

her again, and Hesina probed at a raw spot on her inner cheek in thought.

"Try 906." The year it'd be if the Eleven hadn't started the calendar anew.

Akira entered those numbers. The lock remained firmly shut. Again, he looked to her, this time with skepticism.

"I know my own father's birth year," Hesina said, defensive. When his gray eyes disagreed, she grabbed the chest. Their hands brushed, and Akira's expression lost that chilling focus. He peered at her through the fall of his bangs, as if beholding her bloodless, sweaty face for the first time.

"I know my own father's birth year," she repeated quietly, and Akira nodded. But the damage had been done; her eyes grew scratchy as she stared down at the whorls of patina on the lid of the chest. *She* was the one holding them back, not the Investigation Bureau, because while she knew her father as well as she knew herself, she didn't know her mother. She didn't know what the dowager queen might have set the lock to, if not her father's birth year.

"I'll find the right numbers," she said as Akira picked up his rod. "I promise I will. Just give me some time."

He walked to the door and stopped under the frame. "Are you sure you want to do this?"

"Yes!"

Akira hefted his rod up and down, seeming to weigh it with his words. "Sometimes I lose myself," he finally said. "I get too focused. Forget that feelings matter. I was raised this way, and I'm still trying to change."

Hesina mustered the courage to join him, then the nerve to place a hand on his back. He stiffened as her palm came to rest over the sharp jut of his shoulder blade, and she swallowed, keenly aware of the bones beneath her own skin.

"Sometimes . . ." Her voice caught; she tried again. "Sometimes, I'm afraid of finding secrets I'm not meant to know." Or was deemed unworthy of knowing, in her mother's case. "But I want to be braver. Stronger. I want to be worthy of the truth. And I'd like it . . . I'd like it very much if you could help me."

Please.

After a long second, Akira nodded. Then he moved out of her touch. Her hand fell, but her heart didn't. This was the beginning of their partnership, not the end.

Grateful, Hesina released a breath. "I'm sorry about the lock. I know we don't have much time." It was their investigation against the Bureau's, their suspects against innocents.

"There are other ways of staying ahead," Akira said as they left her mother's chambers.

"Such as?"

"I don't know." He scrubbed a hand through his hair. "It sounded like the comforting thing to say."

Well, that wasn't comforting at all.

After they parted, Hesina racked her brain. She had a list of potential scapegoats that was thirty names long, but after Consort Fei, anyone with the slightest relation to Kendi'a could be fair game. If only there was a way of knowing who would be framed next. She couldn't foresee Xia Zhong's or the director's future moves, but . . .

She stopped between two embroidered facades, the chest heavy in her arms. On either side of her, the silk depicted soothsayers nailed to the stakes, surrounded by flames.

. . . There was someone who could.

ELEVEN

They controlled the people with fear.
                    ONE of the ELEVEN *on the relic emperors*

Fear, and sooths.
                    TWO of the ELEVEN *on the relic emperors*

When had the secret keeping started?

Since Caiyan had become her first advisor, Hesina realized as she turned away from his doors. She left without knocking; she'd come all the way to his chambers only to withhold her intentions of revisiting the Silver Iris. His safety mattered more than ever. If she suddenly died while Sanjing was halfway across the realm, the court and throne would temporarily go to Caiyan. Granted, Caiyan would argue that her safety trumped his. He would win that debate. Which was why Hesina didn't want one in the first place.

On her own, she readied the gold, studied the imperial city map, and then headed for the throne hall to review paperwork on the ivory *kang* while waiting for night to fall. Hours crawled by. Dusk stained the hall when her head page came to deliver the daily report on the realm.

"Any response from Kendi'a?" Hesina asked when her page concluded his updates.

"Nothing, *dianxia*."

Lilian's suggestion of using force had never seemed more appealing. But until her wrist gave out, Hesina would have to content herself with writing letters. Such was the almighty diplomacy of a queen.

"But there is news from the borderlands," said her page as she returned to editing a memorial on infrastructure.

"Yes?"

"Another village is gone."

Hesina's brush streaked across the paper.

For a second, she couldn't think or speak. She stared at the gash of black ink. Her irritation spiked—she'd spent an hour writing this—and she latched on to the simple emotion as the cosmos fell around her.

Another.

Another village.

"Where?"

"A millet hamlet twenty *li* south of the northern loess basin and fifty *li* west of Yingchuan," said her page. "Population was numbered at around sixty."

Was.

The brush dangled lifeless from her hand. Ink dripped onto the memorial, splattering like blood. "The people? The livestock?"

Her page gave a silent shake of his head.

Hesina's vision dimmed. "My brother?"

"According to our most recent reports, the general is still fighting skirmishes along the southern borderlands."

Then he was safe. As long as he was fighting, he was safe.

Hesina wrestled her panic back by the horns. She'd be playing into Xia Zhong's hands if she lost her nerve. "How far has this news spread?"

"We intercepted the messenger dove the moment it arrived. The news is contained."

For now. Hesina doubted it'd stay that way. They were moving along Xia Zhong's ideal trajectory—one where suspicion against the Kendi'ans mounted day after day. The people wouldn't brush off the disappearance of *two* villages.

She crumpled the memorial and fed it to the desk urn, taking measured breaths as the rice paper curled and blackened in the fire. "Set your best eyes and ears on Xia Zhong."

"Xia Zhong . . . as in the Minister of Rites?"

At least she wasn't alone in misjudging the minister. "Yes, the one and only. I want to know of his every movement and word."

"Understood, *dianxia*. Is there anyone else you'd like monitored?"

What about the people close to the king? whispered Akira's voice.

Flame scorched her fingertips. Hissing, Hesina dropped the memorial's remnants.

"No." She'd rather lose the mandate of the heavens than spy on her own family. "That will be all."

She exited the throne hall shortly after her page. The time for indecision had passed. If Xia Zhong got to the suspects first, he'd drive the final nail into Yan-Kendi'an relations. She had to see the Silver Iris before then.

Back in her chambers, she fumbled with her commoner's cloak while Ming'er stood by.

"It's growing dark, my flower."

"I won't be gone long."

She protested as Ming'er took the cloak from her, but the woman fastened the cloth buttons with much more finesse. "Be careful," Ming'er said, notching the last one.

Hesina vowed she would. Then she hurried to the imitation mountain range in the centermost courtyard. The lichen-draped cliffs shielded her from any eyes as she jammed a reed into a hole in the pumice. The mountains split apart.

"Not so fast."

Hesina whirled, brandishing the reed like a sword. "Show yourself."

"Over here."

She spun, but still nothing. Just shadows.

She'll be protecting you from the shadows.

Hesina lowered the reed and sighed. Even when he wasn't here, Sanjing still made her look the fool. "Mei."

"Mmm?"

This time when Hesina turned, a lithe girl stood before her, outfitted from head to toe in black, from her formfitting *hanfu* to the many daggers sheathed at her waist. An equally black braid tumbled out from the side of her hood, and a black cloth covered most of her face, sparing only her russet eyes.

"Well, hello," said Hesina, attempting to be amicable.

Mei didn't reciprocate. "Bad time to be visiting the city."

"Did I *say* I was visiting the city?"

"I've been warned of your tendency for lying through rhetorical questions." Mei ignored Hesina's snort of disbelief and scanned her figure. "No weapons." She did a slow sweep of their surroundings. "No guards."

"How long have you followed me?"

"Since your coronation."

"And nothing bad has happened."

"Yet," said Mei, sounding all too similar to Sanjing.

Like general, like commander. With a huff of exasperation, Hesina took one of the daggers strapped to Mei's broad-belt and tucked it into her own. "Better?"

"Not really," said Mei, but she didn't stop Hesina from entering the passageway.

✳ ✳ ✳

The autumn harvest festival was mere days away. The streets should have been packed. Now was the time to stock up on sorghum wine and cooking oil, or hot *zongzi* sticky-rice triangles wrapped in lotus leaves and red-bean moon cakes stamped with chrysanthemum designs. But the market sector was deathly quiet when Hesina emerged from the abandoned tavern. Vendor stalls stood forlorn without their owners. No palanquins bobbed down the narrow streets. No mule drivers yelled at children in their way. The night was thick with smog, and when Hesina looked to the red-light district, her breath stopped.

The horizon was eerily aglow, baking the silhouettes of the ridged roofs black.

"Seen enough?" came a quiet voice from behind.

Ignoring Mei, Hesina picked up her pace until she reached the first sign of life: a fleeing crowd. People ran past her, away from the red-light district, their faces engraved with terror. Panicked cries and shouted words sailed overhead, cleaved by the blast of the city-guard horn.

"Call for reinforcements!" cried the captain, heading a horde of armored men and women. Their red-tasseled halberds gleamed as they marched past.

Hesina grabbed the cloak of one. His spear jerked to her throat, and black flashed in the periphery, but she dropped her hold before Mei could spill blood. "What's going on?"

The guard stepped back, halberd still raised, and took in Hesina's commoner's garb. "Stay away from the red-light district."

"Why?" Hesina pressed, but he'd already rejoined the rest. As they rushed by, her hand shot to her silk broad-belt, where her imperial seal dangled. Then she froze. She could get the answers she wanted by revealing her identity, but then the guards would swamp her like fifty Caiyans. She'd forfeit any chance of making it to the Silver Iris.

Before Mei could stop her, Hesina turned and ran against the tide. She passed under the west arch, down the streets lined with dingy pawnshops, taverns, and teahouses, not slowing until she hit the crowd that had formed in the middle of the limestone street.

It was a bristling thing of people fleeing and people joining. Guards hemmed it in but did nothing to disperse the mob, or silence the shout that came from the heart of it.

"Another village has disappeared!" Hesina couldn't see the person, only the torch he'd thrust high. "The Kendi'ans grow ever stronger!"

"And why?" cried another torch-holder. "Because of *them*! Their kind live among us! They disguise themselves as beggars and whores, hiding themselves among the dregs of society as they bide time and recover from the blow the Eleven dealt them. But mark my words! One day, they will hatch like maggots! They've oppressed us once with their powers! They will oppress us yet again!"

Arm by arm, torso by torso, Hesina squeezed past the human barricade. It ended abruptly, and she pitched into the clearing.

In the middle rose a hastily erected stake. The girls and boys lashed to it stood out like exotic birds in their brothel colors, but they weren't beautiful. The kohl lining their eyes dripped black over their rouged cheeks, the carmine stain on their lips smeared like blood. They cowered as the crowd raged.

"Sooths!"

"Whores!"

"Maggots!"

"Destroy them now!" screamed a woman. "Destroy them before they destroy us!"

Hesina didn't trust herself to speak. She feared her voice would betray her, that the mere sound of it could reveal her horror and her guilt, for taking from the Silver Iris and giving nothing in return.

So she watched with the rest as one of the men handed off his torch and approached a tied-up courtesan. The girl shrank, flattening against the stake as the man cut her free.

He dragged her to her feet. "From this day forward, we strip them of their disguise!" He turned to the girl. "Burn," he spat out. "Burn, and show us your true identity!"

He raised her arm.

Do something.

Drew something from his belt.

Do something.

It was a sickle, the Eleven's weapon of choice, symbolic of the peasants' struggles against the sooths and nobility. Its sharpened edge grinned under the torchlight, ribboning the air in Hesina's throat. Then it hurtled down in a streak of silver.

It should have been a fast moment, over in a second, ending in a spray of blood, perhaps a flicker of blue flame. But instead, time slowed. Hesina envisioned the Silver Iris again. Saw her back, the monstrous truth of Hesina's kingdom carved into skin. The truth of *her*, if she stayed silent.

"Stop!"

The blade stopped short of flesh.

Eyes fell on Hesina, then flashed up to her jade seal raised high in the air. With her free hand, she tore apart the buttons Ming'er had so carefully fastened. The cloak slid to the ground.

Gasps rose as people fell. The mob, worshipping another leader just seconds ago, dropped into a collective *koutou*. The reverie only kicked up Hesina's disgust. She faced the ringleaders. "Step away from the girl."

Once they did, she spun to the guards pushing through the crowd. "Seize their weapons."

Then she drew Mei's dagger and strode to the young courtesan, who blanched when Hesina grasped her arm.

But it wasn't the courtesan's skin that broke under the blade.

In one heartbeat, Hesina sliced her own forearm and pressed the flat of the blade to the courtesan's bare one, streaking the flawless skin with her own blood. By the next heartbeat, Hesina had let her own sleeve fall over the wound. She spun around and, with her good hand, held the girl's arm up for all to see. "Look! Does it burn?"

People shoved and pushed, fighting for a view. Nothing happened. The girl's "cut" didn't burst into flame.

Hesina dropped the arm and held up Mei's knife. "Does it burn?"

The knife didn't burst into flame either.

Under Hesina's sleeve, warmth vined around her wrist and budded off the knuckles. She desperately hoped no one would notice in the falling light.

"But *she* burned," someone cried.

"Who? *Who burned?*" Hesina demanded when the people failed to answer.

They led her to the tavern by the music house. The path to the counter was strewn with broken tables and chairs, mosaicked with smashed *jiutan* of sorghum wine.

Brushing aside the people's warnings, Hesina strode toward the dark shape in the back, coughing on the gray motes clouding the air. Her eyesight gradually adjusted, and she made out the chair. She made out the person bound to the chair.

Clothes, shredded.

Torso, slit.

Skin, charred.

Eyelids, silver.

Silver like her name, and like her voice, metallic in Hesina's memory. *A nice parlor trick, don't you think?* the Silver Iris had said, lighting the candle with her own blood. But this time her blood had lit *her*, burning from the deepest part of the gash outward, consuming everything in its wake.

Hesina fell to her knees and vomited.

Feet crowded around her, joined by hands and elbows as people offered their handkerchiefs. No one suspected. No one guessed that it wasn't the carnage that revolted their queen, but the world, how easily it turned silver to ash, ashes that were on her skin, in her lungs, on her *tongue*.

Hesina retched again. More hands and handkerchiefs crowded into her vision. She pushed them away. "Get back. Get out."

The commoners rushed to follow orders.

Her guards weren't so obedient. Shakily, Hesina rose and turned on them. "*Get out.*"

Once everyone had retreated to the tavern's columned entrance,

Hesina made for the counter. She didn't know why. She was apart from herself, a spectator watching the queen rummage for a box of matches, watching her strike one, watching her hold it until the flame burned down the stick and then, and only then, watching her let it fall.

With a roar that drowned out the cries of alarm, the spirit-soaked ground came alive with blue flames. The hue wasn't quite the same as what had danced atop the Silver Iris's candlewick, but it was close. Hesina had watched the Imperial Doctress light enough alcohol burners to recall this property of sorghum wine. Now, she made a demonstration out of it. If eyewitness accounts spread like fire, then she would ignite her own. For every person who claimed that the Silver Iris burned blue, there would be three to claim that wine burned blue too. With enough debate, wine would become blood, and blood would become wine. Was there an infestation of sooths in the red-light district or drunkards who spent too much time around flammable liquids? Whom to believe? And whom not to? No one was king in the realm of rumors.

It was already happening. As Hesina joined the commoners and guards outside, disagreements were rising.

"Do you think . . . you think that's why she burned blue?"

"No, she was a sooth!"

"But did you see it for yourself? Did she really burst into flame?"

"No, but that's what the men told me!"

The voices hushed as Hesina threw out her arms.

"The world is full of tricksters," she shouted above the crackle at her back. "And there is no greater trickster than fear. Tonight, we fell victim to fear. We let it blind us. We thought we were hunting monsters . . ."

She stared out into the sea of flame-washed faces. It took all her strength not to look away. *But we were the monsters.*

Then she watched the fire of her own making grow and grow. As the flames leapt to the rafters, her eyes welled. Convincing the people that there were no sooths to hunt was all she could do. Her gift, in return for the Silver Iris's truth, was this lie.

The flames reddened as they finished off the wine and licked the wood. Beams and pillars dissolved. Half of the roof came crashing down, spraying embers into the night sky. It was very black, the night sky, Hesina remembered thinking, before her world went black too.

TWELVE

We will all be reborn as equals.

ONE *of the* ELEVEN *on the new era*

First, the old must go.

TWO *of the* ELEVEN *on the new era*

When she came to, Hesina felt like one of her father's shadow puppets. Her flesh was paper. Her bones were reeds.

"*Jia!*"

A terrifying jolt rocked through her. She clung to the closest solid thing—a wrist—and dreamed it was her father's.

You coddle her, her mother would snap if she saw.

Her father would reply with a smile and a shrug. *I'm the only one who does.*

But the arm Hesina gripped now was too slim to be her father's, even padded with a black leather guard. Reins sprouted from a fine-boned fist, and as Hesina's gaze tilted up, the rider barked another *Jia!*

Another sickening lurch. The world around them blurred faster. But the rider's face remained stationary. Russet eyes. Raven braid.

Mei.

Mei's arm, holding Hesina upright in front of her. Mei's horse, wherever she'd gotten it. Mei's cloak, reeking of rust and sticky to the touch.

"You're bleeding," Hesina whispered, startled by the broken sound of her voice.

Mei kept her eyes ahead. "I'm not, but you are."

An ache fanned from Hesina's wrist. She vaguely recalled cutting it. What a strange thing to do. Her eyes slid shut.

"Stay with me now." The arms around Hesina tightened. "What's your name?"

Hesina. A homophone for "dying cranes," something a younger Sanjing delighted to remind her of. Now he called her "Sina," which was hardly an improvement; its homophone translated as "Are you dead yet?"

Mei seemed to be asking more or less the same question. "Does it look like I'm dying?" Hesina mumbled.

Mei spurred on the horse as if to say *yes.*

Hesina frowned. She was fine. Just tired. Sleep-deprived. Sleep . . .

"Why did you cut yourself?"

Just let me be. "I had to."

"Why?" pressed Mei, and Hesina frowned.

"I wasn't sure . . . if she'd bleed . . ."

. . . Like the rest of us.

Or like a sooth.

The next time she came to, Hesina was in the palace. Moonlight from the latticed windows varnished the silent halls. The coals were banked in the braziers, the incense burned down to stubs.

The fog in Hesina's mind dissipated as Mei carried her, and suddenly she could taste the smoke again, thick with ash.

Her lungs seized at the memory of choking. Then she *was* choking. The world flashed from bright to dark to bright as it all came back, and she was cold, cold to the bone. She wanted to hide behind her father, bury her face in his cloak. She croaked for him, forgetting, for a single second, that he was gone.

Remembering was like losing him all over again. She cried out from the pain of it. Mei went faster, but they were going the wrong way. Hesina didn't need the Imperial Doctress. She needed someone to lean on as she came apart.

"Take me to Caiyan," she gasped.

Mei stopped short of the archway to the infirmary. "I may be in General Sanjing's good graces, but he won't forgive me if I let you die."

"I'm not dying."

"And I'm not soaked in your blood."

Hesina could have invoked all her titles—there were a lot of them—and reminded Mei that her word was final. But she was through with being a queen for the day. "Please, Mei."

Silence.

Mei finally sighed. "May the gods bless me in the afterlife." Then she pivoted, taking them through the pillared gallery connecting the outer palace to the inner. Hesina's stomach tightened as they entered the facades, but Mei didn't slow for the images. The swordswoman set her down when they reached Caiyan's rooms and knocked on the doors before Hesina could attempt herself. When they cracked open, Mei didn't bother with a greeting.

"You might want to summon the Imperial Doctress," she said, then vanished into the shadows.

The doors went wide.

"Milady? What's wrong? Where are you injured?"

Hesina stared owlishly at Caiyan. Whatever the time, it was clearly late enough that Caiyan had traded paperwork for sleep. His hair had been released from a topknot, dark locks rumpled, and he wore his black-and-gold viscount *hanfu* like a cape over his nightclothes. He didn't seem real in his state of disarray. She didn't *believe* that he was real, not even when he caught her by the elbows as her legs gave.

"Milady—" He froze when he saw the blood on her sleeve. Then he helped her to the bed, paneled with carved herons to match his doors. "Let me summon the Doctress."

"*No.*" She grabbed his *hanfu's* cuff. "I just . . . I need . . ."

With horror, Hesina realized that everything she needed was out of reach.

A hiccup bubbled out of her. "She's gone. Th-they're all gone."

Her next hiccup merged into a sob.

Slowly, Caiyan sat. He gathered her close. In the safety of his arms, enveloped by his fresh-ground ink scent, Hesina cried until she could cry no more. Then, scooped clean like an autumn gourd, she drew new air into her lungs and recounted everything that had transpired.

Caiyan stacked his pillow logs behind her as she spoke, but she didn't lean back on them. His support was all she needed.

"There now, milady," he said when she finished. "You're safe. As long as you're safe, everything will be fine."

Normally, Caiyan's words soothed her. They were calm. Steady. They almost masked his heartbeat, jagged against her shoulder.

With a twist of unease, Hesina sank against the pillows at her back. "It was never fine. The Eleven freed the oppressed by oppressing their oppressors."

Oppressed. Oppressing. Oppressors. Everything knotted like string in Hesina's head, until she couldn't distinguish beginning from end. "When will it end? When we will stop paying for the cost of peace?"

"I don't know, milady."

"But you must," said Hesina in growing distress. Caiyan had an answer to everything.

Quietly, he rose. Paced to his windows. "One way or another, we pay. You can't gain without relinquishing. For example, the Silver Iris may be gone, but you have gained your freedom."

"Freedom?"

"From your secret." He stared at the windows, even though it was dark, and even though the blinds were drawn and there was nothing to be seen. He turned back to face her. "No one shall ever know you spoke to her that night."

Hesina struggled to untangle her thoughts. Caiyan was right. Her treason had died with the Silver Iris. But she wasn't free. As long as the Eleven's teachings persisted, fear ruled the people, not she.

There had to be something she could do. There had to—

"Milady, you may not want to hear this, but as your advisor, I must speak."

"I'm listening."

Caiyan paced back to the bed. "Some will doubt your performance today, especially if they saw her burn with their own eyes." He knelt before her. "Some might even suspect you sympathize." He took her hands and squeezed. "Your first priority is to put those suspicions to rest. Make the people feel safe."

"Make the people feel safe . . ."

His hands rose to her shoulders. "If you felt something for her and her people, you mustn't show it. Not through your words. Not through your actions. Promise me, milady." His voice tightened with his grip. "Promise me you won't jeopardize your rule."

Hesina met his gaze. She saw his intentions. Caiyan wanted the best for her. When had he not?

Yet she didn't promise. "You're asking me to do nothing."

"Do you trust me?"

"I do." But she'd never snuck out into the city without him, or kept something as big as starting her own private investigation from him.

She knew they both must have been thinking that, and her guilt rose, compelling her to say, "And I promise."

The tension in his chestnut eyes mellowed. "Thank you." He lifted his hands.

A new force held Hesina still. "Have you . . ." She wet her lips. "Have you ever felt something for them?"

For the sooths.

The question alone, spoken to the wrong person, could have been construed as jeopardizing her rule, and she worried that Caiyan might reprimand her for breaking her promise so soon.

Yet all he did was shake his head. "No."

Her blood cooled, mostly with relief. "Good." She didn't want him haunted like she was. She didn't want him to see the stories on the silk facades, watch the plays of the imperial troupe, and wonder if the heroes of their legends were actually the villains.

But it also meant she was alone in her torment.

After visiting the Imperial Doctress—whose lecture brought her closer to the brink of death than the cut itself—Hesina lay awake. The nights were cooling, but her bed was hot. Her silken sheets cocooned her as she tossed and turned. Her blankets ensnared her limbs.

She hurled them off and sat up, breathing hard.

She had let her people's fear fester while waiting for a Kendi'an reply to her letters. She could wait no longer. If she couldn't quell a war, she would have to find the truth before it erupted.

Hesina padded to her desk and lit a candle. Her mother's chest glowed like a jewel in the flame, the silver lock kissed to gold.

Think, she ordered her mind as if it were a courtier. Somewhere in her memories, there had to be a nugget of information that would explain why her father's birth year was not the combination to her mother's lock.

The number had to be something significant. If not 265, the current year in the new era, and if not 906, the year it would have been by the relic calendars, then perhaps it was the difference of 906 and 265. She knew 641 was the year of the relic emperor's death, the last year recorded before the Eleven reset the calendar to zero—*so that all lives could be reborn*, her father had explained when she'd asked why. *Young, old, rich, poor, male, female—we all became children of the new era.*

Hesitantly, Hesina spun the first dial to a 6, the second to a 4, and the third to a 1.

641.

She tugged on the lock. It didn't budge. She shoved the chest away from her. That didn't budge the lock either, and after a long staring match, Hesina groaned and pulled it close again.

If not 641, then what? 000? The year immediately after 641, when the Eleven had started the calendar anew?

Hesina scoffed, but spun in a 0. Another 0. She almost didn't do the third. It was too simple. Too obvious. Too—

The last 0 slid into place, and the lock sighed apart.

She couldn't lie to herself; part of her had hoped the combination wouldn't work. Her mother's love for her father was the only thing she and her daughter had ever shared, and Hesina wasn't ready to lose it. Still, she grasped the lid with both hands. If the contents of this chest could help her end the trial before it hurt anyone else, then she could squeeze her eyes shut. She could lift.

The weight of the lid swung back. The hinges clinked. In the dark behind her lids, her thoughts unspooled.

The denial will pass, said the Imperial Doctress.

Nothing you do will bring him back, said her mother.

The truth might destroy you, said Akira.

But one voice silenced the others. *Knowledge is truth, Little Bird.*

The edges of her mind feathered like diluted ink, and a conversation from many years ago bled back in.

Why do you think so many scholars live in the imperial city? her father had once asked as they strolled by the city moat.

Because they're wise.

Yes. A ruler must keep the company of sages, because knowledge is truth. Those who refuse to learn live in a world of falsity. Do you remember how the relic emperors stopped themselves from learning?

They burned books.

Her father nodded. *They closed their eyes to the plights of their people and executed their critics.*

But didn't the Eleven burn books too? Hesina asked before she could think better of it.

Her father paused.

Yes, they did. He laid a hand atop her head, eyes crinkling as he smiled. *Which is why you'll be a better ruler than them all.*

The memory melted away as Hesina opened her eyes. Her father's voice faded. But in the near dark, she sensed his presence. He was here. With her. They were looking down at the chest together, at a . . . book.

A book.

Her disappointment outweighed the volume—a light thing, thin as the *Tenets* were fat, and in shockingly abysmal condition. The cover was singed in some places, stained in others, splotched with ink, grease, and a brownish substance that looked suspiciously like dried blood. Three characters ran down the right-hand side, but as luck would have it, Hesina couldn't read the language, nor did she recognize it as Ci, Kendi'an, or Ning.

To make matters worse, the author would have dearly benefited from one of Hesina's mandatory calligraphy lessons. The characters inside the book were squashed, and each short column of text contained several cross-outs. But that wasn't what drove her mad. As illegible as the characters were, they tugged at her mind, and for the life of her, Hesina couldn't figure out why they seemed so familiar.

Several hours and lexicons later, she slammed the book shut in disgust. Another dead end. If only the kingdom would wait for her as she cracked the language. But that was too much to ask for. The sun would go on rising; the court would go on assembling. The Kendi'ans would go on ignoring her letters; the people would go on fearing. All she could do was push up from her seat, pop the kinks in her back, and leave one unfinished duty for another.

She headed for the throne hall. The voices reached her before she reached them, buzzing through the carved double doors like hornets.

Hesina clenched her teeth. She knew what she had to do. What she had to say.

They weren't going to condone the cutting and burning of

innocent people, and they certainly weren't going to perform a citywide sweep of the sooths based on some rumored sighting.

But they also weren't going to stand by and let Kendi'a continue threatening their borders.

They were going to war.

Her vassals hushed as she entered, and the Grand Secretariat scurried forward once Hesina was seated, bearing a reed tube.

"From Kendi'a, my queen," the woman murmured as Hesina loosened the twine securing the clay cap.

Her hands stilled. Then she ripped the cap free from the last of the twine. The roll of parchment slid into her palm.

She unfurled it to characters written in the common tongue.

To the Queen of Yan,

We have received your request for negotiations, and we accept. On the first day of the eleventh month, we will wait for you by the banks of the Black Lake. We hope you find this to be a suitable intermediary location. You may bring six companions of your choice, but no more.

Transcribed by Jikan the Scribe
Dictated by Tasn the Eunuch
Willed by the Dragon Who Wields the Fire, Crown Prince Siahryn, Fifth to His Name

THIRTEEN

The four kingdoms must be kept in peace.

ONE of the ELEVEN on war

At least feed your people before conscripting them.

TWO of the ELEVEN on war

Hesina was going to the Black Lake, and nothing Caiyan did or said could dissuade her.

That didn't stop him from trying.

"If you go," he said on the morning of her departure, two days after receiving the Kendi'an letter, "they might break the truce." The two of them had climbed to the imperial mail room atop the eastern gong tower, stooped between the gabled ceiling and the bird droppings on the slate floor. "They make their demands—land, water, whatever it may be—and attack when you refuse. They may even kill you."

It was troublesome, thought Hesina grimly, that everyone believed her so easily killed.

"In doing so, they force Yan's hand," continued Caiyan. "War will erupt over your death."

"There will always be risks." They'd come to a point in the debate where every argument and counterargument felt like the steps of a well-rehearsed dance. Maybe that's why Hesina improvised with a little wave of the hand. "There might even be sooths."

Caiyan's expression hardened like clay, and she wished she could take back her words. She didn't *want* to believe that the sooths had allied with the Kendi'ans, but she and the rest of the delegation were prepared—as prepared as one could be with anti-sooth paper talismans tucked into sleeves and shoes.

"I understand this isn't ideal." Doves cooed as Hesina passed the cages for Sanjing's birds. "But I have to do *something*. And yes, I know," she said before Caiyan could interrupt. "I know I promised I wouldn't jeopardize my rule."

She unlatched a cage. "But let's consider the alternative: I don't go. Kendi'a continues threatening our borders while the trial frames more suspects. The people grow more paranoid by the day. War erupts, I enact the first conscription in centuries, and my rule is jeopardized anyway."

Caiyan pinched the bridge of his nose. "You're comparing plums to persimmons."

They weren't all that different, in Hesina's opinion.

"Any danger can be faced from the throne," Caiyan insisted. "But out there? Without support?"

"I have protection." The falcon Hesina chose gave her a reproachful look as she tied a matchstick-sized tube to its leg. "And I have a backup plan."

Caiyan eyed the falcon. "That backup plan being General Yan Sanjing."

"Who happens to be at the borderlands." She carried the bird to the slatted window, which she opened to the overcast day. Fog blanketed the farmland beyond the city walls. "You're the one who always advised me to use my immediate resources."

"The Black Lake is not an immediate location."

Hesina sighed. There was no winning against Caiyan, who sensed his advantage and pressed it.

"Send someone on your behalf, milady. Send me, if you don't trust anyone in the court."

She let the falcon go and waited until it was a speck against the clouds before she faced him. "You're right. I *don't* trust anyone but you in court."

"That's why—"

"That's why you must stay." She grasped his hands, willing him to understand. The journey to and from the Black Lake could take upward of a month . . . far too long to leave Xia Zhong to his own devices. "Only you can keep the officials in line while I'm gone. I need you."

And I need to protect you. Hesina remembered that winter day. That terrible crack. The black pond waters. Blood on ice. Caiyan had almost died once. If the Kendi'ans really broke the truce, she wasn't sure she could save him again. She couldn't lose the one brother as close to her as kin.

"I need you," she repeated, quieter this time.

Not enough to take me, he could have retorted if he knew where to dig the knife.

But Caiyan wasn't Sanjing. He simply sighed and bowed. "Then use me as you please, milady."

* * *

A crowd of commoners had gathered at the base of the gong tower; they knelt when the queen and her first advisor emerged. Some reached to touch the hem of her *ruqun*, and Hesina couldn't help but flinch away. These hands had killed the Silver Iris. She wanted nothing to do with them.

"A word or address?" suggested Caiyan as they proceeded through the crowd.

Words? Her brain was millet mush. Caiyan's reservations weren't unfounded. Negotiations might fail. Sanjing might not pull through. A thousand things could go wrong on her first journey past the city walls, to the borderlands no less.

But what queen left her people without so much as a parting?

Without anger or grief to inflate her, Hesina felt small before the crowd. "The Eleven hoped to build a kinder era," she said, then caught herself invoking the *Tenets*. The taste of ashes returned to her mouth. "They gave us a peace that has lasted three centuries, a peace I go forth to protect."

The people lapped it up. Hope opened faces. Chants parted lips.

"*Dianxia! Dianxia!*"

"*Wansui, wansui, wan wan sui!*"

Unease rolled over Hesina, followed by the sensation of being watched. Over the heads of the commoners, she spotted a group of court officials. Xia Zhong stood among them. Their eyes met, and his lips curled.

What do you think you can do? he seemed to ask. *The pieces have been set; you can't stop this war.*

They'd see about that.

At the Eastern Gate, Lilian waited with a bundle of cloth that she stuffed into Hesina's arms. "If you're going to negotiate, you should do it in style."

Hesina shook out the black silk *ruqun*. A coiled dragon—the Kendi'an insignia—wrapped from front to back, very fierce, very beautiful, and very . . . headless.

Looked like she'd attend her funeral in style too. "It's . . ."

"No need to thank me," said Lilian as Hesina touched the red embroidery spewing from the severed neck. "I've woven threads of silver into it as a sad excuse for armor. Still, better than nothing if they're dumb enough to cross you."

Now that Lilian mentioned it, Hesina noticed that each scale had been rendered with iridescent thread. The entire dragon must have taken days to stitch. Her gaze cut to Lilian's. "You didn't have to."

For once, her sister's eyes were solemn. "It's the least I can do."

No matter how tightly Hesina laced back her emotions, Lilian undid her. There were so many things she wanted to say, but all she managed was, "I'm sorry I'll be missing the harvest festival."

The sentiment came out stiff; expressions of love didn't come any easier to Hesina than speeches to the people.

"I'm not," chirped Lilian. "I get to eat your share of moon cakes."

"You would have done so anyway."

"Hey!" Lilian scowled, then poked her in the arm. "You better return in one piece. I'll never forgive you if you leave me with the stone-head. He's been reading so many books recently that you'd think he's trying for immortal sagehood."

Caiyan cleared his throat. "Didn't know you still believed in children's tales."

"Oh yeah?" Lilian raised a brow. "When did you outgrow them for erotica—"

"Ready, milady?"

Hesina nodded, hugging Lilian before entering the tunnel that bore through the city wall. Caiyan accompanied her. His footfalls stopped short of the other side. Hesina fortified herself against another barrage of reasons as to why she should stay, but he only said, "Be careful."

Then he stepped back and erased the worry from his face.

The gesture moved Hesina more than any logical argument could. "I will."

With one last breath drawn under the cool shade of the stone tunnel, she stepped out into the daylight. She swung into her saddle and surveyed her entourage.

Four guards, one scout, and Akira, the recipient of some dubious glances as he trotted his steed to her side. The others hadn't seen him fight. They didn't know he was helping her find the truth outside of the trial. Hesina wanted to keep him close as he investigated the gas in the vial, so that she could track his progress and perhaps share hers—and the existence of the book—once she made headway worth speaking of.

But right now, he felt a little *too* close. The rising sun that gilded the hills and valleys between them and Kendi'a gilded him, too, lightening his hair to wheat and plating silver over his gray eyes. It stole Hesina's breath to see the ex-convict thoroughly transformed—before he opened his mouth, at least.

"You sure you want to give a robber a horse?"

Her head cleared. "Representative," she corrected. "Remember that."

Then she snapped the reins.

She had the Eleven to thank for her passable riding skills. They'd decided that no ruler, man or woman, was above learning the grit of their own lands. The journey would be rough, but she could weather it. Negotiations could fail, but she had to try.

"*Jia!*" she cried, leaning into the wind. The world whipped past. This time, she was the one making it fly. "*Jia!*"

* * *

They set a hard pace, stopping only to change horses every fifty *li*. Aches and pains plagued Hesina, hindering her ability to appreciate the crystal-clear basins, emerald rice paddies, and bamboo forests around them. But gems of life were sewn into every corner. When they cut through mountain passes, golden-tailed monkeys chattered on the crags overhead. When they forded streams, red-crowned cranes, rumored to be the animal counterparts of immortal sages, crossed alongside them.

With every gasp and glimpse of beauty, Hesina found it harder and harder to accept this fertile, dew-crowned land as hers. Rather, it became easier to accept it *hadn't* always been hers. In ancient times, cranes had been the size of horses. Now their heads only came to her stallion's chest. The relic emperors, believing the blood of the birds to be an ingredient in the elixir of immortality, had hunted them to near-extinction.

The land also bore scars of the past. Tombstones appeared on the roadside as they approached Tricent Gorge at the end of the week. The water levels had receded under the Eleven's reign, but the gorge, exaggerated in myths to be a thousand *li* deep—hence the name *Tricent*—had flooded biannually in the past, drowning tens of thousands at a time. On the morning of the crossing, even the toughest of Hesina's guards forewent breakfast. Their faces were as white as the rapids below by the time they cleared the swaying bamboo bridge.

When night saturated the sky, starting from the distant Ning peaks, the scout would ride ahead while the rest of them pitched camp. The guards would draw their shifts, and Hesina would go to Akira. He'd packed a small burner, jars filled with multicolored powders, a set of silver spoons, and the vial of golden gas. Except that it wasn't a gas anymore. And it wasn't gold. He had condensed the poison into an orange-toned liquid that Hesina watched him dilute with water, boil off, and dilute again. Whenever she inquired after his process, his responses ranged from "I'm not sure" to "thinking" to "burning things."

Sometimes there was no response. Akira would merely finish whatever he was doing, take up his rod, and begin to carve.

"Monsters roam at night," he'd say, and Hesina would stare, unsure how to take his words. But she'd grown accustomed to uncertainty around Akira, to the point she didn't mind it. She was content to watch him work until he eventually dozed off. Then she would remove her mother's book from her satchel.

It was infuriating, the book. It would trick her into thinking she was reading it. The characters would crawl through her pupils and chant their secret language, and the itch of *knowing* would fill her subconscious as if it'd been etched upon her bones. But the second her mind cleared, the knowing vanished. The characters devolved into many-legged insects again. Night after night, Hesina found herself at the edge of this precipice. And night after night, she resigned herself to three pathetic observations.

The first: Each column of text was short. The entire book seemed to be composed of quotes rather than paragraphs.

The second: A set of three characters always appeared at the end of each quote, as if the authors all shared the same surname.

The third: The book had doubled as a travelogue. Sketches of foreign plants, landscapes, and weaponry were crammed in the margins, and drawings of Kendi'an sandstone citadels, Ning ice pagodas, and Ci porcelain-tiled mansions were stitched between the pages.

There was a fourth observation, if it counted: The book refused to be deciphered.

More than once, Hesina caught herself looking to Akira for answers. Yet she never woke him. He didn't mutter or stir in his sleep, but the space between his brows would knot. A knot would form in Hesina's own chest, and she'd keep an eye on him until his brow smoothed and his head settled. He was no more than a boy, really, a boy with powder-stained fingertips and hair that was always falling out of its tie, begging to be brushed back by a careful hand.

It wouldn't be hers. That much Hesina knew. She had enough on her mind, and she had no intentions of losing it to some idyllic fantasy.

* * *

They arrived at the Black Lake on the day of the harvest festival. As Hesina and the rest tethered their spent mounts in a cypress grove between the nearest village and the banks, the scout rode out to survey the region. She returned with a report on the terrain, and Hesina took particular note of the best retreat routes in homage to Caiyan.

The scout seemed more concerned about a cypress tree. Hesina followed her to the tree in question and looked to where the woman pointed.

"It followed me."

Yellow eyes peered out from the dark net of needles. Her brother's falcon. The message tube was still attached to the bird's leg, but the letter was gone, replaced by a scrap from one of Sanjing's banners.

Hesina wanted to shake the scrap at the heavens and demand an answer in plain Yan. "Any sign of my brother or his men?"

"Not in the radius of a *li*."

So Sanjing hadn't moved yet to answer her call. *He knows what he's doing*, said a little voice inside Hesina. But it was drowned out by a louder voice that said *Caiyan's right. You're wrong to rely on him.* For all she knew, her brother could have torn her letter apart and shown the shreds to his lieutenants. *See this?* he'd drawl. *My sister only writes when she needs me.*

The worst of it was that he was technically right.

Her mood darkened as dusk fell. The guards built a bonfire, and laughter and cypress smoke soon filled the air, along with stories of the Thousand-Faced Ning Spy and the Ci Whisperer of Secrets, legendary antiheroes Hesina had read about between her *Tenets* studies. She wanted to join in but couldn't bring herself to. Her presence would stifle things.

Alone, she wandered back to the tarps containing their supplies. She picked up the unreadable book, tried to read it, threw it, picked it up again, tried to read it again, and threw it again. As she picked it up a third time, she noticed Akira's rod on the ground.

That was strange. Akira never neglected his rod. Frowning, Hesina glanced back to the fire. He wasn't with the guards. He wasn't in any of the other tarps either. That left the lake. With the full moon as her guide, she started for the banks.

"Must we go through this again?" came a voice from behind.

Hesina spun—into Mei.

Splendid. She'd found herself some unwanted company instead of Akira. "Why are you here?"

Mei leaned against the gnarled trunk of a cypress tree. "I go where errant queens go." Her hood was down but her mask was up, and she wore her braid wrapped twice around her neck. "Has your arm healed?"

The question caught Hesina off guard, and she forgot to sound cross when she said, "It has." She pushed up her sleeve and showed

DESCENDANT OF THE CRANE

the scab to Mei. Then she remembered how unabashedly she'd bled over the swordswoman and figured some gratitude was in order. "Thank you for helping me that night."

Mei's russet gaze lingered on the scab.

Hesina dropped the sleeve, her embarrassment curdling to unease. "I didn't happen to say anything . . . strange, did I?"

"No. Just the usual rhetorical questions." Mei pushed herself off from the tree. "You should get some rest. For tomorrow."

Tomorrow. The thought of it compressed the breath in Hesina's chest. "Will you be coming with us?"

"Am I needed?"

Hesina toed the gravel by the tree roots. "No."

"I'd recommend sleeping instead of wandering," said Mei. "And on the subject of recommendations, be wary of those you trust."

Hesina knew whom Mei was referring to; distrusting Caiyan appeared to be a prerequisite for Sanjing's friendship. "Not you too."

Mei pulled up her hood. "I'm suspicious of all the secretive ones. It's a trade necessity."

"*You're* quite secretive."

"Once again, a trade necessity." Mei turned to go, then stopped, glancing over her shoulder. "Your brother cares, you know. I wouldn't be here otherwise."

Then she retreated into the shadows.

Your brother cares.

Like Elevens he did. Thinking about Sanjing cast another cloud over Hesina's mood, which continued to blacken when she tried—and failed—to find Akira. That's what she got for pardoning a convict. He'd run off. Left her alone with his stupid rod. The guards, on the other hand, couldn't leave her alone. They didn't actually want to bring her along to celebrate the harvest festival at the nearby village, but they, like she, had no choice. Hesina followed them, sulking the whole way. Then, just as a cramp panged through her abdomen, explaining her mood but not helping it, villagers swarmed her and she had to smile through the pain. Couldn't they see that it was a lie?

Apparently not. She wasn't Hesina anymore. She was the queen, a firm but doting mother to the people, a mother she had been without. Perhaps that was why Hesina didn't resist the village girl who took her hand and pulled her into the newly threshed fields. She let the elders sitting on bales of sorghum rope her into making lanterns, and after several attempts, she fashioned a passable one for Sanjing. When it came time to write her wish on it, she wished for his well-being.

Then she made more. Her pile grew. The elders offered her a fishnet to carry the lanterns to the village square where people were setting them aloft, but Hesina thought of the lake and the moon and made the journey back to the encampment.

She passed the cypress grove and went down to the inky waters. Tomorrow, she would come here again and negotiate with the Crown Prince. There could be only two outcomes: war or peace. Success or failure.

But it had to be done, and she had to be the one to do it, underprepared or not.

With unsteady hands, Hesina set to work, stuffing oil-soaked cotton gauze into each lantern's bamboo cradle, transferring her watch lantern's flame to the cotton with a reed, setting them free in the order they'd been made: Sanjing. Lilian. Caiyan. Ming'er. Akira.

But Akira's never took off. A gust of wind killed the flame mid-ascent. The lantern floated down, drifting several reed lengths out into the black water.

According to the *Tenets*, the Eleven had tipped in five thousand barrels of ink, lured both relic and Kendi'an troops into the lake, and escaped while the two armies decimated each other, foe and friend indistinguishably dyed.

And that, explained Hesina's tutors, *is why the waters are black*.

She could take their word for it without a midnight swim. But the lantern taunted, its pale paper sphere bobbing like a second moon in the expanse of black.

Elevens save me. Sighing, Hesina knotted up her skirts and shucked off her traveling boots. The freezing water didn't agree with her cramps, and as she waded deeper, she concluded that the night couldn't possibly get worse.

Then it did. The lantern finally drifted within reach, but before she could grab it, Hesina collided with something. Her hands shot out—a feeble attempt to stabilize herself. The water punched into her face as she fell, and she choked as she sloshed, her limbs tangled with ones that weren't her own.

Spluttering, she resurfaced and stood. Beside her, another form broke out of the water.

Hesina couldn't believe her eyes. She wiped at them, just to be sure. "*Akira?* What are you *doing*?"

He sat up, coughing, fully clothed and soaked. "Floating." Inky rivulets snaked down his temples. "Well, not anymore."

She would not be reduced to speechlessness. She would not. "But *why*?"

"Er. Moon-gazing?"

Moon-gazing.

Speechless, Hesina raised a sleeve. It was drenched in black. That settled one matter; she would have no choice but to wear Lilian's *ruqun* to the negotiation.

A perplexed laugh escaped her, then another. Before she knew it, she was doubled over in laughter, teeth chattering in the cold. Who would have known that a good, icy dunking was what she'd needed all along?

It was Akira's turn to stare. "You're not here to moon-gaze, I'll guess." He looked about, his eyes landing on the lantern. "Is that yours?"

"No." She sounded out of sorts and out of breath. "Well, yes, but I made it for you."

"Leave it. I don't need people making lanterns for me."

"Too late." She lifted her sopping skirts and resumed wading. "I've already fallen into a lake for you."

He reached the lantern first and scooped it from the water. "What did you wish for?"

She snatched it before he could see. "For you to be free—"

From the things that trouble you in your sleep.

"—From your crimes."

"All of them?"

"Yes, all of them."

Akira rubbed the back of his neck. "You'll need more than one lantern, then."

"How many merchants did you rob?"

"I don't remember, but definitely more than one."

Another laugh burst out of Hesina. She welcomed it and the bewilderment from which it was borne. It freed her from all the things she was supposed to do, feel, say. "Well, have you had your fill of moon-gazing?"

"After this?" Akira pushed back his wet bangs. "For a few years, yes."

Said the one who'd been half-submerged in the first place.

With a shake of the head, Hesina offered him her hand. "Let's go back."

Her heart did a funny little dance as he grasped it. It was as if she'd never held a hand before, which was almost as preposterous as floating in a lake to moon-gaze. But she couldn't stop from homing in on the feel of his hand in hers, and how hers might feel to him. Was it too cold? Too pudgy? Could he detect her quickening pulse?

Better question: *Why* was it quickening at all?

She almost pitched forward again when Akira pulled himself up.

The camp was still empty when they returned. Hesina built up the fire and set the lantern on the embankment of stones to dry. Then they sat to dry themselves. A zither melody warbled in from the direction of the village. She recognized it from a play the imperial troupe performed every autumn.

It was said that nine suns once flamed in the sky, roasting rice paddies and people alike. A great warrior rode out in her chariot and shot down eight. The ninth consumed her. Her mother spent the rest of her life reading all the scrolls in all the libraries of the world, looking for a way to recover her daughter. She breathed her last over an open book, and the gods, impressed by the tenacity of the mortal mind, brought the woman back as a sage. They blessed her with immortality and gifted her with a giant crane that flew her up to the lunar palace, where the warrior's spirit resided. Thus, mother and daughter were at last reunited.

It was a story as old as the sun and moon themselves, inscribed on turtle bones by shamans that predated the sooths. The relic emperors had interpreted the crane as the key to immortality. The Eleven had interpreted it as wisdom. Hesina picked neither. She didn't care for living forever when one lifetime was hard enough, and she was, in general, biased against stories of devoted mothers.

But tonight, it occurred to Hesina that she envied the daughter for her courage. She'd confronted not one sun, but nine. Hesina could barely face her own destiny.

"What is destiny?" she wondered, half to herself.

Akira, the master of saying random things, wasn't perturbed. "When you're really good at something."

Hesina hadn't thought about it that way. Now that she did, it was depressing. She wasn't good at much. A long, long time ago, she thought she had a knack for acting. She took to lying, and she preferred living in someone else's skin as opposed to her own. But nothing squelched childish dreams quite like inheriting the throne. Learning to rule was an all-consuming pastime.

"What would you say I'm good at?" she asked Akira.

"Making lanterns."

She glowered and he smiled, the corners of his mouth soft.

"The truth," Hesina demanded.

"I didn't say you were good at retrieving them."

She snorted, then rather wished she hadn't. It made her sound like a pig, and apparently she still had *some* dignity left to lose in front of Akira.

"What about you?" She blamed the fire for the warmth in her chest. "Were you a good robber?"

Akira poked a twig into the flames. "Good robbers aren't caught." The twig burned down to a nub, and he dropped it. "I knew someone who was better than the rest of us. His skill defined him. But one day he took too much. I haven't found him since."

"Was he a friend?"

"You could call him that."

"You must miss him."

He gave a noncommittal shrug that she understood better than any *yes* or *no*. Missing some people was like missing air. You did yourself no favors by wondering how you survived without them.

But tonight, Hesina let herself miss her father. She missed him. She missed him a lot. As the distant chords flowed into their little clearing, winding with the strings of her heart, she imagined herself riding on a chariot to face the Kendi'an Crown Prince. And later, when she slept, she dreamed she died, but her father read her back to life, and together they flew to the lunar palace on the backs of their giant cranes.

* * *

Of course, the next morning, she wasn't a warrior. She didn't ride a chariot in blazing glory to the Kendi'ans. She was a queen whose hands were shaking so badly she could barely dress herself.

"We counted six, *dianxia*," reported the scout from the other side of the tarp, her shadow faint against the oiled fabric.

Hesina coached herself through putting on the many components of her clothes. *Cross-wrap the* ruqun. *Strap the sword between the shoulder blades. Tuck in the bombs. Fasten the broadbelt, string on the royal seal, the jade mandalas, the trio of knotted cords.* "Are you certain?"

"Yes," the scout confirmed. "Six, excluding the Crown Prince himself. Four slaves, two advisors."

Now the cloak. She drew the tassels tight at the hollow of her neck, hiding every speck of headless-dragon embroidery.

The Crown Prince had honored the terms of negotiation. No army awaited them. Maybe Hesina wouldn't even need Sanjing's help. She had every reason to relax. "Have you concealed your weapon?"

"Yes, *dianxia*."

"Good." Her voice didn't betray her nerves, but her hands did, twitching, sweating. She curled them into fists. "We depart in ten."

Overnight, black-and-scarlet tents had sprung up along the far lakeshore, pitched against the golden dunes. Kendi'an pennants of the same colors flew high, snapping in the desert wind.

One last time, Hesina checked that her sword and bombs were all in place. Then she marched herself and her entourage across the gritty plain to the largest of the tents. A Kendi'an advisor greeted her in the common tongue, instructed her guards to wait outside, and lifted the dragon-emblazoned flaps.

Yan Hesina wasn't ready.

But she wasn't Yan Hesina when she stepped into the Crown Prince's lair. She was a warrior, a queen, fully costumed and ready to bluff her way to success.

FOURTEEN

No human shall be owned by another.
　　　　ONE *of the* ELEVEN *on slavery and serfdom*

Freedom is everyone's right.
　　　　TWO *of the* ELEVEN *on slavery and serfdom*

She wasn't the first queen to negotiate with Kendi'a. She wouldn't be the last. Generations of Yan monarchs had tried to establish something more than a trade partnership with the land of sand and fire, and generations had failed.

It became obvious why, once Hesina's eyes adjusted to the dim. Icy Ning was like an older sister, swampy Ci a younger cousin. Their differences existed, but they were reconcilable.

Kendi'a was oil to Yan's water. Yan philosophers and literati lauded cooperation; Kendi'an ones encouraged competition. Yan aesthetics drew on complementary colors and motifs; Kendi'an ones favored contrast. This tent was a classic case: panels of red and black silk fanned the circumference, and bronze dishes filled with flames dangled from rickety chains hooked to the wooden crown above. Any moment now, a chain might break, a dish might fall, and the whole tent would burn. That would be one way to die—if Hesina didn't asphyxiate herself first.

Breathe. As she tried to, her eye caught on the salt picks strung across one of the hide panels. They weren't so different from the sickles used to reap millet in the northern provinces. If it came down to it, Hesina could fend off an attack with one. Her breathing picked up speed.

"Seen enough to your liking?"

Slowly, she brought her gaze to the hypothetical attacker.

The Crown Prince sat on a rattan divan next to a tapestry-covered mound. He wore a loose, burgundy robe with a V-neck that slashed down to his lean stomach and disappeared under a jade girdle. Hesina scanned his body for concealed weaponry, and he grinned wolfishly. "Or would you like to see more?" he asked in accented common tongue, fingering the girdle's lacings.

She flushed, and he laughed.

"I imagine your life must be boring." He rose. "A queen without a harem." He was around Caiyan's age. Perhaps a year or two older. Hesina focused on that fact as he circled in. "A queen without slaves."

He stopped several reed lengths away. "What is the point?"

She shrugged like a puppet yanked into the motion. "I rule. Every now and then, I also travel nine hundred *li* to see princes like you. Now, make it worth it."

"I will." He went to the covered mound and yanked off the tapestry.

Salt. Hexagonal pillars of it, stacked like honeycomb. It was more than Hesina had ever seen in one place. Ground down, it'd make for a hundred sacks at the very least.

"We have fifty more waiting for you," said the prince.

She wet her lips. "We'll match you with water."

"Oh no. We do not want water."

He came close, and closer. Hesina envisioned molten steel funneling down her spine, branching through each leg and pooling in her heels, melding her to the ground. *Don't move*, she ordered herself as he leaned in from the waist.

Soot darkened his lashes. Silver studs arced over his brow. His breath brushed her nose when he spoke. It smelled of star anise and copper.

"We want your soothsayers."

The steel of her spine liquefied.

This was just bait. He was waiting for the right moment to pounce. She had to tread carefully or end up cornered.

Buy time to think. "For?"

It'd seemed like the safest reply. But when the Crown Prince smiled, Hesina's stomach sank.

"So the rumors are true," he mused. "You know nothing about them."

"Nothing" seemed like an overstatement, but Hesina wasn't in a position to argue that when the Crown Prince snapped his fingers.

Two figures emerged from the shadowy interior of the tent. Hesina tensed, relaxed when she realized they were children, then tensed again when she saw the chains between their wrists and the iron collars around their necks. A red lily had been tattooed below the gray shadow of their shaved hairlines. The Kendi'an slave mark.

"Do not be alarmed by what you see next," said the prince. "I hear your kind fears them, but there is no need to fear anything in chains." Then he waved a hand. "Show her."

Their eyes slid shut.

The air chilled. Hesina's clothes clung to her skin—and not from sweat. Tiny, clear globules oozed into existence, condensing midair into a globe the size of a summer cantaloupe, a globe of water.

"Enough," ordered the prince.

The globe splattered on the ground, immediately swallowed by the parched earth. The children swayed as their eyes blinked open. Beads of blood rolled from the inner corners. One swiped at her cheek and licked her knuckles clean. The other was slower. He whimpered as the smeared blood sparked, flamed blue, and died, blistering the skin.

Sooths had just bent reality before Hesina's very nose; she should have fainted from terror. Instead, her hands balled. These were children. They shouldn't have been slaves.

But they were because the Eleven had forced their ancestors from their homes. Because all the Yan kings and queens since then had failed to expunge the hatred.

Including Hesina.

Her fury congealed to nausea. For a dangerous moment, she thought she might sicken at the Crown Prince's feet and reveal not only the contents of her breakfast, but also her biggest secret: she was a sympathizer. Her heart didn't beat to the rhythm of her people's. And now, as the Crown Prince watched her, it hammered to no rhythm at all.

"Away, my little monsters. You are frightening my guest."

The chains clinked as the children retreated.

"Soothsayers," he mused when they were gone. "The name brings to mind the ones that See into the future. And yet—"

He glided to the decanter resting on a stool and poured some ruby-red liquid into a ram's horn. "It fails to describe the ones that can actually *manipulate* the future.

"You think Kendi'a is dry," he said, sipping, making Hesina all the more aware of her own parched mouth. "You are not wrong to think so. Kings have been killed in times of drought. Citadels have fallen over wars for water." His thumb journeyed around the rim. "But come morning, even the air here is filled with dew."

He began to circle her. The surge of bile in her throat had settled, but Hesina didn't trust herself to speak or move.

Sooths who manipulate the future.

The dews come morning.

"Imagine summoning the dew of tomorrow morning to today." His breath caressed the nape of her neck. She resisted the urge to spin around.

When he spoke next, it was to her right side. "Imagine summoning the dew of a thousand tomorrow mornings."

Comprehension dawned. "You'd be moving the air into a future state."

And with the future air came the future dew.

Dew. Water. This was how Kendi'a planned on getting the water it so desperately lacked: through the slave labor of sooths.

Hesina didn't know what to think or feel. She imagined it was like learning, as a relic emperor, that the elixir of immortality could be derived from the blood of humans instead of cranes. A horrible but painfully obvious revelation.

"Yes." The prince circled back to face her. Hesina fought to keep her surprise hidden, but his lips drew back as if he detected it all the same. "Your old emperors kept this knowledge of how the magic worked to themselves. Your eleven saviors too."

The Eleven. Her head churned, frothing with memories of old lessons and histories, of the miracles that'd occurred shortly after the Eleven's ascension. The sudden recession of water levels. The calming of torrential rains. Blessings from the heavens, One and Two claimed. Signs that they'd been anointed to rule. But what was the line between miracles and magic? Where did heaven-ordained end and sooth-made begin?

"So, Queen of Yan, do you find the conditions to your liking?"

Just as the Crown Prince intended, the extra information muddled Hesina's brain. For a split second, she couldn't remember what the conditions were.

Salt. Sooths.

A trade.

It didn't matter what the prince threw at her. Hesina already knew her answer. Once the trial was over and stability returned to the realm, she would reject the word of the *Tenets*. She would fight to create a kingdom for sooths and non-sooths. Before then, she would not forsake them to a life in chains.

"I'm afraid you're mistaken," she said. "We have no sooths."

"My sources say the remnants live in hiding."

Concede, Caiyan would have advised, *and approach from a new direction*. "If I give them to you, what will you do? Make them slaves?"

"You should not care."

The prince was right. Hesina shouldn't care. If she were truly a Yan queen, she'd agree to this trade in an instant. Salt for sooths—an exchange that cost them nothing.

Righteousness never fails. "The *Tenets* forbid Yan from involving itself in any part of the slave trade." But the words didn't sound nearly as convincing from Hesina as they did from Xia Zhong.

The prince's smile turned scathing. "You think you are better? You are wrong. You are no better. You killed them. I make use of them because I see their value." His gaze narrowed. "Is there something wrong with the terms?"

Trying and failing wasn't a method. The longer this went on, the more she stimulated the Crown Prince's suspicion. How could she reject the conditions without revealing her true heart?

Slow down, Little Bird. Her father's voice came to her as Hesina scrambled to think. *If you want to understand a person, peer at their heart through the window of their prejudices and assumptions.*

Her mind stilled.

The prince had nothing to gain by divulging his plans of enslaving the sooths. He'd only done so because he believed Hesina was like any other Yan, that she would rather kill the sooths than copy his idea.

These were his assumptions. This was his heart. Now he would be in for a little shock, for Hesina would use them against him and offer the last reason he expected.

"As a matter of fact, there is something wrong with the terms."

"Oh?" The prince lifted his brow.

She lifted her chin. "They're insulting."

"Please, explain."

"Think of it this way, Siahryn. You offer me fish and ask for a boat in exchange. Eventually, we'll run out of fish, but you? You have the means of getting all the fish you desire." Hesina took up pacing as she spoke, trying to fill the tent with her presence. "Who knows how many resources a kingdom stands to gain from using sooths?" She spun on her heel. "The uncharted potential! You must take me for a fool if you think I can hand them over."

The prince regarded her strangely, as if she were prey that had suddenly erupted claws and fangs. "You cannot use them. Your people would denounce you."

Improvising, Hesina closed in and placed a hand on his chest. "Do you want the truth of me, Siahryn? My heart is not that of my people's. They might be good. They might be righteous. But I will resort to whatever means necessary to get the things I want. If it's salt I want to make, I'll use the sooths. If it's villages I want to demolish, I'll use the sooths. And if they refuse to do my bidding, I'll put them in chains myself."

She relished how his heartbeat quickened under her palm. He started to move away, but Hesina lifted her hand first. She was an actress. With a costume, a mask, and a mouthful of lies, she was powerful.

And now, it was time to make her exit. She turned for the tent flaps. "Should you continue terrorizing our borderland territories, you'll find I have no qualms about using the sooths against you either. But Yan honors generosity. Desist from your raids and agree to resume trade, and I won't abuse the knowledge you've shared today."

Her guards sprang to attention when she emerged into the daylight, but Hesina didn't give the signal that something had gone awry. If the Crown Prince believed she could and *would* harness the sooths' powers if pushed, then perhaps she'd successfully repaired trade and diverted war. They could end this negotiation peacefully.

But that naive hope died when his voice followed her into the open.

"You will honor me with a toast, will you not?"

He was striking in the sunlight. The piercings above his brow flashed gold, and the sands swirled at his feet as he lifted his horn of wine. "It is a custom of ours to end a discourse with a toast. I hope you will partake."

With that, he drank. Deeply. Hesina's stomach pulsed with each undulation of his throat, and she scowled when he refilled the horn and held it out to her.

It was impolite to refuse the wine. But it was even more impolite to expect her to poison herself, which was almost certainly the prince's play here. Had *Hesina* made the mistake of seeding dangerous ideas in the head of a rival queen, she would have done the same. The wine was spiked; she would die if she partook. The kingdom would weep, war would erupt, and Xia Zhong would drink libations in her name.

And here the prince stood, licking his lips as if to say: *I'm fine, aren't I?*

Hesina would be, too, if he did her the courtesy of sharing the antidote.

Think of a plan. Slowly, she reached for the horn; to refuse it was to tarnish an otherwise pristine negotiation. *Think of—*

A hand beat hers to it.

"*Vrakan,*" said Akira, bowing over the rim. "*Hahzan un dal.* I will make this toast."

The prince's brows lifted. "Who is this one that speaks the Kendi'an tongue?"

A convict who kept too many secrets for his own good and left Hesina speechless more often than she liked to admit.

"Just the queen's representative," Akira answered. "Which, if I remember the customs correctly, allows me to partake on her behalf."

Then, before anyone could stop him, he drank.

He displayed the emptied horn, and Hesina wanted to smack him. Elevens. Her knees went weak. What had he *done*?

"I wanted a taste," Akira said without looking at her. His eyes were fastened on the prince, who appeared equal parts amused and irritated. "I was told Siahryn the Dragon never fails to serve his finest." He glanced down at the horn. "Sadly, I'm disappointed."

Hesina didn't care who Akira was, what crimes he'd committed, or how many languages he could speak. *He'd* drunk the poisoned wine. *He* was about to die, not her. The breath in her lungs moistened with a mixture of emotions she couldn't name, and she grabbed Akira's hand and dragged him to her while signaling to her guards.

"We take our leave," she said to the prince.

"That will not do."

A wave of desert wind rolled over the banks, but it wasn't strong enough to explain why entire mounds of sand shifted back.

Hesina's guards pressed close as black-hooded figures rose out of the ground.

"Stay a little longer," rasped the prince. "And I will serve you the finest."

FIFTEEN

Ignorance leads to the spreading of lies.
ONE of the ELEVEN on edification of commoners

If you listen to what the sooths say, you'll never be free.
TWO of the ELEVEN on edification of commoners

Twelve mercenaries sprang from the sand like bamboo shoots.

Hesina's hand tightened around Akira's before she realized she was still holding it. Dropping it, she glanced toward her men and women. Their gazes had hardened. They might not have understood *what* magic entailed, or *how* it worked, but they knew it when they saw it. It was abnormal, just like the ones who wielded it. This—the shifting sand, the rising mercenaries—was unquestionably the work of sooths.

"Make it quick," ordered the prince with a flick of the hand.

Blades whispered out of sheaths, and in unison, the mercenaries charged.

"Kill only if necessary," Hesina hissed to her men. Then she drew her bombs and flung them high.

Red smoke shot into the sky, mushrooming outward and drifting down over them.

Please, Hesina prayed, hoping Sanjing would see. *Hurry.*

"You cannot run!" cried the prince from somewhere in the red haze, mistaking the signal as a diversion. A yell burst at Hesina's left, a clash of metal to her right. When the smoke cleared, she found her guards fighting in formation around her. But they were outnumbered. Several guards dealt with two or three mercenaries at once. As they overextended, the formation cracked.

They scattered over the banks, with Hesina ending up near the scout. A mercenary launched himself at them. Hesina slashed him down. The man hadn't even fallen when two more appeared. One attacked the scout. The other came at Hesina.

She deflected his first blow and met the second. Their gazes locked with their blades. A black scarf had been pulled tight over the man's skull, and he wore an animalistic ritual mask that cut away at the mouth. The stench of rotting gingko eked past his teeth, which clenched as he jerked his sword up.

The hilt of Hesina's jumped out of her hand. She recaptured it and, without dwelling on the close call, transitioned left. The mercenary swung in from the right. She spun away from the silver slice of his blade. It was too late to escape the blow, but if she could avoid the brunt of it . . .

It connected. Sensations came to Hesina in fragments: a blooming warmth, a sticky trickle, a pain that scaled over her ribs and resonated in the spaces in between.

Her fingers fumbled to her right side, meeting the shredded cloak, the torn *ruqun*, all wet with blood. Her thoughts ran hot with panic. Where was Mei when she actually needed her?

But the cut could have been worse. The mercenary had given everything to that swing. He'd expected Hesina to fall. He was still riding the momentum when she raised her forearm in the move Sanjing had helped her perfect. Recognition flared through the man's eyes, and he fought to regain his center.

She cut to the right before he could.

Her blade took to him like a wire through clay. His blood splattered her cheek, but it was his gasp that made Hesina stumble. She watched, paralyzed, as he clutched his arm, ropes of scarlet gushing through his fingers.

His roar snapped her out of her daze. It was primal and raw, and when he ran at her, sword held high, she knew better than to meet him. She dropped and rolled and rose—valiant for all of a second before someone crushed her back down.

Hesina had had enough. She bucked her head back, and something clicked. Someone oofed. The weight shifted, and Hesina wormed free. She grabbed her attacker by the neck and was midway through grinding his face into the sand when she noticed the twine securing his hair at the nape.

"Stay down," coughed Akira as throwing stars volleyed overhead.

He helped her to her feet once the danger passed. "Turns out sand doesn't taste half bad." Then he whirled behind her and hefted his rod. "Not that I'd like to try it again."

He sounded fine. He *seemed* fine, apart from the sand burns she'd given him. Had the wine *not* been poisoned?

No time for questions or apologies. The next wave of attacks bore down. Together, they parried and slashed. Akira filled in her openings. Hesina covered his back. Their movements were one, an alliance of steel and wood, and when it broke, it wasn't because of a mercenary.

It was because Akira had come to blows with their very own scout.

"What are you doing?" snapped the scout as the mercenary she'd been fighting slipped away.

"That one's on our side," said Akira.

Hesina scanned the fighters in puzzlement. "That one" had already moved on to his next opponent—one of Hesina's own guards. The guard swung. "That one" ducked, letting the sword befall the oblivious mercenary behind him while he dashed on, a raven-black braid whipping out from his hood.

Her hood.

Before Hesina had a chance to draw a breath, Mei blurred between a two-on-one fight, slashed the kneecaps of both mercenaries, and sidled up beside her queen.

"You came," Hesina said, her shock fizzing to somewhat inappropriate elation.

Mei wiped her knife clean. "It seemed like my presence might be appreciated. Do you have a plan?"

She did. She had. A plan contingent on Sanjing answering her call.

But she could do without him. "No. Just fight."

With a curt nod, Mei set to work. The tide of the fight turned with her help. Eight standing mercenaries became seven, seven became five, five became four.

Three.

Two.

Then one. Akira and Mei finished him with a rod between the legs and a knife handle to the skull.

Sweat-soaked and blood-soaked, Hesina lowered her sword. Her entourage followed in suit and faced the Crown Prince with her. They weren't a pretty sight, but the same could have been said for the fallen mercenaries. All were bruised and bloody.

And none, not a single one, had burst into flames.

Adrenaline addled Hesina's mind. Slowly, too slowly, she realized that the mercenaries weren't responsible for the trick with the moving sand. Neither were the children, who'd barely managed to summon dew. But then, who was?

"Impressive," said the prince, smiling even as his forces moaned on the ground. "But you have not won."

At his beckon, one of his advisors stepped forward. She removed her screened hat, revealing a face that was young and smooth and—to Hesina's surprise—oval, hinting at Yan blood. What was a Yan doing on Kendi'a's side?

As if in answer, the sand beneath Hesina fell away.

A shout tore the air as she plummeted to her calves. It wasn't hers. Hesina was too stricken by that oval face watching her sink.

She was the culprit behind the vanishing villages, the reason Yan was on the brink of war. The prince murmured something into her ear and she responded, raising both hands.

Hesina and her guards sank deeper. Sand encircled her hips, her chest, her limbs.

Persuasion was futile, but so was everything else. *"Don't do this!"*

The sooth's eyes flickered open to a blank, uncomprehending stare. Hesina faltered. The girl couldn't understand her. She was of Yan descent, but she'd never known her motherland or its tongue.

Because of your ancestors, growled the monster in her gut. *Because of you.*

"*Dakan.*"

Akira's voice silenced the monster's. Hesina stared as he repeated the strange word. "*Dakan.*"

She didn't know what it meant, but she understood it by its texture and weight. It was a mirror to her heart, a translation of her intent, and it reflected courage back into her. "*Don't listen to your prince. Join us!*"

"*Dakansan Vrakan uz. Siubtehn.*"

The prince laid a hand on the girl's shoulder. "*Tulsan, cricholon uz. Senyn cricholon.*" Then, in the common tongue, with his eyes on Hesina: "Join them, and they will kill you after they use you . . ."

Sand coiled around her neck.

"Like their eleven killed your ancestors after using them."

Hesina's throat closed, preparing for the deluge. But there was still her nose. Her ears. Doors to a granary, about to be filled. Her terror blazed anew, and she screamed. She didn't want to die. Not like this, not by being buried alive. She'd rather drown. Burn. Hang.

She'd rather be shot.

The second she had the thought, something silver streaked through the air. An arrow, released from behind.

It struck the sooth in the breast.

The sand stopped. The girl looked down. Her mouth rounded to an O. Her hands fluttered to the shaft as if to pull it out, and Hesina's vision went glassy. For that fraction of a moment, before the girl folded forward like a paper screen, they were the same. Powerless and helpless. Trying and failing.

But in the girl's case, no brother had come to rescue her.

"I'd prefer if you didn't bury my sister alive," rang out Sanjing's voice as Yan banners crested the dunes. Cavalry dismounted and closed in, yet all Hesina could see was the blood trickling out from beneath the body, smoking like a fuse in the sand.

Sanjing had shot the girl.

He'd had no choice.

Neither had the sooth, nor any of the sooths working for Kendi'a.

Hesina suddenly wished she *had* been buried alive.

But the act wasn't over yet. As Sanjing's men and women helped her out of the sand, Hesina gathered her fragmented wits and, in her best imitation of authority, ordered them to retrieve the salt from the tent.

Then she faced the Crown Prince. Sand streamed from the folds of her cloak, leaving Lilian's *ruqun* exposed. The headless dragons drew the prince's eye.

"The barrels of water I promised will be delivered to your markets before the gibbous moon wanes." Her voice broke like the rest of her. She was back to being Yan Hesina, not strong enough, not smart enough, a heart full of secrets and a bellyful of contradictions. "Accept them, and I'll take it as a sign that you remember what we discussed."

The Crown Prince cocked his head to the side. For a fraught second, Hesina swore he saw through her to the impostor of a queen she was. The smile he flashed—nowhere near as rakish as before—didn't put her at ease. "I will remember."

* * *

If only a prince and his smiles were all that troubled Hesina for the rest of that long, long day.

Instead, the moment they made it back to the encampment, Akira started vomiting blood.

"Just an adverse reaction," he gurgled, raising a red-smeared hand as if to hold their concern at bay. Hesina shouted for the guard who'd apprenticed as a healer, and Sanjing's people pressed in to help, but Akira waved them all off. "Water . . . will do."

If water was the cure, Hesina would bring an ocean to him. But there were no oceans, or rivers, or streams. There weren't even any full waterskins; it took combining three to fill one. By the time she ran to Akira with it, he had already started a fire at the pit and was reducing sticks to charcoal. Calmly, as if his hands *weren't* shaking, he tipped the charcoal into the waterskin. Hesina watched, chest locked, as he drank. She waited, breath held, as he frowned at his bloodstained *hanfu* skirt. She blinked, pulse slowing, as Akira proceeded to use the rest of his lifesaving concoction to rinse the cloth out.

Hesina lost it. "Why did you do it?" she snapped as Akira wrung his *hanfu*. She snatched the cloth from his hands when he didn't reply. "You could have died!"

Her throat stung, and she wasn't even the one who'd eaten sand.

Akira blinked. She'd startled him for a change, and he looked . . . young, with his eyes wide, the spread of his pupils black as ink.

Then his face closed. "Unlikely."

She shook her head. "Who *are* you?"

He rose and tugged his *hanfu* free. "Someone queens shouldn't get close to."

He made for the horses, and only the pain in Hesina's side stopped her from throwing her hands into the air. Princes. Brothers. Ex-convicts. Everyone was utterly maddening. She glared at Akira's back when they started to ride, a detail that didn't escape Sanjing's attention.

"I see you've expanded your entourage," said her brother as he pulled up beside her. "At least this one has a spine."

The not-so-subtle jab at Caiyan might have gotten to Hesina

if this day hadn't already. "His name is Akira," she said coolly, then paused. Sanjing was returning to the imperial city so that they could make a joint announcement on the cessation of Yan-Kendi'an aggressions. She wouldn't be able to hide the trial from him there. "And he's my representative."

She summarized the last two months, her hands clenched around the reins. She braced herself when she finished, but Sanjing was uncharacteristically silent.

"So the people think the Kendi'ans killed our father," he finally said.

"And sooths," Hesina added quietly. "Because of the vanishing villages. And, well . . . because of your scout."

"My scout."

"Yes. He came to my coronation and said the soothsayers were working with the Kendi'ans." And he hadn't been lying. They were—against their will as slaves.

"Where is he now?" asked Sanjing.

Hesina didn't answer.

Sanjing wheeled his stallion in front of hers. For the first time since their reunion, she saw the chips and cracks in his bone laminar. "Where is he, Sina?"

She looked away, cheeks burning. "He's dead, Jing. I'm so sorry. We couldn't save him."

"All my scouts are alive and accounted for." Her gaze snapped to her brother, but Sanjing didn't give her a moment to think. "Six's bones. A captured scout is a security liability. You think one would be able to ride up to you at your coronation, just like that?"

"I—"

"No, you didn't, because you never think," Sanjing continued, relentless. "The guards should have stopped him. It's a red flag if they didn't. You should have closed the investigation immediately."

"And leave the question of who murdered Father unanswered?" What could she have possibly said to the people? *I take it back! Forget everything I said about the king dying before his time!*

"Who urged you to go on with it?" demanded Sanjing. "Your manservant?"

Evading the inevitable was not a strategy, and Caiyan had seen that. But Sanjing wouldn't understand, so Hesina didn't explain.

Her brother cursed at her silence. "You don't listen to me, but you listen to him. I warned you from the start, but you—"

"So I made a mistake," she snapped. "Haven't you? Or have you forgotten about that day on the pond?"

Then, before she could see his expression, she steered her mount around and trotted ahead.

They stayed apart for the rest of the ride. Hesina filled her mind with the logistics of resituating the returning militia members and passing new salt taxes to reflect the normalization of trade. But it was like applying a thin bandage to a wound; her thoughts bled through the administrative work and returned to her brother. She didn't know what pained her more—that they brought out the worst in each other, or that they hadn't always.

When they stopped for the night and set up camp in a bamboo thicket at the juncture of two streams, she put aside her pride and went to Sanjing's tent. She was two steps short of entering when her brother spoke to someone inside. "I can explain."

"Yes," came a voice that sounded like Mei's. "I'm sure you can. But that doesn't change what you did. You loosed that arrow."

"What did you want me to do? Let my people capture her? Have her brought back to the palace, where she would have died by a thousand cuts?"

"She hadn't flamed yet."

"She didn't need to. She was dead the moment she moved the sand. You haven't been on the front, Mei. You haven't seen what my men and women have seen. They can spot sooth work from a *li* away now."

Silence.

Mei broke it. "I think I understand why you ordered me to stay behind. You said it was for your sister. I believed you. But it was also to keep me from seeing this side of you."

"What? No," Sanjing said earnestly—*too* earnestly, like that time he denied filling Caiyan's pillow log with dead tadpoles. "Mei—"

The flaps parted without warning, and Mei flitted by like a wraith.

Blinking, Hesina cleared her head. She wasn't here to eavesdrop. She pushed through the flaps and almost ran into Sanjing, who looked to be in midpursuit but froze at the sight of her, deliberately turning away as she approached.

Her wound, surprisingly shallow thanks to Lilian's gown, still throbbed under the bandage when she reached for his shoulder. "Jing . . ."

The harder her brother tried to hide his emotions, the more they bristled. She could practically feel the spines of his confusion and guilt. She withdrew her hand. "This is about the sooth, isn't it?"

"So what if it is?"

"I . . ."

What did she want to say?

The truth. Tell him the truth.

But what was the truth?

Recently, it was the thing she found hardest to admit. "I would have done the same." She would have killed the girl to save him too.

"I know," said Sanjing, and Hesina relaxed. Then he faced her, black eyes burning. "You're like all the others."

"The . . . others?"

"What are you here for?"

Hesina couldn't remember. She did remember that she'd come grounded with intent, with justification and reason and solution, all blown away as they coasted toward the same old ruts. "I—I just wanted to say thank you. For coming. For helping." Her throat went tender. "I'm glad we could work together."

"Of course. Issue the summons anytime you need a hand in killing some helpless slaves, and I'll drop everything and come running like I did today."

His words dashed over her like cold water. When he brushed past, she couldn't grab him or order him to stay. Her lips parted with the tent flaps, and the air leaked out of her after he left.

This was what they did, Hesina reminded herself, too weary for anger. They broke themselves. They took the shards and drove them up the chinks of each other's armor.

She stayed in the tent for a little longer, unready to face the world. When she finally did emerge, the moon was high and round, just as it had been yesterday. But everything else had changed. No legends circulated around the bonfire tonight. Sanjing's soldiers had joined Hesina's guards, whispering about sooths who aged young children to death, sooths who, with a single blink, turned breathing livestock into steaming meat.

"But what about the women?" ventured Hesina's scout, her face lit by the flames. "What happens to them during their *yuejin*?"

"They burn," said a clean-shaven soldier, yelping as his female comrade elbow-locked his neck and knuckled his head.

"Jun, you idiot," sighed the girl, before looking to the scout. "Don't listen to him. The monthly cloths you and I use? Sooths stuff theirs inside so the blood can't evaporate. But that's where our similarities end. Want to know what mothers do to their new-borns?"

"What?"

The girl released the clean-shaven soldier. Leaned toward the fire. "They blind them," she whispered. "With the same bloody knife used to cut the umbilical. Makes the Sight stronger—"

Stomach clenched, Hesina escaped to the banks, where the autumn breeze drowned out the bonfire stories but also combed goose bumps over her arms. As she rubbed them away, tempering her nausea, the shadows beside her rippled with a familiar presence.

She let out a heavy breath. "Don't be angry at him."

"Why? You are."

No, Hesina should have said, *of course not.* A queen had better people to be angry at—hotheaded Crown Princes and two-faced Ministers of Rites, for example.

"Anger is a form of confidence," Mei said when Hesina didn't reply. "A hope that the ones we admire will change for the better."

But why be angry at all? No one else was upset at Sanjing. They celebrated the death of a sooth.

"Something wrong?" asked Mei.

"Nothing." But a strand of woodsmoke and laughter strayed their way, and Hesina shivered.

Mei watched her carefully. "Do you believe what they say?"

"I'm not sure." Could she believe in anything else when she knew nothing? "Do you?" asked Hesina.

"I believe sooths are human. There are the good, the bad, and all the ones in between."

It was obvious, in retrospect. "You're a sympathizer."

"I'm not the only one."

Mei didn't say Hesina's name. She didn't need to. Her words connected with their target even before her gaze hit Hesina's arm, the one she'd cut in front of the mob.

Irrational relief filled Hesina. She wasn't alone. Someone finally knew the princess who'd committed treason and been foolish enough to let it change her.

She couldn't reveal that, of course. She'd made a promise to Caiyan, and now she kept it by stepping back. "Don't be so sure," she told Mei.

She retreated to her tent. Within its dark privacy, she pushed up her *ruqun* sleeve. The cut she'd given herself had been shallow and clean. It should have healed without a scar. But no queen had time to apply tiger balm twice a day, and a bumpy seam of new skin gleamed under the lantern light.

Hesina traced it, recalling that night. The blood. The shouts. The fire. The ash.

She slid the sleeve back down.

The Crown Prince had tried to kill her for what she'd learned today. Would he have done the same had her father also possessed forbidden knowledge? Could it be that the Kendi'ans really *were* behind the king's death? No outsiders had been in the palace that late summer day, but the murderer didn't have to be an outsider. Xia Zhong couldn't be the only one in secret correspondence with the Kendi'ans.

Speculating in the outskirts of Yan was no use. Hesina had to get back to the imperial city.

They'd ridden out at a hard pace; they rode back harder, push-ing the limits of what their mounts and bodies could take. Soon, the last stretch of land disappeared. The rolling hills flattened. When the imperial city walls teethed on the horizon, Hesina's doubts broke the surface too. No one knew how the Eleven had breached the massive structures of pounded earth and stone. Scholars had hypothesized everything from gliding over to tunneling under, but was the Crown Prince right about the Eleven using the magic of sooths? Hesina wasn't sure. She wasn't sure of a lot of things any-more. *Knowledge is truth*, her father had said, yet all knowledge had done was unveil a world of lies.

News of their return preceded it, and throngs of people paved the limestone boulevard wending to the Eastern Gate to welcome them back. They chanted the name of a queen who'd kept her promise to avoid war and secure salt. But it was also the name of a girl who'd broken her promise to protect all, regardless of blood.

Again, Hesina tasted ash. The flavor fermented as they rode into the eastern tunnel, becoming more sour than bitter, more dread than regret. Dread of what, Hesina didn't know. That happened to be the nature of dread.

No one ever knew what they dreaded until it came to pass.

The moment they emerged from the tunnel, city guards poured into the gateway and surrounded Hesina and her entourage.

"Seize the suspect!" shouted the director of the Investigation Bureau, who stood behind the regiment. "Protect your queen at all costs!"

Hesina's stallion startled. For a dangerous moment, she slipped in her saddle. Then she jerked the reins tight, wrangling back con-trol. "What is the meaning of this?"

The director bowed. "A grievous oversight on the Bureau's part.

We couldn't find the next suspect when we went to apprehend her. We scoured the city, thinking she'd gone into hiding. Little did we know . . ."

Two guards passed by Hesina and her mount, dragging someone between them. They kicked the person to her knees and yanked her head back by the hair.

By the braid.

The russet of Mei's irises became the red of Hesina's shock, then rage, as the director gazed down at the swordswoman and sniffed. ". . . the vixen was with you all along."

SIXTEEN

The person purchasing rights sets a price others cannot match.

ONE *of the* ELEVEN *on corruption*

Weed it before it's too late.

TWO *of the* ELEVEN *on corruption*

It was the director who arrested Mei, his men who dragged her away.

But it wasn't the Investigation Bureau that Hesina stormed.

Ten sets of heads turned as she burst into Xia Zhong's residence. She stared at the young courtiers, kneeling on thin reed mats, brushes poised over note-taking paper. They stared at her, their faces slack with awe and shock—and terror, too, when she started laughing.

Marvelous. To think that Xia Zhong was grooming the young officials of her court, lecturing them on the values of—Hesina glanced at one courtier's notes—honesty and humility.

"Class dismissed," said Xia Zhong, clutching shut the scroll in his hands.

Books went into bags. Brushes slid into oxhide wraps. The courtiers rose, bowing at Hesina and murmuring *dianxia* as they passed. The doors had barely shut behind the last one when she spun on Xia Zhong, who had lowered himself to his hands and knees and was rolling up each mat.

"Release her." Hesina loomed over him as he continued his busywork. "We both know she isn't the murderer."

"Of course she isn't." Xia Zhong stacked one rolled mat atop two others. Hesina wanted nothing more than to kick them apart. "She wouldn't have stayed around if she were, unless it was to kill you, which means she would have attempted on the road."

"You—"

"You made your move. An elaborate one, at that, traveling a thousand and eight hundred *li* just to stop a war. Now I make mine." With a groan, the minister rose, knees popping, and shuffled to the mats on the other side of the room. "I thought you knew the rules of the game, my dear."

His not-quite-black robes bunched as he squatted again, reminding Hesina of a roosting pigeon. A pigeon, she realized with a burst of fresh fury, who pecked at her as if she were millet on the ground.

"It doesn't matter who you frame. You won't get your war."

"What's to stop me from trying? Do you propose that I sit idly by and accept 'fate'?" Xia Zhong chuckled, shaking his head. "You sound like a sooth."

Ice speared up Hesina's spine, but the minister had already moved on to gather all the mats. She followed him warily to the partition of gridded shelves dividing his inner chambers from outer.

"Why?" she demanded as he stuffed the mats into the grid holes. "What are you doing all of this for?"

"You know why, my dear. The letters are still in your possession, if you need to refresh your memory."

Hesina could accept sooths drawing water out of thin air, but she couldn't, no matter how she tried, stomach the idea of Xia Zhong going to such lengths to increase his personal wealth. It had to be something more, something to explain the fire in his eyes.

His hand went to the beads around his neck, an accessory Hesina had found monk-like before. Now that she was close enough to count the liver spots on his drooping face, and his head wasn't bowed in obeisance, she saw that the beads were actually onyx, polished to a wood-like matte.

"Have you ever heard of the Xia family, my queen?"

"Which?" There were only a hundred or so surnames in the Yan language, and sharing one didn't necessarily mean sharing blood.

Somehow, her question seemed to be enough of an answer for Xia Zhong. He dropped the beads. "The Eleven destroyed more than just the sooths. They tore apart the fabric of society."

He paced to the other side of the partition, the grid coming between them. "The Xia family used to be one of the greatest patrons of the arts and culture. They sponsored academies across the kingdom, including a minority that instructed the sooths.

"They brought us down by affiliation, those ingrates. Now, the only names the people worship are those of eleven thieves." His gaze pinned her through a hole in the grid. "I will regain what we lost, ingot by ingot, right under the nose of this dynasty."

Unasked-for empathy stole away Hesina's words. A lost legacy wasn't so different from an untold truth. She identified with the weary anger in the minister's watery eyes, the mirthless mirth.

She would never admit that, of course, and when Xia Zhong went on to say, "Yet, you and I, we're the same," she found her voice again.

"We're not."

"The world denies us the things we desire. We go to great

lengths to secure them. You blackmail me with letters; I arrange a little tragedy at your coronation. You ride to Kendi'a; I—"

"The scout at my coronation was *your* doing?"

"I'm surprised you didn't realize sooner, my dear."

People had alarming amounts of faith in her ability to notice every tiny detail while running a kingdom.

"You are many things," Hesina spat, empathy evaporating. "But I didn't think 'murderer' would be one."

"He was a leper who knew his time in this world was nearing its end. I gave him enough gold so that his family would be provided for after his death. It was a transaction, much like ours."

A transaction. The words jarred purpose back into Hesina. She hadn't come for Xia Zhong's tragic backstory. She'd come for Mei.

"Release the suspect, and I'll give you whatever riches you desire."

Xia Zhong went to his *kang* and sat. "I can't release her," he said as he spread out rolls of parchment. "It would interrupt the interrogation."

Interrogation?

"I *can* grant you visiting privileges, seeing that the Investigation Bureau has suspended them."

Interrogation. Torture. Imprisonment. None of this had happened to Consort Fei. Hesina's mouth opened, then closed. What could she do? Accuse him of being unfair? The game they played wasn't fair.

Visiting privileges, Xia Zhong had offered.

It was better than nothing, and nothing was all Hesina had.

"Write the document," she ordered.

The minister already was. "What would you like to trade?" he said as he stamped it with his seal and held it up to dry.

Too late, Hesina realized she had nothing on her. Nothing but her travel-worn *ruqun* and her imperial seal, the dusty slippers on her feet and the hair on her head.

And the pins in her hair. Most were small, whittled from whalebones imported from the Aoshi archipelago, hardly worth a silver tael combined. Knowing what she knew now about Xia Zhong, they wouldn't satisfy him.

Only one pin would.

She hadn't removed the crane pin since her coronation. Slipping it out now felt like relinquishing another piece of her father. Recognition lit in Xia Zhong's eyes, and Hesina's throat squeezed as his fingers pinched the jade length. She forced hers to let go.

The minister pocketed the pin and lifted the document. "Not your father's daughter after all," he said as she, in exchange, pocketed the visiting privileges.

Hesina froze.

Anger was a form of confidence, Mei had said, but her anger toward Xia Zhong was fire and acid. It corroded rationale, reducing her to pulse and impulse. She was a reaching arm. A seizing hand.

She wrenched the minister's beads into a noose around his neck. "You're wrong."

He had the audacity to laugh. But then she gathered beads into her clutch, and the laughter stopped. His face reddened. Purpled. Spittle frothed at his mouth, and Hesina knew she was close. To cutting off his air. To appointing a new Minister of Rites.

All it'd take was one more bead.

It shouldn't have been a decision. She'd come to bargain, not murder. But there was a moment of teetering, of peering into an abyss that called to her, before she pulled herself back and yanked.

Xia Zhong fell to his knees, gasping as beads bounced around him.

Hesina's hands rose to her own throat. Flesh and blood. That was all they were, even Xia Zhong. Had she really considered ending him?

No, she was just trying to scare him.

She was sending a message.

She was asserting her power.

Her hands twitched as she told herself these lies.

"There is only one thing we have in common, Minister Xia." Clenching her hands, Hesina turned for the threshold. "We're not who we think we are."

With a sweep of brocade, she crossed into winter's chill.

* * *

If she regretted choking Xia Zhong, she didn't the moment she saw Mei. The swordswoman lay unmoving in the corner of the cell, her fingers swollen to the size of baby daikon radishes. Scarlet and plum banded around the knuckles, hallmarks of the bone-cruncher. It was the only legal interrogation instrument of the new era, able to inflict excruciating pain without breaking skin.

Caiyan went straight to Mei's side, setting his lantern onto the hay-scattered prison cell floor and unstacking his medicine box. Lilian joined him, removing instruments from the trays.

"Get away from her," Sanjing growled, advancing.

Akira checked the general with his rod at the same time Lilian said, "Touch one hair of his, and I'll castrate you myself."

Sanjing's fury jolted Hesina out of her own, and she seized her brother by the arms. "Control yourself, Jing."

"Control myself?" Sanjing barked a laugh. "You bring *him* and expect me to control myself?"

"You asked for Caiyan."

"I asked for anyone *but* the Imperial Doctress. I guess I should have known that you'd run for your manservant."

"He knows what he's doing."

"In your eyes, he knows everything under the sky. What's the worst injury he's seen?" snarled Sanjing. "A paper cut? How many broken bones has he set?"

"More than you." Lilian handed off a roll of gauze to Caiyan and rose, bringing herself chest to chest with Sanjing. "And if you don't shut up, he'll have to set yours too."

A muscle ticked in Sanjing's jaw. Hesina tried to pull Lilian back, but Akira took Hesina's arm first, shaking his head.

Then Caiyan finally spoke. "She's going to be all right," he said, his hands deft at work, applying poultices, binding linen, aligning splints. Sanjing was right in thinking that most courtiers wouldn't know the medicinal arts, but most courtiers also hadn't grown up in the slums, where brawls led to broken bones, and broken bones led to infection and death. Caiyan tied off the last splint, and with a twang of nostalgia, Hesina recalled the time he had done the same for an injured sparrow in the imperial orchards. They'd been twelve and ten, respectively, but the gap between them was one bigger than age.

Yet unlike Sanjing, Caiyan had done his best to bridge their differences. "The bones will heal in four to six weeks," he said as he packed away his supplies. "She's out from the pain right now but will come around in an hour or two."

"If she doesn't—" started Sanjing.

"Then you know where to find me." Caiyan rose, tucking the chest under his arm. "Lilian, step away from the general."

"But—"

"Please."

With one last glare, Lilian obliged.

Sanjing didn't move. Not immediately. His black eyes fixed on Caiyan, and for an absurd second, Hesina thought he might express a word of thanks.

Instead he said, "My sister might not blame you, but I do."

"*Jing.*"

"While she was away, you were here," continued her brother, unremitting. "You were supposed to stand sentry over this palace in her place. You failed her."

"Jing, that is *enough.*"

Sanjing held Caiyan's gaze a heartbeat longer. Then he went to Mei's side, sinking to a crouch beside her. With a knuckle, he cleared her forehead of sweat-dampened hair.

As much as Hesina wanted to stay angry, she couldn't. Her composure came untethered, and her voice splintered when she said, "Leave us for a moment."

Quietly, Caiyan bowed and filed out. Akira followed, draping his cloak over her shoulders.

Lilian left last, giving Hesina a squeeze of the hand.

The doors shut, and Hesina swayed. But she didn't deserve to buckle. She had to bear her own weight, be there for Sanjing when he rose and faced her.

"Prove her innocent."

He spoke as if she were a soldier under his command, not a sister, not a queen.

At least she was still someone to him. "We will. But understand this: Xia Zhong wouldn't frame her without reason. Akira will need to know everything you can provide on Mei's background."

"You trust him completely?"

Hesina hesitated. Did she? She didn't know his past. Didn't know what crimes he'd committed. She wouldn't be awfully surprised if she didn't even know his real name. But he'd fought for her, taken poison for her. He'd seen her at her cowardly worst and believed in her all the same.

"I do," she said. "Will you meet with him?"

Sanjing nodded, but the wariness didn't melt from his face. "Don't let them hurt her," he said as they left the cell, and Hesina understood very well that his distrust wasn't just meant for the dungeon guards they passed. She'd failed to foresee Xia Zhong's counterattack. She'd lost this match.

She wouldn't lose the next.

* * *

Hesina woke, neck stiff, cheek on an edict, and immediately jerked upright. Then she sagged even though the throne wasn't made for sagging and rubbed a hand over her face.

She'd come to the throne hall after visiting Mei, determined to defeat the paperwork that had accumulated in her absence. The stacks on the ivory *kang* were particularly imposing with the civil service examinations nearly upon them. Erected by the Eleven to replace nepotism, and hosted in the imperial city, the exams were the reason why Caiyan, with no noble blood to his name, was a court official at all. He'd already volunteered to oversee them—from the appointment of registration officers in provinces as far as Anmu to the regulation of roads as the returning militia overlapped with traveling hopefuls.

But each action required ten edicts, which—considering how she'd dozed off—induced sleep more efficiently than medicinal candles. Now a migraine pounded behind her eyes as she stared at the edict she'd used for a pillow. The words were smudged, but the fact that there were words at all, when she didn't remember writing them, had Hesina frowning and leaning in.

The edict was filled out. The necessary revisions and signature— *her* signature, in her hand—were in place. So was the edict beneath it. So were all the others. The mountain of paperwork was still a mountain, but they required only the stamp of her insignia.

Had she signed them in her sleep? If so, that was a useful talent to have as a queen.

But on closer inspection, Hesina realized the handwriting wasn't hers; it was *better*. It had her weight, her style, but lacked all the little imperfections that drove her calligraphy tutors mad. This was especially apparent in the three characters of her name.

You never form your "si" correctly, sounded Caiyan's voice in her head. *The tail of the third stroke doesn't quite wrap around the first.*

As children, he would guide her hand through the strokes. Now she pulled out a fresh piece of paper, lifted her brush, and wrote her name. She stared at it, side by side with one of Caiyan's renditions, and crumpled up hers.

He was better at this than she'd ever be.

Thoroughly defeated, Hesina left the throne hall for her chambers, where she let Ming'er help her out of her wrinkled *ruqun* and run a bath she arguably didn't have time for. To hell with ruling. Why even try? But when Ming'er removed the pins from her hair, Hesina remembered everything she'd already sacrificed, and when she looked into the mirror, she saw her mother's face.

You can bring this kingdom to its knees, for all I care.

Gooseflesh tickled her skin. "Leave me."

"But the bath—"

"Leave." Hesina closed her eyes, not wanting to see Ming'er's expression, and reopened them when all the maids had swept out.

Her chambers were deathly quiet as she rose from the vanity and went to her desk. She removed the bundle from her satchel and peeled back the crude silk, corner by corner, until the book lay revealed at the center.

Again, Hesina traced the three characters on the cover with a forefinger. Again, she swept a hand over the crinkled first page, as if she could dust away the barrier between the words and her mind. She needed answers more than ever, but the book didn't care.

"I'm lost," she admitted to the silence. No matter where she turned, she couldn't find a way out.

Lost and trapped, like the time she'd made a wrong turn and found herself in a secret passageway longer and wider than any of the others she had known. It was her father who found her hours later, who brought her back to his rooms, brewed a pot of chrysanthemum tea, and lit every single candle. He rocked away her fears. He taught her how to never lose her way again.

How do you learn one passageway? You don't start by looking at the differences. You look for the similarities, the patterns that link the new to the old. Now, how do you learn all the passageways of the world?

Memorize them?

Even Caiyan can't do that. No, you breathe, and follow the way.

What way?

The way of the breath. The way of things we know, but do not notice. Instinct, you could call it. The most basic of truths. So breathe. And again. And again, until you forget you are deliberately breathing. Search until you forget you are deliberately searching.

From the start, she'd been fighting against the book. Now she surrendered. Just as the pitch-black of a passageway would help her pick up on a change in the cut of stones, or a whistle of air signaling an exit nearby, the utter darkness of unknowing opened her mind to the words—not their meanings, but their shapes, the rhythm of their march up her skull, the clicking of their secret language. She ingested one unreadable character at a time, then faster, until they filled her like cicadas in a jar, scrambling over one another, fighting to be heard.

Breathe, her father reminded. She'd lost him, lost her most treasured possession from him, but his voice lived on in her ear. *Breathe.*

And again.

And again.

One insect clicked louder than the others. It was a thing of many legs, but its core was composed of three downward strokes sitting atop two jagged, overlapping lines.

Look for the similarities.

It could have been three downward strokes atop the character for *mountain*.

It could have been the Yan word for *truth*.

Every muscle in Hesina's body stilled. How had she not seen? And how could she have forgotten? When the Eleven burned the relic books and opened schools to commoners and women, they hadn't invented a new language. They'd merely pruned the complex version, removing extraneous strokes, sometimes by the dozen, condensing core radicals. But roots of the new language extended back to the old.

To learn, her mind had needed to unlearn. Different associations now chimed, brought together by that missing breeze.

Slowly, Hesina flipped the book back to the first page. Swept her hand over the creases, and lifted it away to the column of words beneath.

Some were too far removed from the simplified characters for her to read. But others she could guess:

What is truth? 畺希 *seek it.* 駗夭 *write it. Good kings pay* 畚 *to hear it. But in trying times, truth is the first thing we* 肯肵.

—ONE *of the* ELEVEN *on truth*

She shut the cover. Traced over the three characters running vertically on the right-hand side. Two she could read. As for the one she couldn't . . . the longer she stared at it, the more it looked like what it represented. Short, vertical strokes nestled within a box of closed strokes.

Quotes on a page.

Adages in a tome.

Tenets.

TENETS OF ELEVEN

Hesina kept her finger on the cover, convinced that in the next moment, the next breath, the characters would turn to insects again, and this whole revelation would be some hallucination born out of frustration. But it stayed solid under her fingertip, this book that'd shaped their laws, their customs, their minds and hearts and souls. The original *Tenets*. A relic, lost—until now.

SEVENTEEN

Instinct is the most basic of truths.

ONE *of the* ELEVEN *on truth*

It's also damn stupid at times.

TWO *of the* ELEVEN *on truth*

Book in hand, Hesina plunged into the secret corridor connecting her study to Akira's. The shadows accepted her as if she were one of their own. But she wasn't, not like Mei. The swordswoman had worn darkness as a cloak, though it hadn't been enough to protect her in the end.

Hesina hadn't been enough.

But now she had answers. She had hope. She tore past the lacquered panels, steps never surer. She picked up speed until not even the shadows could cling to her, pushing through the panel at the corridor's end without pausing for breath.

"Akira?" She cleared the linen tapestry with an arm as she entered. "Akira, are you—"

She stopped in her tracks.

The burner in the center of the floor was still going. It belched out smoke that clouded against the beamed ceiling while Akira sat in the corner, unmoving.

The book in Hesina's hand hit the ground.

She rushed to his side. Was he sleeping? In this smoke? Elevens, was he dying? Was it the poison? Had his charcoal-water concoction been just that—charcoal and water?

"Akira." She clutched him by the shoulders, giving him a hard shake. "Wake up. *Akira*."

His eyes flashed open.

The breath thudded out of Hesina as she slammed into the wall. The rod bisected her throat. Light and dark blotched her vision. Ringing filled her ears. Smoke clogged the rest of her senses, dulling the pain, the shock.

Akira pressed the rod closer. The fire backlit his face in washes of red and umber. His hair was down, out of its tie, brown bangs screened over gray eyes devoid of recognition.

This wasn't Akira. This was somebody else. A stranger. A *killer*. A scream rose in Hesina's chest, but her throat clamped down. No. She couldn't. She couldn't bring the guards running unless she wanted to lose her representative.

"Akira . . . it's . . . me . . ."

Somehow, someway, she got a hand between the rod and her throat. As she strained, something twitched in Akira's expression. The death-like stillness to his face cracked, and the pieces scattered like mah-jongg tiles.

The rod clattered as it fell.

Hesina slumped, choking on air. Akira lifted a hand as if to pat her back, but withdrew when she flinched away. He removed a jar from the cross folds of his *hanfu* and tossed its contents over the flames. The fire died under the rain of white powder.

He retrieved the vial of poison from the ash and embers and showed her what once had been the orange-toned liquid, now reduced to a gray powder. He explained his process of condensing the gas into a liquid and distilling it, outlined further tests he planned to conduct. It was more than he'd ever spoken at once. It was a plea to forgive and forget.

He was talking about how all substances had distinct boiling and disintegration points when Hesina couldn't take it anymore.

"Stop that." Akira fell quiet, and she leaned her head against the wall, wheezing. "Are you okay?"

He wouldn't meet her gaze. "I should be asking that of you."

Hesina was a little shocked, a little bruised, but mostly she was fine. *She* wasn't the one who'd drunk a horn full of poisoned wine. "I'm summoning the Imperial Doctress if the poison is still bothering you."

"Not the poison." He gathered his hair back and retied it at the nape. "It's okay. This is normal."

Sleeping through fires wasn't Hesina's definition of normal. And Akira didn't *look* okay, upon closer inspection. The skin under his eyes was creased and translucent. His face was sallow. His collar had shifted to the side. Again, Hesina caught sight of that inked leaf, hooking over his shoulder like a demon's claw.

She made up a story of a boy who'd done terrible things in his past. It was a tale of names shed like leaves, and old ghosts that visited when he slept—*if* he slept.

Am I right? Hesina wanted to ask. But it didn't feel right to take his secrets from him, so she took his face instead, cupping it between her hands.

"Akira, I'm here." She searched his eyes, willing him to understand. "I see you. You could be a convict or a merchant robber, and I would still see you as you are now. My representative. My friend."

His lashes beat once as he blinked. Slowly, he closed a hand over her wrists and eased her hands off his face. But he didn't drop them. The pulse in Hesina's veins went erratic, and without thinking, she gave a tentative tug on her wrists.

He didn't resist.

She drew him to her. The crowns of their heads met. Their breaths mingled, mismatched, her inhales his exhales, his exhales her inhales, tasting without touching, stealing what they willingly gave. His hold on her wrists tightened. Thin skin and warm air stood between them—nothing else. Nothing could stop Hesina from giving more.

"Don't."

The whispered word warmed her lips. Then it was gone, snuffed like a flame as Akira pulled back. "Do you know why I'm helping you?"

"To watch the spectacle."

But Hesina knew it wasn't true even before Akira shook his head. It was just another one of his non-answers.

"You seemed so certain of what you wanted." Akira released her wrists, and her hands dropped to her lap. "I've never been. I helped you, hoping to find myself along the way."

He lifted his rod and considered it. It'd gained several nicks from the journey, but his gaze glossed over the imperfections and flicked to her throat.

"But you haven't," she guessed. It wasn't her fault, but she felt as if she'd let him down.

"No." His lips quirked with a rueful smile. "Only I can help myself."

"That's not true."

The smile disappeared, and Akira shrugged. "You say you see me, but you don't. And trust me, you wouldn't want to."

His words unmoored her, left her floundering with no reply. She cast her gaze out to everything but Akira before anchoring on the book on the floor.

"I can read it." She could almost hear Lilian's groan. *Tactless.* Luckily, Lilian wasn't here to see Hesina flush when she realized she'd never shown Akira the book. "It was the item in Mother's chest."

To his credit, Akira took it in stride. "The title?"

"*Tenets of Eleven.*" She opened it to the first page. "The original."

She prickled from head to toe as Akira leaned in. But then sensation faded. Her mind quieted as she read out loud, sinking herself into worlds and words forgotten.

What is truth? 彙耤 seek it. 黔天 write it. Good kings pay gold to hear it. But in trying times, truth is the first thing we betray.

Akira turned the page. "What is this language?"

"Complex Yan."

"Can you read the rest?"

With practice? "Probably."

"Why would your mother have it?"

The question tripped her. "I don't know," she said after a pause.

"Then what do you know about her?"

Much less than she should. Her hand drifted to the back of her skull. The pin's nick had healed. A shame, Hesina thought tartly.

Pain always reminded her of her mother. "She was the daughter of a baron from the northern provinces," she started. "My father met her when he was touring the realm on his eighteenth namesday. They married a year later, and had me the next."

Images came to her unbidden. Snuff bottles stoppered with nubs of red coral, scented sachets stuffed with ginseng and angelica, *ruqun* hems embroidered with autumn leaves. It was easier to think of her mother in components. "Father said Mother was whip-smart and brave. But the mother I knew was . . . different. She was mercurial. Distant." Her voice lowered. "Frightened." Hesina hadn't been able to admit that as a child, not when her mother frightened *her*.

"How so?" asked Akira.

She focused intently on a scuff on the *zitan* floor. "She had nightmares." A fact that Hesina was ironically privy to because her mother would punish her and forget about her, leaving Hesina kneeling well after the maids retired from the queen's chambers.

"And sometimes she spoke to people." The words tasted acrid, secrets not meant to be swallowed in the first place. "She had conversations even when she was alone. There was also . . ."

Hesina broke off. Her hands grew clammy. ". . . There *is* also a scar, around her neck. And I . . ." She hadn't told this to anyone. Not Caiyan, not Lilian. "I've seen it bleed."

"An old scar?"

She managed a nod. Perfectly healed too. It shouldn't have reopened. It made her queasy, remembering.

"And your father?" asked Akira. His expression was as impassive as ever. "What did he do?"

"Everything. He summoned the best physicians of Kendi'a,

Ci, and Ning to court. He even sent out explorers for the mystical Baolin Isles and the panacea rumored to grow there." An action met with public criticism, since the relic emperors had done the same in hunting for the elixir of immortality.

There was some criticism in Akira's voice, too, when he said, "Then he sent her to the Ouyang Mountains."

"It was for the best." Hesina spoke in her father's defense. She heard him as if he were here, alive, his shoulders under her legs, her hands resting atop his head, the mist on their faces as they watched the queen's carriage fade into the gully. *The mountains will do her good, Little Bird. The clear waters and pure spirits will heal her.*

She'd believed him then. She'd tried to keep that belief alive with each passing year.

Her breath went shallow, as if to suffocate the embers of pain sowed among the memories. But she could face them. Akira could make her face them, push her past her discomfort. She waited for him to do so.

Instead, he simply lifted the vial of gas. "This poison was more complex than I expected. I'm close to isolating the final components, but I'll need a new sample. The body should have continued to emit the gas—"

The body?

"—as time went on. We can collect traces from the coffin. It wouldn't need to be opened, if it can be unearthed." His gaze swung to her, inquiring. *Can it?*

Coffin. Unearthed.

"That . . ." Hesina's mind darkened, shuttering against Akira's request.

Unearth her father's grave. *Unearth her father's grave.*

No. We can't. It's not possible. Never mind what the people would think, what the court would think. How could *she* bear it?

The answer was easy: she had to. For Mei, and all the other innocents to come, Hesina had to end this trial once and for all by finding the truth, no matter what it took, even if it was unearthing her father's grave.

Could she bear it? No. But could it be done?

Yes.

Her lips molded around the word. Whispered it. She rose, lurching when she realized what she'd agreed to. Akira reached to steady her, but she wrested away, grabbing the book as she went. "I'll read the rest of it."

Hesina stepped into the corridor. Let the panel fall shut behind her. She stood in the dark, motionless, breathless. Moments ago, she'd run through this passageway, the book a key in her hand.

She should have known better.

This book wasn't a clue. She was wasting her time.

Tears welled in her eyes. Books and snuff bottles, goblets and costumes, medallions and wedding locks. She couldn't remember why she'd ever thought these objects precious. They were just fragments. If her father were whole, he'd take her hand and call her a silly Little Bird for even thinking of unearthing his grave.

Hesina dragged back her tears, sinuses smarting. Then she returned to her chambers and muscled through a dozen pages of the real, original *Tenets*. One of the Eleven, in particular, said things that resonated through the pulsing of her head, and she went to bed troubled by how she related to them.

In trying times, truth is the first thing we betray.

She had lied for the truth, blackmailed for the truth, implicated innocents for the truth. Soon she'd unearth her father's grave for the truth. But could she face the truth? Hesina had once known the answer to that question.

She no longer did.

EIGHTEEN

One act of treason paves the way for a thousand others.

ONE of the ELEVEN on law

If the people approve the law, it must be followed.

TWO of the ELEVEN on law

Na-Na?"

Lilian blinked from the opening in her fuchsia-and-gold fretworked doors. Hesina knew how she looked. It was two gong strikes past midnight, and snow dusted her hair; the first flurries of the season had started coming down after she left Akira's rooms. "I couldn't sleep," she whispered.

It was all the explanation Lilian needed. "Don't mind the silks," she said, ushering Hesina in.

The silks were partly why Hesina had come to the Western Palace. She couldn't seem to face her own chambers after Akira's proposition, and the clutter and color here chased the demons from her head. She lay on the bed, and Lilian flung down beside her. It'd been a long time, Hesina realized, since the days when the two of them would hide here. They'd make a tent of the blankets, and Lilian would speak of all the rainy nights she and Caiyan had huddled beneath crumbling awnings and stone bridges, of orange rinds chewed to paste and roach bites that ripened with pus. She'd hug Hesina tightly afterward, and later, when she snored, Hesina couldn't bear to wake her.

Now, like before, Lilian rolled over and threw her arms around Hesina, enveloping her in a cloud of osmanthus and peach-blossom perfume. Her sister's breathing evened. Slowed. The snores started, and a smile curled on Hesina lips.

Then came the unbidden image of Lilian thrown into a cell. Lilian, interrogated like Mei.

Lilian, framed by Xia Zhong.

Impossible. Lilian didn't have blood relations other than Caiyan, Kendi'an or otherwise. She was just Hesina's sister, for whom Hesina would do anything—perhaps even declare a war.

Her bones filled with ice. Slowly, she wiggled free, pulled the blankets up to Lilian's shoulders, and stepped out, closing the doors behind her. She tilted her face to the heavens, snow landing on her lashes, and made a promise.

She'd go to the Ten Courts of Hell for unearthing the grave of the deceased, but she'd take Xia Zhong with her.

※ ※ ※

In the morning, Hesina went to Akira with an armful of star charts.

"We'll need to wait," she said, pointing to a date before Mei's trial the following week. "When Shu's two minor moons intersect in orbit, the arc of the sun drops one degree. We can unearth the tomb under the pretense that it must be propped at an angle for the spirit to receive the most direct rays."

Akira scratched his head. "That's very elaborate."

Elaborate and vague—two things any good cover story required.

She was about to become the first Yan ruler to unearth a tomb. This white lie would pacify the people if they found out, but to perfect it, Hesina needed the Minister of Rites' seal.

Suffice to say, Xia Zhong wasn't thrilled to see her so soon. He kept his distance as she made her request, a scarf wrapped around his neck. She almost sympathized—until he made his counter-request. He'd sanction her unearthing the tomb if she let him open a silver coffer for "provincial shrine projects." She had no choice but to agree.

In the evening, Sanjing met with Akira to disclose information pertinent to the trial. Hesina was present to facilitate, but her brother got along with Akira just fine.

"You seem like another mysterious one," mused Sanjing at the end. "My sister certainly has a taste for them."

Hesina's blush ruined her glare.

"At least you can fight. The guards say you were a formidable opponent."

Akira lifted his rod. "With this?"

"Anything you master can be called a weapon."

"I'm afraid I'd disappoint. I've never played the flute before."

Sanjing blinked, then pretended Akira hadn't spoken. "When all this dies down, find me. I'll see that your talents aren't wasted."

"Stop trying to recruit my representative," Hesina said to Sanjing after they left Akira's room.

"Stop letting him delude himself. That thing can't possibly be a flute."

"It has holes. And it's hollow." *I think.*

"Flutist or not," said her brother, "he's a swordsman, through and through. Did you see the way he was positioned?"

"Positioned?"

"Yes. He angled himself toward my dominant side immediately."

"Jing," said Hesina carefully, "you were both sitting."

"All the more impressive, for him to be able to sense it."

"Jing, you don't *have* a dominant side."

"Exactly. He sensed my ambidexterity, Sina."

She held back a snort but let him go at it, grateful he was thawing a bit. Still, he wore his tension like a heavy mantle. Her pages reported that her brother spent most of his nights guarding Mei's cell, and as they came to a split in the corridor, Hesina wanted to tell him to take care of himself and leave the worrying to her.

He left before she could.

* * *

Today was the day.

Hesina began it like any other—first by attending court, then by visiting Mei. The swordswoman raised a brow as Hesina slid steamers of crystal shrimp dumplings and *shaguo* of chili-oil jellyfish noodles through the cell bars. "I feel like a hog being fattened before my execution."

Hesina grumbled something about food improving any situation. Lilian believed in it, but Mei seemed skeptical, and to be quite honest, Hesina was too. Her appetite had shriveled, and with hours still to go before the unearthing, she skipped supper and went to her rooms.

The space was empty, lifeless, the cranes embroidered on her screens punched black by moonlight. Carefully, Hesina retrieved her mother's chest from under the floorboards, where it rested next to Xia Zhong's letters. She undid the silver wedding lock, removed the original *Tenets*—disguised as *The Medicinal Properties of Exotic Fungi*—and sat down with it at her desk.

She read until the gong strike, then met Akira in his room, handing him a fur cloak. Together, they made for the eastern courtyard, where a covered palanquin awaited under the snow-covered plum trees. Servants helped Hesina in. Once they were both seated, pole-bearers hoisted them up, and they were off.

The night was clear and sharp, with a slight musk to the air when Hesina pushed aside the brocade curtain. The palace gates groaned shut behind them, and the palanquin jolted as they descended the terraces.

She let the curtain fall. "I finished the book," she whispered, facing Akira.

He took to the dark like a blade to a sheath, eyes alert, yet also at ease. He was no stranger to these soulless nights, and with that in mind, Hesina added a stroke to her story. The boy was an assassin who used the night as his cover. He gave his targets no time to scream. A shiver fingered her spine—and not entirely in fear.

"Is it the hair?"

Hesina blinked. "What?"

Akira pushed a hand through his bangs. "You're staring."

"No. I'm not." She wheeled her thoughts around. "I was just thinking about the book."

And then she really was. Her heart stopped doing clumsy acrobatics, and her voice dripped with disappointment when she said, "It was exactly what it claimed to be. A book of tenets." One's sayings weren't answers, regardless of how they resonated, and Hesina was almost grateful when they reached the imperial tombs not long after. She didn't want to dwell on her inroads—or lack thereof.

The *paifang* archway to the tombs rose just outside the city walls, facing the nearby Shanlong mountain range. The pole-bearers set the

palanquin down before the tall pillars, and after Hesina instructed
them to wait, she entered with Akira.

She'd been wise to fast; acid shot up her throat as they traveled
through the concentric tombs. Each was a couch of granite curved
like a womb; together they gleamed like rings and rings of verte-
brae.

Wrapping her fur-muffed cloak closer, Hesina passed kings,
queens, princesses, and princes, some competent, some inept, but
all checked by the six ministries, and none as corrupt as the relic
emperors. She made for the center, where the gazebo for One and
Two, first rulers of the new era, towered.

Her father's tomb was one ring away. The gravediggers waiting
by it helped Hesina and Akira pour boiling water over the frozen
ground, melting it to sludge. Shovels soon rasped in and out of the
earth. The sound scraped Hesina's insides raw. It went on for what
felt like hours before the diggers struck the coffin. They climbed
out of the pit, and Hesina handed each a small pouch of *banliang*.
She waited until they were gone before nodding at Akira.

The real work began when he jumped into the pit and bored
a hole into the coffin's side. He hammered in a metal spout, then
inserted a ceramic pipe that fed into a vial he had depressurized by
burning out the air. Before Hesina knew it, he was climbing back
out, gas collected.

"Got it."

Perfect, she should have said, then gotten them out of this place.

Instead, Hesina wandered over to the still-steaming pit. Here lay
her father, or what remained of him. The least she could do now
was look at his final resting place with fearless eyes. She leaned
over, straining to see the coffin.

"The edge—" Akira started to say.

—was unstable. The sopping earth fell out from under her, and Hesina tumbled down in a flurry of cloak and skirts, her fall broken by something hard.

Seconds passed as she lay winded. Then she scrambled upright, rolling off the coffin. She thought she heard Akira's voice, but the world above was muffled, the moon and stars distant. Down here, the gleam of her father's lacquer coffin was her only source of light.

Queasily, Hesina crouched at the coffin's side. The *zitan* was carved into a simple log shape. Kings in this era no longer had mausoleums built in their names, or ordered their concubines to follow them into the tomb and play the *pipa* until they suffocated.

"Are you hurt?" asked Akira, landing beside her.

She shook her head, her eyes pinned on the hole that Akira had made in the *zitan*. It was no wider than her little finger, but the darkness beyond appeared to contain a universe.

Vertigo washed over Hesina. She forced her attention down from the hole to something beneath it.

A rim of silver, half-buried in loam.

She brushed away the dirt—and jerked her hand away as if she'd been bitten. Her breath came fast. "Akira. *Look*."

Moonlight embossed an etched vine and trumpet-blossom motif. Swirl for swirl, line for line, the design was the same as what graced her mother's wedding lock, like one in a set. One in a *pair*.

The realization—that this was the other wedding lock, given by her mother to her father, protecting the secrets of a coffin instead of a chest—rocked Hesina onto her heels. She glanced to Akira and found him studying *her*, as if the lock was no surprise.

"Why didn't you tell me?"

"I don't know," Akira said quietly.

But Hesina knew.

It was because she had to make this choice on her own.

Her heartbeat was a gallop, thudding in her ears. Her fingers shook so badly that she spun past the 0 on the first try.

0.

Ba-dum.

0.

Ba-dum.

0.

Ba-dum. Ba-dum. Ba-dum.

The lock dropped into the mud.

Akira moved to the foot of the coffin. Hesina placed her hands on the head. She wasn't ready to do this. She never would be.

But then she envisioned Lilian's candlelit face again, and her jaw set. She couldn't ignore the significance of the matching lock. She had opened her mother's chest.

She could open her father's coffin.

Together, on the silent count of three, they lifted, revealing her father's legs, torso, neck, face.

His face.

Hesina's thoughts took off like startled birds. Her extremities numbed, and Akira saved the coffin lid from crashing down. He heaved it to the side as she stammered, "This . . . this isn't right." She shook her head, mouth dry, gaze unfocused. "This can't be."

Then her gaze focused, but not on her father. He wasn't there. In his place was a young man wearing his silk *hanfu*, everything about him perfectly preserved.

This is a dream.

Hesina pinched herself. The boy remained.

Grave robbers.

But he was wearing her father's clothes, her father's mandalas, and worst of all . . .

Akira caught her shoulders as Hesina stumbled back.

. . . her father's face.

The angles were softer. The hollows weren't quite so prominent. But there was no mistaking it; the boy wore a younger version of her father's face.

Hesina quivered in Akira's hold. "Tell me we're seeing the same thing."

"We are."

She whirled to face him. "You suspected something all along, didn't you?"

His grip around her shoulders loosened.

"When?"

For a second Akira seemed on the verge of letting go. Hesina was glad when he didn't; he held her wits in his hands.

"When I realized the poison was actually a mixture of fifty," he finally said. "Some come from vents deep in the Baolin Sea. Others . . . I've never encountered, only read about their properties in theory books. The same goes for this particular mixture. It's something of a legend. Intended to kill a legend."

"To kill a legend? *What* legend?"

Akira took a measured breath. "To kill immortals."

Immortals . . . immortals? As in the immortal sages? If so, Hesina knew all about immortals. Children's tales. Tutors' slogans. Giant cranes and moons and suns that consumed daughters. Her brain prattled off useless information, guttering to a stop when Akira spoke again.

"I'd assume . . ." He trailed off. His eyes flicked down to where Hesina had wound both hands into the front of his cloak. She didn't let go. She didn't care how it looked as she clung to him, her breath clouding with his in the narrow space between them.

"Tell me." She meant it as an order. She spoke it as a plea.

Akira drew another breath, no longer so measured. The space between them suddenly seemed like a ravine. She stood on one end and he on the other, his voice so very far away.

"I'd assume the poison would still destroy things, even if it failed to kill. If it broke the illusion work wrought by sooths, it would explain his current appearance. He must have stopped aging the moment he became immortal. The face we're seeing now must be his true face . . ."

If it failed to kill . . . became immortal . . . true face . . .

Failed to kill.

Failed to kill.

Hesina released Akira.

She knelt by the coffin's side, the ground seeping damp past her skirts, and pressed her cheek over her father's chest.

There was a heartbeat in her temples, a heartbeat in her throat. But the heartbeat that filled her ear was not her own.

Ba-dum.

Ba-dum.

Ba-dum.

NINETEEN

When we make up stories about the things we can't see or grasp, we are simply lying to ourselves.
                    ONE *of the* ELEVEN *on superstition*

It's good entertainment, but never education.
                    TWO *of the* ELEVEN *on superstition*

F*ather?"*

A dragonfly lands on his nose, but he doesn't twitch. Seconds later, a magpie swoops by, and white droppings splatter dangerously close to his head.

She laughs and wades through the flowers. "Even the birds are telling you to wake up."

It's late summer. The irises are in full bloom. Their bladed foliage grabs on to the layered skirt of her ruqun. She tugs free and comes to loom over him, folding her arms. "Now you're just pretending."

Her father's very good at pretending. They've spent hours rummaging through his costume chest, donning different kinds of garb. She's watched him transform into an artisan, a merchant, a *courier right before her eyes. He may be a king, but he can play the other roles too.*

With a dramatic sigh, she uncrosses her arms and plucks an iris. "Wake up and smell the flowers."

She tickles him under the nose. She prods his cheek with the end of the long stem. He continues to sleep. The sun continues to shine. It beats down on her back. Reflects off the emerald koi pond nearby. Everything is a bright, prismatic haze.

"Father?"

Wake up.

Please, wake up.

* * *

They tried to wake him.

Akira tried, that was, poking and prodding at a series of vital energy points on the body. Hesina sat frozen. Someone had callously rearranged her insides and mixed everything up. Half of her would have betrayed the world to hear her father's voice again; half couldn't accept this boy, who looked no older than herself, as a father of any kind.

Which half was better, and which was worse? Hesina didn't know. Past became present as they failed to wake her father, but unlike before, she experienced no grief. No denial. How could she deny something already denied by the laws of nature? If anything, she felt anger.

She shouldn't have had to relive this nightmare.

Blood rushed to Hesina's head as she staggered to her feet. Her father wasn't dead, but he wasn't alive either. He couldn't comfort her. Couldn't explain *why* his heart was beating months after it'd stopped. Nothing had changed; it was all up to her.

Mechanically, Hesina returned to the coffin side. *Examine the body, Hesina*, she ordered herself. So she did. She checked her father's clothes, her motions rough and jerky. A thought slithered into her mind, and she pushed apart the silks covering his abdomen.

The incision was gone. The stitches were still there, but his skin was smooth and even in tone. As if the dissection had never happened.

Darkness fuzzed like mold over Hesina's vision. A face that hadn't aged. A body that hadn't decomposed. A scar that had healed without a trace.

Was there a difference between *immortal* and *abomination*?

Stand, Hesina, she ordered herself. So she did. Her knees wobbled as she pushed to her feet. Akira followed seconds later.

Speak, Hesina.

"Is—" Her voice came out like a wisp of smoke; she tried again. "Is there an antidote?"

Akira shook his head. "The poison shouldn't even exist outside of arcane theory."

Yet here it was, in existence. "But there's an antidote in theory?"

"In theoretical theory."

Her head swam. Theoretical theory. It was the kind of ridiculousness that the imperial alchemists had entertained in their search for the elixir of immortality. Then it struck her like a knife to the chest—the *elixir of immortality*. To the relic emperors, immortality was neither a myth nor a means of tricking children into studiousness. They'd believed it was real, and it could be attained with the right combination of ingredients.

But none of the emperors' alchemists had derived it. And the Eleven had dissolved the guild, deploring the epic waste of resources. That had been three centuries ago—though what did three centuries mean to an immortal? How long, exactly, had her father been alive? Did he have other children? Was *she* immortal too?

The questions existed in a swamp: venturing into one meant losing herself to the downward suction of all the others. The night around Hesina warped as she dragged her gaze to the body. Without an antidote, she didn't know how, or when, her father would ever speak again. It could be years. It could be never.

Consider the logistics, Hesina, she reminded herself as her hands, arms, shoulders shook. *Logistics.*

She couldn't bring the body back to the palace and risk discovery. She had to keep it in a place no one would think to look: here.

She took up her end of the coffin lid. Akira took up the other. They lifted. They lowered. With Akira's help, Hesina clambered out of the pit, seized one of the discarded shovels, and began reburying the coffin.

Thud went the first shovelful of dirt onto the *zitan* lid. The loamy scent of it filled Hesina's mouth, packing onto everything she'd tamped down: tears and bile. Grief and revulsion.

Thud.

Her father was immortal.

Thud.

The face she'd known all her life was a lie, aged forward by a sooth.

Thud.

How? *Thud. How?*

Thud. Thud. Thud.

It took them an hour to refill all the dirt. By the end, Hesina's hands were an abraded mess. Yet she barely registered the pain as they returned to the palanquin and headed back toward the palace. Broken skin could heal. Maybe even hearts. Not trust.

Stay calm, Hesina. But the mental trick had lost its effect. As they reached the terraces, Hesina's stomach surged like a fist, punching her lungs. She grabbed for the palanquin's side.

"Go on without me," she gasped to Akira. Then she ordered the bearers to set her down.

She staggered out, gulping air. They'd only climbed halfway up the terraces, but it was enough for her to see the city sprawl below: the courtyard compounds, the limestone alleyways, the black tiled roofs shimmering like scales in the predawn. The glow encapsulating the red-light district dimmed as other quarters blinked awake with lanterns. Merchants would be loading their wagons. Raft pushers would be heading for the moat, sedan carriers for the main boulevard. The rest of the kingdom would soon follow in waking, living, and believing their king had been murdered by some Kendi'an assassin, by some poison lethal to an ordinary, mortal human being.

Wrong! Hesina wanted to scream from the terraces. *You're all wrong!* But she was the source of all their misbeliefs. Without her, there would be no trial. No search for a truth that ultimately implicated the sooths.

Without her, the ghosts of a previous generation wouldn't have returned.

She buckled under the load of her guilt, but an arm caught her. It drew her close and supported her. *Everything will be fine*, Caiyan would have said, and Hesina almost expected to see his face when she raised her watery gaze.

Instead it was Akira, hair in his eyes, dirt on his cheekbones, insubordinate as usual.

She pushed at him. "I told you to go."

"I did. I went and came back down."

"I'm going to be sick."

Akira released her, only to sit her down on the terrace. He slid a hand over the back of her neck, his touch featherlight as he coaxed her head to her knees.

Her nausea passed; her need to cry didn't. But after several minutes, Hesina found the strength to stand. She climbed the terraces. Akira didn't stop her. She waited for him to tell her it was going to be okay, but he didn't do that either. He simply followed her to her father's study, where she instructed him to wait. Then she headed for Caiyan's chambers.

She made it halfway before her body spasmed. She clutched at the facades, breaking into a cold sweat.

Her father wasn't dead.

Yet someone had tried to kill him all the same.

Who?

Someone close, close enough to have known about his immortality. Closer than Hesina herself.

Black lines zigzagged across her vision, carving up her mind like strokes of ink. Together, the strokes formed the characters of her mother's name, a name that had never made it onto the suspect list. *And the dowager queen?* Akira had asked, brush hovering beneath *Xia Zhong, Lilian,* and *Caiyan.*

Hesina had rejected the idea, but no one else could have known about her father's immortality. No one else had an army of attendants to act in her absence. The snuff bottle made sense. The matching silver locks made sense. Everything blended like segments on a painted top, fusing in motion.

Her mother.

It could only be her mother.

A hiccup escaped Hesina, the beginning of a sob, a scream. If she didn't reveal this, Mei would stand trial tomorrow for a crime she didn't commit, but if she did reveal this, then what about her mother? She clapped her hands over her mouth and ran the rest of the way to Caiyan's chambers, until her lungs seared and there was no air left for sobs or screams.

"She's going further than I expected."

Hesina skidded to a stop at the sound of Lilian's voice.

"Give her time." Caiyan's voice. Hesina approached his door, then flinched back when he went on to say, "Sooner or later, she will break from the truth."

Her blood froze over.

"And if she doesn't?" asked Lilian. "What if she decides it's up to her to mend things?"

The ice melted, and her veins throbbed with heat.

They were talking about her.

"It won't come down to that," Caiyan said, but Hesina didn't hear the rest. With a bang, she burst through the doors, whirling on her siblings.

"Perfect," cried Lilian in delight, without a fluster of guilt. "More brains to solve this problem for my apprentice."

Hesina narrowed her eyes. "Your apprentice."

"Yes. Panling. You remember her, right?"

"No."

"Fine if you don't. You can still help. So here's the thing: she's besotted with this poet who thinks he's oh so special when he's about as evocative as a donkey in heat. But the *real* problem"—Lilian lowered her voice—"is that he's already married and leading her on."

Pieces of what Hesina had overheard slid nicely into this new framework—except for one.

She turned on Caiyan. "You know her?"

"He more than *knows* her," Lilian answered for her twin. She pinched his cheek, and Caiyan, to Hesina's dazed surprise, flushed. "Which is why I can't let her be blindsided by that pretentious ass."

"Oh," said Hesina. She should have said more; this was the first time she'd ever heard of Caiyan having a love affair with something outside of academia. But all she said was "oh" again, too relieved and too ashamed to have suspected anything in the first place. "Just tell her the truth," she finished.

"It's not that easy," said Caiyan. "It would hurt her."

Lilian sighed. "You two are useless. I'll deal with it on my own. So, why don't you explain your new aesthetic?" She flourished a hand at Hesina's *ruqun*. "There are easier ways of dyeing something brown, you know."

Brown? Hesina looked down and saw the mud reaching up from the hem of her skirts. To explain it would require explaining everything, including her father's not-dead state, his theoretical immortality, the poison meant to kill him, and the dowager queen who'd done it.

The words pushed against Hesina's lips. She could have vomited them out. But not here where the maids might overhear.

"Father's study," she croaked, and the blush immediately cleared from Caiyan's complexion. Lilian straightened. The twins followed Hesina through the knit of corridors into the king's study. Hesina bolted the *zitan* doors.

Akira came to stand by her, and she braced herself before facing the twins.

The hardest part was starting. Once she opened her mouth, she couldn't stop, and when she finished, Hesina felt ten times lighter— lighter and barer. There. She'd given Lilian and Caiyan every reason to walk away from her. She was their sister, but not in blood. She didn't have a choice but to accept her father. They did.

Her fear spiked when Lilian frowned. "Na-Na . . . have you been dipping into the *jiutan*?"

"I'm not drunk, or hallucinating. I saw it with my own two eyes." *And felt the beat of his heart, and the brush of his breath.*

"It's true," said Akira, earning himself a grateful glance.

Of the twins, Caiyan was more likely to reject myth and superstition. But when he said, "I believe you," and Lilian sighed and did too, Hesina loosed a breath of appreciative relief.

Caiyan started pacing, a fist cuffed over his chin in thought. "Why do you suspect the dowager queen?"

"Why shouldn't I?" Hesina had been justifying her mother's actions for too long. Was she wrong to see the facts for what they were?

"Do you have hard evidence?"

"I have the poison."

"But can you prove that she was the one to set it?"

"Still trying to identify the residue on the goblet," said Akira.

The whirlwind of her thoughts slowed, and Hesina nodded. If the residue matched the poison in the vial, then the poison had been served in the goblet. The next step would be to trace the goblet's origins. Whoever had delivered it would be their first true suspect.

But none of that was going to happen before Mei stood trial tomorrow. "I have to stop the trial."

Lilian went to her favorite daybed but didn't lie down. "How?"

If Hesina could commit treason to bring the trial into existence, she could commit treason to end it. But it was out of her hands, sustained by the machinery of court and law.

She joined Caiyan in pacing the length of the study, then came to a stop at the wall of books. She'd been thinking in the wrong direction.

The solution wasn't to commit more treason.

It was to admit to what she'd already committed.

"I can show the people that the trial was never legitimate."

"How—"

Hesina whirled on Lilian. "Xia Zhong," she said breathlessly. "If the court learns that he didn't select Akira at random, the trial will be terminated."

Lilian blinked. "But won't he claim you forced him to? I'm all for taking out the slug, but not if it means implicating yourself."

"She's right," said Caiyan. "He's not worth it, milady."

"Are you saying Mei isn't worth it? Or the others who will inevitably be framed?" Hesina's voice rose as her fears spiraled. "This isn't about Xia Zhong. This isn't some scenario where I can cut my losses and walk away. Yes, this trial will come to an end, but only on the day I let it claim an innocent as its victim."

The study had gone deathly quiet.

"If I sink," Hesina said firmly, "Xia Zhong sinks with me."

"Na-Na . . ."

"Have you thought about the people, milady?" Caiyan stopped midpace and faced her. "Ending the trial prematurely won't answer the question of who killed the king. The uncertainty will poison their minds. Suspicion will mount against everyone, not just the Kendia'ns."

People aren't like that, Hesina might have once said. But she no longer could.

"Let Akira acquit Mei the way he acquitted Consort Fei,"

continued Caiyan. "Gain another victory over the Investigation Bureau. Rattle the court, and show them who the villain really is. Then . . ."

"Then?"

"Frame Xia Zhong for the king's death. Kill two birds with one stone. Rid yourself of an enemy, and avoid condemning your own mother for the king's death."

"For once, I approve of this political underhandedness," said Lilian as Hesina stared at Caiyan, dumbstruck. He wasn't suggesting anything beneath what Xia Zhong might do himself, but the proposal, coming from her brother's lips, unsettled her.

"How confident do you feel about acquitting Mei?" she finally asked Akira.

"If it's fabricated evidence again, decently confident."

Hesina didn't like this plan. But the same could have been said for every plan she'd made since rising to the throne. And Caiyan had a point. He always did.

"I won't reveal my treason yet," she said, and relief fanned over Caiyan's face. "But we'll discuss this again after tomorrow."

Then, one way or another, either by condemning herself or framing Xia Zhong, the trial would end.

But first, she had someone to write to.

* * *

Caiyan's chambers overflowed with organized stacks of books, but Sanjing's were spare. The *kang* tabletops were clear, the *zitan* cabinets empty, and everything was filmed with dust, as if the maids knew better than to clean for someone who came home so sporadically. Ever since taking over command of the Yan militia at the tender age of fourteen, Sanjing had divided his time between the palace and the various fronts.

Now, walking into his rooms felt like walking into his mind. In this forlorn space, it occurred to Hesina that her brother's jealousy might not have been jealousy at all, but rather fear that she'd replaced him in his absence.

Was it true? Hesina didn't know, nor did she have the time to ruminate. She'd come as an intruder.

She'd come as a thief.

Quickly, she pulled open his drawers. Most, like his cabinets, were empty. One held a sad ball of twine, a whetstone, some ink sticks, and an inkstone. The drawer beneath it was promisingly heavy, and Hesina jerked it open only to find a stack of letters, from their mother no less.

A lump grew in her throat before she reminded herself this was exactly why she was snooping through her brother's things. She used to write to their mother, too, always waiting for a reply, somehow convincing herself that each and every one of her letters—so carefully sealed with rice glue and posted by dove—had gotten lost. Her delusions died the day she caught Sanjing receiving replies to his.

Hesina hadn't written since.

She found what she was looking for behind the stack of letters: a plain *huanghuali* box filled with an assortment of seals carved with her brother's name. In her triumph, and in her dilemma over which to pick, she missed the sound of the door opening behind her.

"Fancy seeing you, Sina. You never do guard your back, do you?"

Hesina froze, then deliberately turned, leaving the drawer ajar like a childish challenge. *Go on*, it seemed to say. *Fight me.*

Sanjing regarded her coolly. "And what, may I ask, brings you here?"

"To borrow a seal."

"Borrow, you say."

"Steal." She would confess to the theft, but not the reason behind it.

"Ah." Sanjing took a step into the room. The space between them suddenly shrank tenfold. Hesina tensed, and her brother stopped in his tracks, tilting his head to the side. "Why? Did you suddenly end up with a shortage of your own?"

"No."

"Then did you tire of your name?"

"Just let me have a seal, Jing."

"Not until you tell me what you need it for."

She was at the end of her patience. She snapped a random seal into her hand, but her brother blocked the doorway with an arm. "It's a simple question, Sina, that requires a simple answer. Preferably the truth."

The truth.

"Though a lie will also do, if it's easier for you," Sanjing said as Hesina turned away from him, clenching the seal so tightly that it hurt the bones in her hand.

The truth.

The truth was that their father had deceived them.

The truth was that she suspected their mother.

The truth was that the dowager queen would only read a letter marked with Sanjing's seal, and this, on top of everything, was more than Hesina could take. Tears rolled down her cheeks before she could wipe them.

"Sina." Her brother was suddenly standing before her; he held her by the arms. "Sina, what's wrong?"

There were no simple questions, or simple answers, Hesina decided bitterly. There were only truths sacrificed for other truths.

"I need the seal for Mother." She threw off Sanjing's hands. "Because I want to write to her."

She read Sanjing's emotions like clouds in the sky. The confusion, the skepticism, the confusion again, scattered by sudden understanding. Then there was only vast, blue pity.

She didn't want his pity. "You should have just said so," he said as she made for the doors. "Wait, Sina."

It wasn't enough to stop her, not like what came out of her brother's mouth next:

"I'm sorry."

In disbelief, Hesina turned.

"I know . . ." Sanjing broke off, sighed, and pushed a hand through his hair. "I know you didn't mean for this to happen. It's just hard." He opened a palm and fisted it. "It's hard feeling helpless." He met her gaze, and she was perplexed to find guilt in his. "But I know you must feel helpless too."

Her confusion cleared.

Her brother thought he was to blame for her tears.

Fresh ones filled Hesina's eyes. She wanted to close the distance between them, smooth down his cowlick, and tell him she was sorry too.

But if she did that, she would be tempted to share the burden of the truth.

"I'll see you at the trial tomorrow," she managed before making her escape. After Akira acquitted Mei, she would tell Sanjing everything. Until then, she would spare him this pain.

TWENTY

Equality is not the natural way of the world. It must be nurtured.

ONE of the ELEVEN on the natural order

Who isn't powerless against the will of the cosmos? But who doesn't try all the same?

TWO of the ELEVEN on the natural order

It was the day of Mei's trial, and Hesina hadn't slept. After talking with Sanjing the night before, she'd stayed up in her study to draft the letter, telling her mother that she'd found the chest, the book, the truth about her father—and that now she wanted to hear it from the dowager queen herself. Hesina had summoned her to court by the full moon, stamped the envelope with Sanjing's seal—a strange-looking thing chiseled with a half-lion, half-dog creature—and handed the letter off to her page. Then she'd taken out her father's box.

Once more, she spread out his possessions. The snuff bottle. The *Tenets*. The courier's *hanfu*. The paring knife. The corded medallion. All that was missing was the goblet, still in Akira's room.

The objects themselves hadn't changed, but through the refraction of what Hesina now knew, they appeared like artifacts from another realm. She touched a trembling hand to the character for *longevity* carved onto the medallion's surface, and suddenly remembered seeing the same character within a book about sooths. The book claimed that sooths could extend their lives by speaking true visions. It was supposed to be a rumor. A myth. But was it possible her father had been a sooth himself? Hesina wasn't—she'd cut herself in the red-light district, been wounded at the Black Lake, and her blood hadn't burned. But she also wasn't sure if she had ever seen her father bleed. There'd been no blood when the Imperial Doctress dissected him, and every memory Hesina had of her father seemed distorted.

He wouldn't have lived long as a sooth anyway, Hesina thought numbly as she set the paring knife back in the chest and strung the corded medallion onto her own sash for further inspection. He'd told too many lies.

She returned to her bedchambers, but didn't try for sleep. She watched the stars set and the moon turn fish-scale transparent in the lightening sky, and when her eyes tired and she closed them, all Hesina could do, it seemed, was cry. She didn't want to suspect her mother. Didn't want to distrust her father. She hadn't asked for any of this—or had she? Hadn't she gone so far as to commit treason for this trial?

Come sunrise, the face reflected in Hesina's bronze mirror was blotchy and red.

"More," she ordered when the maid stopped powdering.

"*Dianxia*, I really don't think—"

"I said more." She could afford cakey powder. What she couldn't afford was walking into the most important trial of her life looking like she'd sobbed into a pillow.

Ming'er sent the younger girl away and took up the brush herself.

She swirled it through the powder jar and tapped off the excess, resting her pinkie against Hesina's cheek to steady her hand.

When Ming'er was done, Hesina studied the results. She didn't look her best, but she didn't look like a flaky winter-melon pastry either. Her true face was hidden. It would always have to be, just like her father's.

Ming'er helped her into her trial robes, cross-wrapping the collar of the dove-gray *ruqun*. Anticipation and dread broke against each other like waves, and sweat drenched Hesina's back when it came time to affix the *bixi* panel to the skirts.

"Will you wear a hairpin today?" asked Ming'er.

Hesina hesitated. None compared to her father's gift. All reminded her of Xia Zhong. But she didn't know her father anymore, and Xia Zhong's influence over her was nearing its end.

At her nod, Ming'er inserted a red coral pin to complement the scarlet phoenix embroidery on the *ruqun*'s sleeves. She accompanied Hesina down the Hall of Everlasting Harmony, adjusting the gown's train one last time outside the court doors.

The sight of Ming'er on her hands and knees, fussing with a hem as if it meant the world, fogged Hesina's chest. She bent and raised her lady-in-waiting by the elbows.

"My flower—"

"Thank you," Hesina interrupted firmly. Then she said it again, more quietly, to the woman who had wiped her tears with her own brocaded sleeve, who had sewn rose petals into her pillow logs and braided trumpet lilies into her hair. Ming'er had made Hesina her princess before the people had made her their queen.

Hesina stepped into the court, sweeping past the ranks that fell in *koutou* and up the suspended walk, reaching the imperial balcony just as Sanjing made his entrance.

"He's a bit overdressed," remarked Lilian as Hesina sat.

An understatement: Sanjing was dressed for war. He strode down the aisle as if it were a battlefield, his *liuyedao* sheathed at his side, the clip of his horn-heeled boots stunning the court into silence.

Then the mutters broke. They trailed Sanjing as he ascended the steps to the imperial balcony, and Hesina sighed as he took the seat beside her. "Are you planning on killing someone today?"

"Many, if I must."

She couldn't tell if he was joking or serious; she wasn't sure she wanted to know.

The doors parted, and they both tensed as the guards dragged in Mei. Her fingers were still bound, her beige dungeon issues smudged with grime, but her braid was sleek and her eyes defiant as they pushed her up the dais.

Mei's representative was to enter next. Hesina fidgeted as she stared at the great doors. Xia Zhong had surely selected a more competent scholar this time.

But no one came through the doors, and it was the director himself who climbed the dais. "Last time, we witnessed the unprecedented act of the plaintiff's representative volunteering as the defendant's. In the spirit of fairness to both parties, the Investigation Bureau has decided to do a thorough debrief before proceeding with the trial. Let us review the evidence together, shall we?" he asked Akira, smiling. "We wouldn't want you missing anything."

So *this* was their play. Do away with the representative entirely, thereby allowing the director to personally oversee every beat of the session. Smart, and probably against the rules written in the *Tenets*, though Hesina shouldn't have been surprised. Xia Zhong held the *Tenets* in lower regard than she did herself.

"Fine by me," said Akira, unruffled. "Again, I'd like to see the maid you have listed as a witness. Please," he said when the girl stepped to the front of the witness box, visibly trembling. She was young and scrawny, and though she was about to deliver whatever incriminating evidence Xia Zhong or the director had prepared, Hesina could commiserate. "Share your account."

"It was morning . . ." Her eyes darted about before fixing on the director. "It was morning, and I was bringing the king's breakfast to his study."

Hesina's mouth thinned. The first of many blatant lies to come. No one had delivered any food or drink to her father on the day of his death.

"And what might that have been?" asked Akira.

"Congee and cider." The maid bit her lip.

"Please continue."

"Right before I reached the hallway to the study, she . . ." The maid pointed at Mei. "She attacked me."

Mei snorted, and the maid flinched. She shrank as Akira approached the half wall between them.

"Define 'attack.'"

"W-what do you mean?"

Akira motioned for a nearby page. "Pardon me," he said, then grabbed a fistful of the boy's *hanfu* and reared a fist back. "Like this?"

"N-no."

"Are you part of the imperial troupe?" crowed a marquis from the upper ranks.

Sanjing seethed. "How do you stand this? Do you just take it?"

"Yes," Hesina muttered. "Even better, you pay them no mind."

A skill Akira seemed to have mastered better than her. He

released the page and faced the maid again. "Describe the attack the way it unfolded."

Her hand fluttered to her left shoulder. "She grabbed my shoulder and tore my dress."

"Just condemn her already, *dianxia*!" called one of the viscounts. "She's the murderer!"

Sanjing touched a hand to the hilt of his *liuyedao*; Hesina yanked it away.

Akira scanned the witness stand. He beckoned for the page again and whispered something into his ear. "I'd like to see the ruined dress," he said as the page hurried off.

The *ruqun*, torn at the left shoulder as described, was delivered to him on a gilded tray.

Akira lifted it. "Is this silk?"

"Yes. What do you wear?" jibed a baron. "Cotton?"

It was almost comical, how many officials Xia Zhong and the director had so obviously paid off. But Hesina was not amused.

The page Akira had sent off returned with someone in tow. It was none other than the Imperial Tailor. The cross collar of his *hanfu* gaped open, and his long locks flowed free. "Did you really have to enter without *knocking*?" He sighed as the page pushed him up the dais. "I hate leaving a partner unsatisfied."

"Discussing his own sexual prowess in court?" muttered Lilian. "What a pretentious ass."

The tailor's sexual prowess was the last thing on Hesina's mind when Akira held out the torn *ruqun*. "Lend me your eye on this one matter: Which direction was the pull in the torn weaving?"

The tailor examined the gash. "This is no pull. Something sharp cut it."

"How certain are you of that?"

"Everyone knows the silk looms weave one way."

"And what would that be?"

"Double stitching, of course!" cried the tailor, brushing lint off his shoulder. "Only through double stitching can Yan silk live up to its lifetime guarantee. So it's not going to simply *tear* without creating pulls in others parts of the fabric. An apprentice of mine could tell you that. Now, I'd really appreciate it if you never interrupted—"

"Thank you," cut in Akira. "You're free to leave."

Still muttering, the tailor descended the dais, blowing kisses at the noblemen and women at each step. Lilian sighed, but all Hesina could hear was Akira as he spoke to the maid.

"You say she tore your gown, but you didn't say it was with something sharp . . . a sword, for example."

"I—I was surprised." The maid sounded on the verge of tears. Hesina's wrath toward Xia Zhong and the director bubbled. They bent these girls like saplings to a trellis.

"Yet you still managed to deliver the tray in one piece," observed Akira.

"We're trained never to drop things."

"Fair enough. So you didn't hear the unsheathing of the sword beforehand?"

"N-no."

"So she unsheathed at the last possible moment and cut your gown in the same stroke. A quick draw."

"If you're going to talk about swords," the director interjected, "then I have just the witness for you."

A maid brought forward another gilded tray, draped with a sword belt fashioned from black brocade.

"This was found on the floor outside the king's study," said the director. He summoned a middle-aged woman wearing a brown *hanfu* cinched by an iron girdle. With a start, Hesina recognized her as the Imperial Blacksmith.

"Did you fashion this for the swordswoman?" asked the director, waving the tray over to the blacksmith.

The blacksmith ran her hands over the proffered sword belt. "Yes, I did. I carved these markings myself."

Hesina's heart plummeted.

"Then it's settled. The evidence undeniably—"

"Wait." Akira gestured for the sword belt. He gave it one glance and said to the blacksmith, "A traditional belt has the scabbard sling on the left, but this one is on the right."

"The traditional design is meant for a right-handed swordsman or woman."

"So the suspect wasn't right-handed," said Akira.

"Correct," said the blacksmith. "She was left-handed."

"And that's why the sling is on right."

"Correct."

"And can you confirm that the left-handed wielder reaches to the right side when unsheathing into a quick draw?"

"Yes, that is the correct method."

Akira thanked the blacksmith and turned back to the maid. "You claimed she grabbed your shoulder."

"Y . . . No."

"Right. Because you then claimed she didn't grab your shoulder but instead cut you with her sword."

"Yes."

"Are you sure?" asked Akira.

"I-it all happened too quickly."

"Why do you think a member of the imperial militia decided

to slash you? To poison the king's cup? But why would she do so if that meant killing you on the spot and then disposing of your body? When it would be easier to poison the cup in the kitchens? Forgive me, I'm getting carried away. Ah, where were we? Yes, she slashed you. Are you still not sure?"

The maid wet her lips and glanced toward the ministers. Without looking, Hesina could guess which one. "I'm sure now."

"Then let's have a demonstration." Akira gestured for a page.

"I never expected you to take me seriously," said the same marquis who'd invoked the imperial troupe.

Akira scratched his head. "Would you prefer to be taken as a joke next time?"

The man went red.

"Stand in front of me," Akira directed the page. "Yes, like that. Now start walking." Akira grabbed at his right side with his left hand and unsheathed. The imaginary blade flashed upward in a distinct bottom-right to upper-left movement.

"An excellent draw," appraised Sanjing. Then he stiffened. His mouth parted. Comprehension lanced Hesina a second later, and voices gusted through the court as Akira displayed the tear. Half the nobles, all trained in swordsmanship, nodded in affirmation.

The tear spanned from bottom left to upper right. It was the undeniable cut of a right-handed wielder.

But Mei was left-handed.

Hesina sagged like a flameless lantern. It was over. It was finally over. Everyone else seemed to think so too. All throughout the ranks, people were rising, muttering. Another case, debunked by Akira. But then:

"Enough!" boomed the director. "We've been strung along by this jester for far too long! Guards!"

Startled, Hesina rose as members of the imperial guard streamed through the doors and down the walk. They seized Mei by the arms, and the unit leader at their head approached with a dagger.

In a flash, Sanjing launched himself over the imperial box. He tucked and rolled as he hit the floor, then shoved to a sprint. Hesina performed the maneuver less gracefully and ran after her brother. Something was wrong. She didn't know what, but there shouldn't have been this many guards, or a dagger, a dagger that sliced into Mei's arm just as Sanjing reached the dais.

A roar of rage, a swish of a blade, a piggish squeal—the last sound that registered for Hesina before shouts overtook the court. The clamor of the ranks only faded to the background when Hesina reached the dais herself—in time to see Akira seize some noble's ivory cane. He raised it not a heartbeat too soon; Sanjing's *liuyedao* clanged off the ivory.

Sanjing. Akira. Fighting.

Why?

"Stand aside," Sanjing snarled. Belatedly, Hesina noticed the director cowering behind Akira's legs. He squealed as Sanjing broke away and bore down again. "Don't think I'll spare him . . . or you."

Akira met the blow, and the next. "You might regret this."

"I've never regretted anything less."

"If you kill him, he'll have won."

The word *kill* revitalized the director. He clutched at Akira's ankle. "Guards!"

Sanjing let out a cruel, low laugh. "I don't think that's his idea of winning."

Then he slid into the deadly quick-draw stance he was known for.

The sight shunted Hesina's spirit back into her; she grabbed her brother's saber by its base. The blade was dulled there, but still sharp. Warmth welled in her palm. "Step aside, Jing."

The pain in her hand couldn't compare to the pain of betrayal in her brother's eyes. For a split second, it didn't look like he'd spare her either. Then his face crumpled. "You're always protecting the wrong people."

His *liuyedao* fell to the ground.

The court breathed a collective sigh of relief—until Hesina picked the saber back up. The director scrambled away, but she swept right by him and strode to the guards.

"Stand aside."

"It's dangerous, *dianxia*."

"As is this," she said, pointing the blade, still red with her blood.

Slowly, the guards parted like reeds, revealing Mei.

The swordswoman clutched at her arm, her eyes fixed on the dagger, lying where it'd fallen, the blood on its blade already dry. Her gaze flickered to Hesina's. The russet of her eyes was fierce yet frightened, unapologetic yet guilty.

"Protect them," Mei whispered, right before the blade burst into blue fire.

TWENTY-ONE

They were in a position of power. They could have served the people. Instead, they served the emperor.

ONE of the ELEVEN on soothsayers

I'm willing to give them a second chance if they join us.

TWO of the ELEVEN on soothsayers

The court plunged into pandemonium. Nobles fled from the upper half, commoners from the bottom. Those sitting closest to the suspended aisle made leaps for it. Crowds ran, pushed, hobbled for the great doors only to collide with the director's reinforcements.

In the thick of it, the guards grabbed Hesina by the arms. She dug in her heels, screaming and biting as they pulled her away from Mei. Mistaking her ire for fear, the guards tried to reassure her: the sooth was in chains and would be executed by the coming dawn. Their words only incensed Hesina, and by the time they'd made it into the Hall of Everlasting Harmony, she'd punched one guard and clawed another. They were all too happy to pass her on to the maids.

The maids, too, tried to placate Hesina, but their eyes showed fear. Was her carefully pinned chignon coming apart, her powdered mask streaking? Had they finally seen the truth of her, and was it too ugly to behold?

So be it if it is.

Hesina flung off their hands and ran back toward the court, stopping when she physically couldn't break through the human river. Fleeing people streamed past her. She was their queen, but in this moment, she was nothing more than a pebble in their current, destined to be eroded by forces larger and older than herself.

This isn't how it's supposed to be. She lurched to the throne hall, down the enamel walk and through the faux gateways, up the dais and into the cold throne with the soapstone reredos at her back. *This isn't how it's supposed to end.*

The caisson ceiling overhead had been commissioned by emperors regarded as gods. Hesina was far from one. The throne hall was a temple. She was unworthy of worship. When she closed her eyes to it, she saw Mei's face. Heard her voice. Remembered all the times they'd spoken.

Realized all the things she had missed.

You're a sympathizer.

I'm not the only one.

How had she not put the pieces together?

Worse—why hadn't Sanjing told her?

She found her brother in his rooms, bent over his desk, the drawers pulled out and sifted through. He turned when she passed through the open doors, his lips parting, but she grabbed him by the collar before he could speak.

"Why didn't you say anything?"

Push me off, she willed him. *Shout at me.*

But all he did was stare, eyes empty and dull.

"What would it have changed?" he croaked. "What would it have changed?" he repeated, as if he actually wanted an answer. "We could have had the strongest case, the weakest case, and it'd all be the same. She was guilty. In their eyes, she was guilty from the moment of her birth."

Hesina couldn't accept this. She *wouldn't* accept this, truth be damned. "You could have said *something* to Akira."

"I didn't know if you trusted him."

"I said I did!"

"You hesitated."

"That wasn't—"

"I didn't know if I trusted *you*."

Hesina released Sanjing. Staggered back. Her blood had roared thick and furious only seconds ago, but just like that, his words drained her dry. "I never said I hated the soothsayers."

"You never said you didn't."

"I—" *I used one. I wept over her death. It still haunts me to this day.* The words caught in her chest, so used to being suppressed.

A snick came from behind. Slowly, Hesina turned.

Everyone was here. Lilian. Caiyan. Akira. Even Rou. They stood in the doorway, watching her come apart, their thoughts loud in the silence, crashing over her.

"Na-Na?" Lilian was the first to close the distance. She wrapped her arms around Hesina.

Hesina broke free. She wanted to storm the dungeons. Rescue Mei. She needed to, or she'd never free her conscience.

But Mei hadn't asked to be saved.

Her final request was *protect them.*

Hesina spun on Sanjing. "Does she have family?"

"Yes," he answered, still looking dazed.

"Take me to them."

His eyes cleared, and he nodded.

Hesina glanced out his windows, to the sun hung like a silver disk in the sky. The taste of ashes returned to her tongue. They had to act quickly. If the people had gutted the Silver Iris because they'd *heard* about a vanishing village, they would do much, much worse now that hundreds of eyes had confirmed a sooth's existence in the imperial court.

"*Now*," she ordered Sanjing, a plan coming together.

He'd already advanced to the door. "Step aside," he barked at the others, fingers wrapping around his hilt.

No one moved.

"We're coming with you," said Caiyan.

Sanjing started to unsheathe. Hesina stopped him. "It's not safe," she said to the others.

"*You* can come with us," Sanjing said to Akira. "As for the rest of you, give me a good reason why I should trust you. Then prove to me you won't slow us down."

"We care about your sister as much as you do," said Caiyan. A vein twitched in Sanjing's neck, and Hesina clutched his arm tighter despite her stinging palms. "And you may need more than two people. Abandon us, if we slow you down."

"Fine," Hesina said. It was decided. Sanjing might not have trusted them, but she could—with the one exception.

She turned on Rou. "Why are you here?"

"B-because—"

"Are you a sympathizer?" Sanjing pressed.

Rou swallowed and nodded. "My mother always says we fear what we don't know. She says it's why people stay away from her and spread rumors about her face. I . . . I don't think I'll ever fully understand what it's like for the sooths, but I can understand a little."

Hesina exchanged a glance with Sanjing. Rou was right. They feared the things they didn't know. They made them less than human.

And Caiyan was right too. Time was of the essence. They would need all the help they could get.

"Change your robes," Sanjing finally said to Rou. "I can spot that color from a *li* away."

* * *

They emerged from the secret passageway and into the abandoned tavern, then stepped straight into the midday hustle. Wheelbarrows and sedans clogged the limestone alleyways ribbed with vendors and their stands. A number of young men and women milled through the streets with rucksacks and bedrolls strapped to their shoulders. The first wave of civil service examinees. They were both a blessing and a curse, stopping every few steps to admire some cultural relic, but also helping Hesina's group blend in.

That didn't deter the vendors from foisting their wares onto them.

"Bream!" cried a man, shoving a fistful of the iridescent fish into Rou's terrified face. "Fresh bream!"

"*Hongmu* coffins! Genuine redwood! Buy one for your aging parents today!"

Hesina took their harassment as a good sign. No one would be hawking coffins or fish if news of today's court had reached them. They had to find Mei's parents before the mob did.

Sanjing led the way to an apothecary on the far edge of the western market sector, squashed between an antique shop and a wine seller. A man stood behind the medicine counter, weighing piles of dried herbs and fanning the knob-handled *shaguo* on the burner beside him.

"Good afternoon," he said as they entered. "Are you looking for a preprepared decoction, or . . ."

His voice trailed off as Hesina lowered her hood. His eyes widened to the whites, and before she could stop him, he thumped to his knees and flattened into *koutou*. "*Dianxia!*"

"What's going on?" A woman emerged from the back cellar with a clay jar under her arm. Strands of gray hair escaped the wrap of her linen kerchief. Her russet eyes shot to her husband, prostrate on the ground.

"You fool! Have you forgotten about your arthritis?"

"T-ting . . ." Trembling, the man inclined his head in Hesina's direction, keeping his gaze respectfully lowered.

The woman looked directly at her. "What do you want?"

Hesina hadn't thought of what she'd say. How did she break it to them that their daughter was to die at sunrise by a thousand cuts?

Directly, perhaps, as Caiyan did. "Your daughter bled in front of the court."

The father fainted.

The mother stood, still as a figurine. Then, with a crack, the jar under her arm split into a dozen hovering shards as if it'd been smashed. She seized one of the pieces and dropped by her husband, lifting him by the hair, exposing his throat, slashing toward it with that winking ceramic lip—

The shard struck the wood of Akira's rod.

He wrenched it away and swept the rest of the shards out of reach. "Let's not be so hasty," he said as Hesina struggled to make sense of what she'd seen.

Sooth work . . . Her husband . . . She'd just tried to kill him—

"Take me to my child," said Mei's mother. "I'll come willingly. Take me, but let me spare him."

Spare him.

Understanding stabbed Hesina, a knife wrenched sideways by guilt. A person was a soothsayer by blood, and blood was passed from parent to child. By coming here, by declaring Mei a sooth, she was essentially sentencing the entire family to death by a thousand cuts. She'd forgotten because she could afford to forget, having never lived a life of terror and fear herself.

Hesina crouched, met the woman's eye, and made her voice steady even as she shook inside. "I'm here to lead you to safety."

"Lies."

"No." Her brother joined her, his expression strained. It must have cost him to be here instead of with Mei. "It's the truth. It was her wish."

Recognition sparked in those russet eyes, lighting into rage. "*You*," hissed the mother, and Hesina flinched even though the anger wasn't directed at her. "I warned her that day. I told her not to follow you out of this apothecary."

Sanjing stilled to stone—as did Hesina, when distant shouts floated through the oil-paper windows.

"Milady," Caiyan murmured in warning.

Hesina seized Mei's mother by the arms. If a sooth could break a jar by moving it into a future state, maybe a sooth could break Hesina too. She didn't fully understand their powers.

She didn't care.

"Mei's been put into the *tianlao* cells of Heavenly Sin," she said, enunciating each word clearly. "Cells that not even my master key can open, patrolled by a dozen of the elite guards at all times.

"Tonight, I will go to her. No matter what, I will tell her I carried

255

out her last wish and moved both of you to safety." Hesina released Mei's mother from her hold, but not her stare. "I hope I won't have to lie."

Then Hesina rose. Straightened. Exhaled. "The people will be scared. Their fear will overpower their humanity. You may remember some as neighbors, friends, and customers, but they won't remember you. To them, you'll just be monsters. Maggots." Her voice fell quiet. "Something to be destroyed."

Outside, the shouts drew closer.

"There is no safety in this city," Mei's mother finally said. Her gaze flickered around their little shop, to the wall of medicine cabinets, the red paper cutouts pasted on the rafters for luck. They'd carved out this fragile existence for themselves. Hesina was taking it away.

"Maybe not," she said. "But I know of a place where you'll be safe for the time being."

"I won't hide and leave the others to die."

Convince her. Lie if you must. "Then we'll lead them to safety as well."

The shouts turned their way.

"Come," Hesina begged. "Please."

Dismay strangled her as Mei's mother turned away. But then the woman slapped her husband into semiconsciousness, coaxing him up to his feet. She draped his arm over her. "He's not as light as he looks," she warned as Lilian took the other.

"No man is," Lilian grumbled.

They went through the back cellar and out the half door, checking both ways before slipping into the alleyway. They were but twenty paces down when shouts erupted from the apothecary.

Hesina quickened her lead.

"Where are we going?" Rou asked as she took them past the tavern from which they'd come.

She let the way answer for her.

They went down a set of crumbling, moss-covered steps and came to the shrine. Not the imperial-sanctioned one where commoners went to pray for healthy children and grandchildren, but a dilapidated structure that kings and queens before Hesina had considered tearing down and replacing with a public well. Ministers of Rites had advised against it, citing the presence of vengeful spirits Hesina had never encountered herself. Only thieves visited this shrine, and they'd pilfered everything but the praying mats, furred with mold, and the altarpiece, veiled in spider silk. The tablet underneath was etched with strange symbols, but Hesina's heart stopped as symbols became words.

To the gods who betrayed us.

The characters were complex Yan. Just like the original *Tenets*, the shrine must have existed three centuries ago. Everything in this kingdom was older than Hesina expected, and with a spurt of vexation, she yanked aside the hemp skirt encircling the altar base, revealing a hole in the ground.

They crawled in one after another, with Hesina going last. She fixed the altar skirt behind her before turning, momentarily disoriented by the dark. A hand caught her wrist, and she followed its pull down the steps, bumping into Akira once they reached flat ground. Rou complained about the low visibility. Hesina, red in the cheeks, thanked it.

"Hold on to the person in front of you," she ordered, then strode down the very passageway in which she'd lost her way so many years ago. After her father had rescued her, she had returned, determined to learn it once and for all. Something about being here again, in this place where she'd conquered her fears, made her bolder.

Rasher.

The need to do the right thing took root in her mind, and as they went down a slope, the tunnel yawning ever wider, Hesina faced Mei's mother. "Tell us where the others are."

The population pockets of sooths, she learned, were scattered all across the imperial city. Hesina was suddenly glad the others had insisted on coming. Once they reached the cavern, she turned on her group.

"Do you all remember how to get here?"

They nodded.

"Rou, gather the sooths in the red-light district." Her half brother flushed, and Hesina backtracked. "Lilian."

"On it."

"Sanjing and Akira, to the trading sector. Caiyan—"

"I'm coming with you," he said, his voice leaving no room for argument.

Hesina shook her head. "I'm going to the moat."

"Then so am I."

"No."

"And I," said Mei's mother, coming up beside her.

Absolutely not. "Neither of you," Hesina said at the same time Caiyan said, "That won't be necessary," which Hesina found dreadfully hypocritical.

"You don't know their faces," said Mei's mother. "And they won't trust you."

"Then give us a sign, a code, something that will *make* them trust us," said Hesina.

Mei's mother considered for a long moment. "Tell them the crane has died."

"What about me?" piped Rou.

"Stay here to receive the newcomers and keep order," said Hesina. Rou nodded. If only all her brothers were as obliging.

Together, Caiyan and Hesina headed for the main boulevard, where mobs barged into shops, demanding that everyone submit to a cut on the palm, while the city guards stood by, letting it happen—condoning it, probably. Disgust rippled through Hesina, but Caiyan tugged her down a side alleyway before she could act on it, and soon, they were at the moat.

It snaked through the market sector and the residential wards like a silver chain strung with small barges and passenger rafts. The pushers whistled and hollered their fares, blessedly oblivious to what was happening elsewhere in the city.

Hesina wished she were a pusher. She wished to be the one wearing the broad-rimmed straw hat, leaning idle against a long bamboo pole, and not the one tasked with marching up to a raft and blurting out, "The crane is dead."

The raft rocked as the pusher straightened. "Eh? Is it now?" Hesina held her breath, but the man simply sang, "A shame, a shame. But there are many more to be seen, just around the bend. I can take you to them for two *banliang*. Consider it a deal . . . just two bronze!"

It sounded like a lovely deal. Hesina hated to turn it down.

"It really is a fine day for a ride!" the pusher called as Caiyan ushered her away.

"We should try under the bridges, milady." Caiyan nodded at the one up ahead, and Hesina discerned a group of workers sitting under the arch. "It's more efficient—"

His hand tore from hers as a gaggle of giggling noblewomen swept between them, wrapped in rabbit-fur-lined cloaks dyed in sepias, grays, and roses—all the colors that Lilian had made fashionable this winter season. A mule-pulled wagon stacked high with porcelains barreled by next.

"Caiyan!" Hesina rose to the balls of her feet, relaxing when she spotted her brother's topknot beyond the rattling pots.

He would catch up to her. Alone, Hesina hurried onward to the bridge, down the pebbled slope, and through the frozen cattails. She ducked under the spandrel arch and stumbled into the company of men and women. There were six in all, either drinking wine, playing the trick-taking card game of *madiao,* or both.

She interrupted with, "The crane is dead."

And now, thanks to her, so was the conversation.

A young man lowered his hand of cards, setting it facedown as if he expected to return to the game. "Who are you?"

Hesina ignored the question. "Your lives are in danger. You need to follow me to safety *now.* Gather the others, and I'll explain as we go."

"Really, A-Lan?" sneered one of the women as the young man pushed to his feet. "We don't even know who she is! Lose the hood," she snapped at Hesina.

"Bring the others first," Hesina snapped back.

The one called A-Lan left and returned with three men. One had a mass of angry-red scar tissue in place of his right eye. Hesina drew back as he leaned in and sniffed.

"A-Lan claims we have a brethren among us. A brethren who hides her face." He chuckled as she took another step back. "There's nothing to be scared of, darling. I know all the people in this city."

He made a grab at her hood. Hesina, seeing the attack from a *li* away, snatched and shoved two of his fingers back, wringing out a howl. She dropped his hand like a hot coal, and he cradled it to his chest and laughed.

"A little skittish, aren't we?"

He whistled. In an instant, someone grabbed Hesina's arms and yanked them behind her. She bucked, but the person was too tall, and her head thumped against a chest.

"Skittish, so skittish. Why?" mused One-Eye. "If you're really one of us—"

He stripped away her hood.

"—then you should know we have only one enemy." His left eye studied her, slow and thoughtful. A smile spread over his pock-marked face. "And that enemy would be you, *dianxia*. Well, well." He twirled one of his good fingers, and the person holding her spun her around for the others to see.

Cards went down faceup. Wine *jiutan* overturned as people leapt to their feet.

"What do you know?" said One-Eye, licking the pad of his thumb. "It seems that we've caught ourselves the queen."

Hesina was in danger, but so were her attackers. She'd made a promise to Mei and Mei's mother, and through the thrum of her panic, she told the situation as she had before.

She finished to laughter.

One picked up a rock. Another seized a piece of frozen driftwood. The others pushed up their sleeves, crowding in, forcing Hesina back until the underside of the bridge curved cold against her spine.

Someone swung the driftwood. She dodged right. The blow connected anyway, and white fire blazed from Hesina's temple to neck.

Insults. Jeers. They'd predicted her dodge. Of course they had. They were sooths. Hesina was a descendant of the Eleven. Worse, she'd claimed that they were all going to die unless they followed her. It was no surprise they didn't trust her.

The laughter died, and they began discussing how they should kill her. Slowly or quickly. Painfully or humiliatingly. Their words should have inflamed Hesina, but her limbs were leaden with defeat. She didn't fear death any more than she feared life, where every choice of hers determined the life and death of others. And if she was anything like her father, maybe she wouldn't die at all.

But as one of the sooths lifted a rock, her heart ricocheted against her ribs.

Let it end quickly.

"Go on," came a sudden voice from behind them. "Kill her."

The rock wielder froze. So did Hesina's heart.

Because she knew that voice.

It was Caiyan's.

TWENTY-TWO

The past is destined to repeat unless we learn from it.

ONE of the ELEVEN on histories

Read. Need I say more?

TWO of the ELEVEN on histories

W ho the hell are you?" growled the woman.

"Kill her," Caiyan repeated, a calculating glint in his eyes as he neared. "Go on. Finish it."

Hesina's stomach fell and kept on falling. She couldn't move. Couldn't think. Then instinct kicked in. It didn't matter if Caiyan was giving up on her; she needed to protect him.

"*Run!*" she screamed. He was no Sanjing. He wouldn't be able to defend himself if they attacked.

But Caiyan did the opposite of run; he came closer. The edge of his black cloak spilled off the pebbled banks and trailed into the icy current. "Bring the fury of the kingdom to your doorstep, to your husbands and wives and parents. Have your little bonfire now, and sizzle later like moths in a flame."

Hesina almost wept. Caiyan was here to *save* her—with sense, of all weapons. Elevens, they were both fools.

"There we go again," sighed One-Eye. Hesina's heart filled with dread as he limped up to Caiyan. The sooth was a whole head shorter, but his slight frame crackled with suppressed energy. "Lofty proclamations of doomsday. Grand, just grand. But I believe you were asked a question."

"I am the viscount."

"*The* viscount? Was *a* viscount not good enough for you?" More guffaws. "Today certainly has been full of surprises. First a queen, now *the* high and mighty viscount, all so concerned about our well-being." One-Eye turned and threw his hands wide. "I believe our futures have changed, brethren!"

Earsplitting laughter met his words.

"Yes. I am the viscount," said Caiyan, ever composed. "But are you even soothsayers? The future is hurtling down these city streets as we speak. Why don't you look for yourselves?"

More laughter.

"I See," came a whisper.

The others turned to look at A-Lan. He'd gone very pale. "I See."

Silence.

"Drop the stone," Caiyan ordered. "Drop the wood."

Hesina waited for them to laugh as they had before.

Instead, One-Eye nodded at the others.

Driftwood and stone fell to the ground.

"Now release your queen, and follow her."

* * *

Hesina didn't pass out from the blow to her head, but she almost did from relief when she saw that Lilian, Sanjing, and Akira had returned safely to the cavern, along with the sooths they'd convinced to come. Rou was helping some settle down with the scanty belongings they'd managed to toss together. Others milled about, examining the torches mounted on the slate walls. Hesina had been awed by the torches, too, when she'd first found this place. They never burned out, never flickered, their flame sustained by something more than the usual sulfur and saltpeter. Now, her hairs rose as she watched them burn. The flames were unnatural, just like her father.

Tamping down the thought—and the bile that rose with it—she conducted a count. Her heart sank. They'd convinced thirty-eight to come. In a city of one hundred thousand, this was likely a small fraction of the sooths.

Lilian joined her. "Many didn't want to follow."

Hopefully many had also hidden themselves so well they simply couldn't be found.

"They'll need more provisions," said Sanjing from her left.

"Should I rob some merchants?" came Akira's voice from behind.

"I forbid it," Hesina said at the same time Rou said, "I can go. N-not rob merchants," he stammered when they gawked at him. "A vendor is indebted to me, so I can get us free supplies."

Rou left, and Lilian, Akira, and Sanjing dispersed to tend to the people. Caiyan came up beside Hesina.

"How is your head?"

"Fine," she lied, wincing as he examined the knot swelling at her temple.

"It missed the artery."

"I don't think I'd be standing if it hadn't."

Concern pleated Caiyan's brow. "Be careful, milady," he finally said. "Always assess the situation and your audience first. Then tell them the narrative they tell themselves."

"You're right." Hesina picked at a loose thread in the brocade of her sleeve. Once, she'd envied Caiyan's intelligence. Theory came to him easily. So did reading massive tomes and calculating impossible sums on the abacus. But it was hard to be envious of someone who learned for the love of learning, and she admired Caiyan for always admitting ignorance whenever admission was due. She still struggled with that.

"There's still so much I don't understand," she confessed. "I want to help, not make things worse."

"There will be time to learn, milady."

Would there be? Mei's execution was at dawn. After that, it was a matter of time before word reached the Kendi'an Crown Prince. Once Siahryn realized Yan was killing sooths instead of enslaving them, he'd see Hesina's threats of harnessing their powers for what they were: hot air. Kendi'a would attack their borders again. That would trigger another wave of anti-sooth sentiment. More anti-sooth sentiment would lead to more Meis.

Everything would crumble. Everything already was. Just considering the chain of events crushed Hesina's will. "I can't be the only one, right? To realize there's something wrong with this kingdom?"

"I don't think so."

Caiyan didn't sound nearly as confident as Hesina would have liked. "Then why hasn't anything changed?" she asked. "It's been three whole centuries since the fall of the relic dynasty, but everyone . . . everyone's still the same."

"Memories are short. History plays out in cycles. Tables turn; the sufferers rise and make their oppressors suffer. This is simply human nature."

"But that's terrible." Terrible to be a sooth. Terrible to be a human. Terrible no matter how Hesina looked at it.

"Stone-head!" Lilian's voice echoed across the cavern. "A little less pontificating and a little more help, please? I think this man has a broken wrist."

"Excuse me, milady." Caiyan went to his twin, leaving Hesina on the periphery. She wanted to help, too, but the encounter under the bridge had shaken her. How could she do anything when she represented everything the sooths feared?

What would Father do?

Simple. He'd be himself. Elders regarded him as a son; grown men and women regarded him as a brother. Children chased him, begging for a ride on his shoulders, and he'd always oblige, sometimes carrying one on each just like he'd carried Sanjing and Hesina. He treated them like his own. He told them the same truths. The same lies.

Hesina's hands closed into fists. He had no reason to tell the people about his immortality. But he should have told *her.* She was his daughter. He had named her and raised her. She deserved his honesty more, for example, than the little girl who tugged on her sleeve.

"When can we go back home?" asked the girl. Her hair had been parted lovingly into three pigtails for luck, and a jade mandala rested against a padded coat with pink cloth-nub buttons.

"Ailin!" A woman ran over, scooping the girl into her arms, shielding her from Hesina. "D-*dianxia.*"

Hesina should have acknowledged the woman. She should have soothed her fears, told her that she'd never harm a child. But the girl's innocent question had netted her, drawing her into the harsh reality she had created.

When can we go back home?

She passed the mother and child. She passed the group of raft pushers. Their scowls glanced right off her.

When would these people be able to return to their lives?

Would the commoners notice their absence? Would they guess that the missing *mantou* vendor or the sedan carrier had actually been a sooth? Perhaps Hesina had saved them. Perhaps she'd also condemned them to an eternity in hiding.

Different conversations and voices all washed into one, asking the same question:

When can we go back home?

Hesina backed into the cavern side, then into a random tunnel opening. The voices eventually faded, but she kept going, sloshing through pools of stagnant rainwater, pushing onward until she came to a dead end of stones, perfectly stacked to form a wall.

Who had sealed this passageway? And why? What lay beyond?

Hesina froze. The cavern was somewhere beneath the eastern market sector. She'd come a long way from it. In fact, she must have been nearing the city walls.

Aboveground, the hour struck. Each note was muffled, dulled by layers upon layers of earth, yet the air about Hesina vibrated as if the gong tower was directly above her.

Four notes passed.

Could it be . . . that this tunnel ran all the way to the city walls?

Was *this* how the Eleven had breached them?

Impossible. The Eleven were heroes. They hadn't brought an entire era to an end by worming through underground tunnels. No, the passageways were Hesina and her father's little secret, a puzzle they had worked on together between the tedium of ruling and imperial lessons.

Unless their cherished secrets were sketched out of lies too.

Hesina shivered, shrinking into herself, but that brought her closer to the ache in her heart.

I miss you. I miss you, even if you were a lie. I hate the truth of you.

I hate you.

"I hate you," she whispered aloud. "I hate you." She whirled and screamed into the yawning tunnel way. "*I hate you!*"

Her words echoed back threefold.

She ran. Just as she had that day in the gardens, she ran as if she could outstrip the terror of finding her father's body. Then, the ground had been soft and squishy underfoot, summer nectar florid in her nose, tears in her eyes, and disbelief in her chest.

Now, anger drove the ground hard into her heels. She pounded down the tunnel. Flew past the branch she was supposed to take, stumbled blindly up a set of stairs, tripping more than once on her wet skirts, but never falling. The pathway narrowed. She didn't stop, and her shoulders scraped against the stone.

The bottleneck widened abruptly, spitting her into an open space. Gasping, Hesina looked around, trying to regain her bearings.

She was in another cavern. Again, it was lit with torches, and again, the flames didn't waver in the dank. Alkaline water and coppery earth staled the air—and the smell of something else.

A man-made tang . . . a piney spice with a hard-candy finish.

Varnish. The place reeked of varnish and cinnabar. It reminded Hesina of the throne hall, with its varnished dais of black lacquer and ruby-red cinnabar pillars.

Gingerly, she picked her way to the cavern walls and placed her hands on them. Her palms met cold, slick stone.

Soapstone. A whole expanse of it, utterly smooth except for the seam where one panel met the next, and the next, and the next, and the next, and the next, and the next, and the next, and the next, and the next, and the next—and the next.

Hesina jerked her hands away with a sharp intake of breath.

Twelve panels in all.

Only one twelve-paneled screen existed in the entire palace, and that was the reredos that rose tall behind the throne. If this was it, then that meant—

She took a step back.

—this place smelled like the throne hall because *the throne hall lay beyond this wall.*

Hesina had just entered the Eastern Palace complex undetected. Anyone could have done the same. Her heartbeat raced, and when the torchlight flickered, she spun, convinced that someone had snuck up on her.

But no one was there.

In the breathing silence, every song, every performance, every story told about the Eleven rushed back to Hesina.

They breached the city walls. They stormed the palace gates. They beheaded the emperor where he sat on his throne.

How? generations of scholars had asked.

Now she knew how.

She returned to the wall. Her legs weakened with disbelief. A hundred times, she must have sat with this screen at her back, and a hundred times, she'd dismissed it as yet another gaudy antique from the relic days. She never would have guessed what lay behind it. Neither had the last emperor. How shocked he must have been, when One of the Eleven materialized out of nowhere. Hesina could imagine the iron tang of his fear. She could taste it—because she'd bitten her cheek.

There was writing on the walls. She rubbed at her eyes; the words remained. Columns of characters, crawling down the soapstone like ants, the calligraphy shaky, as if the writer were unfamiliar with the strokes.

But Hesina knew them well. This was simplified Yan, the language of her era. Without realizing it, she'd already read the rightmost column.

TODAY, A RULER WILL DIE.

The crackling of the torches quieted. The distant tunnel wind sang to a stop. Woozy, Hesina leaned on the soapstone. Her forearms bracketed the words.

TODAY, A RULER WILL DIE.

She'd found him. The murderer was the writer of this line; no ruler of the new era aside from her father had "died" before his time. But she didn't want to read on. It wasn't too late to walk away and pretend she'd never seen this.

Knowledge is truth, Little Bird. Those who refuse to learn live in a world of falsity.

Hesina let out a sob of a laugh before choking down the tears. She'd believed him. Deceit was in her nature, but for her father, she had tried to be better. She'd chased the truth for him, even though it hurt. What reason did she have to chase it now?

To be better than him.

Her arms trembled as she pushed away from the wall.

To be better for no one but yourself.

Her spine twinged as she straightened.

TODAY, A RULER WILL DIE.

She took a deep breath and read on.

Nine says it must be my hand. I said that he'd be better suited for the task. That got a rare laugh out of him.

"I belong in the dark," he said. "You belong in the light. I can end our villains, but you must end the era, starting with the emperor."

I told him he wasn't making any sense. Even now, writing this out in an attempt to clear my mind, I still don't understand why it must be me. He claims the people will follow me because I have a good heart, but we both know Six has the best heart out of us all.

"It's because of your childish idolization of the truth," Two says. "This world has gone to rot. The throne needs someone pure."

"It's because you know what you want," says Three, "and how to get it."

"It's because we believe in you," says Six. "We were orphans and consorts and fallen princes. You gathered us and gave us something to live for. When we were reeling over our losses and on the verge of scattering, you held us together. You will do the same for the people."

They make me feel like some sort of god. Maybe I am—I'm definitely not human anymore. But at least they know me, the real me. The people don't—and won't, not after I kill the emperor of their nightmares. I'll be given a hero's narrative. There will be songs and operas and epic poems composed for this very moment, and none of them will mention the scared boy, the shaking boy, the boy who wanted to drop his too-heavy sword and walk away.

But I can't walk away. I've given up my mortality to come this far. We all have sacrificed so much. Our fallen ones are watching from the heavens above. Their deaths must not be for naught.

All I want is my name. I want it back, if just for a moment. Nine reminds us that we don't belong to ourselves anymore, that we forfeited our identities the moment we took on the people's cause. But right now, right here, I wish to be remembered as myself. I wish to remember the others not as Two, Three, Four, Five, Six, Seven, Eight, Nine, Ten, or Eleven, but as Moxia, Jin, Wang A-bao, Wang A-dou, Su Ennei, Zifen, Guo Xiao, Shi Ling, Kaishen, and Sima Lan.

May we go down as legends.

May we live on by the truth.

Li Wen
One of the Eleven
Year 000

Hesina's legs gave.

I've given up my mortality to come this far, One had written.

She fell to her knees, but instead of meeting hard stone, they sank into wet dirt. She was back at her father's coffin side, the beat of his heart against her cheek.

Father. Immortal.

She was in her room, spinning her mother's silver lock, the metal bands slick under her fingertips.

0
0
0

000. The start of the new era. The day One of the Eleven was born as a ruler. The year her father had been born as a ruler too.

She was eight years old and sat on her father's knee, sheltered in his candlelit study. *Why did the Eleven restart the calendar, Father?*

So that all lives could be reborn. Young, old, rich, poor, male, female—we all became children of the new era.

She was reading the *Tenets*, comforted and unsettled by the kinship she'd felt with a revolutionary, a murderer, his beliefs echoing with hers.

"We will all be reborn as equals." —ONE *of the* ELEVEN *on the new era*

Knowledge is truth, her father had said. *Those who refuse to learn live in a world of falsity.*

"Knowledge is truth." —ONE *of the* ELEVEN *on edification of commoners*

When you become queen, Little Bird, you must never abandon your people, even if they appear to have abandoned you.

"A ruler who abandons their people is no ruler at all." —ONE *of the* ELEVEN *on monarchs*

The best way of controlling a person is by reading their heart. And the clearest window to any heart is prejudice and assumption.

"Our prejudices and assumptions reveal our true selves." —ONE *of the* ELEVEN *on human nature*

Hesina let their voices fuse. Two halves of a whole. Two lies of a truth.

Li Wen.

One of the Eleven.

Actor, legend, sooth-slayer.

King of the new era.

Her father.

TWENTY-THREE

Everyone, regardless of gender or social standing, will have a
fair chance at education and occupation.
                        ONE *of the* ELEVEN *on the new era*

It'll be something spectacular. Trust me.
                        TWO *of the* ELEVEN *on the new era*

Hesina didn't know how long she stayed like this—on her knees, a thousand of her father's gestures soaring past her as she plummeted, a million of his words kiting above her head as she fell further and further from the sky of his love.

She had loved a mask. She rejected the man beneath.

She rejected herself.

Betrayal buzzed up her veins, stinging. Her insides erupted with hives. Hesina scratched until it hurt to scratch, then curled in on herself with no intentions of uncurling ever again. *Here lies Queen Yan Hesina*, the histories would say. *Lost her way in a tunnel and died from dehydration.* They'd never know the real story—she'd died under the crushing weight of the truth—and it'd be for the better.

But the voices came before death could. Distant, at first. Hesina prayed they would go away. Then they grew closer, louder, until she could make out the words—and their speakers.

Caiyan, Lilian, Akira, Sanjing, and Rou.

They were searching for her.

She couldn't be found. Not like this.

Hesina made herself stand and went out to meet them.

"Where have you been?" demanded Sanjing when she emerged from the narrow bottleneck of stone.

"We looked all over for you," said Lilian, rushing over to clutch her.

"You were missing for an hour," Caiyan added gravely.

Rou shivered. "We hit so many dead ends."

"I—I got lost." That was true. "I . . . I didn't know what happened." That was true too. For a flash of a second, she imagined telling them the *whole* truth. She craved to. She dreaded to. She yearned for their acceptance and shunned it at the same time. Because if they accepted her, she might too.

But she wasn't ready. She couldn't even think of the blood in her veins without wishing to drain it.

Caiyan suggested taking her to the Imperial Doctress. Sanjing snarled something back. Lilian smacked him, and Rou mentioned staggering their departures. Somehow, the argument ended with Akira leading her away after assuring the others that he knew the way back to the palace.

"I don't actually know the way," he said under his breath once they'd left the tunnels for the open streets.

Hesina directed him to the abandoned tavern and showed him how to dribble water down the guardian lion's throat. But when it came time to descend into the passageway, her chest constricted as if they were going underwater. Each breath felt like taking in a lungful of memories. She must have made it a total of five steps before she heard her father's voice.

Watch the drop, Little Bird.

She went sprawling so fast, dry heaving, that Akira couldn't catch her. He crouched beside her, but she turned away—only to heave again. Her eyes watered with embarrassment as he held back her hair. She could never be a girl who blushed over simple things. Not as queen, not as . . .

She swallowed and squeezed her eyes shut.

Not as the daughter of One of the Eleven.

Murderer. Hero. Monster. Savior.

She hurled again.

"I learned something about my father," she gasped throatily when she was finished. At the very least, she owed Akira an explanation after nearly spewing on him. "But I need time . . ."

To accept? To heal? To vomit some more?

"To think," she finished.

Akira nodded, then guided her back to her chambers. There, he made his one and only demand: that she drink a goblet of water.

"All of it," he insisted when Hesina tried to get away with half. "Your insides need it."

What her insides needed was a break from the truth. Her father had the face of a boy, yet was apparently three centuries old. He'd lived during the relic reign. Lived during the hunt for the elixir of immortality, which the Eleven had denounced. But if Hesina knew anything about the Eleven, it was that they did not do as they said.

She downed the rest of the water, knocking back a resurgence of acid. That seemed to satisfy Akira. He turned to go.

"Akira?"

He stopped.

She wanted to ask him to stay. She could have drunk a second goblet, just for him. But in the end, Hesina said a quiet "never mind" and let him go.

Alone, she took a long, shaky breath. Then she selected a lantern with very little wick left, tucked a medicinal candle that the Imperial Doctress had prescribed for insomnia into her sleeve, and threw on the thinnest of her winter cloaks.

I am the daughter of One, she repeated to herself as she made for the dungeons. She liked to think she shuddered a little less each time. *I am the daughter of One*. She passed through the facades and the Eleven's stories—her *father's* stories—stitched upon the silk. *I am the daughter of One*.

And she was on her way to see a sooth.

Tianlao was a misnomer. It literally meant prison in the sky. But these cells had never seen the light of day and were reserved for those who'd committed the highest treason. Hesina shivered as she descended. This was the underworld in flesh, a place to rot and die. The dark wound around her, judging her with its sightless eyes.

You belong here, don't you?

The stairs bottomed out, bringing her before an arcade of black-iron gateways. A line of bronze-mailed guards stepped forward and bowed.

"Take me to the soothsayer."

"*Dianxia*—"

"The people are scared. I'm here to see for myself that she is secured."

They insisted that the sooth was, indeed, secured and warned her against proceeding farther.

Hesina didn't speak. She used her silence to bleed their persuasion dry. Then, when they had nothing left to say, she took one step forward.

They reacted as she'd predicted, immediately circling her, their gazes fine-combing. They'd be patting her down if she weren't their queen. But she had nothing to hide. She was weaponless; she wasn't about to murder her elite guard. She was keyless; the *tianlao* key was melted down after every execution and reforged the dawn of the next. She gave them no reason to turn her away, and at last they escorted her down the arcade.

Doorways opened in the stone, leading to the crypts. The relic emperors had crammed them full of commoners suspected as rebels, left to defecate and die on top of one another. Hesina's hand involuntarily rose to her heart. The emperors had committed unspeakable crimes. But her father—*One*—had too.

At the arcade's end, five guards posted themselves at the final gateway, while two ducked under a smaller archway with her, leading her to the cell.

It was a protrusion of solid stone, curved like a kiln with thin, vertical slats carved at its base. When Hesina envisioned Mei carrying on in that lightless space, her throat closed. She set her puttering lantern to the ground and reached into her sleeve, drawing out the replacement candle. The guards at her sides didn't move.

As she transferred the dying flame to the candlewick, Hesina launched a volley of questions. What kind of stone was the cell made out of? How durable was it? Was there enough oxygen within? Was there any way Mei could hurt herself?

"I can't have her dying before the execution," she added sharply, detesting the words.

The guards assured her the sooth had no chance of dying before the execution. There was enough air in the cell, her hands were bound, the walls were padded. The medicinal candle burned as they spoke, and Hesina took shallow breaths. With luck, Mei would know to do the same by seeing into the future.

And the future arrived—quickly. The guards buckled, put to sleep by the candle fumes. Hesina lugged them to the wall as quietly as she could, trying not to alert the ones standing guard outside. By the time she managed to prop them in a sitting position, she'd gulped several mouthfuls of air and her own head spun.

Hurriedly, she unfastened her cloak. She drew it over the guards' helmeted heads and slid the lantern beneath the silken canopy, where the fumes might be somewhat contained. Then she knelt by the cell, pressing her lips to the slats. "Your parents are safe. So are many others."

Her anxiety swelled with the silence. Was Mei gagged? Hurt? Unconscious?

There came some hmming, some shuffling, a quiet breath, and—Hesina's heart jumped—words.

"Thank you." Muffled, quiet, but audible.

Hearing Mei's voice brought Hesina little comfort. In the morning, the swordswoman would be cut a thousand times, kept alive to the very last slice by a silt-coated knife that would clog the wounds and prevent them from flaming. Mei would die because of the Eleven's *Tenets*, and because Hesina was a queen. She couldn't bring down entire kingdoms for a single soul. She could do all she wanted in the dark, but in the light, she had to choose her people. She always had to choose her people.

Still, desperation made Hesina forget herself. "I've put the guards out," she whispered, tripping over her tongue in a rush to speak. "I can try to think of a way to distract the others. But I can't open this cell. Can you . . . can you do anything like the girl who manipulated the sand?"

"Hold out your hand."

Hesina did as Mei instructed. She bit back a gasp as her hand vanished. She could still *feel* it, but it had melted seamlessly into the cell's shadow, which had simultaneously grown bigger. She wiggled her fingers, and they remerged.

"All light dims," said Mei. "So it's as simple as moving light to a future state of darkness."

Simple to a sooth, perhaps. "That's how you make your shadows."

"Yes, that's how I make my shadows. But light and dark are no match for rock."

"It's possible though? To change the stone?"

"Yes. Some sooths were so powerful that they could See the future right up to the world's end. They could turn anything into ash, stone included." Mei paused. "But they don't exist anymore."

The blood in Hesina's wrists throbbed. "Because of the purge."

"Yes, but not in the way you think. Do you know why our blood flames?"

Hesina shook her head before remembering Mei couldn't see.

But Mei had already Seen. "It's because our power *is* a flame," she answered without missing a beat. "But untamed power is like a flame that has overtaken its wick. It may illuminate; it can also destroy. Every sooth used to undergo years of training at the imperial academies, learning to tame the flame. The purge killed that institution. Now, the powerful ones can't access their powers without literally burning up."

There were other limitations to what sooths could do. They

couldn't See their own futures, and the futures they did See came in brief flashes, one in a hundred possibilities. The most talented sooths could narrow a hundred down to ten, but the future was volatile whenever people were involved. Predicting the fate of a kingdom was a tall order.

"It's why the emperor's sooths failed to foresee the overthrow," explained Mei. "The Eleven were supposed to die, but in the darkest of moments, humans surprise."

Mei was trying to distract Hesina, and to Hesina's chagrin, it worked. For once, knowledge *did* feel like truth. Everything she learned filled in another blank the books hadn't.

Were sooths able to detect other sooths?

Not in any special way. There were small behavioral tells, but nothing was as reliable as blood.

How many had both the Sight and magic?

The Sight existed independently, but the Reel ("magic" was simply reeling in the line of time, moving future to present) required the Sight. One in every five used to be born as Reeler. Now, with the loss of so many strong bloodlines, it was closer to one in every twenty.

A thought crept into Hesina's mind. "Have any been able to See into the past?"

"Theory on that remains sparse," said Mei. "Kings never cared about the past. All they wanted was to know how to conquer the future."

Hesina could have listened to Mei talk forever. But they didn't have forever. These were Mei's last hours, and here she was, giving them to her.

"Mei . . ." Hesina started, then stopped. She couldn't apologize, or make empty promises, or comfort her, not when she was so scared herself. "Did you know?"

That I would fail you?

That my kingdom would fail you?

All this time, Hesina had acted strong for Sanjing. She didn't want to pretend anymore.

"Did you?" she choked out when Mei didn't answer.

"Hesina, let it end here."

"Stop."

"I See a future without me."

"Stop."

"I See a future where the people are convinced I killed the king, and I was rightly put to death. I See this kingdom moving beyond this trial, healing, growing stronger. Let it end here. With me."

No. Hesina should have listened to Caiyan. She should have framed Xia Zhong when she'd had the chance. She should have done a thousand things differently. She should have had no regrets.

"Will you be there at dawn?"

Mei didn't specify where. She didn't need to for Hesina's stomach to plunge. She'd read about sooth executions, how terrible they were to watch after the hundredth cut, how some sooths were force-fed concoctions, kept alive until the very end. Her voice wobbled when she said, "If you want me."

"I'd like a familiar face in the crowd."

"Then I'll be there. I'll be at the very front."

"Promise me you'll keep your brother from going."

"I promise." She'd have to lock Sanjing up, perhaps employ his own soldiers as guards. He'd hate her, but no more than he already did.

"He'll forgive you," said Mei. "One day, you'll forgive yourself too."

One day could be a century away.

"Listen to me, Hesina. In the times ahead, you may not know whom to trust. So trust in yourself, and trust in your beliefs."

Hesina choked on a wet laugh. "I don't know what I believe in anymore."

"The things you search for. The truth. *You will* find it," insisted Mei when Hesina shook her head. "And when you do, you'll have to make a decision."

"On what?"

"On whether—" Mei broke off. "Leave!"

Not so loud, Hesina would have said, if the edge to Mei's voice hadn't startled her.

"Leave! You have to go *now*!"

"Why?"

"Just go! Hurry," Mei urged as Hesina pushed to her feet, her body heavy, as if in the throes of a dream. "Leave the lantern and run."

"Where?" Only the arcade of gateways waited beyond this cell.

"Into the crypt—" Again Mei broke off. "It's too late," she whispered, almost to herself. The next thing Hesina knew, the two sleeping guards disappeared under a pall of shadow. "Come back. Come close," Mei said as Hesina crouched again. "Make yourself smaller."

Hesina tucked into a ball. The cell's shadow expanded, swallowing her knees. With Mei's next breath, the rest of her disappeared as well.

"Mei, what's—"

"Quiet. Stay still."

Why? What's happening?

Two thumps sounded in answer from the direction of the archway. Someone gurgled and choked, then fell silent. Moments later, feet whispered across the ground behind Hesina. Two pairs . . . maybe three.

"What are you doing here?" demanded Mei. "With *them*?"

"We're getting you out."

Hesina nearly groaned. Sanjing. Of course. Who else would have had the audacity?

"What did you do to the guards?" asked Mei.

"It's funny how so many people have love in their futures," piped a new yet eerily familiar voice. "And how stupid it makes them when it's Reeled into the present. All we had to do was ask for the way, and they led us right here. As for the unlucky ones . . ." Something *swished* through the air, and droplets rained onto Hesina's back. ". . . Consider it merciful that we saved them from their loveless futures."

Hesina's pulse spiked with urgency. Where had she heard this voice?

"Sanjing, take these people away."

"Mei—"

"Leave, or else I'll never forgive you, not even after I die."

"But you won't die. Don't you see?" Her brother sounded so hopeful that it hurt. "You don't have to die. I won't let you." The volume of his voice dipped as he turned to someone else. "Unlock her."

"Can't," replied the person, voice gruffer than the first stranger's.

"I saw you split that rock in the cavern."

Cavern?

"Oh, no, no," said the first voice, and Hesina smothered a gasp. She remembered. His face, pockmarked, scarred, and one-eyed.

One-Eye.

"What Tong means," he said, voice creeping closer, "is that he can't unlock the cell without a price."

"I've already paid it," said Sanjing.

"And I was hoping for a bonus. I thought we might find a queen down here, but sometimes you mis-See things."

Hesina's heartbeat thundered, as if to announce her presence. She envisioned Sanjing tightening his jaw. "What do you want with my sister?"

"Well, if there's no queen, we'll have to settle for second best." A pause. "Huh. You're a tragic one. Nothing but heartbreak ahead of you. Guess we'll have to fight this fair and square."

Something struck the stone above Hesina's head and rung metallic. A blade. A blade that'd missed her brother. A silent scream skinned her throat, and she uncurled before she could help herself.

"*Don't.*" Mei's shadows rippled before Hesina could protest, and darkness engulfed the space.

"Darling," sang One-Eye. "You know I can See still him. How he's going to feint. How he's going to attack. And I think, if I'm not wrong, in the next moment—"

A knife whistled through the air.

"—how he's going to die."

Hesina moved without thinking, scrabbling for the lantern pole. She stood, swinging.

Bamboo, reed, and paper smashed with a crackling pop.

The shadows shattered. One-Eye stumbled. Sanjing knocked out the other soothsayer and spun, covering his back. "Sina?"

"I knew it!" crowed One-Eye in glee, with a dozen splinters in his face and a hand cupped over his nose. "I knew I could trust my Sight."

It took all of Hesina's willpower to drop the broken lantern and spread her empty palms. "Here I am. Fight me, but don't touch . . ."

She trailed off as One-Eye uncovered his crushed nose. Blood ran, then dried, over his lips and chin.

"You'll—"

Smoke curled into blue flame.

—*Burn*.

One-Eye winced as the fire crackled over his skin, but he didn't put it out. "I know what you're thinking, darling. This pain is nothing. You know what pains me more? Seeing my people grow content with their scraps, then lured by a queen into hoping. Do you know what happens when we hope?" He glanced at the cell. "We end up like her. She trusted your kind; she burned for it. A couple more like her, and we *all* burn.

"So thank you for coming here today." He withdrew a linen-wrapped package from his cloak. "And thank you for saving me the trouble. I was never good at striking the flint."

He tossed the package onto the lantern's flickering remains. The smoke of burning linen immediately scratched at Hesina's nose. A second smell reminded her of the annual spring festival.

The tang of newly minted *banliang* coins.

The warm musk of firecrackers.

Metal and black powder.

No.

Hesina ran for Sanjing, but her legs were pushing through tar. She screamed his name, trying to reach him, grab him, but she was so, so far away.

Then the distance vanished. Space and time snapped together, and she was flying, flying, flying, the dark bleached to white around her, its flesh sheared right off its bones.

III

TRUTH

In the beginning, One gave up his name. He killed the king and surrendered himself to the legend he was fated to become. As the years stretched on before him, never ceasing, he assumed other names and other roles. But he always cradled the true one in his heart. Sometimes, he said it, just to himself. In the twilight hours when the rest of the world forgot, he remembered.

He'd wake in the morning still as One. Bloodstained, revered One. He'd look at his kingdom from the terraces and see what it'd become.

He didn't tell anyone else—not even his daughter—because he knew they wouldn't be able to accept. It was unnatural. Unreal. People feared what they couldn't grasp. He didn't want to be feared.

But he should have thought of that before he burned the first sooth.

TWENTY-FOUR

Tyrants cut out hearts. Rulers sacrifice their own.

ONE of the ELEVEN on ruling

It's not about what you want. It's about what the people need.

TWO of the ELEVEN on ruling

"Milady."

"Na-Na."

"Sister."

"Sina."

"Hesina."

Their voices darted like minnows across the surface, their shadows barely filtering through the depths. Hesina reached for them as she plunged. Her life flashed through the spaces between her outstretched fingers.

She drowned.

* * *

"What happened to your knees, Little Bird?"

She poked at the swollen flesh and winced. "Mother made me kneel all night."

"What for?"

"I wore white chrysanthemums in my hair." Lilian said it was in style. Hesina was never trusting her again.

"What does white represent?" her father prompted gently.

"Death."

"Yes. The absence of color is the absence of life. And if you witness enough death, it can take the color out of you too."

"Has Mother seen a lot of death?"

"Yes. We both have."

"But you're not unwell."

"We all handle loss differently."

"Right," she muttered. "Differently as in she'd be sadder if Sanjing died."

Her father hoisted her onto his knee with a grunt of effort. "No one's going to die."

"But if I did, Mother wouldn't cry. She doesn't love me."

"She does."

"She doesn't."

"I love you. Isn't that enough?"

"No," she said, but inside, a small, less-stubborn part of her said yes.

* * *

"Fever . . . burning up . . ."

". . . pulse erratic . . ."

"Bring . . . the needles . . ."

* * *

"Father," she asked, putting on an imperial troupe mask, "do you believe people change?"

He donned a blacksmith's arm guards. "Of course they do, Little Bird."

She dug through his costume chest, looking for her favorite brocade cape. "Then do you believe the sooths have changed?"

"I'm sure they have."

"Good. Because Scholar Niu says they did bad things three centuries ago, but he never listens when I say three centuries is an awfully long time."

✢ ✢ ✢

"We . . . wait much longer . . ."

"We can't . . . decision without her . . ."

"But the people . . ."

". . . More guards . . ."

"At this rate . . . revenue . . . lives . . . destroyed!"

". . . Wait until the queen wakes—"

"*If* she wakes!"

"She will wake," said one voice above the others. Then softer, but steady with conviction. "Milady will wake."

✢ ✢ ✢

"There's something I must tell you, Little Bird."

She braced herself for another lecture on the growing tensions between Kendi'a and Yan.

"I may not always be here for you."

She missed the father whose smile was given freely.

"In my absence, there will be others who want the best for you."

The years have passed. She no longer believed that her father could keep all his promises—even the impossible ones—but she wished she could go back to those summer nights of cicada song floating through his fan-shaped windows, of falling asleep on his lap with his hand crowning her head, of stories and explorations of passages yet to be discovered.

"But only you can decide the life you want to live."

Maybe if she weren't heir to the throne.

"Carve your own fate. Understand, Little Bird?"

She didn't, but for her father, she lied. "I understand."

* * *

A hand rested on her forehead, cool and dry against her hot skin.

"Queens are supposed to stay away from bombs."

That sounded reasonable enough to Hesina.

"And assassins," said the voice, much quieter.

Probably. Some assassins carried bombs and knives and poisons. But maybe there were other assassins who only carried rods.

Some, she wanted to say, *but not all.*

* * *

Wake up, Little Bird.

* * *

She shouldn't have woken up.

She should have died. Mei had died. *Gone without a trace,* whispered the Doctress's apprentices when they thought Hesina was unconscious. They puttered around her, dabbing her forehead with a damp washcloth. *Not even a body to collect.*

They squeaked when Hesina asked, "Where's my brother?" They flinched when her voice rose. *"Where is he?"*

"In better shape than you," answered the Imperial Doctress as she swept in. And then, before Hesina could cry ugly tears of relief, a medicinal candle was lit and the fumes sank her into a drug-induced sleep. Dreaming of One-Eye's leering face, she convinced herself that *he* was her father's poisoner. Never mind the logistics of how the sooth would have procured some legendary poison and known how to use it. He hated her. He hated the Eleven. It made perfect sense to her murky unconscious. In her dreams, she hunted him down and avenged Mei.

But when Hesina next woke, she stared at the turquoise-stained wood of the ceiling—adorned with golden turtles and *yuanyang* ducks and ginseng sachets looping down like vines—without emotion.

She should have died.

Why hadn't she?

Was it because she was an abomination, just like her father? Had she died and somehow come back? Was Sanjing an abomination too?

Alive. The Imperial Doctress said he was alive. But the Imperial Doctress had also claimed her father was dead. Who could Hesina believe?

Only herself.

She needed to see her brother with her own two eyes.

She deforested her arms of acupuncture needles. They pinged onto the floor. She sat up—and almost fainted. Her back was a map of pain.

Gut twisting, Hesina drew her hand away from the valleys and ridges of burned flesh and slipped her legs over the bedside. The air felt cool on her shins, the *huanghuali* floor solid beneath her feet.

Stand, Hesina.

So she did.

She tried and failed, in her usual fashion.

She hit the floor with a thump that rattled her teeth and quaked through her skull. But nothing was as loud as her scream. The skin on her back was melting off. It had to be. Tears swam down her face by the time the Imperial Doctress flapped through the fret-worked doors, a horde of apprentices trailing her.

"Fools! Who let the candle burn out?"

Three apprentices rushed to relight the medicinal candle. Four surrounded Hesina, dabbing at her face.

The explosion of activity was too much. "*Don't touch me*," ordered Hesina, and the apprentices scampered back.

"*Dianxia*—" gritted out the Imperial Doctress.

"Take me to my brother." Hesina let some of the more seasoned apprentices help her to her feet.

"I'll summon him."

"No." She couldn't meet him in a room that reeked of her weaknesses. "I'll go to him."

"In due time," said the Doctress. "You've been bedridden for eight days."

Too long.

"When your strength returns, we—"

Hesina grabbed on to a shelf lined with delicate ceramic jars of the Doctress's precious tinctures. She made her threat clear.

"Take me. *Now*."

The Doctress didn't need to be told twice.

The apprentices rushed for a stretcher, but Hesina stopped them. She would walk to her brother, even if it killed her. She had the strongest ones support her by the arms, and together, they made the slow, awkward hobble out of the infirmary. Sweat crowned her brow as they entered the facades. She pushed on.

Confusion clouded Hesina's mind when they passed her brother's rooms. Then they arrived at hers, and there he was, facing her desk, alive, *standing*, the bandage around his head the extent of his visible injuries.

Hesina could have collapsed right then and there.

But she didn't. She left the apprentices at the door and entered on her own.

"They say you threw yourself on top of me," Sanjing said when she was halfway to him.

She wobbled to a stop, and he spoke again, still facing away. "You shouldn't have bothered."

"Jing—"

"Do you want to know the first thing I thought when I came to?" He turned. His face was pale but uninjured. It was his eyes, the black of them matte like Go stones, that sapped the last of Hesina's strength.

"When I learned she was gone, I blamed you. I blamed you for the explosion, for the fact she was in that cell to begin with. I told myself nothing would be this way if it hadn't been for your trial."

His first words pierced her, needles to her heart. His next tugged, drawing out the crimson threads.

"Then I saw you. You were on the bed next to mine. I woke. You didn't. I was walking the next day. Your fever didn't go down for a week. When the Imperial Doctress changed your bandage—"

He broke off, throat bobbing.

"They say you threw yourself on top of me," he whispered after a long silence. "They say they had to pry you off. And too late, I . . . I—I realized—"

"Jing."

"—you still saw me as your brother—"

"I always—"

"—when I didn't deserve—"

"*Jing.* Stop."

He did, and silently began to sob.

She lurched over and pulled him into her arms. "It's okay." She didn't mind that he blamed her, or that they only knew how to make each other whole when they were broken. For once, she didn't want anything more than just to hold him. "It's okay."

He shook harder, his fist clenched around a figurine. It was the seal Hesina had taken from him, not quite lion, not quite dog, a funny-looking thing that Sanjing wouldn't have picked for himself. A gift.

He held on to it as though it was the only thing he had left.

Her throat closed. "What happened to . . . to the others?"

He shook his head.

So they were dead like Mei. Gone. Blown to pieces. Irretrievable.

Then why, why, *why* were they still alive?

Sanjing wanted to know the same thing. "Why?" he gasped when the sobs racking his body diminished to spasms. "Why are we still here, Sina?"

"I don't know, Jing." She didn't *want* to know. But if the reason was what she'd suspected, she'd never tell. She'd taken away her brother's only friend. She wouldn't also take away his memory of their father.

* * *

After Hesina's little act of rebellion, the Imperial Doctress stationed imperial guards outside the infirmary doors. Hesina pleaded for her release. The most secure dungeons in the entire kingdom had just been breached. Five of the elite guard had died, along with the first soothsayer convicted in the last thirty years. The people could be razing the city to the ground, for all she knew, while she lay in bed and let it burn.

Her arguments would have impressed Caiyan, but the Doctress was immune to rationale. "The people want to see a *healthy* queen," she said testily. "Not a fainting queen."

Hesina railed and hissed and downright threw a fit, but mostly, she hated the woman for being right. Her back was healing at the rate of a silkworm's crawl. Her thoughts ran sluggishly, like a stream choked with sediment, and if she wasn't hallucinating hummingbirds into the beamed ceiling, she was pining for Akira, which, in Hesina's opinion, also counted as a sort of hallucination. But she didn't mind those as much. Akira slowed the pace of the world around her and made it easier to breathe. She wanted him here with no words, no gestures, no intentions between them, just the quiet rain of wood chips from his rod pattering onto the floor.

He didn't come. Neither did Caiyan, much to Hesina's consternation. When the Imperial Doctress could finally be persuaded to allow visitors, Lilian and Rou were the first to bear news of the outside world. Hesina asked after Mei's parents and the sooths in the caverns. Safe and provisioned for, they reported. Hesina let herself relax for all but a heartbeat before asking about the state of the kingdom.

Lilian and Rou glanced at each other.

"It's not pleasant," Lilian finally said.

"Show me," Hesina ordered as the Imperial Doctress ushered them out.

Several folded papers made their way onto her breakfast tray the next morning, tucked beneath the steaming *shaguo* of black sesame porridge. They were torn, their ink characters smudged, as if hands had grabbed them fresh off the printing blocks.

TERRORIST ATTACK IN IMPERIAL
DUNGEONS
SOOTHSAYER PRISON BREAK ENDS IN
MURDER AND DESTRUCTION
QUEEN HESINA ON BRINK OF DEATH
KINGSLAYERS AGAIN ATTEMPT REGICIDE

No wonder Caiyan hadn't visited yet; Hesina could only imagine the state of the court. Appetite gone, she set the tray aside and hobbled to the fretwork sliding doors, pulling them apart to reveal the patio.

Another dawn. Another view of the mists enshrouding the silk ponds, the banks cottoned with snow, lily pads dotting the surface like little white islands. So peaceful.

So false.

Her mouth soured. She turned away from the patio, hands balled, her heart jittering behind her ribs like a caged bird. She'd reached the end of her patience. Tomorrow, she was getting out.

She had one of the apprentices send a message to Rou.

＊ ＊ ＊

In the morning, Yan Rou of the Southern Palace came down with a dreadful case of diarrhea that required the Imperial Doctress's immediate attention. The moment the woman left, medicine chest packed for the hike across the imperial grounds, Hesina glared the apprentices into submission and had her pages call an emergency meeting with her vassals and ministers.

She summoned her maids to help her prepare. Some gasped upon seeing her back, but Ming'er worked silently, putting Hesina in a black *ruqun* embroidered with white camellias, their glossy, teardrop leaves rendered in emerald silk on the *bixi* panels draping the skirts. It was a prudent choice. The black drew out the olive undertones of Hesina's skin, and she left the infirmary looking more alive than she felt. Sanjing offered his arm at the doors, and she leaned on him as they made for the throne hall.

"*Dianxia!*" Ministers dropped into *koutou* when brother and sister crossed the threshold. "*Wansui, wansui, wan wan sui!*" Ten thousand years, ten thousand years, ten thousand of ten thousand years.

Forget about years. Hesina just wanted to live through today. It hurt to walk. It hurt to *breathe*. Yet somehow—thanks to Sanjing's iron grip—she reached the dais just as the enamel pythons laid into the walk began to ripple and swim.

She sank into the throne with a wince of relief. First order of business, done; she'd made it to her meeting in one piece. Next order of business: Bring the realm back from the brink of self-destruction.

Elevens help her.

Sanjing positioned himself at her left. Caiyan was already at her right. Hesina assumed he hadn't visited her in the last four days because he was busy, but now he didn't even look at her. Her anxiety spiked. She tried to tame it before facing the sea of kneeling officials.

"Rise."

Everyone had answered her summons, from minor courtier to the six ministers. They forested any space between the pillars, standing so close to one another that the black wings of their *wusha* caps brushed.

One by one, Hesina called them forth.

The Minister of Works reported that all industry within the city walls had halted, and cases of looting and public works defacement had skyrocketed. The Minister of Personnel reported that sector magistrates could no longer keep their residential wards under control, and that neighbors had turned on one another, demanding proof in blood. The Commandant of the city guard reported that his forces were spread thin in restraining the vigilante groups.

So this was why the Imperial Doctress had been so keen on keeping her locked away. Hesina's back tingled as the blood required for healing rushed to her heart. She tried to will some to flow to her brain. "How many vigilante groups?"

"Roughly twenty. The largest one is composed of blacksmiths and skilled laborers. They call themselves Children of the Eleven."

The irony. She wanted to laugh. She wanted to cry.

The explosion had unleashed suspicion among the masses. Not only did people believe soothsayers were living disguised as their neighbors and friends, but they also believed the king's real killer remained unfound among them.

"But the perpetrators are already dead," Hesina said. "So is the convicted." Her mouth went grainy, and Sanjing tensed.

"Who's to say that the perpetrators weren't working as part of a bigger group?" asked Xia Zhong. His neck was bare of scarf and beads. His bruises, Hesina noticed tartly, had finally healed.

"As for the convicted," said the director, and Hesina glowered at both men, "it turns out your representative presented *quite* the convincing defense. She was guilty of being a sooth, yes, but few believe she was the king's true murderer."

Akira *had* constructed a solid defense. Would things be different if he hadn't?

But the reality couldn't be changed. Fifty-two civilians were dead. Hundreds were injured. One sooth had been identified by the vigilante groups and hastily executed. He'd burned to death on the seventieth cut.

Just when Hesina thought it couldn't get any worse, it did. Secretariats approached with sheaves of papers. As Hesina spread them out on the ivory *kang*, they explained that messenger pigeons had been flying over the imperial city and the surrounding provinces for days now, dropping Kendi'an stamped leaflets. The city guard had tried to collect as many as they could, but some, inevitably, had fallen into the people's hands.

TO ALL THE SOOTHSAYERS
WHO DISPLAY STRANGE AND UNUSUAL
POWERS,
YOUR KINGDOM HAS ABANDONED YOU.
OURS WELCOMES YOU.
SEEK SANCTUARY ACROSS THE BORDER.

Hesina envisioned the Crown Prince, lips draped with a smug smile. *You are no better*, he'd say. And he was right. By dropping these letters, he was fanning bloodthirst against the sooths. All he needed to do now was sit back and watch her people tear themselves apart before striking.

She managed to set down the letters without crumpling them. Her gaze sliced to the assembly ground. "Kendi'a lies. Their goal is to enslave the sooths."

Her officials tutted in disgust. At least they could be trusted to condemn slavery, which the Eleven had outlawed along with serfdom.

"Grand Secretariat Sunlei, see that this corrected information is posted around the imperial city and flown into the affected provinces."

"Understood, *dianxia*."

Hopefully, it'd calm the people's anger against the sooths. And hopefully, it'd stop sooths from seeking "freedom" across the border.

But Hesina wasn't optimistic, and her hands balled as she realized something else.

"Eleven days." Her voice boomed through the faux archways. "It's been eleven days since the explosion. The fastest falcon takes twelve to reach Kendi'a, and another twelve back. Do you know what this means?"

She met the gazes of as many as she could. A minister. A viscount. A marquis. A page. She let her eyes fall on Xia Zhong as she said, "We have turncoats in this city. People are printing these letters as we speak."

A stir went through the ranks.

"And I have an inkling who they might be." Neighbors looked to each other, and a pathetic trill of satisfaction went through Hesina. If she couldn't out the minister, she'd at least raise the collective vigilance.

"Any news from the borderlands?" she asked the Grand Secretariat.

"Not as of this point."

Good, because another disappearing village would be the people's final straw.

Hesina was done playing games with Xia Zhong. She couldn't sit around and let Kendi'a ambush Yan in its weakest moment. She had to make the first move, even if it meant conceding defeat.

"The truce ends here," she said. "I want militias of the western provinces mustered, organized, and stationed at the border by the end of the week."

"They'll need a leader," piped a marquis.

"I'll go." Sanjing stepped forward. "I've dealt with the Kendi'ans before. I know their tricks."

His bandage had been removed; the cut on his temple had scabbed. But his real wounds were invisible, and Hesina didn't want to send him away so soon. The kingdom had already taken so much from them. Why give more?

You must always love your people, came her father's voice.

He must have conveniently forgotten that the sooths were people too. But his teachings were a part of Hesina. His love was the sky she turned to when she couldn't breathe in this lacquer box of a home. She couldn't forgive One, but One wasn't the man who'd shown her how to plant a persimmon tree from a branch, or the man who'd spent so many nights entertaining an audience of one.

And now he spoke to her, whether Hesina wanted to hear him or not.

You must give them your heart.

And then? she thought bitterly. *What do I give up next?* But she already knew the answer.

Her name.

Her life.

Her ideals.

Right after she gave Sanjing up to his duty as her general. "Then I grant you high command."

Her brother bowed. "I'll ready myself now."

This is what he wants, Hesina reminded herself as he went down the dais in two quick strides. The vassals bowed as he swept past. *It's too painful for him to stay here.*

Still, something in her closed as the doors groaned shut behind him.

Exhausted, Hesina gripped the throne's arm. "On to the matter of restoring order to the imperial city."

Officials came forward with their proposals. Some pointed out that the majority of sooths were likely living in the underground sewage system and suggested burning them out. Others argued for letting the vigilante groups do the dirty work. Issues of costs and efficiency were raised, but no one, not a single soul, voiced Hesina's thought: the majority of sooths were innocent. She ached to say it, but at a time when she needed the support of *all* her subordinates, she couldn't alienate them by revealing her true heart.

She looked to Caiyan. He hadn't said a word this entire time. A silly part of Hesina was waiting for him to swoop in with the best solution. But there wasn't any. The people had decided.

What is power? Hesina had thought it was wielding the knife, or getting someone to wield it for her. Now she realized it was neither. Power was yielding. It was taking the bloodstained knife out of a thousand frenzied hands and making it hers alone.

"Silence."

The court hushed.

"Tomorrow—" Her voice cracked; she tried again. "Tomorrow, I will make a tour of the imperial city. We will show the people I am alive and well. The procession will start and end at the terraces with the sharing of my decree. I—"

Her throat was in her stomach, and her stomach was in her throat, and her heart was somewhere between them, clawing to resurface.

"I will sanction a citywide cutting, to be conducted by the imperial guard and *only* the imperial guard, enacted sector by sector, ward by ward. Magistrates and hand-selected officials will oversee that everyone in the population records is processed equally. Any discovered soothsayers will be detained . . ."

Not at the palace, not after what had happened.

". . . in the city guard barracks," she finished, "where they will await further processing."

"Death by a thousand cuts?" piped up an official.

Placate the people, and buy time. "We must wait to learn the total numbers of sooths before we decide how to proceed," Hesina said before she could come up with the proper justification.

Caiyan provided it. "If the number of discovered sooths is high," he said, his voice unusually gravelly, "then we can't afford to carry out the executions to their fullest extent."

The officials grumbled, protesting that forgoing the executions went against the *Tenets*.

Caiyan continued, his words hoarse and strained. "Every province is watching this city. Should we publicize that soothsayers comprise ten, fifteen, or twenty percent of our population, surpassing all prior expectations, the entire realm will turn on itself. The Kendi'ans will advance, and the militia won't be able to stop a two-front war." He glanced to Hesina, his chestnut eyes unreadable. "The queen is right. What happens after identifying the soothsayers will be determined by the numbers."

The protests died down to mutters.

"If you still object, speak now," Hesina ordered.

A minister shuffled forward. "It will take time . . ."

Another took a stand to her right. "It will be expensive . . ."

A third joined on the left. "But it'll cap the chaos and curb the infighting."

Then suddenly, there was an outpouring of support.

"It will reinstate order."

"If everyone is subjected to a cut, private disputes will no longer lead to fights to the death."

"It returns power to the imperial guards."

"Good." Hesina rose—a terrible mistake. Caiyan caught her arm as she stumbled. "It is settled then," she said through her teeth, gritted against the pain. "Grand Secretariat, prepare a procession route for tomorrow and select the palanquin bearers."

"Understood, *dianxia*."

She would round up the sooths and strip them of their cover, giving the people half of what they wanted. Then the real test would begin. Could she reverse centuries of hatred and turn this city into a sanctuary before it became a burial ground?

Or would she become a murderer no different from her father?

TWENTY-FIUE

Nurture the people as if they are your children.

ONE of the ELEVEN on ruling

The masses may be misguided, but their hearts are true.

TWO of the ELEVEN on ruling

As the ministers streamed out, the weight of what Hesina had decided came down on her shoulders alone.

She'd had no choice. They'd come to an impasse. It was her ideals against the people's. One side had to give, or more would die.

Still, the thought of tomorrow horrified her, and it wasn't until Caiyan had walked her back to the infirmary and was turning to go that Hesina realized he hadn't said a thing since leaving the throne room.

"Wait."

A wince cracked Caiyan's face as she caught his right arm. Hesina froze. He started to pull away, but she was faster. She pushed up his sleeve, recoiling at the sight of his skin. It was black and blue and red and swollen, as if something heavy had fallen and crushed the very bone.

Her hand dropped as he doubled over, grabbing the bed frame as his body convulsed with coughs.

This was why Caiyan had seemed so strained in court. Why he hadn't visited all this time. Why he was so eager to make his escape.

The reason behind his injured arm.

"Look at me," she whispered.

Caiyan smoothed down his sleeve. Adjusted the brocade cuff. Hesina was on the verge of ordering him again when he raised his head.

"You were there, weren't you?" she whispered. "Right after the explosion?"

Caiyan didn't answer.

He must have been one of the first responders. He must have inhaled all the smoke and ash in the immediate aftermath, rushing to rescue her as the prisons came down around them.

He'd put himself in danger.

Hesina couldn't keep the tremble out of her voice. "How did you know—"

"You promised you wouldn't jeopardize your rule."

She flinched, then recovered. "You shouldn't have risked yourself. You shouldn't have acted on your own."

"You shouldn't have been there." Caiyan's words landed like the strokes of a whip. "You shouldn't have survived."

He left her in stunned silence as he paced to the fretworked doors. "I moved both of you up the arcade before summoning the guards. If they found you by the sooth's cell, spared by an explosion that had blown the rest to pieces, how would they have explained it?"

The fight trickled out of Hesina. She could see it all too well. Caiyan, immediately realizing how suspicious the scene looked, struggling to drag both Sanjing and her out of it. Always thinking ahead, even in the face of peril.

"Let me call the Imperial Doctress," she said through the pressure in her throat.

"There's no need."

"Please." It was getting harder to breathe. Hesina couldn't see his arm anymore, but now she was visualizing the hilly scar that gouged up the crook of his left elbow, white like the new ice on the koi pond that winter morning. Sanjing had just turned seven. He'd lured Caiyan out onto the ice, expecting it to crack, hoping to give his rival a good scare, but never imagining that broken ice would cut skin like knives, or that Hesina would jump in to save a brother.

One prank gone wrong. Dozens of apologies she never accepted. The ice on the pond melted in the spring, not the ice between her and Sanjing's hearts.

"Please," Hesina begged when Caiyan remained silent. The notion of his pain rivaled the pain in her back.

"I'll see to it myself." Again, he turned to go. "You should rest, milady."

"Wait."

He stopped at the doors, a hand on the latch.

It wasn't fair of Hesina to ask more from him, but she needed his opinion. "Did I make the right decision today?"

"Yes."

"It doesn't feel that way."

Caiyan said nothing for a second. "There's a tale. The tale of Yidou."

"Tell it to me?"

"You really should rest, milady."

"Just one story."

She waited for him to come back and sit with her on the bed, but he stayed by the doors, the distance between them feeling as large as it had that winter day when she'd run across the ice to save him.

"A boy by the name of Yidou had lost his way in the Ebei Mountains," Caiyan began. "Out of food and facing the first snows, he had been resigned to death.

"That's when the wolf had appeared. Yidou had a knife. He had his two feet. He could have fought. He could have fled. But he knew he was weak, so instead, he turned the knife on himself and cut off a finger. He fed it to the wolf. He cut off another, laying a trail of his own flesh, feeding the wolf's very desire while luring the beast farther and farther down the icy pass."

"And then?" she asked, breath held, voice hushed.

"He survived," Caiyan said simply. "He gave the wolf a piece of what it wanted without sacrificing all of himself. Tomorrow you will do the same. It may hurt, but it's the only way." Then his voice softened. "Lilian and I will be there on the terraces with you."

"Is that my name I hear?"

The story's spell broke as Lilian came through the doors, *ruqun* silks spilling out of her arms. "A little bird told me that you have an important tour tomorrow. I'm here to make you presentable. What?" she asked as Hesina frowned at the flashy selection. "A queen should decree things in style."

"Pretty sure you said the same thing about the negotiations." That had ended well.

"Pretty sure my gown saved your life." Lilian turned on Caiyan. "Shoo now. You have ink on your nose, by the way. Not that it really ruins the I-will-forever-be-a-bachelor look."

Caiyan bowed. "I'll see you tomorrow, milady."

"Make sure you see the—"

The doors slid shut behind him.

—*Doctress.*

Lilian laid out the *ruqun* on the neighboring bed. "How's your back?"

"Fine," Hesina muttered.

"You sound glum about that."

"He's upset with me."

"The stone-head? Since when?"

Since Hesina started getting caught in explosions. "He didn't take my injury well." She picked at a loose thread in the silk blankets. She hadn't placed the bombs in One-Eye's hands, but they'd gone off because of her. Because of her, Mei was dead and two of Hesina's brothers were injured.

The bed dimpled as Lilian sat beside her. "And you think I *did*? We all hide ourselves, Na-Na. You most of all."

"What do I hide behind?"

"Lies. Duty. The things you *think* you should do and love, but that you actually hate. You don't owe the people some better version of yourself. In fact, you owe this world nothing."

Hesina dragged out the thread, undoing the feather of an embroidered phoenix. Easy for Lilian to say. The kingdom was currently falling apart because no better version of herself had arrived to save the day. "I'm the queen."

"It's not too late to run away. I'm being serious, for once. We can go to Ning."

"And freeze?"

"Their smoldering men make up for the cold," said Lilian with an eyebrow wiggle. "Besides, I hear they have sapphires as big as your fists."

"Xia Zhong would love it." Hesina had finally handed him the war he wanted. As she sat here, picking dresses, he was probably throwing a feast.

"Okay, forget about Ning." Lilian tapped her lip. "We could go anywhere, do anything. We could ride serpents in the Baolin Isles, soak in the floating hot springs on the Aoshi archipelago." She leaned in, chestnut eyes hopeful. "If I asked you to come, would you?"

Yes, Hesina desperately wanted to say. *Let this kingdom burn. Let the people kill. I want nothing to do with them.* But if she didn't rule, who would? Sanjing? Although he was next in line, he was no more suited to this fate than she.

"I can't," she whispered.

She'd said no to Lilian before. To pranking the Imperial Tailor, to skipping lessons and countless other things. But this time felt different. The air went too still, too silent, and Lilian's smile wavered before it brightened again. She gestured at the gowns. "Then shall we?"

Narrowing down the pile of *ruqun* was easier than it looked. Applying Hesina's stipulations (no inappropriate embroidery) took them from a dozen options to three.

One *ruqun* was cut from crimson silk. Golden sun rays fanned from the sleeve cuffs. Light-blue clouds scalloped the hem.

"Too conservative," declared Lilian when she caught Hesina eyeing it. She laid out the coordinating sash and *bixi* brocade panel anyway, found a chiffon wrap, dip-dyed to resemble mist. She suggested a mink-trimmed cloak and a gold hair comb to match.

Hesina lifted the comb. Its shaft was wrought with serpents, their scaled bodies weaving in and out of a cloud bank. Russet jaspers had been set for their eyes, reminding her of Mei's. The comb grew heavier in her hand. She set it down.

"Lilian."

"Hmm?"

"While the people are distracted by the tour tomorrow, I want you to visit the caverns. Take some sticks of black powder with you and find the passageway sealed with stones. It goes to the city walls." It had to, given what Hesina now knew about her father's identity. "Blast away the stones, and lead Mei's parents and the others out of the city before I read the decree." *Before it's too late, in case I fail.* "Can you do that for me?"

Lilian took her hands. "Of course, Na-Na."

Hesina gave Lilian's a grateful squeeze. Then she looked past her sister, across all the empty beds in the infirmary.

You hide, Lilian had said, but Hesina didn't want to hide. To Lilian, she wanted to be herself. Be true.

"I'm scared," she admitted. "If I give the wolf a piece of what it wants, won't it hunger for more?"

"What are you talking about?"

"The tale of Yidou."

"That macabre thing?"

"You know it?"

"'Yidou, Yidou, a finger, a toe, tricked the great beast and struck down the foe.'"

"Wait. He *killed* the wolf?"

"And ate it. How else would he have survived to pass on the tale?" Lilian asked, and Hesina paled. "Anyway, it's just a silly little story. We used to tell it to each other when it was bitterly cold and our stomachs were empty. But now we have all the pork buns in the world. Why think about wolf meat?"

Why indeed.

But it wasn't a wolf hunting Hesina. It was the people's fear.

She'd either rule with it, or be ruled by it. Either way, blood would spill.

* * *

The rest of the day passed in a blur. Ministers scrambled to prepare for the tour. Scribes hurried to transcribe the time and location of the queen's decree reading, and couriers ran to post the notices all over the city. Pages streamed in and out of the infirmary with route proposals, guard numbers, and weather forecasts.

Sanjing stopped by in the middle of everything to bid Hesina farewell. He was dressed to ride and had a bronze helmet cradled in his arm. Hesina almost asked him to send a commander in his place before swallowing the words.

He guessed them anyway. "I'm useless here."

"How do you know that? What if I need someone beheaded?"

Turn to your manservant then, she imagined Sanjing saying. Instead, he replied, "My place is on the field. Remember my promise?"

How could she forget? Long ago, before the incident on the pond, they would sneak out into the courtyards at night to practice their swordsmanship. Afterward, they'd throw themselves down on the watercress, the stars bright above, and Sanjing would turn to her and say, *When you're the queen, I'll be your general, the best this realm has ever known.*

Now he said, "I keep my word."

Then he tossed her something.

It was the dog-lion seal. Hesina barely managed to catch it; she nearly dropped it when she did.

"I don't want this." She tried to give it back. "It's yours."

"Keep it," said Sanjing. "And stay out of my rooms."

His bravado was his shield. Hesina saw past it to a boy still hurting. She grabbed his wrist, pressed the seal into his palm, and curled his fingers shut over it. "Holding on to something isn't weakness."

Sanjing's grin faltered. His throat bobbed. He turned to go.

Wait.

Tell him to stay.

"Jing."

Her brother turned.

Hesina fumbled with the words. They'd only ever existed in her mind or on paper. "Stay safe."

He blinked, slowly. Spoke, gruffly. "Don't worry. Whatever happens, I can't end up as badly as you."

She grimaced. "You kill me."

"You kill yourself." But there was a catch in his voice and a hitch in Hesina's heart. She watched his shadow fade through the oiled-papered fretwork panes, until she could see it no more.

How long would he be away this time? Three months? Six? Or longer? They'd lost those simple days; a single misstep from either of them might send Yan spiraling into war.

Night fell. The golden turtles and *yuanyang* ducks on the beamed ceiling shimmered to life as apprentices lit the candles and laid fresh coals in the braziers. The Imperial Doctress examined Hesina's back and, deeming the skin fully sealed, removed the bandages so the wound could breathe.

Once everyone was gone, Hesina spread the blank decree scroll; she'd been saving it for last. She put brush to silk, and wrote.

On the twentieth day of the first month, a citywide cutting, enacted sector by sector, ward by ward, will be conducted by authorized members of the imperial guard. Those who flame will be held in the city guard barracks and await further processing.

Her hand lost its steadiness.

The strokes bled.

Her head page came in just as she was stamping the yellow silk with her seal. "Minister Xia is throwing a feast in the Northern Palace."

Could she even be surprised? She lifted her seal, revealing a perfect impression, the red ink crisp and not the least bit smeared, each squiggle of her name bold and unforgiving. She set aside the decree to dry.

"Relieve your people from watching him." Xia Zhong had gotten what he wanted. There was no need to spy on him out of spite. These words made sense, unlike her next: "Reassign them to watching Yan Caiyan."

"Understood, *dianxia*."

It's because I'm worried about him, Hesina told herself. She cared for his well-being, just as she cared for the well-being of a certain dowager queen. "My mother. Has she written?"

"There's been no word from the dowager queen."

"I see." Hesina rubbed her temples. She didn't have the energy for disappointment, let alone anger. The full-moon deadline had come and gone, but what would she even ask her mother? *Did you know Father was One of the Eleven? That you married a man as old as the new era itself?* She couldn't justify sending a cohort to the mountains for an answer so obvious. And though her father's poisoner remained unfound, she couldn't justify searching for the assassin either. The truth couldn't quell the chaos. The truth couldn't bestow the power she desperately needed.

"*Dianxia?*"

Hesina had pressed her head to the bed frame. She never wanted to lift it.

"Is there something wrong?" asked her page in concern.

Yes. Everything is wrong. "No. That will be all."

And then, because her head was simply too heavy, Hesina rested it on the pillow log.

✳ ✳ ✳

She stumbled down a steep mountain pass, her bare feet bleeding into the snow, her ears numbed by the wind, which howled so loudly it almost drowned out the snarl.

She spun. The beast emerged from the rocks, shoulder blades jutting as it stalked in, ribs heaving as it inhaled.

She fumbled for her knife with half-frozen fingers.

Kill it, *urged a voice in her ear.*

Kill it, or be killed.

She bared the blade, and the wolf stopped short. Its raised haunches lowered. It sat, black lips pulling back over teeth as it spoke.

It spoke.

"*Hey.*"

✳ ✳ ✳

Hesina opened her eyes to a pair of pale ones peering down at her.

She bolted up. Her head cracked into something hard, and pain watered her eyes. Even then, she made out his lean shape, ash-colored *hanfu*, and tail of darker ash hair falling over his shoulder.

"Akira? What time is it?"

"Early. Or late."

"And what are you doing here?"

He rubbed his temple. "Waking you up from a nightmare, unless I guessed wrong."

"I mean, what are you doing *here*?" Hesina gestured at the infirmary, then flushed, as if he could see into her mind and count all the times she'd waited for him to step through those sliding doors.

He sat at the foot of the bed and placed a ceramic jar on the sheets. "I meant to deliver this. Earlier. It took a couple tries to get right."

Either she was groggy, or he was more disjointed than usual, because she struggled to understand what he was talking about. "What is it?"

"Ointment." He rubbed the back of his neck as she removed the lid. "Or should be. I'm out of practice."

It *looked* like ointment, which was more than she could have said for his flute. "Um, thank you?"

"It's for your back."

"Oh."

"Er, you should probably test it . . ."

Hesina turned her back to him and loosened the sash of her underrobes.

". . . later," Akira finished.

"Close your eyes." If her words didn't fail her tomorrow, her back might. She'd do whatever needed to be done—including baring her hideous blisters and taking a chance on Akira's ointment.

Applying it to her lower back hurt only a little. Reaching her middle back was trickier, and her scars protested against the contortion.

"Here." A hand brushed Hesina's arm. Her gaze whipped to Akira, but his eyes remained closed as he took the ointment pot from her palm. "You can guide me."

Her pragmatic side approved of the plan, and an "okay" slipped past her lips. Having Akira apply ointment for her was efficient, expedient—and not embarrassing at all! *No, further left, to that grosser scar! Yes, that's the one!*

"Actually—"

Hesina's thoughts petered out at his touch. The air in her lungs solidified, leaving no room for breath. Goose bumps erupted across the small of her back, along her shoulders, over her *knees*, for Eleven's sake.

"Actually . . . ?" His finger stopped between her shoulder blades; her whole existence boiled down to this point.

Hesina moistened her lips. "Actually, I . . . I didn't know merchant robbers made ointment."

For a second Akira didn't speak. "I'm not a merchant robber."

She'd guessed as much, but she couldn't say that. Couldn't admit that she'd been making up his life story all this time. "What about your friend? The one who stole too much?"

"My friend." His fingers skipped down her spine; her heart doubled its pace. "That was me."

His voice sounded strained, as if he didn't want to be talking about this at all. But Hesina played along. "What did you steal?"

Slowly, he lifted his hand. "Lives."

Akira was talking about his past. The sun was setting in the east. Akira was an assassin. Hesina's silly little story about him had been right.

Akira was an assassin.

She was sitting on a bed with an assassin.

Nothing had changed, she tried to tell herself. He was still Akira, her representative.

He went on to say how he'd specialized in poisons. It was so obvious in hindsight. His knowledge of them, his relative immunity to them, his skill at making antidotes—and now ointments. But:

"Why are you telling me this?"

Akira fell silent.

Hesina turned, remembering to clutch her collar shut, and watched as his eyes lifted to the ceiling.

"I never got the chance to tell someone else," he said to the ginseng sachets. "They died thinking I was someone I wasn't."

Then his gaze swung to hers. In it, she read everything he couldn't express. Fear—*I thought you were going to die.* Resolve—*I had to tell you.* Rue—*even if I lost you.*

"Okay," Hesina managed, feeling just as defenseless.

"Okay?"

"Yes. Okay."

His gaze hardened. "I've killed people."

"I know." Well, now she really did.

"Nobles. Serfs. Elders. I killed them just because I could."

"I don't believe that."

The corner of his mouth jerked up in cold amusement. "It's the truth."

"Then what about the monsters that roam at night?"

"I am the monster."

"What about the ghosts that haunt you to this day?" Hesina pressed. "Without remorse, you think you'd still have nightmares about your past?"

Akira didn't speak for a long time. "You should be scared."

Are you? his eyes asked.

Hesina was scared of her people. She was scared of herself. But Akira? She looked at him and all his little imperfections, like the nick interrupting the arch of his right brow, the scar breaking the dip of his upper lip, the blue tinge of a vein lurking under his left eye, almost covered by the fall of his bangs.

She gave her answer—by curling a hand into the front of his *hanfu* and rising up on her knees. She cut short his intake of air and spoke it to him without words.

A thousand moments fused into one. Maybe it was a second—maybe it was a hundred—before Akira reacted.

He jerked back. They were both gasping. The shine of moonlight was on his lip. The taste of him was on hers.

Hesina caught her breath. "*You're* the one who's scared," she realized out loud. *You're scared of being accepted as you are.*

Akira passed a hand over his eyes as if he didn't want to see her, or for her to see him. "I'm really not the person you think you know."

"Neither am I." Who was she? *What* was she? If she told Akira the truth about her father, would he think of her as the descendant of a murderer or the descendant of a savior? Or would he think of her as just . . . her?

"I can't change how people see me," Hesina said. "Just as you can't change your past. But I can choose to accept."

Akira got off the bed.

She lurched to follow. "I accept you."

He walked to the doors.

She stumbled in front of him. "As you are, as I am, I accept you."

He tried to cut around her. Hesina backed up against the fretwork, one hand still clutching her collar shut, the other spread out beside her to block his escape.

"So please—"

Her breath hitched as he braced a forearm above her head, gray eyes locking on hers.

—*Stay.*

* * *

He did.

He carried her back to the bed and sat on the floor beside it. They stayed in each other's silent company. There was so much that Hesina wanted to ask, but she didn't press for more, and eventually Akira began speaking on his own.

He told the story of a boy, orphaned by the Kendi'a slave trade, raised by a poison master, a boy just shy of eleven who'd joined a guild of twenty-three other assassins. By day, he killed for the usual clientele—paranoid princes, greedy barons, estranged lovers. By night, he killed for a sect called the Red Amaryllis. Anyone connected to the Kendi'an slave trade was fair game. The masters and their families. The landlords and their overseers. The accountants and shippers and secretariats. *Evil must be weeded by the root*, the sect leader often reminded the gray-eyed child, a child who listened closely and took the words of others as his truth.

The people renamed the child the Specter because he killed without a sound. Even his own guild brothers and sisters regarded him as a threat. None of the twenty-three noticed when the boy didn't show up at the mess hall one night, or saw the blood on a brother's hands. They laughed and joked as a family while the boy lay in the gutter of some sandstone alleyway, split from throat to navel like a hog, silent as always because he didn't think anyone would come.

He was wrong.

From the start, the boy and the girl lied to each other. She wasn't the manor's healer that she pretended to be, but the daughter of a baron who'd died some months prior. He wasn't the alchemist's apprentice that he pretended to be, but the assassin who'd poisoned that baron at the sect's bidding. Theirs was a friendship born out of ignorance. He recovered under her care and stayed at her request. They passed the days on the manor grounds, climbing pear trees and looking for treasure in the sandstone wells. He didn't contact the sect. He didn't return to his guild.

The servants liked him because he lacked the usual airs of apprentice boys. One evening, he overheard them speaking of an appreciation banquet the manor's young heiress was throwing for twenty-three scholars. The boy thought twenty-three was a strange number.

A familiar number.

He arrived too late and not late enough. He saw his guildmates slumped over the banquet table, punished for the murder of a baron that was his alone to bear, killed by a tasteless, scentless poison he'd created out of simple curiosity in the manor's workrooms. When a masked figure approached the last breathing guildmate, the boy acted without thinking. He saved the brother who had once tried to kill him. He killed the masked one, the girl who'd saved him, and with her penultimate breaths she had asked: Was he dead? Was the Specter dead?

The boy lied.

"As for the rest," said Akira, "well, it's not that interesting. You already know it. Merchant robbing. Touring the realm, prison by prison—"

"You didn't lie."

A beat of silence. "The last time I checked, I was still alive."

"But the Specter died." Hesina pictured Akira as the boy he had been, a boy swallowed by a cause. She didn't know what it meant to be an orphan or an assassin, but she knew how easy it was to adopt another's values. "He died when you left the name behind. It's why you won't touch a real weapon, why you question things and think for yourself." She dangled a hand over the bed and onto his head. "Why you're Akira now."

"Am I? You can bury a body," Akira continued, "but the bones don't go away."

That's not true. But who was she to say what was?

"Will you show me the tattoo on your back?" Hesina asked instead. She didn't know where her inhibition had gone, and she didn't much care. She'd already confessed to watching him sleep.

"It's only fair," she added sternly when Akira said nothing.

"It's not pretty."

Then her back must have been ghastly, because she thought the tattoo—which was of some sort of flower, yanked up by the root and clenched in a fist—almost looked noble. It spanned from Akira's shoulder to the curves of his ribs. He stiffened as she covered the tattooed hand with her own.

Hesina thought of all the ways stories could be conveyed. Inked on flesh. Sewn on silk facades. She thought of her father, beheading the relic emperor. Purging the sooths. An era drawn from blood. A throne erected upon bones.

If she could extend acceptance to Akira, but not her own father, did that make her a terrible daughter?

"Not sleeping?" asked Akira some time later.

"Thinking."

"Sleep," said Akira. "Thinking can wait."

Nothing can wait. A queen cannot stand still as everything and everyone rushes past her. But that had already happened, and Hesina, though arguably worse off than before, had survived. So she listened to Akira and closed her eyes.

✵ ✵ ✵

Come morning, the skin on her back felt supple, and the blisters were no longer unpleasantly tight when Hesina raised her arms.

It worked, she wanted to tell Akira, but he was gone. The only physical evidence of his visit was the jar on the floor. Hesina's hand drifted to her lips, then quickly dropped. It was morning. Time to be queen again, and to stop a citywide massacre.

She dressed herself and twisted up her hair without Ming'er's help, steeling her heart as she dabbed vermillion onto her lips, polishing her words as she swiped her cheekbones with the pearlescent powder of crushed dragonfly wings. Identifying the sooths and placating the masses was only the first challenge. The next—wiping out the masses' hatred—would be even harder. To think she could do it was perhaps downright naive.

Hesina snapped the powder box shut. The opposite of naive was jaded. Her reign had just begun, and her one talent was her bullheadedness. She owed it to the Silver Iris, to Mei, to all the sooths in this kingdom to make full use of it.

Mask perfected, she exited the palace by way of the Hall of Celestial Morality. In the mist-swathed courtyard, two lines of guards stood at the ready by the palanquin. It was a jewel box of a thing fashioned out of lacquered *zitan*, with rounds of jade implanted beneath the pole brackets, the imperial crest of the water lily and the serpent rising in low relief from the green stone.

Hesina was pleased to find the litter uncovered; she wanted the people to see her for themselves. But she began having second thoughts after they went down the terraces and took the main boulevard to the eastern market sector. Stakes had been driven into the roadside, and skewered objects—pigeons, she realized with a lurch of nausea—topped them like human heads.

"Kendi'an," whispered the guard on the palanquin's right. "It's the people's response to their leaflets about the sooths."

The messenger pigeons were hard with frost, their necks twisted at odd angles. Plaques hung from the grasp of their claws:

LET NONE ESCAPE
LEAVE NONE ALIVE

It was the beginning of a very long tour.

The imperial guards announced their arrival at the market sector. Hesina hardly recognized it. Vendor stalls had been burned or picked clean like chicken carcasses. Broken curios littered the icy ground. The few remaining sellers had set up makeshift tarps.

"The queen's ashes!" hawked one such merchant. Customers were pulling out *banliang* for the little silk pouches he offered. "Her only remains! Retrieved from the depths of the dungeons!"

If only. Then Hesina wouldn't have to suffer through this. "Why haven't these ventures been stopped?" she asked the guard sharply.

"We shut them down, but they pop up again overnight because . . ." He trailed off.

Because there was a demand. Even with all the notices papering the limestone walls, how many still thought she was char on the ground?

"Bring me to him," she ordered.

As her palanquin drew close, the bystanders fell to their knees. "*Dianxia!*"

"*D-dianxia!*" stuttered the merchant.

She considered his prostrate frame. A man in his midthirties and in decent health, robust enough to withstand a lesson. "You dishonor your name by profiting off lies."

"I-I'll pack up my wares—"

"No, leave them. Watch him," she ordered a guard. "If anyone touches his wares, treat them as robbers." Then she addressed the bystanders. "The rest of you are relieved."

They wished ten thousand years unto her life and rose. The merchant started to follow.

"Halt." Hesina sounded so much like her mother that she shivered at her own voice. "Did I say you could rise?"

"N-no, *dianxia*."

"Remain as you are, and meditate on your crimes for the next four hours."

"Thank the queen for her mercy," ordered the guard.

The merchant's jaw snapped shut. "Th-thank you for . . ."

She waved her guards onward.

The residential wards were next. Again, Hesina wasn't prepared. A shoeless child wandered through the crowds, bleeding from a long cut on his arm. Magistrates and their residents clustered the limestone corridors and their moon gate cutouts. Some sought her blessings, but many more simply continued their fights.

"Oh, so you think *I'm* a sooth?" screamed a woman. "*You're* the one who proposed joining our families through marriage!"

"*Marriage?*" The man had a kitchen cleaver in his hands, and only his children were holding him back. "Forget about marriage. I'll have your life!"

Hesina intervened where she could. But some battles were already lost. At the moat, vigilante groups circulated pages torn out of the *Tenets* and spewed their convictions. A number were about Hesina. If she wasn't secretly backing the perpetrators, she was conspiring with the Kendi'an Crown Prince and plotting ten other things. Whoever this queen was, she surpassed Hesina.

"Don't engage," she warned her guards. The tour had to go on. Still, she gritted her teeth as they left the moat. The muscles of her face ached from maintaining a mask of indifference, and she almost cracked when they came to the Eastern Gate.

Three bodies swung like tassels in the archway's crown. One was badly burned. The others had been cut so many times that they were equally unrecognizable.

One sooth.

Two colluders.

People like her.

You deserve the same fate, their mangled faces said.

Anger, sorrow, and fear brewed up Hesina's throat. "Take them down."

A crowd gathered to watch as the guards cut the ropes.

"Should have let them hang longer," spat out an old man. Others echoed his sentiments, but followed the palanquin when it continued to the terraces.

A crowd had already gathered on the Peony Pavilion. Many wore white *hanfu* cuffed and collared in black—the uniform of young scholars and civil service examinee hopefuls.

"*Dianxia!*" they cried. "*Dianxia! Dianxia!*"

Hesina ordered the litter to halt and stepped out.

"*Dianxia!*" People craned their necks to see her. "*Dianxia!*"

The guards pressed them back, but Hesina held up a hand. She approached a girl near the front of the crowd. "What is your name?"

The girl blinked, then bowed over her clasped hands. "Family name Bai, given name Yuqi."

"Do you have a favorite text, Bai Yuqi?" asked Hesina, nodding at the sack of books slung over the girl's shoulder.

"Th-the *Tenets*, *dianxia*."

Of course. What had Hesina expected her to say? *Assassins through the Ages*? "And why is that?"

"The past is a timeless teacher, *dianxia*."

"Raise your head."

Hesina touched two fingers to the girl's temple once she did. "The mind is a timeless teacher." She tapped the girl's collarbone. "And the heart. The past must be filtered through both to mean anything in the present."

"Bai Yuqi will commit that to memory, *dianxia*."

Hesina tucked her hands into her sleeves as she turned. "I'll walk the rest of the way," she murmured to her guards as they came forth to help her back into the palanquin.

Her legs were still weak. By the time they made it to the terraces, Hesina had cold-sweated through her underrobes. Still, she rejected any assistance. There was a time to lean on others, and a time to stand alone.

She raised her gaze.

The steps, swept clean in preparation, were already dusted with fresh snow. Imperial guards outfitted in ceremonial jade laminar flanked the ascent, the crimson-dyed tassels of their halberds stirring in the wind. The palace loomed over them all, growing larger and larger as Hesina huffed and puffed her way up. She braced a hand on her thigh once she reached the landing, caught her breath, and straightened.

Caiyan was here as promised. So was Lilian, her chin smudged with soot. She gave Hesina the smallest of nods. No matter what happened today, Mei's parents and the others were out of this city. They were safe.

Relief bolstered Hesina and gave her the courage to remove the hand scroll from her sleeve.

She faced the pavilion. The sky teemed above their heads, a billowing sea of gray. Her people stood minuscule beneath it. They shouldn't have had to claw for air, yet when Hesina opened her mouth, she suddenly felt like she was suffocating.

Then wind blasted through the crowd, cleaving Hesina's core with icy clarity.

There's a tale. The tale of Yidou.

A tale of a life for a life, flesh to sustain flesh.

But feeding the people's fear wasn't giving them sustenance. It was poisoning them.

She clenched the scroll shut. She wouldn't read it. She wouldn't divide this kingdom any further. She wouldn't be like her father and give up her ideals.

"When the Eleven created this new era," she began, "they simplified the language so everyone could learn. The ability to think for oneself is the kind of power neither blood nor status can confer.

"To learn, we must understand the facts. I won't hide them from you. Twelve days ago, the palace dungeons were breached—"

"By sooths!"

"—by unidentified persons," she continued over the shout. "One of the elite guard was injured; three were lost, their bodies unrecoverable. Their names shall go down in the *Imperial Histories*, and their families will be honored.

"We also failed to recover the bodies of the convicted and the perpetrators. I know this is a frightening time." She raised her voice to be heard. "An unprecedented time. But in the absence of information, we mustn't draw dangerous conclusions."

"So who killed the king?"

Who killed the king?

Who killed the king?

Who killed the king?

I don't know: the truth. *Xia Zhong*: a lie. *Mei*: a lie the people would take as truth.

"Was it the convicted?" they cried when Hesina stood silent, paralyzed by the choice facing her. "Was it the sooths?"

"It was the sooths!"

"The sooths! The sooths!"

Truth or lie.

Before Hesina could decide, the cold edge of a knife sliced her throat.

TWENTY-SIX

What you value manifests in the way you treat your blood.

ONE *of the* ELEVEN *on family*

What can I say? I abandoned my family to protect them.

TWO *of the* ELEVEN *on family*

The hand on Hesina's shoulder held her still, even though she couldn't move. The other edged the knife closer. Warmth trickled down her neck.

"It was I." A gale buffeted them, tossing strands of black walnut-colored hair against Hesina's cheek and wrapping her in the scent of osmanthus and peach blossom. She knew it as well as her own. The winds strengthened but failed to steal away Lilian's voice. "It was I who killed the king!"

The ground dissolved. Faces merged, shades of skin becoming one. Commoners, guards . . . everything was gone, eroded by Hesina's horror. "Lies," she whispered.

Lilian replied in a shout that tore right through the blanket of silence. "I killed him for this kingdom!"

"*Qui—*"

The knife cut deeper. The trickle quickened, slipping past her sternum. Her thoughts ran with the blood. Lilian couldn't really mean it. This was a script. An act. It had to be. Her sister couldn't have "killed" their father. She—

"I, too, thought the king was benevolent and righteous. I thought of him as a father. But his benevolence hid his ineffectiveness. His righteousness was an excuse for his past crimes."

The world bled back in: the hundreds crowded on the pavilion below, the guards on the stairs, their halberds and gazes pointed at the knife at Hesina's throat.

"This kingdom is my home." Lilian's voice pealed above the wind. "I wanted better for it, so I ended him."

Hesina's mind thawed. Whatever Lilian's motives, she had to silence her, stop her from condemning herself any further.

"I placed my hopes in this queen," said Lilian.

Elbow to the ribs, hand to the wrist. Seize the knife. Everyone is watching; you have one chance.

"Again, a mistake—"

A shudder rocked through Lilian before Hesina could act. Her sister's gasp warmed her cheek.

The knife fell.

Lilian fell next. Hesina barely caught her, staggering to the ground under her sister's weight. Her perfect features crumpled in pain, and Hesina's heart spasmed. "Speak to me, Lilian. Tell me what's wrong."

"Na-Na." Lilian grimaced, her teeth inked in red. Hesina's mind iced back over. *No. No, no, no.* She frantically searched for the source of the injury. Her hand knocked into an oblong object in Lilian's back. Her trembling fingers curled around a handle, a hilt—a dagger planted beside the left shoulder blade.

The snow's descent slowed.

This . . . wasn't happening. Not for real. This was just pretend. Any moment now, Lilian was going to leap up and cry *Surprise! I got you!*

But the terrible, sticky wheeze of her sister's breath went on and on. A shadow waxed over them, and Hesina's gaze lifted, climbing the length of a black-and-gold *hanfu*, stilling on a pair of hands.

Caiyan's hands, right hand clasped over left, knuckles flecked with blood. He was the only one who'd been standing behind them, the only who could have . . . who could have . . .

Who could have . . .

"Na-Na." The rasp of her name rescued Hesina from the torrent of the truth. "All the ministers—" wheezed Lilian.

"S-shhh. We'll get you to the Imperial Doc—"

"—are stone-heads. They couldn't even think of this solution . . ."

Solution. The word threshed the breath from Hesina's lungs. Solution? What sort of solution was this? What could this possibly accomplish? "H-hush."

Lilian smiled that horribly red smile. Then, with a gasp of effort, she flung out a sleeve.

A package tumbled down the steps. The guards rushing toward them barely had enough time to stumble away before it exploded. Chunks of stone rocketed into the air, and the commoners screamed even as the smoke cleared. The resulting damage was incomparable to what happened in the *tianlao* cells.

But the people didn't know that.

The people would link the two as congruent events.

The smoke of Hesina's confusion cleared, too, and comprehension flayed her.

Lilian was scapegoating herself before an audience of hundreds.

Word of her confession would flood the provinces, the streets. *Who killed the king? None other than the queen's adopted sister.* They had all the evidence they needed. The knife to Hesina's throat. The scripted confession. The bomb, a prop.

"Why?"

Lilian closed her eyes. "Now you can protect them . . . all of them . . ."

"Shhh." Tears spilled over Hesina's cheeks, hot like the blood soaking her skirts. *Tell me you're not doing any of this for free. Tell me you want your payment of candied hawthorn berries.* "S-shhh."

"You're ruining another . . . gown . . ." Lilian's lips quivered with a smile. "Though . . . it was bland anyway . . ."

Voices swelled from down below. *Blood . . . not burning . . . not a sooth . . .*

Hesina's jaw trembled as she bit back a howl of rage. The people could have her heart. They could have her life. They could have everything she had to offer, but Lilian wasn't theirs to take. She wouldn't allow it.

"You're going to be okay. The Doctress will make you okay. Stop talking," she said as Lilian opened her mouth.

"Promise me . . ." The boots of the imperial guards pounded around them, nearly drowning out Lilian's whisper. She raised a hand, struggling to reach Hesina's cheek. "Promise . . . you'll finish this . . . in style."

Her hand wavered. Hesina clasped it before it could fall and squeezed, just like she had when they'd waded into the ponds together, or flown down the corridors with hot *mantous* clutched in their skirts, the cooks in fierce pursuit. She held on so tightly that she never felt the exact moment when Lilian stopped squeezing back.

* * *

Hesina didn't change. Didn't have someone see to her neck. She finally looked the part she deserved: bloodstained.

She swept into the throne hall like a squall, her ministers scrambling to assemble in her wake. From the dais, she ordered members of the Investigation Bureau to search Lilian's chambers and return with an immediate report. As they waited, a few of the younger vassals snuck glances in her direction. If they were hoping to see a reaction, they'd sorely be disappointed. Hesina was amber and stone, a fossilized cicada shell with dust for innards, a cavity for a heart, and a single thought for a mind:

Finish this in style.

The thought anchored her when members of the Investigation Bureau came back carrying gilded trays.

"*Dianxia*," addressed the director. "Per your orders, we searched the kingslayer's rooms and found the following items."

He proceeded to identify them: a vial containing crane's crest, an arsenic-based poison, and a forbidden tome criticizing the Eleven and the new era.

Hesina gripped the arms of her throne as the items emerged. Lilian had staged her exit well. *Too* well, for the girl who wore ribbons in her hair and dye on her apron, shunning politics and its players.

But she had played them all.

"Excellent," said Hesina, her voice hollow, hurt dripping into her heart like water in an empty cave. She should have grown accustomed to people keeping secrets from her by now. "Today marks the conclusion of this case. Vigilante groups who fail to disband will face death by hanging. The same goes for anyone carrying out an unauthorized cutting. Grand Secretariat Sunlei, see that these penal laws are posted throughout the city within three days."

"Understood, *dianxia*."

Hesina moved on, issuing reparations to businesses and vendors, matching the silver outflow with a tax raise on millet, and backing a public effort at reclamation and restoration of destroyed property. Word by word, decree by decree, she stitched her kingdom back together.

"And what of the disposal of the kingslayer's body?" asked Xia Zhong from the ranks.

Hesina met his eye unflinchingly. "That matter falls under your jurisdiction, Minister Xia. By the Book of Rites, how should the body be disposed?"

"They are to be burned in public, their ashes scattered into Tricent Gorge to be forever tormented by the rapids."

No tomb. No ceremony. Nothing to bury or to mourn.

Hesina forced her fists apart and flattened her hands upon the throne. "Then see that the rites are observed."

It wasn't Xia Zhong who made her falter, but Caiyan, whom Hesina summoned from the ranks next. She thought she could barrel through what needed to be done, but as he stepped before the dais and bowed, time slowed as it had on the terraces. A hundred heartbeats raced by before Hesina tore her gaze away from his hands— clean now, but bloodied in her memory—and managed to speak.

"Kingslayer or not, she should have faced trial like everyone else. That is the law of the *Tenets*. You"—*killed her. Killed her killed her killed her*—"didn't afford her the chance."

"Forgive me." Caiyan's head was still bowed; the ground received those two words, not Hesina. It gave her small relief. She wasn't sure if she *could* forgive him, even if Lilian had willed her twin's actions. Lilian had damned herself, but Caiyan had driven in the knife. Hesina couldn't forget this any more than she could bring her sister back to life.

The Minister of Works stepped forward. "If I may, *dianxia*," he ventured, breaking the extended silence. "I'd like to defend Viscount Yan Caiyan. He acted as he saw necessary. No one else was in the position to do the same, not without putting your life at risk."

The others echoed in agreement. They could just as easily have been demanding Caiyan's arrest, but by quite literally cutting his blood ties, he appeared to have dodged any and all suspicion.

Unnerved, Hesina raised a hand, and the assembly quieted. "What Minister Zhou says is true," she forced out. "For saving my life, I am in your debt. You shall have anything you request."

Caiyan deepened his bow. "I'd like to be granted command of the city guard."

She stilled. "You are a court official of great learning." *You are inexperienced with martial matters.*

"They require a disciplined leader dedicated to maintaining the newfound peace."

"You are currently overseeing the examinations." *You are preoccupied.*

"The first round is set to begin tomorrow."

Her eyes narrowed. *You are in mourning.* But she couldn't say it. No one in this hall was supposed to mourn a kingslayer, not even her.

There were a hundred other things she couldn't say: *Who are you, Yan Caiyan? My advisor? A viscount of the court? A brother—who killed his own sister? Why do I find it harder and harder to read you?*

But it was too late to retract her offer. "Then the city guard is yours to command."

Caiyan lifted his head. For the briefest of moments, an indescribable emotion darkened his features. But maybe Hesina was seeing what she wanted to see, because by the next second he was kneeling in *koutou*, rising, and melting back into the ranks without so much as a flicker of remorse.

The director of the Investigation Bureau came forward to take his place. "There is one last matter, *dianxia*."

"Speak."

He turned to the guards flanking the doors. "Bring him in."

I am amber. I am stone. But then the double doors opened and the guards dragged in Akira. Two shoved him before the dais. Another threw down his rod. Reflexively, Hesina rose.

"At the fifth gong strike this morning," said the director, "this young man was caught in an act of thievery."

"What did he steal?"

Xia Zhong stepped forward. "My finest collection of *Tenets*."

There was something lewd about the minister and the director standing side by side, both knowing very well that Hesina could do nothing to stop them. Her gaze tore to Akira, who'd dragged himself up. He didn't look at her. He must have learned of Lilian's fate, must have realized that Hesina would fail him like she'd failed her own sister. Wiping the blood off his split lip, he reached for his rod.

A guard struck his sword down. The rod split in two with a crack that halved Hesina.

"I don't require remuneration," prompted Xia Zhong. "I raise my concern for the sake of palace security."

He said this all with a glint in his fishlike eyes. *Pardon him, if you dare.*

In another life, Hesina would do more than dare. She'd pardon Akira and finish strangling Xia Zhong. But with every eye pinned on the imperial city, she couldn't risk compromising her position, not by issuing suspicious pardons or by ruffling the feathers of her oldest minister.

Defeated, she sank back into the throne.

Finish this in style.

"Arrest him," Hesina said, closing her eyes so that she wouldn't have to see the order carried out.

She should have covered her ears instead.

"The dungeons aren't a bad place to stay." The low lilt of Akira's voice punctured her, and the willpower keeping her in the throne gushed out. "No rules, no expectations, no poison in the goblet—"

The doors shut with a resounding groan.

Hesina stayed behind after everyone left, until the urge to bolt to dungeons and explain herself to Akira withered, along with every other sensation.

Numb, she descended the dais. She wandered through the facades, letting her feet lead the way, and almost laughed when she saw where they'd guided her.

To be fair, she *would* have come to Caiyan in the past. If she were a house, he was the beam holding her up. But now she couldn't even look at the carved herons rising out of his chamber doors without seeing his hands all over again, right clasped over left, knuckles seeded with blood.

She squeezed her eyes shut, spots of light puckering beneath the lids. She reopened them. Stared at the doors. Lifted a hand to knock. Dropped it. Let his name rise in her throat. Swallowed it. Hesina wanted answers, but what did she have to give in return? *I'm sorry*

I couldn't protect her? Sorry I couldn't even secure a proper burial? Caiyan might have driven in the knife, but Hesina had capitalized on Lilian's sacrifice.

Neither of them had the face to confront each other.

She turned to go. Four steps forward. Four steps back.

She barged through the doors.

Caiyan's rooms were cold. Dim. The braziers had not been lit, and Hesina could barely make out his form at the foot of the bed, but she saw him. A brother who needed her.

He didn't acknowledge her when she sat beside him. She pressed her palms to his damp face, and he pulled back. She wrapped her arms around him before he could withdraw again.

They stayed that way for a long, long time.

Eventually, she coaxed him into bed and rummaged under the frame until she found his secret stash of literature.

Lilian had lied. Wang Hutian didn't write erotic novellas, but sappy, melodramatic poems. Hesina read them out loud, finishing one collection and moving on to another, until the words stole away her voice and dreams stole away Caiyan's troubled breaths.

"'Then morning came cloaked in dew./I drank to the sight of your fading ghost,/and you raised your glass to your lips/for one final toast . . .'"

The sheaf quivered in her hands. Hesina set it down. Instead of distracting her from her emotions, the poems had filled her with borrowed ones. The longing of Wang Hutian's fair fox spirits became *her* longing for respite. The righteous rage of his *qilin* hunters became *her* righteous rage against her kingdom. And the guilt of his mistress-taking scholars became *her* guilt over everything she had done since her father's death.

Her bottom lip trembled. She bit down until she tasted copper.

Your fault. Your fault. Your fault.

Hesina lurched out of Caiyan's room. She shut the doors behind her. She stuffed her fist into her mouth and screamed. Her fault. Lilian's death was her fault. Had she not opened a trial, there would have been no question of who killed the king.

The king wasn't even *dead*.

It was *his* fault for keeping so many secrets, *his* fault for teaching her to believe in justice and law.

His fault.

Hesina clutched herself, and something cut into her stomach. Her father's medallion. The one she'd oh so carefully strung onto her sash in search of the truth he claimed to love. She tore it off and hurled it at the ground. The jade broke with a crack, and she breathed hard from the satisfaction of it.

Then her breathing stopped.

Golden gas curled up from the medallion's shattered remains.

The same golden gas that'd risen from her father's body.

Akira's voice suddenly sounded in Hesina's head. She'd been trying so hard to ignore it in the throne room that she hadn't deciphered what he was trying to say.

No poison in the goblet.

Still holding her breath, Hesina crouched. She lifted the shards. They were curved. The medallion had been hollow. Hollow to carry the poison. Not the goblet. Not her mother's snuff bottle.

The poison came from the medallion that'd been on her father's body all along.

She dropped the shards, shaking her head in dry-eyed confusion. What did this mean?

Go back to the place where all this started. Before the red-light district, where the Silver Iris had said *I See golden gas rising from a pile of shards*. Before the imperial gardens, where Hesina had discovered her father's body among the irises.

Go back to the place where he left pieces of himself behind.

Hesina made for her father's study. She strode to his desk. Quaking, she sat in his tortoiseshell chair, just as he probably had.

What did he do next?

The chair scraped as she rose. Pain bloomed in her chest; she was reliving his final moments. But she pushed on, kneeling by his costume chest. She riffled through the costumes, just as he probably had, ran her fingers across the textures. Silk and hemp.

He hadn't pulled the courier's costume out at random. He'd searched for it with deliberate intent.

Why?

What had he done next? Opened the *Tenets* to a page of One of the Eleven. Entered the secret passageway that would lead him to the gardens.

Fueled by pure instinct, Hesina staggered to the wall of books and pulled out *The Cosmic Cycles*, *Pangtie's Reflections*, and *The Rise and Fall of the Relic Reign*. The shelves split down the middle, and the varnished corridor that appeared gleamed like a secret river. She stepped in and pulled the lever protruding from the side panel. The river plunged into darkness.

A shred of old panic curled up in Hesina. She'd gotten lost in a passageway as lightless as this one. But her father had told her to breathe deeply and use the walls as a guide. So she did. She inhaled the piney varnish, felt her heart calm, then placed her hands to the side panels—

And froze.

There were knife marks gouged into the wood, each stroke forming characters.

LITTLE BIRD...

Somewhere in the palace, maids were dusting. Cooks were plucking geese. A hundred thousand others breathed, walked, talked in the imperial city, a million beyond the walls. But they didn't exist in this moment. Hesina's entire world throbbed in the words at her fingertips.

LITTLE BIRD,
   BY THE TIME YOU'RE READING THIS, YOU'LL KNOW. YOU'LL KNOW THAT YOUR FATHER WAS A LIAR, A SINNER, A MURDERER. YOU MIGHT EVEN KNOW, AS HARD AS IT IS TO ACCEPT, THAT I—

Hesina jerked away.

YOU MIGHT EVEN KNOW, AS HARD AS IT IS TO ACCEPT, THAT I—

She backed up and thumped into the opposite wall. She was gulping air and drowning in it. Laughing was the only way she could breathe.

AS HARD AS IT IS TO ACCEPT.

Still laughing, she pawed at the panels until she found the lever. She pulled. The wall of books fissured apart. She escaped the darkness for the study's ashy light, but the truth followed her out.

The truth of who'd poisoned the king.

YOU MIGHT EVEN KNOW.

But she hadn't. Not when she'd seen his body in the iris beds, impeccably costumed, hands folded across his stomach, the perfect image of death without a struggle. Not when the cooks and kitchen maids reported that no one had delivered food and drink to the study that day. She hadn't considered the significance of the *Tenets* being left open to a biography of One of the Eleven when her father *was* One of the Eleven. She'd repressed any subconscious realizations, just as she'd repressed her motives. She'd never been looking for the truth. She'd been looking for someone to blame.

All the pieces fell into place. The snuff bottle on her father's desk had led Hesina to her mother's rooms. There, she'd found the chest. The contents of her mother's chest had led her to the *Tenets*. Now, she saw that it verified her father's identity as One of the Eleven.

Meanwhile, her father had flipped the book open to One of the Eleven before rising from this desk. He'd strung on a medallion carved with the character for *longevity* because he'd *wanted* her to know. He'd taken his paring knife with him not to cut up persimmons, but to carve his final message onto these walls. And he'd put on a courier's *hanfu* to deliver it, this truth that Hesina had paid a price in blood to find.

The pitch of her laughter shot high.

"So now you know."

That voice.

The laughter died on Hesina's lips.

"Well?" The train of her mother's scarlet *ruqun* whispered over the floor as she swept to the square *zitan* table in the center of the lower study.

Hesina stared blearily at the dowager queen. *A ghost.* She couldn't actually be here.

But a ghost's words didn't cut the way her mother's did. "Does it hurt? I imagine it would, going through all this trouble, just to find that he ended himself."

TWENTY-SEVEN

We believe the things we want to believe.

ONE of the ELEVEN on human nature

I'd like to think that my choices are my own, but how many truly are?

TWO of the ELEVEN on human nature

They sat across from each other, the letter Hesina had written and inked with Sanjing's seal on the *zitan* tabletop between them.

It hadn't even been opened.

Hesina didn't speak. If she moved a single muscle in her face, she feared she might cry, and she was pitiful enough in her mother's eyes.

"Why did you keep this from me?" Hesina finally whispered, hovering her gaze over her mother's shoulder instead of her face. It was easier to coexist this way.

The dowager queen gave a cold chuckle, and Hesina's hands tightened in her lap.

"If you'd told me from the start . . ." Hesina's voice broke. *None of this would have happened. No one would have died for my trial.*

Her mother chuckled again. "Four months ago, I offered to rule."

"That's not my question."

"I said you would bring this kingdom down to its knees—"

"You should have told me the truth!"

Silence quivered in the wake of Hesina's scream. Her vision blurred, and she pulled back the tears with a rough inhale. "You should have told me the truth."

The dowager queen raised a brow. "Was that not the truth?"

Hesina expected nothing less from her mother.

"This was his final wish."

But she hadn't expected *that*. "What? For me to think he was murdered?"

"No one forced you to think that. No one forced you to declare a trial. No one forced you to continue searching for the truth on your own."

"I—"

"How many times did you think about giving up? Why didn't you?"

Hesina had no answer.

Her mother sighed. "Stubborn as always."

Hesina was too shaken to even bristle.

"Leave with me," said the dowager queen without warning, and Hesina's gaze jerked to her mother. Again, she was startled by how much they resembled each other, down to their oval faces, the mid-parts in their hair. But the mother she knew didn't say things like, "Pack what you need. A second carriage is waiting by the northern entrance."

"Is that it? After seventeen years, that's all you have to say? To ask me to give up my throne, my kingdom, with no explanation?"

"You think they're yours? That you can control the people? That you can tell them what to think and believe?"

"I can help them."

"Oh? Like you did today?"

She gutted Hesina like a fish.

"Show me the book."

Hesina feigned dumb. "What book?"

Her mother buffed her nails against her *ruqun* cuff. "The one you stole from my room."

Get it yourself. But predictably, Hesina went to her chambers. She got down on her hands and knees, on the verge of lifting the floorboards when she stiffened.

The hair she always stuck between the boards was gone.

She yanked the boards apart. The original *Tenets* and Xia Zhong's letters were still here. The sprint of her heart slowed. She was being paranoid. The floorboards looked shinier than usual, and the citrus tang of bergamot perfumed the air. The maids must have just oiled them. The hair could have been swept away. Even if someone had stumbled upon this nook, they would have found a worthless copy of *The Medicinal Properties of Exotic Fungi*.

Regardless, Hesina made a note to change the hiding spot.

When she returned to her father's study, her mother flicked a finger at the desk. "Place it."

Again, Hesina obeyed, setting it beside a miniature *jiutan* of sorghum wine that had appeared in her absence. She knew better than to question it.

She sat as her mother flipped the book open, and stared as the dowager queen tore out a fistful of pages.

Hesina was too stunned to make a sound. A relic, destroyed just like that.

But then the pages floated out of her mother's hands and fused back into the book.

Hesina had seen sooths draw water from air. She'd seen whole pots crack into shards. But this defied everything she knew. If all magic stemmed from reeling the future into the present, how could this be? Paper couldn't heal itself.

Yet it had. Gingerly, she pulled in the book and ran a finger down the pages. Smooth. Seamless. The tear gone without a trace, much like the cut on her father's abdomen.

Her head spun. "What was that?"

"The same magic that makes us immortal."

"You—"

"I am Two."

The gong struck six. In the gathering dark, Hesina stared at her mother. Two was characterized as brave and spirited. The dowager queen was neither of those things. But now Hesina saw the way she looked at the book, her gaze heavy. These words were her words. The stories they told were her stories. A part of her remained preserved in those pages, no matter how she'd changed.

"How?" she still asked. If her mother was in fact Two, *how* was she immortal? By enlightenment or elixir?

Her mother took a long draw from the *jiutan*. "When we finally breached the imperial walls," she said, voice like ground glass, "there were only five of us left. We couldn't have defeated the emperor. It was Kaishen—your so-called Nine—who suggested we seek out the most powerful sooth in the kingdom. She saw a future in which your father and I lived on in the commoners' hearts, our names and feats kept alive in tales and sagas. She Reeled the immortality of legend into our flesh."

Her gaze slid to the *Tenets*. "Unbeknownst to us, she did the same to this book. Its teachings will forever prevail. The commoners worship every word we wish we could take back."

So this was why the commoners were so opposed to war. Why they hated sooths and couldn't be persuaded otherwise. This . . . *book* was the source of Hesina's plight. She didn't care if it'd heal itself; she wanted to shred it.

Her mother took another swig. "Wen suspected the book's indestructibility was tied to our own." It took Hesina a second to place her father's name. "We tried to kill ourselves. Burning. Drowning. Beheading—we've done it all." She tapped the scar at her throat, and Hesina blanched. "Some attempts healed worse than others. When all failed, we faked our deaths to give other rulers a chance to right our wrongs."

She raised the *jiutan*.

Hesina seized it before it met her lips. "Why are you telling me now? Why did the two of you return after your first reign? And if Father faked his death again, why leave any clues for me to find at all?"

"*Let go.*"

She did, and her mother tipped back the *jiutan*. "Tell me," murmured the dowager queen, setting it down hard. "Was the truth worth it?"

Another deflection. Hesina's jaw tightened. "No."

"Good. Pack your things, and—"

"But searching for it has opened my eyes to the kingdom's wounds. I want to help it heal."

"It's rotten, not wounded. Can you be the knife to cut away the parts that fester?"

It doesn't have to be that way. But words and reason could sway people only so much, and there wouldn't always be a Lilian to take the fall. "I can."

"You'll ruin yourself," snapped her mother.

"Someone has to."

"Foolish girl." The dowager queen lifted the *jiutan* again, frowned, and set it back down. "So be it. You want to know why we returned for a second reign? It was for you."

"You came back just for . . ." *Me?* Hesina couldn't repeat the words without the risk of laughing out loud.

"We'd adopted children, but never had our own. You were the first. Wen saw you as the kingdom's hope." Her mother chuckled without warmth. "A dreamer to the bone."

"Hope. I'm to be the kingdom's hope."

"Ludicrous, am I correct?"

Yes, very. "If what you say is really true, then why haven't I been told this before?"

"Your father decided that the best way to tell you was to show you. He faked his death prematurely knowing very well that you'd pursue a trial, that your actions would throw everything wrong with this kingdom into sharp relief. Now you know exactly what you're up against. To stay or to leave is your choice, and your choice alone. This was his wish."

The knowledge settled over Hesina like cold mist. A choice. Her father's wish was to give her a choice.

Is that all? But then she thought back to the cavern behind the reredos, those words on the walls. Her father hadn't wanted the mantle of a hero. He was giving her the choice he hadn't been given himself.

And he'd done so at a cost she couldn't accept.

"And what is *your* wish?" asked Hesina, to her own surprise.

Her mother blinked. "Forget your silly ideals, and leave with me. You have no one left. What is the point of clinging to a world that has abandoned you?"

"It may abandon me, but I can't abandon it."

She waited for her mother to call her a fool. Instead, the dowager queen stared at her, dead silent.

Then she threw her head back and laughed. That was more like the mother Hesina knew. "Stay, leave, what do I care? Tomorrow, I return to the mountains. Don't bother seeing me off."

Hesina rushed to rise with her mother. "I'll have the servants ready your chambers—"

"Spare me." Her mother swept to the doors.

"Wait." Hesina drew a deep breath. She wanted an answer to one last question.

Did you ever love me? But that was too bloated with hope, too painful to ask, so instead she asked, "Why do you hate me?"

Deny it. Say you came back and asked me to leave because you want to protect me. Say—

"For the same reason I hate this palace." The words were like metal, the blade of them wicked sharp. "For the same reason I hate that book," continued her mother, even though Hesina had heard enough. "For the same reason I hate looking in the mirror with a face that belongs to a person I can never be again."

* * *

Akira was gone, but the smoke stain on the ceiling of his room remained. The dark patch gazed upon Hesina like a bruised eye as she entered. She remembered that night with the fire and his face, a breath away. The memory tasted sweet. It made her throat ache.

She went to the bed. Reclined. She stared at the beams overhead and wondered what thoughts flitted across Akira's mind as he did the same. He had suspected many things. What would he think now if she shared what her mother had said to her, asked of her? Would he advise her to leave or stay?

Hesina imagined his voice. *Leaving doesn't sound bad.*

It didn't sound bad at all. If she stayed, she could end up like her mother. Cold, sardonic, and embittered by reminders of the person she used to be.

Sighing, Hesina rolled onto her side and buried her face in the pillow. It didn't smell like Akira. It occurred to her that he probably didn't sleep on the bed at all.

She laid herself down on the floor and thought of sitting on the throne, standing on the terraces, thought about how it all felt and how it couldn't compare to the ground. This was where she truly belonged.

For the first time in days, her sleep was sound.

✻ ✻ ✻

She took her cup of tea on the infirmary patio the next morning, watching the rain pour off the upturned awning and melt the snow.

If she left with her mother for the mountains, this peace could be her reality. She wouldn't have to worry about the kingdom. Caiyan could rule in Sanjing's absence. But the image of his blood-flecked knuckles reared again, and a tremor shot through Hesina. Hot tea sloshed onto her hand. Her grip flinched open.

The teacup fell.

The sounds of rainfall quieted as she stared at the shattered pieces. Once, she'd done the same. Stared at her mother's spilled concoction, the heat of humiliation in her cheeks, and begged for her blessing. She was no longer so stupid.

No longer so brave.

"I don't see your things," said her mother when Hesina met her by the northern gate. The dowager queen's carriage was plain and her attendants few. No one would know that she'd come and gone, or that Hesina, like a coward, had considered going too.

"I'm staying."

Rain pattered off their paper parasols.

Hesina waited for her mother to persuade her, but with a shrug and a turn, the dowager queen allowed her attendants to help her into the carriage. "Suit yourself."

A familiar emptiness yawned in Hesina as she watched the carriage rattle off. She no longer had a father to take her to the persimmon grove, or a sister to drag her to the textile workshops, where they would dye bolts of white silk into pinks and turquoises and violets until Hesina forgot all about the dowager queen.

Except that she didn't want to forget about her mother this time. Hesina had always been so singularly focused on what *she* might have done to make the dowager queen hate her. She'd never bothered to see it wasn't about her. It'd never been about her. Not all stories were hers to tell.

Alone, she returned to the Eastern Palace and readied herself for court.

* * *

The rain didn't let up the next day. Under a weeping sky, hundreds turned out for Lilian's cremation. Their impatience smoked the air when the firewood didn't; the first few attempts at lighting the pyre guttered under the lashing winds, and Hesina had to order the guards to douse the bed of branches with oil before flame finally caught. As black smoke billowed in choking clouds, she left the dry safety of her palanquin to stand under the downpour, letting the rain be the tears she couldn't shed.

The rain turned to ice overnight, and the streets glittered as Hesina rode out to the pavilion once more at dawn. This time it was to see a vigilante leader hang. Crowds again flocked as the guards marched the young man to the gallows.

"The maggots are hatching!" he cried as they put his neck to the rope. "I may die today, but you will all die tom—"

The trapdoor gave; the rope jerked taut. Hesina looked away. When the thrashing and kicking stilled, she ordered that the body be left to hang one night and one day as a warning.

She turned to leave, but not before she heard a muffled sob. The sound wrung her heart. From whom had it come? A mother, mourning the loss of a child? A sister, mourning the death of her brother? There would be hatred in their eyes, if Hesina dared to look, and she dared, because she deserved it.

A hand grasped her elbow, stopping her.

Silently, Caiyan drew a cloak over her shoulders. He guided her down the pavilion before she could resist, standing behind her as if to shield her from all the hatred in the world. He helped her into the palanquin, and suddenly, Hesina found herself sitting knee to knee with a brother she hadn't seen since that night in his room, hadn't *spoken* to since that day in the throne hall.

She ought to say something now. She tried to work up the nerve for words.

Caiyan beat her to it. He reported on the progress of the examinations (they were past the preliminary rounds) and updated her on the movements of the city guards. Numbers and statistics passed his lips, his voice smooth and calm.

Hesina wanted to shake him. *Stop pretending we're fine. Tell me you hate me, blame me. Give me your hurt to work with, but don't hide yourself like this.*

But she was tired, and she was cold, and she was weary of battles she could not win. So she nodded along and listened and made all the right comments, and when they came to the palace, Caiyan bowed like a proper advisor and left Hesina standing before the throne hall doors.

Letters from Sanjing awaited on the ivory *kang* table inside. They'd been posted from Qiao, one of the three major merchant cities halfway to the front. Hesina carefully sliced them open. Her brother's squared-off strokes were comforting, even though the words themselves—*the Crown Prince has rallied a force of three thousand sooths, war is likely*—were not.

She burned the letters once she finished reading and leaned her head onto her fingertips. Stability was only beginning to burgeon again; Kendi'a would kill it like a hard frost.

She spent the rest of the night drafting a missive to the kingdom of Ning. The *Tenets* forbade military alliances with any of the other three kingdoms, but she had chosen to stay. She had chosen to rule. Books and laws be damned—she had to do *something*.

She spent hours in the archives, seeking a way to destroy the book, skipping meals and forgoing sleep. A sooth had done the Reeling. Surely a sooth could reverse it. But considering her history with sooths—the two she knew were dead—Hesina wasn't in a rush to befriend another.

Life went on as such for two weeks, until the evening Ming'er barred Hesina from the archives and insisted that she take a bath. Following a debate about hygiene, wars, and the pressing priority of both, Ming'er triumphed; a tub was filled with steaming vats of water carried in from the Imperial Laundry.

As Hesina soaked, her thoughts softened. Sleeping was also low on her list of priorities, but she couldn't find a good reason not to close her eyes.

When she reopened them, seemingly seconds later, it was to the sight of her sister.

Hesina's heart froze midbeat. "L-Lilian?"

Leaning her arms onto the rim of the tub, Lilian rested her chin atop her fists. "We could go anywhere, do anything."

Hesina raised a dripping hand.

"We could ride serpents in the Baolin Isles, soak in the floating hot springs on the Aoshi archipelago."

She reached for Lilian's cheek.

"If I asked you to come, would you?"

Her hand went through air.

Hesina woke with a shudder, then shivered. The water had gone cold. She sat for a moment longer, staring at the empty space above the tub's rim, then splashed out and grabbed the underrobes draped over the silk folding screen. Her sash crinkled as she tied it. She'd sewn Xia Zhong's letters between the layers of fabric and hidden the original *Tenets* in plain sight on the shelves in her father's study, the last place people would look.

She threw on a winter cloak and headed for the gardens, cutting a healthy branch from the peach grove before making for the persimmon. Under a moonlit sky veined with silver branches, Hesina set to work, clearing the snow, loosening the hard earth with a rock. She patted it all back in place around her inserted peach branch and studied her handiwork.

This was winter. Her first attempt was unlikely to succeed. But she would plant as many peach trees as it'd take for a lone one to stand among the persimmons. It wasn't the same as a tombstone, but Lilian wouldn't mind. In fact, thought Hesina with a watery smile, Lilian might have preferred it.

Then she rose and took in the surrounding gardens. She'd grown up here, seen ants swarm the peonies in the spring, tadpoles spawn in summer, gingko leaves ferment in autumn, camellias bloom in winter. She knew the paths and where they all led. That one went to the gazebo on the lotus pond. That, to the rock gardens.

And this, the one she ended up on, went to the place she'd sworn never to visit again.

Time had diluted her grief. Secrets had polluted it. Still, her pulse thrummed when she entered the iris beds. They were covered in snow, the flowers long dead. But they were preserved in her mind's eye, just like her father, and Hesina knelt over the place she'd last found him, spreading her hands flat before her and pressing her forehead to their backs.

She stayed in the deepest *koutou* until her skin burned, itched, numbed. Until her form wilted and her shoulders hunched. She wished she could have said that she cursed this snowy spot, or wept solely for Lilian and Mei.

But that would have been her greatest lie of all.

* * *

Later that night, her page visited her sitting room. "I found your former representative's cell number, *dianxia*."

"I didn't—" *I didn't ask for it.*

But she had. She remembered now. In the twilight hours, after spending a whole night with dusty tomes that revealed no answers, drunk on hopelessness and helplessness, Hesina had buckled. She had asked.

Tell me, she wanted to blurt out. She would visit Akira. She

DESCENDANT OF THE CRANE

would explain everything to him. But she wouldn't be able to free him. Seeing him would reignite her agony, and whatever they had between them would decay, just as it had with her and her father.

It was time she learned to let go.

"I don't want to know," she gritted out, then crossed into the corridors even though she had nowhere to go, no place to be.

Except one.

✳ ✳ ✳

Like last time, the doors to Caiyan's rooms were unlocked.

"Caiyan?"

His bedchamber was empty, but a flame twitched in the oil lamp on his study desk, and a lynx-fur brush, still wet with ink, had been left propped against a porcelain rest.

Hesina could wait. She sat on his bed and brushed a hand over the pillow logs, the same ones she'd leaned upon after the Silver Iris's death.

Promise me you won't jeopardize your rule.

She had done worse than jeopardize her rule. She had jeopardized her life. Lilian was dead as a result. Mei too. The blood of shame rushed to Hesina's cheeks, and the urge to bolt stiffened her legs. She wanted to escape this chamber and every reminder of the brother she'd failed so badly.

But she forced herself to stay. The night deepened. The lamp burned out. In the dark she sat, ears pricked for the sound of his return, a sound that never came.

✳ ✳ ✳

"Dianxia. Dianxia."

Hesina had no sense of place or time. The blinds were uniformly dark, and she could barely make out the face of her page.

She rose, palming her eyes. "What's the hour?" Her voice sounded frog-like.

Her page's was oddly strained. "Just past the fifth, *dianxia*."

"Then why am I awake?"

"The court is in session."

"*Court?*"

"Yes, *dianxia*. Here, in the Eastern Palace."

"I know where my own court is," Hesina snapped, then regretted it. Her page had never done anything to earn her wrath, unlike the rest of the people in this palace. "Who called the session? Director Lang?"

"No—"

"Is she awake?" interrupted a rough voice from outside.

Hesina held up a hand before her page could answer for her, then rose and went to the doors. Caiyan's doors, she realized, taking in the carved herons with a drop of the stomach. He hadn't returned all night.

Five guards stood in the corridor outside. "What's the meaning of this?" Hesina demanded.

"Viscount Yan Caiyan requests your presence at court."

Her irritation died. "Did he say what it was for?"

"He only said that your presence is required."

Her hair was a mess, and she was still in her underrobes. But Caiyan wouldn't have called a court session at this time unless it was an emergency.

"Fetch me a gown and a pin," she ordered her page.

He scurried and came back with an onyx pin and a sepia *ruqun* bordered in gold.

Hesina cross-wrapped the *ruqun* over her underrobes, stabbed the pin through a hasty up-twist, and followed the guards out of the inner palace without a second word. But as they neared the Hall of Everlasting Harmony, uncertainty crept into her step. She stopped halfway down the hall, mother-of-pearl pillars towering tall, much like the guards on either side of her.

"The court is waiting, *dianxia*," prompted a guard from behind.

You're tired. You're paranoid. You're not thinking clearly.

But once the doors creaked open, the guards seized her. They dragged her up the dais. They shoved her to the floor. And when Hesina finally managed to push onto her elbows, what she saw next hit like another blow.

Black-and-gold *hanfu*.

Hands clasped, right over left.

His shadow, waxing over the stairs as he descended from the imperial balcony. His voice, soft as if he were speaking to her and her alone.

"I, Yan Caiyan, first viscount and son of King Wen, accuse Yan Hesina of high treason."

TWENTY-EIGHT

A meaningful life is lived for others.
ONE *of the* ELEVEN *on the natural order*

Live for yourself if you trust yourself.
TWO *of the* ELEVEN *on the natural order*

Just like that winter nine years ago, Hesina was falling into freezing water. But this time, Caiyan wasn't rapidly sinking, someone to rescue and protect. He was the one who had pushed her in.

She stumbled to her feet just as a minister spoke. "What is the offense?"

The woman was fighting a yawn. She wasn't the only one. *Hanfu* were rumpled, broad-belts crooked, *wusha* caps tilted.

Caiyan's next words woke them all up. "For colluding with a sooth."

The court went still as new ice.

Then the full weight of the accusation landed, dragging Hesina under.

Keep calm, Hesina, she ordered, even as she fought for breath. She wasn't guilty until proven so . . . the last of the evidence had died with the Silver Iris. Not even the madam of the Yellow Lotus music house could give testimony because Hesina's hood had been up and Caiyan's had been down and he couldn't summon her as a witness without implicating himself and yes, it was fine. This was fine. It was going to be okay.

It's going to be okay.

Yet she shrank back as Caiyan continued his descent down from the dais, drawing closer. "Though the sooth in question perished a few months back, I think you'll find my evidence sufficient."

Why? Simple. She hadn't heeded his advice. She should have framed Xia Zhong and let him take the fall, not Lilian.

But . . . this was Caiyan. The brother who had withstood all of Sanjing's jibes without lashing back, who had helped her through her imperial lessons.

Considerate, reliable Caiyan, who now ordered the first witness forward.

Hesina stared, breathless, pulseless, her heart fished out of her chest and left flopping somewhere on the limestone walk between them.

The witness came to the stand's edge. It was a stern-faced woman in her forties whom Hesina didn't recognize.

"State your name," said Caiyan.

"Meng Hua."

"Give your testimony."

"Wait!"

Heads turned.

"Y-you can't call these witnesses," stammered Rou as every eye swung toward him, including Hesina's. "That's the Investigation Bureau's job."

Heavens be kind to him.

"The Investigation Bureau has signed off on the case," said the director.

"Then this is a trial," said Rou. "If this is a trial, Queen Hesina deserves a representative like anyone else."

"I'm afraid you're forgetting the first tenement of the *Tenets*, Prince Yan Rou of Fei." Heads now turned to Xia Zhong. "If this were any other charge," continued the minister, "the queen would indeed be granted a fair trial and have a right to a representative. Sooths and their colluders are the one exception, as stated in Passage 1.1.2 of the *Tenets*. But there is nothing to fear. Should Viscount Caiyan's evidence prove flimsy by the court's ruling, then we'll go through the usual rites of selecting representatives."

The rest of the court murmured in agreement. What the minister had said was, indeed, true. Hesina had known it even before she'd decided to seek out the Silver Iris. All she could do was send Rou a silent thank-you before Caiyan's voice overtook the court again.

"Speak," he ordered the witness. "How did you come to witness the event two and a half months ago?"

"I run a carpentry shop with my husband in the eastern sector. That day, the talk of the marketplace was of a borderlands village vanishing like a puff of smoke. Our customers said the Kendi'an sooths were to blame, which was no surprise to me. Maggots are born without souls. We all saw what happened to that scout at the queen's coronation."

"Did the rioters do anything else?"

"Yes. They stormed the red-light district because . . . Well, it's obvious, isn't it?" The woman's upper lip curled. "That place is a maggot breeding ground."

"Did you follow along?" asked Caiyan.

"Yes."

"Did you see what the group did?"

"They rounded up some whores. Killed one."

"Was the one they killed a sooth?"

"That's what we thought, yes."

"Did you see the blue flame yourself?" asked Caiyan.

"I was standing in the back of the crowd—"

"'Yes' or 'no'?"

"I did," confirmed the woman. "I saw it. But then the queen came along and made a whole show out of burning the place down. Those flames were blue, too, from all the spilled wine. It made some of us doubt, but I know what I saw. Blue flame, brighter than any flame I'd ever seen, erupting from the whore's body."

"Do you remember the queen's reaction to seeing the body?"

"Yes. She was visibly upset. Threw up too. I didn't think much of it then, but . . ." Her voice trailed off.

"Continue," said Caiyan.

"How do I put it?" The woman shuddered. "It almost looked as if she mourned."

Murmurs rustled through the court.

This was all some terrible fluke. Hesina clung to this belief, though it contradicted everything she knew about Caiyan. He succeeded in whatever he undertook. Her fate was as good as sealed. She should have been prepared.

But she wasn't.

Without pausing for breath, Caiyan summoned the next witness.

When she saw that cream *ruqun* edged with hydrangea blue, Hesina felt like she'd been punched in the gut. Tears sprang to her eyes, hot and embarrassing. She was eight again, crying over some injustice she'd suffered at her mother's hands, except this time there was no one to wipe the shame from her cheeks.

"State your name and occupation," said Caiyan.

"Ming'er. I entered the imperial service sixteen years ago and have served as the queen's lady-in-waiting for fifteen."

"Tell us what you found in the queen's chambers."

"I came across a loose floorboard while I was oiling the wood-work last week. It led to a hidden compartment stacked with drafts of letters written in the queen's own hand. I didn't intend to read them at first. I only handled them to clean off the oil that had dripped onto the paper. But I couldn't help but notice a word."

"What word?"

"The 'Sight.'"

Hesina stared at Ming'er with glazed eyes. *Why?*

"To whom were they addressed?" asked Caiyan.

"Someone by the name of the Silver Iris."

Why am I losing you too?

"Yes," said the previous witness from the box. "That was her name."

"Lies." Hesina found her voice. She whirled on Caiyan. "You planted those letters."

He ignored her. "Match the handwriting."

Pages came forth bearing Hesina's most recent decrees and spread them beside the letters on the ground.

Caiyan summoned the head of the imperial scribes. "By your expertise, are these letters forged?"

The man leaned over the spread of papers, gaze twitching between the letters and decrees.

"No, they're not forged. See?" The scribe held up a decree in one hand and a letter in the other. "A skilled forger can replicate the form of someone's character perfectly but still fail to transfer the imperfections. If you look closely here, you can see that the queen doesn't quite wrap the tails of her 'si,' 'su,' and 'shao' characters correctly. Her hand wavers, and the ink feathers as a result. This is consistent in both the decree and the letter."

Caiyan ordered that the letters and decrees be circulated. As pages ran them to the rest of the ranks, Hesina snatched a letter off the ground. Her gaze raced up and down the columns of characters.

Every stroke of ink was identical to hers, right down to the imperfections. Who—

"Last but not least," Caiyan said, but his voice faded, replaced by the memory of the two of them sitting side by side, his hand around hers as he helped her with her characters.

You never form the "si" correctly. The tail of the third stroke doesn't quite wrap around the first.

That memory bled into another, of the throne room, where Hesina had marveled—and lamented—over Caiyan's perfect rendition of her name.

The letter fell from her hand. Colors, shapes, lines kept morphing, as if she were looking through a waterfall. Someone bumped into her from behind, and it took Hesina a full second to register, process, and step aside.

The page scurried past, a gilded tray in his hands. Caiyan lifted an item and held it up. "Do we all recognize this?"

Pinched between Caiyan's fingertips was a white-jade hairpin with a crane unfurling at its end, last seen disappearing into Xia Zhong's pocket.

Let this be a dream. Hesina's heel slipped over the dais edge. She regained her balance, but not her sense of self. Hazily, she took in the commoners down below, the nobles up above. *Please, let this be a dream.* In nightmares, she could run. She could jump off this thin suspension of a walk and bolt upright in a sweat. Here, she was trapped. Perspiration trickled down her back.

"I remember that," said one of the ministers. "It was a gift from her father."

"Yes, for her first namesday," said another.

"And when was the last time the queen wore this pin?" asked Caiyan.

"That . . ." The ministers glanced at each other. "We can't be certain."

Caiyan looked pointedly at Ming'er.

"The queen hasn't worn this pin in quite some time," she murmured. "It's been missing from her drawers for four months."

Four months? It had to have been one month, at most—

"That's because this was found in a particular courtesan's chambers." Caiyan turned, holding the pin out for all to see. "A courtesan by the name of the Silver Iris, the same sooth who burned in the riot."

The court erupted with voices. A page pounded a staff for silence, but questions rang out, one louder than the others:

"What did the queen need a sooth for?"

Without answering, Caiyan summoned another witness—a dungeon guard.

"Did the queen give you strange orders on any occasion?" he asked the woman.

"Let's see . . . She did ask us to search for a convict with a rod."

"When?"

"It must have been four months ago."

"And was such a convict found?"

"Yes, in fact. Convict 315, who'd been charged with merchant robbing, was found in possession of a rod."

Caiyan dismissed the guard and faced a ring in the upper ranks. "Minister Xia, you may come forward now."

A sea of silk *hanfu* parted for Xia Zhong's passage. Hesina stared as he stepped onto the walk.

"As many of you probably noticed," began the minister, "the queen's representative was *quite* adept. That's because she hand-picked him from the highest rank of scholars and planted him in the imperial dungeons. She *tricked* me into selecting him by taking advantage of my egalitarianism."

The pin hadn't been enough to convince Hesina. Ming'er hadn't been enough. But this was.

Caiyan had allied himself with Xia Zhong.

The realization struck Hesina like a hand to a zither. The fibers of her being twanged, and she snapped, shuddering as the marrow returned to her bones, the blood to her veins, her heart to her chest in all its raw fury.

"You forget," she gritted out, "that we sink and swim together."

Now sink with me, Xia Zhong. She tore off her sash, split apart the seam, and flung the letters he'd written to Kendi'a. Five, ten, twenty burst from their stitches and rained over the court below. The rest fluttered onto the walk.

Pages ran to distribute them to the upper ranks. Paper crackled like twigs snapped underfoot.

Hesina held up the letter she'd saved for herself. "Xia Zhong, how will you explain this correspondence?"

A page ran a letter to the minister. Teeth clenched, Hesina pinned her gaze on his bald head as he tilted it down to read.

Finally, it lifted. "Your Majesty," said Xia Zhong. "Or should I say, your disgraced honor."

The last of the letters were opened, and a hush fell over the court.

Hesina's heartbeat slowed as she looked down at the letter in her hand. She wasn't sure what she feared as she unfolded it—she'd sewn them together herself just a week ago—but this . . .

This couldn't be.

There hadn't been an addressee on the letters before. Now there was, and it was Hesina.

There hadn't been an addresser on the letters before. Now there was, and it was the Silver Iris.

The letter wobbled in Hesina's hand. She couldn't read all the characters in between.

She didn't need to.

Howls rose from the ranks, accusations merging like a pack of wolves. They lunged for her, a defenseless queen. They shredded her with tooth and claw.

"Maggot lover!"

"Traitor!"

"Death by a thousand cuts!"

"Take her away," ordered Caiyan, and guards seized Hesina by the arms.

"I admit to speaking with a sooth!" she shouted as they dragged her down the walk. The court went into an uproar. A guard clamped a hand over her mouth; he yanked away when she bit down. "But I will never confess to treason! Speaking to another human shouldn't be a—"

They gagged her. They lugged her through the double doors, which swung in like window shutters, narrowing her view of the court until only Caiyan's figure remained in the sliver of space.

She willed him to look at her. It was the least he could do as he betrayed her. But he simply turned and ascended the dais. He was still ascending when the doors folded him out of view.

* * *

Hesina tumbled into the cell, concrete sanding her palms. The doors clanged shut behind her.

She picked herself up and stared blearily through the bars. A normal cell, she noted. Not a *tianlao* cell, where someone who'd committed her caliber of treason should have been locked. But she hadn't bothered to rebuild after the explosion, and she guessed Caiyan hadn't either. His first and only oversight.

She scooted against the cinder-block walls and hugged her legs tight to her chest, making herself smaller, as if that would diminish everything else.

Caiyan had sided with Xia Zhong.

Caiyan had convinced Ming'er to betray her.

Caiyan had forged letters in her hand. He'd swapped out the ones in her sash, or the sash entirely. It would have been easy for him. He was family. No one would have batted an eye if he visited her rooms one night while she was buried deep in the archives.

Or he could have gotten Ming'er to do it for him. Hesina shook, too stunned to weep. Caiyan had crafted an airtight case, considering that the Silver Iris had died. Had she been alive, he might have dragged her before the court and bled her himself. She'd be executed right alongside Hesina, a means to an end, a pawn on a board. They all were to him.

Even then, guilt fringed the hems of Hesina's mind. When weariness finally overtook her, she dreamed that it was Caiyan who took her place at dawn, his flesh that the executioners carved, not hers. Afterward, she crawled to him, clutched him, and wept.

Before he'd betrayed her, he'd been her brother. Before he'd turned everyone against her, she'd killed his only family. Her tears and remorse could be explained.

His blood and sacrifice could not.

* * *

Beyond the bars stood the Grand Secretariat, a decree scroll in hand. Hesina's own official had come to read her sentence.

For threatening a high minister, Hesina was barred from entering the court for the next three months.

For manipulating the random selection of the representative, Hesina was forbidden from forwarding cases to the Investigation Bureau for a year.

Of course, none of that mattered, because for colluding with a sooth, Hesina was to be executed by a thousand cuts at the sixth gong strike tomorrow.

The Secretariat rolled up the scroll. "You have a visitor," she said, retreating as the newcomer approached.

Hesina braced herself for Xia Zhong.

"My flower."

But if she'd known it'd be Ming'er, she wouldn't have braced herself at all. She had no defenses against her lady-in-waiting, and her heart went brittle as the woman crouched by the bars.

"Don't call me that," Hesina snapped. "And stop crying."

Ming'er wiped at her apple cheeks. She parted her lips.

"Don't waste your breath asking for forgiveness."

"I know," whispered Ming'er. "I just want you to know the truth."

It was a little late for that, in Hesina's opinion. "Hurry up and say what you need to say."

"My fl—"

"Or leave, if you can't control yourself."

"It was Minister Xia." Ming'er's eyes brimmed. "M-Minister Xia found out about my daughter."

Hesina's gaze snapped to her. "You have a daughter?" Maid-servants were forbidden from starting families of their own.

Ming'er nodded. "She was born early. The midwife didn't think she'd live past her first namesday. Now, she's seventeen—"

Hesina's age.

"—still sickly, but so full of life. My sister takes care of her, and I send them my earnings to cover the cost of tinctures."

A lump grew painfully in Hesina's throat.

"I'm sorry." Ming'er blotted at her lashes as tears eked out anyway. "I'm sorry."

What did Ming'er expect her to say? *I understand? I forgive you? You betrayed me, but for a good reason?* Hesina felt a sudden surge of animosity toward Ming'er's daughter. The girl had stolen the one mother Hesina had ever had.

"Get out of my sight." But as Ming'er stumbled away, Hesina thought everything she couldn't bear to say.

I understand.

I forgive you.

She pitied Ming'er, even though there was no one left to pity *her*. She was going to die tomorrow, and there was no kick in her chest, no urge to survive. *What's the point of clinging to a world that has abandoned you?* her mother had asked. Now Hesina knew real abandonment. It was being queen of a kingdom that was clamoring for her execution. It was having nothing to live for.

Some time passed. She wasn't sure how much, but enough for the guards to deliver a meal of watery congee garnished with some stringy scallions. It seemed rather pointless; Hesina wasn't going to starve before dawn tomorrow. She pushed the bowl away, the bottom scraping against stone, almost covering the guards' mutters.

"Serves her right." Their voices were distant but amplified by the dungeon tunnels. "Now this kingdom will get cleaned up once and for all."

Cleaned up.

They didn't need to say "of what." Sooths. Maggots. The feared. The unknown.

Have you . . . ever felt something for them? Hesina remembered asking Caiyan. He had shaken his head. *Don't show your sympathy,* he'd said. *Don't speak your feelings. Don't act on them. Don't jeopardize your rule. Trust me.*

She had listened. She had trusted. She had believed him like a brother.

Not anymore.

Now she listened to Mei, who told her to protect them. She listened to Lilian, whose sacrifice had saved hundreds, perhaps thousands of sooths from losing the only cover they had. She listened to her father, whose heart she finally saw. His words passed on a love for the truth, but his actions passed on love for the people. For them, he'd given up everything, truth included. But bloodstained or hallowed, cursed or celebrated, named or nameless, he had never surrendered. He'd filled the throne hall with ghosts; he'd returned to face them all the same.

Hesina would too.

Because tomorrow at the sixth gong strike, she wasn't going to die.

She dragged the *shaguo* of congee close and choked it down. Then she closed her eyes and began to think.

She couldn't simply escape. If the *Tenets* held her people in the throes of hatred, then she would continue her parents' work of trying to destroy it, with or without her throne.

As she pieced together a plan, the outer prison doors whined.

More visitors? Becoming a fallen queen was doing wonders for her popularity.

"Sister!"

Hesina blinked, stared, and snapped her jaw shut. "What are you doing here?"

Rou splashed through a puddle, his shell-blue *hanfu* too bright for his mildewed surroundings, and knelt by the cell bars. "I can get you out of here. Just tell me where your master key is."

And then he'd unlock her, and they'd stroll out of here and fly away on the backs of giant cranes. "Don't be stupid."

"I have a way."

"Of getting past the guards?"

"You won't believe me if I explain it now," said Rou. "Just . . . trust me."

In other words, *let me put my life on the line with yours.*

Hesina didn't need more blood on her hands. "No."

"Do you want to live or not?"

Stunned, she stared at Rou. It was hard to see past his pale, peaky features, to the boy who'd helped the sooths and spoken up for her today when no one else had. By the time she did, Rou was already blushing and saying, "You have to live, Sister," like his normal self, but then all Hesina could hear was his voice of fire and stone.

Do you want to live?

Yes.

Yes, she wanted to live.

Yes.

But not alone. Not in a world without family or friends. Hesina bit her lip and dared to ask, "Can you get Akira out too?"

"I promise I can."

"Then listen closely. The master key is in my vanity drawer, but you can't be the one to fetch it."

"Oh." Rou didn't bother hiding his confusion. "Why not?"

Many reasons—her chambers were likely heavily guarded, and Rou would be an automatic suspect—but Hesina didn't have time to explain. "I already have a way of delivering the master key to the dungeons. Your job is to keep an eye on my father's study. If you see Xia Zhong or any of his servants entering it, assume that my plan has worked. Return at the second gong strike with your plan at the ready. Can you remember that?"

"Got it. Anything else?"

"Yes." If Rou's voice was fire, Hesina's was ice. A smile frosted over her lips. "Tell Xia Zhong that I have what he wants most."

TWENTY-NINE

Sometimes, it is possible to give up too much.

ONE *of the* ELEVEN *on regrets*

Everything and nothing.

TWO *of the* ELEVEN *on regrets*

Do make it quick," said Xia Zhong, wrapped in a tiger-pelt cloak that appeared to be molting even though the beast was dead. "My bones ache in the draft, and as difficult as you were, I don't take particular pleasure in seeing you in such a vile state."

Hesina had made herself all the viler for him. At the sound of his footsteps, she'd rubbed her hands over the walls and smeared gray grime over her face. She'd tugged at her hair until it was as tangled as a swallow's nest, then bit her lip and smudged the blood with the back of her hand.

That was just setting the pieces on the board. Now she made her first move by crawling to the bars on her knees, clutching them as she begged. "Help me."

"I have," Xia Zhong said. "Twice, if I recall. I believe you repaid me by almost taking my life."

"Name your price, and I'll pay it in full and more."

"Your viscount is quite the generous man," said Xia Zhong. "I have all that I want." Something squeaked in the dark, and he flinched and turned to go.

"Wait!" Hesina's voice cracked convincingly. "I have the *Tenets*."

"I do too. All the editions, in five translations."

"Not the original."

His step slowed.

"Neither do you," Xia Zhong said at last, but something in his voice had changed.

Hesina kept hers as desperate as before. "It's yours if you can get me out of here."

For a heartbeat, the minister didn't speak. Then he chuckled. "You, my dear, have an affinity for lies."

She must have inherited it from her father. "You think I'd lie? With my life on the line?" She shook her head. "I don't want to die." It was the truth, and it made her sound all the more compelling.

"I'll humor you then," said Xia Zhong. "Where is it?"

"Bring me my master key."

"And have you run away first? These tricks won't work on me."

This was it. This was the part where she'd either fail or succeed. "Let me verify the master key. Place it within my sight but beyond my reach. I'll tell you the location of the book. Once you see I'm telling the truth, come back and place the key within reach."

In the dim, Hesina watched Xia Zhong consider her words. Her skin crawled at the thought of his spotty hands on the original *Tenets*, but she needed him to take it for her plan to work.

"You've thought this over," he finally said.

"You would, too, in my shoes. The master key is in the drawers of my vanity. It's silver and shaped like a dragonfly."

Imagine riches. The silence stretched. *Imagine glory.*

Footsteps broke the lull; Xia Zhong had resumed his walk.

Imagine renown and fame, all within your grasp, if you recover the original Tenets *when thousands of others have failed.*

The footsteps stilled at the end of the corridor.

It was funny, thought Hesina, how Xia Zhong could create and destroy opportunities for her all at once. When he said, "I'll see what I can do," it was as if she was kneeling before her mother all over again, with the minister beside her, his words offering hope she didn't dare grasp. He raised her up only to let her fall.

But this time, Hesina could fall no further.

So she grasped hope. Patience had never been her strong suit, but the role demanded it, so she played it. She counted pieces of straw on the ground, then cinder blocks in the wall. Finally, shortly after the midnight gong strike, Xia Zhong returned.

"Show me," Hesina demanded.

He held up the pin, and she loosed a genuine sigh of relief. Silver and dragonfly-shaped—it was indeed her master key. She watched closely as the minister set it down in the corner of the corridor, well out of reach and tucked into the shadows where no guard would bend to look.

"Now," he said as he straightened. "Where is the book?"

"On the second shelf of the king's study, between *The Annals of the Empire* and *Lizhu's Chronicles*. Hurry back," Hesina commanded as Xia Zhong left.

Then she wiped the dirt off her cheeks and tamed her hair.

He wouldn't return. He had no reason to. For all he knew, she was as good as dead. But he'd already helped her—twice. First, by delivering the master key. Second, by taking the *Tenets* with him to his own residence in the Northern Palace. Hesina's blood thrummed in anticipation of reclaiming what was hers, then cooled. It was now Rou's play.

What did he have up his blue sleeve?

Or rather, *who*? For when her half brother returned at the second hour, it was in the company of two. One was a page.

The other was Consort Fei.

That would have been the biggest shock, simply seeing Rou's mother in that iconic, screened headpiece, if the consort hadn't then gone on to remove it.

Rou asked for the location of the master key. Hesina gave it. Rou told her to meet him in the corridor to the left of this block of cells, where he would be waiting with Akira. Hesina nodded. Rou unlocked her, then left with the page.

Hesina stepped out, gaping at Consort Fei. What did she say to her father's concubine? What did she say, upon seeing her face?

"You're . . . beautiful."

Because Consort Fei was. Skin white as jade. Eyes black as jet. Hair like a spill of ink, and lips stained, rather than painted, by the juice of plums, parting in laughter at Hesina's words.

"Hello to you, too, Hesina."

Hello. Hesina should have said *hello.* But she couldn't manage it. How many times had she envisioned a missing eye, a droopy lip, a terrible birthmark, or a scaly scar under that veil?

"Why do you hide?" With a face like that, Consort Fei could have easily garnered respect instead of ridicule.

"A face is an identity." The consort passed Hesina her screened hat, then started disrobing. "And some identities, as you well know, are best forgotten."

"But—"

"Time is fleeting," said the consort, shoving her *ruqun* into

Hesina's arms. Hesina donned the headpiece, which turned out to be opaque only from the outside.

"There." The consort affixed the *bixi* panel to Hesina's skirt, stepped back, and dusted off her hands. "You look just like me."

Belatedly, it occurred to Hesina that Rou intended for his mother to take her place. "Will you be safe?"

Would the page, who she assumed was to take Akira's?

"Safe as a hare," said the consort.

Hesina wanted to point out that hares were hunted animals, and caged ones could not run, but Consort Fei stepped into the cell before she could say anything.

"Now go." She pulled in the door by the bars. "Rou is waiting."

Hesina made it four steps out before stilling. She turned back around. "What was your relationship with my father?"

It wasn't exactly the ideal occasion for a conversation. Hesina realized that. She also realized, since last speaking to her mother, that she had a troubling habit of asking self-destructive questions. But she couldn't help herself. She needed to know.

"It's not what you think," said Consort Fei with a secretive smile.

"Then is Rou his son?"

"Yes and no. Come back when the time is right, Hesina. Then I'll tell you."

Would the time ever be right for a fallen queen? Hesina filed the thought away as a worry for another day. Considering the number of worries she had, perhaps there would never be enough days. "Thank—"

"Uh-uh." Consort Fei wagged a finger. The gesture reminded Hesina of Lilian, and her heart panged as the consort said, "This is my thank-you to you."

Righting a wrong—what Hesina had done by acquitting Consort Fei—wasn't worthy of gratitude. But if she started talking about wrongs, then she'd have to go back to the beginning, to those long nights in the consort's shrubbery in the company of summer gnats and fireflies.

Flushing hot, Hesina hurried away. She wished that they might have met in the Southern Palace instead of here, these dungeons where all her greetings and farewells took place.

And now reunions.

Her heart stopped at the sight of Akira, standing alone up the prison corridor where Rou had told them to meet. Dressed like a page from the back, but with a topknot too sloppy to truly be.

Hesina couldn't speak. The last time she'd seen Akira had been in the throne hall. Half a month had passed since then. Would she ever be able to redeem herself?

She'd start with an apology, one of many she owed.

"I-I'm sorry about your flute," she stammered when she reached him. He turned, and she looked away even though he couldn't see her through the veil. *I'm sorry about more than that.*

The air on her cheeks cooled. Her gaze swung back to find the veil lifted, and Akira beneath it, sharing the headpiece's wide brim.

"I decided it wasn't a flute after all," he said.

Did he realize how very close he was, those eyes gray as stone a breath's space across from hers?

"Just a rod," he said.

Did he realize how much she wanted to throw her arms around him and never let go?

What was stopping her?

"And a rod is very replace—"

He broke off as she hugged him tight. Then, just because she could, she raised herself to her toes and kissed him. It might have been the most awkward kiss in the history of kisses, complicated by extraneous veils and not-so-extraneous noses, but she didn't care because this time, Akira kissed her back. It lasted for all of a second before Rou rejoined them and squeaked, "Ready?"

Hesina inspected her flimsy costume. "Is this enough?"

The consort's *ruqun* was just silk, her headpiece just wood and gauze. And Akira, even with the cap that Rou handed him to hide the topknot, didn't look like any page in Hesina's palace.

"No one notices the attendants," said Rou, nodding at Akira. "They'll be looking at me. And they'll be looking at my mother, and you look like her."

Hesina had to trust. Still, she held her breath as they approached the guards. Nothing came to pass. The guards bowed for them. They made it safely out of the dungeons without trouble, and soon they were traveling down the covered galleries that zigzagged through the snowy jujubes. The maids and pages they encountered hastily moved to the side and bowed, then scurried away, whispering as they went, their eyes darting to Hesina. Her hands balled. She glanced to Rou, but he was reactionless.

"The carriage is this way," he said when they arrived at the courtyards.

She stopped him. "This is far enough."

"Where are you going?"

"Xia Zhong's. He has something of mine," she continued as Rou stared at her, aghast. "I can't leave without reclaiming it."

"But how will you get out?"

By one of the passageways that started in the gardens. None of them led beyond the palace walls like the one behind the soapstone reredos, but she couldn't risk entering the Eastern Palace.

"Don't worry about me. I have my ways." Hesina caught Rou's arm before he could protest any further. "Thank you," she said firmly, meeting him square in the eye. "For everything."

He blinked, then swallowed. "I'll see you again, won't I?"

"Yes," said Hesina with more confidence than she felt. "You will."

She waved him off and waited for him to leave before facing Akira. "You should go too. Take the carriage out."

"I'll come with you. I need to stretch my legs anyway."

So be it. There was a good chance she'd need Akira's help.

"Keep guard outside," Hesina said once they reached the Northern Palace. "I can handle the minister on my own." Then she marched up the steps to Xia Zhong's courtyard house and sidled up against his lattice windows. She poked a hole in the oil paper with her finger and peered through.

Past the partition of antiques and relics, Xia Zhong sat at his *kang* table, reading a bamboo-strip scroll. Alone.

Hesina burst in, and the scroll fell out of his hand. He scrambled back as she climbed onto the *kang* and grabbed the sword hanging on the wall behind. A *xia* was engraved on the hilt. A family heirloom, the length of its steel blade gleaming as Hesina pointed it at the minister. "Where's the book?"

He stared at her blankly. "You . . ."

She ripped off the headpiece.

His eyes narrowed. "*You.*"

"Where is it?"

"I don't have it."

"Lies." Why else would he have given her the master key? "One last time: Where is it?"

"Why don't you look for yourself?"

Hesina was *trying* to part on somewhat civil terms, but Xia Zhong wasn't making it easy. She stalked to a wall of drawers and yanked them out. Scrolls tumbled onto the floor, then books from the next drawer. None of them were the original *Tenets*.

She slammed them in, then stopped.

The impact had caused the walls to jingle.

Hesina stalked to a peeling wall bare of shelves and thrust Xia Zhong's heirloom sword through the seam between two panels.

"No," cried Xia Zhong. "No, no, no—"

Like a painter with a brush, Hesina stroked left.

From the slash poured ingots. Gold. Silver. Bronze. It was like watching someone's innards fall out—ghastly, yet impossible to look away. Hesina slashed another panel. This wound wept red, of rubies. The next wept blue, of sapphires. It seemed that Xia Zhong had stuffed his entire fortune into the walls of a house that was otherwise falling apart.

The minister crawled after the rolling gems, futilely trying to gather them up. Disgust reared in Hesina, and without thinking twice, she'd pinned his hand with his own sword.

"Where have you hidden it?" she asked over his earsplitting howl.

Instead of answering, Xia Zhong howled more. "How could you?"

What a strange question to ask, when it was clear that she could, and had, just shoved a blade through his knuckles. "What do you mean?"

"You're your father's daughter. You said so yourself."

Hesina hardened. "My father is dead. Now, where have you hidden the book?" When he kept howling, she gave the pommel a twist, working the blade a hair deeper into the wood beneath. His screams went shrill. "*Where?*"

"It's not here! It's not here! Th-the viscount was right! He said you'd try to trick me! Now take it out!" he screamed, scrabbling at the rooted blade himself. "Take it out!"

His voice faded as Hesina's blood went cold.

She had forgotten what Caiyan's alliance with Xia Zhong meant in its entirety. That the things she said to the minister would reach her adopted brother's ears. That he would dispense advice. Read her mind.

As if on cue, the sounds of clashing metal rose from outside.

Akira.

This was a trap, and she'd walked both of them into it.

Xia Zhong caterwauled as Hesina yanked the sword free. "If it's not here, then where is it?" she demanded.

He was sobbing too hard to speak. But then Hesina knew. She knew the way Caiyan tackled problems—with parsimony.

The *Tenets* hadn't been moved at all. The book was still in her father's study.

Two guards lay heaped in the snow when she ran out into the courtyard. One clutched his head, dazed, while the other struggled to sit up. Hesina's gaze darted beyond them to the lone, weaponless figure ringed by ten guards.

"*Akira!*"

The snow slowed her run. She was halfway to them when one guard lunged. Akira spun behind and threw an elbow into the man's neck. A second guard closed in, and Akira caught the woman's arm and used her sword to deflect another's blow. One of the swords fell into the snow, but Akira didn't grab it.

Even now, he didn't want to hurt them.

Hesina ran toward him, skidding to a stop as some of the guards broke away from the ring and blocked her way.

"Capture her alive!" ordered one while the others charged. "Save her for the execution!"

Hesina dragged Xia Zhong's blade through the snow, leaving a long, red streak. She flung the snow at the guards when they neared. They slowed, momentarily impeded, and Hesina cut around without engaging, yanking an empty sheath off one of their belts.

"Catch!" she cried to Akira, throwing it.

Akira swiped the sheath out of the air and slid it over his blade, becoming a new fighter—fluid and unrestrained, wielding his sword as he had his rod.

Hesina broke through to him and whirled so that they were back to back. They pushed back the guards, thinning their ranks, until a gap opened and Hesina spun to Akira. *"Run."*

Hurry. They sprinted through the galleries of the outer palace, dashing through the corridors and scattering shrieking maids right and left. Hesina had lost the screened headpiece back in the fighting, and her face was on clear display, but she didn't care. She slowed only to slash the facades. They toppled behind them, choking the path to the inner palace. Anything to buy them more time.

But no guards came after them, or waited in her father's study when she burst in.

Hesina spun with her sword held out, ready to fend off another onslaught, dumbfounded to find none. Then she snapped out of her daze and ran for the shelves, honing in on the rough-bound spine nestled between *The Annals of the Empire* and *Lizhu's Chronicles*.

The pages stuck to her clammy hands as she flipped through,

scanning the insect-like characters. To be sure, she tore out a page and watched it fuse back, whole and unmarked.

"Where to?" asked Akira when she rejoined him in the corridor with the *Tenets* bound to her waist.

Hesina grabbed his hand. "This way."

Once they were inside the throne room, she bolted the doors and faced the dais up ahead. The throne was empty. She wasn't sure why she'd expected Caiyan to be here, or why her heart dropped when he wasn't. Maybe it was because this seemed too easy, to be able to leave without a final confrontation. But she couldn't complain, not when her back burned and her legs throbbed.

She went up to the dais, arm shaking as she pointed Xia Zhong's sword at the soapstone reredos. "Help me destroy this."

Without questioning, Akira unsheathed his sword and struck. Hesina slashed perpendicular to his diagonal. He slammed his pommel into the center of their cuts. Cracks spiderwebbed outward.

One more slam, and the screen collapsed in pieces.

Hesina clambered onto the throne and hauled herself over its back. She thumped to her feet on the other side. Akira landed behind her.

This time, she didn't need to say "run."

The passageway was longer than Hesina recalled. They must have been running for ten, fifteen minutes before the ground grew jagged with chunks of broken rock. She slowed to touch the wall. Her hand came away powdered with soot. Her nose smarted from the musk of black powder. Her eyes smarted from tears.

Take some sticks of black powder with you, and find the passageway sealed with stones, she'd ordered Lilian. *Blast them away, and lead Mei's parents and the others out of the city before I read the decree.*

Lilian must have already been planning on condemning herself at that point. Even then, she had carried out Hesina's final request, and now Hesina smiled in spite of the twinge in her chest. She wiped at her eyes as the gong struck six notes directly above them, announcing the hour of her execution.

It was time to finish this in style.

Hesina faced forward. Behind her lay the lacquer palace she called home. Beyond lay the life of a fugitive. She'd always dreamed of freedom, but this wasn't quite the kind. How were they going to live? How were they going to feed themselves?

"For what it's worth," said Akira, making her realize she'd spoken out loud, "I can return to robbery, and you can . . ."

"I can what?" Pursue the truth? Rule? Hesina had proved herself quite incapable at both.

"Make lanterns."

Hesina smiled—sadly. Wherever she went, she would go alone. She wouldn't bring Akira down with her.

But for now, they crossed this boundary between worlds together, their jog slowing to a walk as they came to a fork in the dirt tunnel. The passageway on the right echoed silence. The left whistled with distant wind, probably leading up to one of the bamboo stands just past the imperial gate. Hesina craved fresh air but knew better than to go aboveground. The whole city would be learning of her escape any moment now, and the palace's vicinity would be clotted with guards. The risk and danger were simply too great.

And they would only grow greater. Her empty hand went into the cross fold of her *ruqun* and came out glittering with Xia Zhong's sapphires. She pressed the fistful into Akira's hand. "You're free to go. Leave."

Then, before she could falter, Hesina turned on her heel and continued down the right passageway.

Footsteps trailed behind her.

She drew up short, her body tensed against her every selfish desire. "What did I say?"

"That I'm free to go."

"And to leave."

"I am. I'm freely leaving with you."

Why did he have to make this harder? "You once told me you were searching for what you wanted, and that I couldn't help you. Now I'm in a position where I can't even help myself. You're better off on your own. Go. Live. Make flutes or burn fires, but don't follow me."

"You did help me," said Akira.

She stalked on, pretending not to hear him.

"You showed me that it's okay to rely and be relied on."

"I ruin everyone I rely on. I turn them into monsters."

"I'm already ruined."

She spun on him. "This isn't a joke."

"I know."

"But you don't." Hesina shook her head and pushed her hands through her hair. "I found the truth, Akira. My father is One of the Eleven. He killed thousands of sooths only to realize his mistake. Then he tried to fix things, and nothing worked because *this*"—she whipped out the *Tenets*—"is cursed. So then he hoped that *I* would be able to change things. He killed himself just to show me everything wrong with this kingdom, so that I could choose to stay or leave. And now I'm leaving, and—and I don't even know where I'm going!" Her breath came in pants. She was quickly unraveling. Maybe it'd scare him away.

But all Akira said was, "There's nothing wrong with wandering." Then he took her hand—loosely, so that she could shake him off if she wanted to. When she didn't, he walked ahead. *Being* led felt strange to Hesina, but she followed. She didn't try to lose him again.

Eventually, she would resume taking the lead, because she was a liar just like her father. She *did* know where she wanted to go.

She needed to reclaim her throne, and her own kingdom wasn't going to come to her aid. Neither would the kingdoms of Ning or Ci.

But Kendi'a would. Kendi'a and its already growing military forces, its parched populace thirsting for her land. In this kingdom of unfulfilled wishes, Hesina would enter with her own. She would wipe her identity. Start anew. Whatever it took—a well-conceived costume, a fabricated backstory—she would infiltrate the court and make herself useful to the Crown Prince. She would gain the confidence of the necessary people while learning more about the Kendi'an sooths. And when the time was right, she would make Kendi'a's wishes serve her own. Together, they would invade Yan.

It was all very ambitious—stupid even. But if brothers could turn traitor, enemies could turn ally. Only one thing was sacred in this world, and that was the vow in her heart, a vow Hesina spoke with every step she took into the dark.

I will be back.

EPILOGUE

He watches her go.

As he does, he remembers their first meeting. He'd been bone and skin and white with fever then, and she'd peered at him from the bedside and said: *The Imperial Doctress says you might die, but sometimes she's wrong. I hope she's wrong.*

She'd looked so serious, brow crunched into a frown, that he'd smiled. His chapped lips had cracked and bled. He'd quickly sucked away the blood and scolded himself for being careless. Carelessness was what got others like him killed, not fevers.

From then on, she'd been determined to become his friend. Not just a friend. *Brother*, she called him, especially in those early days when he refused to divulge his name, not even to the king who'd saved him. The less they knew about him, the better.

But she kept following him around. When she discovered his weakness for books, she carried hers to him. *These are my favorites.*

Assassins through the Ages was a strange book for a princess. Then again, she was a strange princess. She fidgeted through her lessons, but not because she didn't want to learn. She was always trying to figure things out on her own. She liked asking him questions. Easy ones—*Caiyan* (his twin had finally slipped his name), *why do we have to learn history? If fairy tales are set in the past, why can't we just read those? And hard ones—Caiyan, why does my mother like Sanjing more?*

The tutors called her slow. He called her steadfast.

"I don't know what you're looking at," moans the miserable minister, cutting into his thoughts. "But I'm down here."

He kneels by the man. "I was right, wasn't I?"

"Forget about being right. You came too late."

"Do you trust me?"

"Less talking, more bandaging."

He takes that as a yes. Good. He needs them all to trust him.

Only then will his plan succeed.

He tears a strip of his court robes, wrapping it tight around the minister's still-bleeding wound. The man groans. "Is she gone?"

He looks again. She's in the tunnel now, quickly dimming in his vision as the distance between them grows.

"She is. But don't worry. I have the guards hunting her down."

"Good," the minister whispers over him. "Dead or alive, it's good that she's gone." He shudders, clearly shaken.

Caiyan agrees. It's good that she's gone.

※ ※ ※

His memory of that night glistens like a wound that's never closed.

It had been right after the incident at the pond. Water had washed away most of the blood, and the freezing temperatures had crystalized what had soaked through his sleeve. He had told her that he was fine. He told her brother, who'd looked scared for once, that he was fine. Only he knew that he wasn't fine, but he had no one to go to, Lilian least of all. He hated making her worry.

He'd hidden in his room, and when the shaking wouldn't stop, he'd piled on the blankets. That's how the king had found him:

feverish, weak from blood loss, incoherent, but not incoherent enough to forget who he was. What he was.

He had tried lying to the king too.

He remembers everything so clearly. How the king sat at his bedside. How he looked at him with warm eyes, as if he were a true son. How his lips barely moved when he spoke those two words, so soft, so loud.

I know.

The king asked him what the weather would be like tomorrow. In a daze, he'd answered. The king asked him what the cooks would make for a feast a week from now. In less of a daze, he'd answered.

Question by question, truth by truth, the magic in his veins came to his aid, and the wound scabbed over.

✳ ✳ ✳

That had been the beginning. Of late-night conversations over meaningless subjects, debates for the sake of entertaining new perspectives. No question seemed too big in the king's study, and so Caiyan asked the one that'd been on his mind since the night he healed:

How did you know?

After all, he was nothing but careful.

The king poured him a cup of tea. *Long ago, a sooth told me that I'd find a pair of twins, a boy and girl, on the roadside. He said that their veins would contain the blood I helped to spill, and that by protecting them, I might protect my own daughter from my legacy.*

Long ago turned out to be three hundred years. The blood that the king had spilled turned out to be sooth. As for the king's legacy, that was the legacy of One of the Eleven. By the time the king told Caiyan the truth about himself and the queen, the tea had gone cold.

DESCENDANT OF THE CRANE

He never saw the king as his father after that. But he didn't hate him either, despite what the king had done to dismantle the power structures of the old era. Was that betrayal of his kind? He wasn't sure. He'd always been overly rational, and to him, three centuries equaled many a lifetime and many a chance to start anew. The more the king told him about his hopes for a land where *all* were equal, the more he believed that the man once called One was trying to heal the kingdom's wounds.

He still had questions though. *You haven't taught her to love the sooths.*

I taught her to love the truth. You taught her to love learning. Your sister taught her to fight for what is right. Her mother taught her the pain of not being accepted for something she can't control.

Those are things all children learn, he pointed out.

They are.

Not all children can end an era of hatred.

I want to give her a choice. Would you rather force one onto her?

He hadn't known the answer then. But over time, as he read more about exactly what it took to end an era, his opinion began to form. As he watched her grow, he realized he wanted to preserve that smile she'd once shown him. His opinion solidified.

Last year, he'd finally reached the conclusion that it was better for her to never face a choice at all. *He* would end the era for her. He would save her from staining her hands.

Last year was also when the king had deemed it time. *She's ready.*

Caiyan had disagreed.

Do you want to make your people wait any longer?

Of course not. But he could help his people and protect her at the same time.

The king couldn't understand his reasoning. *Love is giving someone the freedom to choose.*

Love, to him, was protecting someone from unnecessary risk. But he didn't say that. Instead he asked the king how he'd present the choice to his daughter.

By removing myself from the picture. My death will set her on the path of a private investigation. I'll lay out all the clues. If she continues on her own volition and learns the truth about who I am, and still desires to rule, then that is her choice. But whatever you do, you mustn't let her pursue a trial.

The king didn't need to explain why. Ministers with political agendas would view a trial that significant as ripe fruit for the plucking. Then, the princess wouldn't be faced with a choice, but a monstrous rupture of everything wrong with this kingdom.

It was what the king wanted to avoid—and what *Caiyan* needed to have happen. A series of monstrous ruptures would break her will. It'd force her to leave. If she left, she would be safe. It'd take a revolution to end the hatred against his people, and revolutions were dangerous things.

Promise me, Caiyan, the king had said. *Promise me that you'll be her guide.*

So he'd promised. Then he'd gone to the queen, suspecting her opinion to be different from the king's.

Why do you think I care? she'd asked after he revealed what her husband had planned.

He was always watching, always listening. *Because she reminds you of yourself, so much so that you can't bear to keep her close.*

So tell me, what will you do? Advise her to go away? You can try, but she won't listen.

She'll want a trial. I'll give her that trial.

He went on to explain what he intended to do, aware of the queen's keen gaze. Few had seen this side of him before.

If it comes down to it, will you help me? he'd asked. *Will you ask her to leave when she's at her most vulnerable?*

The queen didn't say no, which was her way of saying yes.

I wonder, she mused as he bowed and excused himself. *I wonder, Yan Caiyan, if you will go down as a villain or a hero.*

He couldn't be bothered with such trivialities. He was just a means to an end.

* * *

In the end, the trial was born out of her own will. He'd simply helped it along. He'd found her the sooth—the Silver Iris was just one of many he knew in the city. He'd encouraged that the trial go on. And when the pressure mounted, he checked her impulses, kept her from jeopardizing her rule. If all went as orchestrated, she would abdicate peacefully, and he would assume the burden of ending an era, reinstalling her when the worst of the bloodshed had passed.

But he wasn't perfect. For every hundred predictions he got right, there was always one he got wrong.

This time, it was her brother.

He'd known that Yan Sanjing sometimes acted out of heart. He hadn't predicted the *strength* of his heart until the sooths were already in the dungeons and the explosion was going off and it was too late. It was all too late.

He'd meant to break her will, not ruin her. She was never supposed to face the choice that she had, forced into throwing away her ideals because the kingdom demanded it. That was always supposed to be his role. *His* hands were supposed to be the ones wielding the knife.

It was never supposed to end with his twin.

It was supposed to end with *her*—with those russet eyes staring at him now.

She yanks at the restraints on her arms and legs as he takes a seat by the bed. "What do you want?" she hurls at him. Her raven hair is out of its signature braid, half of it lost to the fire. The rest of her is covered in bandages, the white of them a stark contrast to her usual black.

He almost lost his arm rescuing her.

But he never fails what he starts.

"I went through great lengths to save you," he says calmly. "Now I want you to heal."

She pulls on the ropes and they chafe her wrists. Any harder, and she'll bleed and burn this lacquered room down.

He leans close so that she can see his face, see that he can—and will—do everything he says next. "If you can't bring yourself to cooperate, I'll have a medicinal candle lit in this room from dawn to dawn, dusk to dusk. You will heal nicely in your sleep."

"Why? Why are you doing any of this?"

"I need the general to do my bidding."

"I won't be your chess piece."

"Do you have a choice?"

"He'll never believe you! He thinks I'm dead!"

He leans back. "People believe what they want to believe."

He saw this moment coming. The moment when she cracks. When she cries. The sobs rack her chest. The motions are not conducive to healing. He should make good on his word and light the medicinal candle. But he lets her have her grief. Without her, both his queen and the general would be lost. If not blown to pieces, then burned in the resulting firestorm.

Heat, however, is just concentrated light. She used her affinity for the shadows to move the blast into a diminished, future state. She saved them.

She can consider this as his token of gratitude.

※ ※ ※

He has the newest crop of examinee talent, who will help him transform the literature.

He has control over the city guard, who will maintain order in the turbulent days to come.

He has the throne as long as the general stays at the front. He has the means of keeping him there.

But most importantly, he has her out of this city, away from the assassination threats bound to come from sooths and humans alike. Because people detest change. They fight it tooth and nail.

But he will usher it in whether they want it or not.

He will welcome his people back home.

He will restore them as human beings.

There are institutions to end, people to kill. He keeps the Minister of Rites alive simply because that man and his cronies have their uses. But they will not live for long. He will end them himself. They will be the first of many he must end.

So he goes to his twin while he's still the brother she knew. He kneels before her resting spot, her final words to him echoing in his head.

Let me protect my people.

He'd unleashed rationale unto her. They weren't her people. She couldn't share that identity when her blood didn't flame. Because even though they'd both been born from the same womb, at the same time, the power never manifested in her. She could have chosen the life of an ordinary person, a safe life. She didn't have to stay by him. But she had, all nineteen years. And now she was saying goodbye.

He'd given up on rationale; he'd begged.

She'd simply touched his cheek. *Stone-head. You can't protect everyone.*

He can.

He will.

When that day arrives, he will bring his queen back.

But until he has everything he ever wanted, he has only this: a tree that might not even survive to spring, the joss stacked high before it, the horrible candied berries his twin liked so much scattered in place of peach blossom petals.

He didn't bring a flint. He doesn't need one.

He bites his thumb. Lets the blood roll.

It splatters onto the paper money.

The joss catches fire seconds later. Smoke curls heavenward, carrying with it a wish, a promise, a truth yet to be realized.

ACKNOWLEDGMENTS

Not many stories get a first life. I know exactly how lucky I am that this story is getting two.

John and Jen, thank you. None of this would have been possible without you. To Luisa and everyone at Macmillan—thank you for adopting this book. And I'd be remiss not to thank Michael Harriot at Folio. Words have power, I know that. But a single line from you held more power than all the words in this book combined.

To the friends and family from the first acknowledgments, so that your names may live on: Deborah Kreiser-Francis, Anne Cole, Jessie Devine, Rivka Gross, Carissa Taylor, Julia Byers, Kyra Nelson, Molly Calcagno, Mara Rutherford, Michella Domenici, Michelle Armfield, Jamie Pacton, Kristen Ciccarelli, Kat Hinkel, Leigh Mar, Kara Wolf, Megan England, Sheena Boekweg, Allie Schellong, Jenny Chou, Danielle Rebisz Fifer, Jamie Lee, Lyndsi Burcham, Onyoo Park, Jordy Carrick, Marisa Finkelstein, Christine Herman, Amanda Foody, Rory Power, Maura Milan, Judy Lin, Marina Liu, June Tan, Alyssa Carlier, Grace Li, Lori Lee, Hafsah Faizal, Heather Kassner, and Julie Dao. To Rachel Hartman, Laura Sebastian, Adrienne Young, and Traci Chee for the kind words, and again to Eliza Swift, without whom this book would not exist. To my parents and to William, who let me lean on them when things fell apart. The same can be said of Hesina's Imperial Court. Thank you.

To Ellen Kokontis and Feifei Ruan for the beautiful first cover, and to Aurora Parlagreco and Sija Hong for the beautiful second.

Finally, to my readers. To the Fanfiction.net readers who gave sixteen-year-old me the courage to begin, and to my readers now. To everyone who picked up a copy of *Descendant of the Crane* when it first came out in 2019. Hesina gets to stay because of you. Much love to you all.

SPECIAL THANKS TO THE IMPERIAL COURT

FIRST ADVISOR
Vicky Chen

MINISTRIES

礼
RITES

Minister
Jamie Pacton

Marquis
Sara Conway
Maddi Clark
Margarita Cortina
Melissa Lee
Davianna Nieto
Kelsey Culver
Sophie Schmidt
Amy Portsmouth
Dion Alexander
Jasmin Lang
Kaylene
Courtney Browny
Sarah Nizar

Barons
Auburn Nenno
Melanie Parker
Kat H.
Aditi Nichani
Solaceinreading
Asher
Chelsea P.

Justice Hill
Carina
Gauri

Viscounts
Diana Muñoz
Kate Lovatt
Ashley Shuttleworth
Victoria Chiu
Priyanka Taslim
Cassandra Farrin
Adriyanna Zimmermann
Kathleen Nguyen
Sarah Lefkowitz
Sarah Leeman
Ceillie Simkiss
Michella Domenici
Noelle Nichols
Megan Painter
Ann Zhao
Kyra
Trinity Nguyen
Adriana

工
WORKS

Minister
Mingshu Dong

Marquis
Vivian Han
Alex Chen
Melissa Robles
Lauren Chamberlin
Austine Decker
Danielle Iglesia
Jennifer Kaleta
Samantha Beard
Jocelyne Iyare
Mila
Leonie
Ana Elise
Ling
Safa

Barons
Lily Hillary
Anthony G.
Patricia Camille Antony
Felicia Mathews
Bianca
Abbey
Umairah

Viscounts
Alyssa Carlier
Shenwei Chang
Judy Lin

A NOTE TO THE READER

Hello, dear reader,

The first edition of *Descendant of the Crane* released April 9, 2019. In the time that's transpired since, I've met two kinds of readers: those who are satisfied with *DOTC* as a standalone, and those who, to quote a friend, find it akin to reaching the end of a C-drama without a season 2.

As much as I enjoy painful stories, the pain I caused in this instance was not intentional. So, to save you a trip to Google, I'll answer the most frequent query here:

Is there a sequel?

Alas, there isn't. Even if I were to write more books set in the *DOTC* world, they wouldn't be from Hesina's point of view. Her story and character arc were always meant to be 80 percent wrapped up in one book; any future books would have been closer to companion novels. They'd follow characters you haven't yet met and complete the bigger story that's hinted at in the epilogue.

However, due to a number of factors, it wasn't feasible for me to expand on that story for many years. And now, though the book is back in print, the journey of reviving *DOTC* has been long, hard, and marked by eerie similarities to the plot you've just read. Like Hesina, I've learned the price of justice, and like Hesina by the end,

I've learned to walk away. The wound of not being able to continue this journey has scabbed over, healed by all the other stories I wish to tell. I hope you'll follow me to those. Or, if *you* also need time to heal, may I recommend some C-dramas and books? *Nirvana in Fire* was a huge inspiration, and *The Imperial Coroner* has very similar vibes. *The Red Palace*, *A Magic Steeped in Poison*, and *Jade Fire Gold* are also fantastic reads. If you enjoyed *DOTC*, I think you'll enjoy the aforementioned!

Turn the page for more answers to your questions!

Q&A WITH JOAN HE

Were there any tropes that you had wanted to include or avoid from the beginning?
—Yona Siero

Trope I wanted to include: a princess taking the throne.

Trope I wanted to avoid: an empowering coming-of-age story.

Hesina is not unique, as an idealistic, inexperienced, and rash princess-turned-queen. But I wanted to highlight how Hesina *doesn't* cope with the situation she inherits. No mistake of hers goes unpunished, no ideal unchallenged. Her incompetence is underscored with deathly consequences that can't be reversed, and by the time she does grow, she ends up in a "lower" place than where she started. But life goes on. From the start, I set out to write a story of failure, not success. Because that was one of my biggest fears as a teenager: failing at something I had prepared for.

What is the significance of the crane motif throughout the story?
—Grace

In Chinese culture, the crane represents immortality. And immortality was certainly something that Qin emperors literally pursued, in history. But I'm much more fascinated by what lives on, metaphorically. Be they the lessons passed down to Hesina by her father or quotes from Confucius's *Analects*—how do values come to be immortalized, and should they be?

If Hesina could study anything else, what would she pick?
—Asher W.

Hesina wasn't kidding about agriculture! She'd move onto a farm with her siblings and forget about ruling—if she didn't care about the approval of others, that is.

Which character is your favorite, if you had to choose?
—Pilar Festiëns

Probably Caiyan.

What is Caiyan's favorite memory of Hesina?
—Lexie C.

Hmm . . . so many! But the time when Hesina fell asleep while reading *Yingchuan Flora* and woke up with "melon" inked on her cheek definitely ranks at the top. FYI: Being called a melon-head is much worse than being called a stone-head.

Have you ever thought of an alternate ending?
—Elena Y.

In the earliest drafts, Hesina never finds out who killed her father by the end of the book. My agent (wisely) encouraged me to reveal it.

Was any specific scene hard for you to write?
—Fernanda Zuniga

Every scene was quite difficult, but chapter 24 was especially hard, when Hesina makes a decision to order a citywide cutting. I knew it was objectively "wrong," but I wanted to honor Hesina's circumstances and write the scene absent of my own judgment.

If Akira had grown up in the palace alongside the others, who would he have been closest to?
—Kathleen

Sanjing. They probably would have been sparring buddies.

Does Akira actually know how to play the flute?
—Veronica

Yes, but badly. Funny thing is, as I was reading this question, I was slammed by déjà vu. It occurred to me that in a past draft, I *might* have written such a scene. I went back to my emails from 2016 to find it. Please witness, at Akira's expense:

Hesina squinted at the rod. "You're done." She ran her fingers over the holes. Each one was the size of a pewter coin, edges sanded smooth. "Can you play?"

Akira lifted the flute to his lips.

And promptly blew a note that sounded like the cawing of a thousand crows.

He looked down at the instrument and scratched his head. "I could have sworn I was making a flute."

"Here, let me." Hesina took the flute and tried it herself, coaxing out some scratchy notes. Not much of an improvement. "This is horrible," she laughed weakly, then realized her mistake. "I didn't mean the flute. I meant my playing."

"So, is this"—Akira blew another skin-crawling note—"music to your ears?"

From *New York Times*– and Indie-bestselling author Joan He comes an epic fantasy about found family, rivals, and questions of identity.

Turn the page for a sneak peek!

SOMETHING FROM NOTHING

Some say the heavens dictate the rise and fall of empires.

Clearly, those peasants have never met me.

My abilities as a strategist have earned me many sobriquets, from the Dragon's Shadow to the Tactician of Thistlegate. Rising Zephyr is my personal favorite. "Zephyr" will do, if you please.

"Peacock!"

Unless you're Lotus. Then it's too much to ask for.

I struggle to steer my mare around; horses don't appreciate genius.

Neither does Lotus. "Hey, Peacock!" she hollers over the creaking wagons, crying babies, and cracking whips. She urges her stallion up along the other side until we're somewhat eye to eye, the heads of people and oxen coursing between us. "They're catching up!"

Consider me unsurprised. Miasma, prime ministress of the Xin Empire in name, acting empress in reality, was bound to close in on our soldiers and peasants, who now—thanks to Lotus—realize they're about to die. A child bursts into tears, an auntie trips, a young couple spurs their mule faster. No luck. The steep forest path is doughy from last night's rainfall, kneaded to mush by the hundreds we've evacuated.

Still hundreds more to go.

"Do something!" Lotus shouts at me. "Use your brain!" Her hair has frizzed into an impressive mane around her face, and she waves her ax as if she's itching to use it.

Wouldn't help us. It's not just Miasma we're up against: Our own numbers are bogging us down. *We must evacuate everyone*, Ren said sternly when I suggested it was time we flee our current town for the next. *Miasma will slaughter the commonfolk just for harboring us.*

Miasma may still yet, at this rate, but there's no arguing with our warlordess Xin Ren's benevolence. Most strategists wouldn't be able to cope with it.

I can.

"Think of a plan!" Lotus bellows.

Thanks for the confidence, Lotus. I already have—three, in fact. Plan one (ditch the commoners) might be off the table, but there's plan two (cut down trees and pray for rain), and plan three (send a trustworthy general to the bridge at the mountain's base to hold off Miasma).

Plan two is in motion, if the humidity is any indication. I've set General Tourmaline and her forces on felling trees behind us. The trunks will wash down in the coming storm, and the resulting dam should delay Miasma's cavalry by a couple of hours.

As for sending a trustworthy general to the bridge . . .

My gaze cuts from Lotus to Cloud, Ren's other swornsister.

She's helping evacuees farther up the muddy slope, her ultramarine cloak rich against the muted greens of the firs.

Cloud thinks better than Lotus under pressure. A shame, because I don't know if I can harness her. Last month, she released Miasma from one of my traps because *Sage Master Shencius forbids killing by way of snare*. That's all very nice, Cloud, but was Sage Master Shencius ever on the run from the empire? I don't think so.

"You." I point my fan at Lotus. "Ride down to the bridge with a hundred of your best and employ Beget Something from Nothing."

Lotus gives me a blank look.

"Just . . . make it look like we have more forces across the river than we actually do. Stir up dust. Roar. Intimidate them." Shouldn't be too hard for Lotus, whose sobriquet only suits her if you visualize the root, not the flower. Her war cry can shake birds out of trees within the radius of a li. She forged her own ax and wears the pelt of a tiger she killed as a skirt. She's as warrior as warriors come, the opposite of everything I stand for. At least Cloud knows her classical poems.

But Lotus has something Cloud doesn't: the ability to take an order.

"Intimidate," she repeats under her breath. "Got it." Then she's galloping down the mountain on her beastly stallion and referring to herself by name in that gauche way some warriors do before riding into battle. "Lotus won't disappoint!"

Thunder swallows the rumble of her departure. Clouds brew in the sky, and leaves drift around me in a breeze more stench than air. Pressure builds in my chest; I breathe through it and focus on my hair, still clasped back in its high ponytail. My fan, still in my hand.

This won't be the first time I've delivered the impossible for Ren.

And deliver it I will. Miasma isn't reckless; the impending rains combined with Lotus's intimidation will make her think twice before pursuing us up the mountain. I *can* slow her down.

But I'll also need to speed us up.

I jerk on the reins; my mare balks. The insubordination! "Turnips and figs later!" I hiss.

Jerking harder, I trot us down the slope.

"Forget the pack animals!" I bark to the sluggish stream of people. "Leave the wagons! This is a command from Xin Ren's military strategist!"

They do as they're told, scowling all the while. They love Ren for her honor, Cloud for her righteousness, Lotus for her spirit. My job is not to be lovable but to get every peasant off the mountain and into the town over, where Ren should already be waiting with the first wave of evacuees, the other half of our troops, and—hopefully—a boat passage south so that I can secure us some much-needed allies.

"Hurry!" I snap. People plod a little faster. I order someone to help a man with a broken leg, but then there's a pregnant woman who looks seconds away from labor, children without shoes, toddlers without parents. The humid air thickens to soup, and the pressure in my chest climbs to my throat. Harbinger of a breathing attack, if there ever was one.

Don't you dare, I think to my body as I ride farther down the line, shouting until I'm hoarse. I pass a girl shrieking for her sister.

Ten people later, I cross a younger girl in a matching vest, bawling for hers.

"Follow me," I wheeze. I barely see the sisters reunited before lightning strips the forest bare. The animals whine in chorus—my horse among them.

"Turnips—"

Thunder claps and my horse rears, and the reins—

They slip through my fingers.